D1361996

ANDROMEDA'S FALL

COMING SOON FROM WILLIAM C. DIETZ AND TITAN BOOKS

Andromeda's Choice (February 2014)

Legion of the Damned (March 2014)
The Final Battle (April 2014)
By Blood Alone (May 2014)
By Force of Arms (June 2014)
For Those Who Fell (July 2014)
For More Than Glory (August 2014)
When All Seems Lost (September 2014)
When Duty Calls (October 2014)

WILLIAM C. DIETZ
ANDROMEDA'S FALL

TITAN BOOKS

Andromeda's Fall
Print edition ISBN: 9781783290307
E-book edition ISBN: 9781783290314

Published by Titan Books
A division of Titan Publishing Group Ltd
144 Southwark Street, London SE1 0UP

First edition: January 2014
1 3 5 7 9 10 8 6 4 2

A CIP catalogue record for this title is available from the British Library.

Printed and bound in Great Britain by CPI Group Ltd.

For my dearest Marjorie

1

Here the question arises; whether it is better to be loved than feared or feared than loved. The answer is that it would be desirable to be both but, since that is difficult, it is much safer to be feared…

NICCOLÒ MACHIAVELLI
The Prince
Standard year 1513

IMPERIAL PLANET EARTH
THE NORTH AMERICAN CONTINENT

Princess Ophelia Ordanus felt a fierce sense of joy as she led a squad of synths out onto the narrow footbridge that connected the palace to the royal tower. The summer residence had been built on top of a mountain in the Rockies, where, in the words of the first Emperor Ordanus, "I can see the sun rise and feel the urgency of the wind."

And even the ruler's critics had to admit that the soaring turrets, the carefully placed observation platforms, and the frail-looking bridges that tied everything together made for a truly remarkable structure. But in spite of the poetic words, and the almost ethereal beauty of the first emperor's creation, the "sky castle," as the locals referred to it, was far more than a monument to the Imperial ego. Because deep within the heart of the mountain, where it was safe from every possible threat, was the government that bound billions of people together.

And a good thing, too. For there were other spacefaring races in the galaxy, some of which would have been happy to glass Earth. The Hudathans being an excellent example. *But the ridge heads aren't going to get the chance,* Ophelia thought to herself as her heels clicked on the pavers under her boots.

The sheer drop of more than five hundred feet on either side of the causeway meant the tower was an island where the monarch could retreat if necessary. Something Emperor Alfred Ordanus III did with increasing frequency. Not to escape his enemies but to avoid the pressures associated with his position and to pursue his scientific experiments.

But not for much longer, Ophelia thought grimly. *While you play with your toys, our enemies gather all around. And rather than confront them, you continue to dither. That must end.*

A squad of Imperial guards was stationed on the other side of the causeway, which could be blown up if necessary. They crashed to attention as the princess and her escort came to a halt in front of the security checkpoint. "I'm here to see my brother," Ophelia said coldly. "Let us pass."

"Of course, Highness," the officer of the guard responded respectfully. "Is the emperor expecting you?"

"No."

"Then I'll have to ask you to wait for a moment while I…"

The sentence was punctuated by a popping sound as Ophelia shot him between the eyes. The long-barreled pistol had been there all along, hidden within a fold of her knee-length leather coat.

The officer fell as if poleaxed, and his men were still processing that event and trying to bring their weapons to bear when Ophelia stepped to one side. That cleared the way for the synthetics to open fire with their machine pistols. The hail of lead cut the human soldiers down in a matter of seconds. They lay in heaps.

Ophelia nodded approvingly, circled the steadily expanding puddle of blood, and made her way toward the door beyond. There was no going back. Win or lose, the dice had been thrown.

* * *

The "study," as Emperor Alfred Ordanus referred to it, was a series of interconnected rooms that took up one floor of the royal tower. The furnishings included a stuffed velocipod from O-Chi 4, a messy lab, the daybeds that his dogs liked to nap on, alien plants, and at least a dozen androids in varying states of repair. Or what *looked* like androids although they were actually civforms. Meaning cybernetic vehicles intended for civilian rather that military use. Because it was Alfred's dream to grant his subjects something close to immortality by providing them with affordable cyberbodies. The key was to take the technology that Carletto Industries had developed for military cyborgs, simplify it, and scale the production process up to keep unit costs down. Most of the development work had been carried out by Cyntarch (Count) Carletto and his staff.

But Alfred could claim credit for designing a thinner, more sensitive version of the thick MILSPEC "leather" developed for military applications. Unfortunately, there were occasional flaws in the sheets of "synthiskin" as they came off the rollers. Was that the result of a mechanical malfunction? Or a flaw in the mix of materials from which it was made? Alfred had been working on the puzzle for the last sixteen hours.

So he was anything but pleased when his Rhodesian Ridgebacks began to bark and ran skittering toward the main entrance. But since Alfred's staff knew better than to disturb him for anything other than a true emergency, the emperor braced himself for another dose of bad news as he followed the excited dogs to the doorway. A Hudathan attack perhaps? A natural catastrophe somewhere? That was the problem with such a large empire. Something went wrong every day. A tiresome business that consumed most of his time.

And it was then, just as a steel fist punched a hole through the wooden door, that Alfred remembered something important: The officer of the guard should have called him but hadn't. So the emperor was backing away as half a dozen powerful kicks shattered the door, and a synth entered the room.

The killing machine was humanoid in appearance, but only vaguely so, and that was intentional. The synth's uniform had been sprayed on. Its head was made of metal, broad in front, and tapered in back where it formed a vertical ridge. Red eyes stared at Alfred from deep-set sockets, a slight bulge hinted at the possibility of a nose, and a fully articulated jaw moved as the machine spoke. The computer-generated voice was deep and resonant. "Stay where you are. Do not attempt to run."

"Kill it," Alfred said grimly, and pointed.

The ridgebacks, all of whom had been watching their master, growled in response. Toenails fought for purchase on stone floors as the pack attacked. The synth shot the first animal—and batted the second aside. It yowled and hit the wall hard. But the third, fourth, and fifth dogs were in the air by then, and the machine went down under their combined weight.

But the effort was to no avail as *more* synths entered the room and machine-gunned both the ridgebacks and the first robot. Alfred thought about running but recognized the gray-and-burgundy colors the intruders wore and knew all of the exits would be blocked.

Gun smoke hung in the still air. It shivered and parted as Ophelia stepped through the shattered door. Her long, dark hair was swept back over her shoulders, her heart-shaped face was empty of expression, and the pistol she was carrying was pointed at the floor. "What a pigsty," the princess remarked as she stepped over a dead dog. "I'll have to gut the place and start over."

Alfred was more surprised than angry. He knew his sister was ambitious and ruthless. That was why he paid half a dozen people to spy on her—and even more people to spy on *them*. So why hadn't he been warned?

Ophelia smiled thinly. "I know you, Alfred. I know you better than you know yourself. So it wasn't that difficult to spot the people who were supposed to watch me. They'll be dead before the night is over. As will you."

Alfred felt the first stirrings of fear. He'd been careless. Stupidly so. But maybe there was a chance. "Don't do it, Ophelia. There's no need to. You can run the empire. I'll focus on my work. Both of us will be happy."

"Sorry," Ophelia replied, "but that won't work. I plan to rule the way you should have. Everyone who has a reason to oppose me is going to die. And that includes you. Besides, the nature of the so-called work you do runs counter to the needs of the empire. Think about it. If all of our citizens become immortal—how will that affect the economy? And how will they spend their time? Meddling in politics perhaps? And that's just the beginning. Who knows what the rest of the trickle down would be.

"But enough of that… It's time to say good-bye, dear brother. Too bad you won't be able to attend your funeral. I plan to cry. Take him."

Alfred turned and tried to run. But the synths were fast and were on him in seconds. "Be careful," Ophelia cautioned. "Try not to leave any marks."

"*Please,*" Alfred said pitifully as the androids half carried, half dragged him toward a pair of double doors that opened out onto an observation platform. "Don't do this."

"It's too late to stop," Ophelia answered. "Even if I wanted to. Which I don't. Teams of synths have been sent out to kill your supporters and their relatives as well. Because they might oppose me. And I have no intention of dying early—or *ever* for that matter. Thanks to Cyntarch Carletto and you, my civforms are ready and waiting."

Alfred felt a blast of cold mountain air as the doors were thrown open and he was wrestled out onto the large balcony beyond. The synths were going to throw him off. He knew that now. And then what? A claim of suicide? Probably. All of that raced through the emperor's mind as he was hoisted up onto the railing. He could see the lights that were Denver, a couple of early stars, and the glow of a heliostat rising in the east. Then there were no more thoughts. Just the sound of someone screaming as he fell into the abyss below.

ORCAS ISLAND
THE NORTH AMERICAN CONTINENT

The Casino Pacifica was located on Orcas Island in the San Juans. The climate-controlled location was said to be beautiful year-round although Colonel Rex Carletto had a tendency to sleep during the day and hadn't toured the island since his boyhood. He liked the casino because that was where he had won more than 150,000 credits before going up to Vancouver and losing it there. Now he was back at the Pacifica, where he hoped to win again. *Then I'll stop,* he promised himself, even though he knew he couldn't. How much had he lost over the years? Five million? At least that.

But that's in the past, Rex assured himself, as the limo came to a stop under a huge portico. *This time it will be different.* A bellbot was there to open the door as the ground car came to a stop. "Do you have any luggage, sir?"

Rex didn't but tipped the android anyway, knowing the money would be split between the casino's human employees.

A red carpet led Rex to the front door, where a man in a tux stood waiting. Thanks to the video captured by the bellbot and relayed to the casino's computer, the host knew the guest's name. "Good evening, Colonel Carletto, and welcome back."

"It's a pleasure to be back," Rex replied.

"Michelle will get you situated," the host said as a lithesome brunette stepped forward. "Good luck."

The hostess was wearing a low-cut black evening gown, and Rex smiled appreciatively. "Thank you."

Rex allowed Michelle to lead him back past the holo slots and the poker tables to the room where the roulette wheels were. The odds were overwhelmingly in favor of the house, but there was something about the excitement of roulette that he couldn't shake. An all-or-nothing thrill that was reminiscent of combat and the moments when all of his senses were fully awakened.

So Rex allowed Michelle to find him a seat at the table, gave her a chip card that had all of that month's income on it, and felt the usual twinge of guilt. He hadn't done anything to earn the money other than be the second son to Cyntarch Alfred Carletto II, who, having passed control of Carletto Industries to his eldest son, Dor, had seen fit to gift Rex with a large inheritance and a monthly income. The inheritance was long gone, but the payments from the family business were sufficient to keep the retired officer from becoming an embarrassment, and to feed his addiction.

Rex's thoughts were interrupted as Michelle returned with stacks of yellow chips on a silver tray and gave him a receipt. There were other guests to greet, many of whom were better-heeled than Colonel Rex Carletto, but she was happy to spend time with someone who had links to the royal family. The next couple of hours were pleasant if not especially satisfying. Rex won, but lost as well, so he was only slightly ahead when a well-dressed blonde took the seat to his right.

She was probably in her forties but looked considerably younger thanks to some well-executed biosculpting. And since Rex enjoyed women almost as much as he enjoyed gambling, he was happy to reduce the size of his bets in order to focus his attention on her. She was not only attractive but quite witty, and openly curious about the Carletto family.

So when Rex offered to give her a nighttime tour of the Carletto estate near Seattle, she agreed. Her name was Macy Evers. And thanks to a hefty divorce settlement, she was wealthy enough to have her own air car, which made short work of the trip from Orcas to Seattle.

Knowing Colonel Rex as they did, none of the family's retainers thought it strange when he requested permission to land someone else's car on the family's pad, then helped a woman to the ground and led her away. She would, they knew, finish the evening as so many others had—in Colonel Rex's bed.

The air was cool as Rex and Macy followed a well-groomed path past a tastefully lit statue of Emperor Ordanus I. "That's the main house," Rex said as he pointed to a four-story stone-clad building. It was ablaze with light, and occasional silhouettes could be seen as people moved from room to room. "My brother lives there along with his wife Carolyn and their daughter Catherine. Or Cat, as she's known in the family."

"I've read about her," Macy replied. "They say she's very spirited."

Rex chuckled. "You're being polite. They say she's a spoiled bitch. The first part is true. She's touring the inner planets at the moment. And living very well indeed."

"And the second part?" Macy inquired. "Is that true as well?"

"Sometimes," Rex admitted reluctantly. "But she's smart, and on those occasions when she chooses to apply herself to something, she's invariably good at it."

"You like her."

"Yes," Rex admitted. "I guess I do. The building on your

left is the greenhouse. Carolyn loves orchids and grows them herself. The structure directly in front of us, beyond the main building, is the guesthouse. Or would be if my brother could get me to move out."

Macy laughed. "So you enjoy living here?"

"Of course I do," Rex admitted. "I have every possible convenience and don't pay rent. That's hard to beat." He was about to say more when a loud thrumming noise was heard. Rex recognized the sound immediately. And it brought him to a halt. He peered up into the night sky. Why would a troop transport be hovering over the estate? Especially one without any running lights? Unless…

A brilliant flash lit up the night as a rocket hit the security shack next to the landing pad and blew up. Rex said, "Oh shit," and was running toward the main house when the estate's computer-controlled defense system came on. That included banks of lights that were aimed up into the night sky. The transport's alloy belly was clear to see, as were the ropes that dangled below, and the figures that slid down them like beads on a string.

The staccato bark of automatic fire followed, and as Rex came to a stop, he could see muzzle flashes through the windows. Macy had caught up to him by then. She was frightened. "What's going on?"

"Something bad," Rex answered as he took her hand. "Come with me."

Macy had to abandon her high heels and run barefoot in order to keep up with the officer as he led her down the brightly lit path toward the guesthouse. Muffled screams could be heard from the residence, but were cut off as more shots were fired, and flames appeared in a window.

Rex thumbed the door lock, burst into the entry hall, and went straight to his study. There was a *thump* as his fist hit the paneling, a door slid to one side, and a recess appeared. A pistol and three clips of ammunition were waiting. Rex took the weapon, the ammo, and a leather pouch. There were some old-fashioned gold coins in it. There should have been more. Would have been more if he hadn't lost half the stash in Monte Carlo.

Still, the coins made a comforting clinking sound as he dropped the purse into his jacket pocket and slid a magazine into the pistol. The slide produced a clacking sound as he pumped a round into the chamber. That was when Macy screamed.

Rex turned, saw the flat black synth, and shot it in the head. As the machine crumpled, a machine pistol skittered across the floor. But the weapon was electronically keyed to the "dead" robot and therefore useless. "Come on," Rex said. "Those things are linked, so more will arrive soon. Can you swim?"

Macy gave a jerky nod.

"Good. 'Cause we're going for a dip."

Rex led the frightened woman through the house, out the back door, and toward the elaborate swimming pool beyond. It was lit from above, but some carefully aimed shots took care of that. The water was black as they jumped into it, and waves rippled out in every direction.

Rex quickly discovered that it was difficult to swim with a weapon in one hand while holding on to Macy with the other. So he let go of her as they surfaced. He said, "Follow me," and she spluttered by way of a reply.

Rex turned and swam toward the sound of the artificial waterfall to his right. Then, as water began to pummel his head, he made a grab for Macy and towed her through the deluge.

The hidden grotto had been his grandfather's idea. His brother and he had enjoyed the secret hideaway as children. Then, during his early teens, Rex discovered that the secret chamber was a wonderful place to take girls. There were half-submerged benches to either side plus a deep ledge in the back. It was stocked with a supply of fluffy towels and wide enough for two.

The water was warm, but the air was cool, and Macy's skimpy cocktail dress was plastered to her body as they climbed up onto the ledge. It was dark, but Rex could hear her teeth chattering. "Get out of those wet clothes," he ordered. "And wrap yourself in towels. We're going to be here for a while. An hour at least."

Sirens could be heard in the distance, but who was on the way? Firemen? Or more synths? There was no way to know, but one thing was for sure. Cyntarch Dor Carletto and Lady Carolyn were dead. That left Rex and Catherine. *Cat!* He had to warn her. But how? Lights stabbed downwards, found the bottom of the pool, and began to explore it.

IMPERIAL PLANET ESPARTO

Lady Catherine Carletto snapped her lipstick closed and studied herself in the oval-shaped mirror. She had shoulder-length blond hair, wide-set blue eyes, and a softly rounded face. Everyone agreed that she was beautiful. And that was true. In the technical sense, anyway. The problem was that she didn't *feel* beautiful. Or anything else for that matter. No ambition. No fear. No joy. And that didn't make sense since she had *everything*. Or that's what the vidnets claimed. Cat made a face at herself, dropped the lipstick into a tiny clutch, and turned to go. The door to her hotel suite hurried to slide out of the way, and the private elevator surged upwards the moment she stepped on board.

There was a small but tastefully furnished lobby on the roof—and two of the hotel's employees were there to wish Cat a good evening as she passed through. Less fortunate people were constantly wishing her "good morning," "good afternoon," and "good evening." But very few, if any, meant it. And why would they? Everything was for sale—including the most trivial of greetings. So Cat ignored them, followed a green runner out to a waiting air car, and slid into the backseat. A chime sounded as she buckled the seat belt.

Moments later, the limo was in the air and entering the flow of southbound traffic. Esparto was an Earth-normal planet known for its vast grasslands, rich deposits of rare earth minerals, and the glittering city spread out below her. The *only* city on Esparto.

There were townships of course. But laws laid down by the first families limited them to populations of no more than ten thousand people each. The idea was to contain urban sprawl and encourage decentralization. But the unintended consequence of that policy had been to create a city that occupied more than five thousand square miles of land and had a reputation for both sophistication and decadence. That was the main reason why young men and women fortunate enough to be sent on the so-called grand tour wanted to visit Elysium. And Cat was no exception.

Thanks to her family's relationship with Emperor Ordanus, and their considerable wealth, Cat was a much-sought-after guest. It was a role she both enjoyed and despised. Because although she loved the attention, Cat knew it was undeserved and felt a sense of contempt for both herself and the people who fawned over her.

So the socialite took in the view as the car followed a stream of other aircraft south over brightly lit buildings and toward the glowing globe perched atop the one-hundred-story-tall Imperial Tower. If one looked closely, it was possible to see that the familiar outlines of Earth's seven continents had been etched into the opaque structure. The skyscraper had been built by Emperor Alfred II to house the planetary government and to remind the local citizens of where the *real* power was.

Hundreds of people had been invited to the governor's ball, so as the limo circled the tower, and the pilot waited for a clearance to land, Cat had an opportunity to eye the sprawling city below. Elysium's streets were laid out grid-style. But there were so many of them that Cat wondered if anyone could come to know such a huge metroplex.

Rivers of glowing headlights flowed along the main arterials. Commercials, many of which circled entire buildings, flowed snakelike from one section of the city to the next. And blimps that looked like internally lit jellyfish drifted across the night sky, all competing for eyeballs and mindshare. It was both beautiful and horrible. Or that's the way it seemed to Cat as the air car came in for a landing.

At least two dozen landing pads were located in the area just below the gigantic globe. And while vidnet reporters weren't allowed on that level, their airborne cameras were. The machines jockeyed for position as Cat stepped out of the limo. She smiled as the lights hit, and paused to turn a full circle so all the fashionistas could appreciate her ten-thousand-credit evening gown. It was red, with slits up both sides, and glittered under the lights.

Then Cat took the arm of the brightly uniformed militia officer who was waiting to escort her inside. He was a lieutenant, about her age, and clearly enthralled. His carefully memorized words of introduction were lost in the roar of repellers as Cat's limo took off. But it wasn't important since the officer was little more than an accessory and indistinguishable from all the rest of his kind.

Together, they entered a lobby, where Cat was welcomed by some functionary or other, guided onto an elevator, and taken down to the fifth-floor ballroom. It consisted of a huge room decorated in the early Imperial style. Heroic 3-D murals covered all four walls and morphed into fresh perspectives every three minutes.

Hundreds of less important individuals were already present, and most turned to stare as her name was announced, and cameras swarmed around her. Then it was time to greet the governor and her husband. Both wore perpetual smiles, claimed to know her parents, and were clearly wary. And for good reason. Though nothing in and of herself, Cat could do them harm by dropping a few carelessly chosen words to the cameras.

After exchanging pleasantries with them, Cat allowed herself to be steered over to a reception line, where a line of lesser functionaries were waiting to greet her. It wasn't long before their faces became a blur, their names merged into a meaningless drone, and she was grateful when the last sweaty hand had been shaken.

That was the point when things took a turn for the better as a group of chattering young people closed in around her. She knew many of them and was barely aware of the manner in which the disappointed lieutenant was shouldered aside by a fop decked out in a vid suit. Pictures of Cat and her friends roamed his body, and everyone laughed as the likeness of a girl with spiky pink hair slid down into his crotch.

During the next hour, Cat gossiped with her friends, took a moment to flirt with a moody sim actor, and consumed three cocktails. She was about to visit the buffet when a formally dressed hostess appeared at her side. "Lady Catherine? My name is Stevens. A man is here to see you. We told him you were busy, but he claims to have an urgent message from your uncle."

Cat frowned. "My uncle? You're sure?"

Stevens had closely set eyes and thin lips. "That's what he claims," she said noncommittally. "But I have no way to be sure."

Since she departed Earth two months earlier, Cat's parents had sent her messages every couple of days. Each of which had to be recorded on a chip, loaded onto a message torp, and sent through hyperspace the same way a full-sized ship would be. A very expensive process indeed. And since most of the holos were admonishments to take care of herself, or queries regarding some of her more notorious exploits, Cat had a tendency to let a few days pass before sending a reply. Or, in some cases, she ignored the missives altogether.

But Uncle Rex *never* sent messages. And being the official black sheep of the family, he was in no position to complain about public intoxication, partial nudity, or the provocative statements Cat made to the press. Was a member of the family sick or something? So, fueled by both curiosity and a rising sense of concern, Cat agreed. "Okay. Where is this guy?"

"He's in the kitchen," the hostess explained. "We couldn't bring him into the ballroom because… Well, you'll see."

Cat followed Stevens through a pair of swinging doors and caught a glimpse of a busy kitchen before being led into an office labeled Food Service. The man's head was bare, his cheeks were covered with at least two days' worth of stubble, and his clothes were filthy. And because his torso was resting on an argrav platform that floated just inches off the floor, he had to look up at her. "Good evening, miss. You look just like the pictures I seen."

Cat glanced over her shoulder, saw that Stevens had withdrawn, and wished she hadn't. A mistake had been made, and she'd been left with a vagrant. All she could do was play the farce through. "You have a message for me?"

"Yes, ma'am," he replied respectfully. "My name's Toshy. *Sergeant* Toshy back before I lost my sticks in the battle of Ripper's Ridge. But Major Rex don't forget. The money comes every year. Right on the anniversary of the day I saved his life. It helps me and the missus to get through. So I owes him just like he owes me."

Looking down at the ex-soldier made Cat feel uncomfortable, so she sat on a chair. The socialite hadn't heard of Toshy, but Uncle Rex had told her stories about his career in the Legion, and the battle of Ripper's Ridge. A hellish assault that left half of his battalion dead. So there was reason to hear Toshy out. "When my uncle retired, he was a colonel."

"Really?" Toshy inquired. "I didn't know that. Well, good on him. He was a fine officer."

"You have a message for me," Cat said flatly.

"Right you are," Toshy said as he fished a chip out of his pocket. "It came yesterday. And there was a note. 'Get this to Lady Catherine Carletto,' it said. And don't tell nobody.'"

Cat frowned. Rather than send the chip to her hotel, Uncle Rex had chosen to entrust it to Toshy. And cautioned him to keep it secret. *Why?*

"Thank you," Cat said as she accepted the chip. "It was very kind of you to come and find me."

"I saw you on the news," Toshy said proudly. "They said you'd be here."

"I'd like to give you something for your trouble," Cat said, and opened her purse.

"No thank you," Toshy said stiffly. "The chance to help Colonel Rex is payment enough. Give him my best."

And with that, the ex-legionnaire used two blocks of wood to propel himself toward the open door. Moments later, Toshy was gone. He was, Cat knew, one of thousands of badly wounded veterans who had been handed a severance check and put on the street. In all likelihood, Toshy had been issued a pair of bionic legs but, lacking the means to maintain the prosthetics, had sold them to pay the rent or gambled them away. Of course, that was *his* fault, or so many people maintained, her uncle being a notable exception.

Cat stood, took a quick look around, and spotted a holo deck. Having closed the door into the hallway, she went over to the player, slipped the chip into the slot, and touched a button. A cloud of confetti-like motes of light appeared, were attracted to each other, and combined to form a three-dimensional image.

The lighting was poor, as if her uncle had been forced to make the recording in a dark room, and there was a momentary buzzing sound as his face disintegrated and came back together again. "Cat... It's me, Uncle Rex. I'm sorry, honey, but I have some very bad news for you. The emperor committed suicide.

That's what the vidnets say, but I don't believe it. First, because Alfred was anything but suicidal, and second, because hundreds of his close friends and supporters have been killed during the last week."

At that point Cat felt a sudden emptiness at the pit of her stomach. Because her parents fell into both categories. Friends *and* supporters.

"They were killed in air crashes, diving accidents, and house fires. And that's what supposedly happened to your parents, Cat... Except I was there. And before the house caught fire, a military transport lowered at least two dozen synths into the estate. And they killed *everyone*. Servants and family alike.

"So it's clear that Princess O was behind it. Except that she's the empress now, and judging from the way Alfred's associates continue to drop left and right, she's determined to purge anyone who might stand in her way. And that includes relatives who might want revenge. You and I are bound to be on that list, pumpkin. So listen carefully. Drop out. Hide as best you can. And don't use your credit cards or try to contact any of the people you know. Because if you do, they *will* find you."

There was a noise in the background at that point and, as Rex turned to look over his shoulder, Cat saw the gun in his hand. When he looked back there was concern in his eyes. "I'm sorry, Cat. So very sorry. Find a hole to hide in, honey... And don't ever come out." The image broke into pieces at that point. They were sucked inwards and disappeared.

There was so much to absorb, so much to accept, that Cat was numb. Then, as the full weight of her uncle's words began to sink in, she started to cry. Deep sobs racked her body, and her stomach hurt as she rocked back and forth. Her mother. Her father. Both dead. It seemed impossible. Yet there it was, and having seen the look on her uncle's face, she knew it was true.

The crying lasted for a good five minutes; tears were still running down her cheeks when someone knocked on the door. It was Stevens. "Lady Catherine? Are you okay?"

Cat *wasn't* okay. But she couldn't say that. So she said, "Yes, I'll be right there," as she plucked tissues out of a box. Then, having wiped the tears away, she removed the chip from the player and stuck it into her bra.

The door whirred out of the way, and judging from the expression on the other woman's face, she knew something was wrong. Together, they walked back through the kitchen and out into the ballroom. And that was when Cat saw the synths. There were at least six of the Carletto Industry ALF-46s (Artificial Life Form model 46s). They crisscrossed the floor, pausing occasionally to stare at particular individuals, while the pale-faced governor was forced to look on. The room, which had been so noisy before, was eerily silent.

Cat stopped, and was trying to decide what to do when a robot spotted her. The machine fired a pistol and a bullet ripped through Stevens's throat. There was a look of surprise on her face as she crumpled to the floor. Life as Cat had known it was over.

2

There is, in the flow of events, a time to run.
AUTHOR UNKNOWN
A Dweller folk saying
Standard year circa 1950

IMPERIAL PLANET ESPARTO

As Stevens collapsed, Cat instinctively held up her hands as if to stop bullets with them and backed through swinging doors into the kitchen. The shock of what she had witnessed, plus the certain knowledge that the synths had orders to kill her, caused Cat's heart to beat like a trip-hammer.

It was noisy in the kitchen, so the culinary staff hadn't heard the gunshot. They looked up in surprise as a wild-eyed young woman in a red evening dress appeared and looked around. Having spotted the back door, she turned and ran. By that time, Cat was focused on only one thing, and that was the desperate need to escape the building. Her spirits rose as she entered the service corridor and saw the elevator. All she had to do was jump on board, get off on the first floor, and run like hell. Simple.

Except that it wasn't. According to the indicator over the polished metal door, the elevator was on the sixteenth floor. And Cat knew the synths would catch up with her in a matter of seconds. So she glanced both ways, spotted a distant EXIT sign, and headed in that direction.

Cat hadn't gone more than a few feet before she tripped, fell, and skinned a knee. The five-hundred-credit Horace Latimer high heels were the problem. So she stood, kicked them off, and continued on. Seconds later, she realized that leaving the shoes behind would show the synths which way she had gone. But there wasn't enough time to go back and correct her mistake.

Cat heard a shout as she jerked the exit door open and began to race down the stairs. The duracrete was cold under her bare feet. Cat knew she wouldn't be able to go all the way to the ground floor because the androids were in constant communication with each other.

Her worst fears were confirmed as she looked down through an opening at the center of the staircase and spotted a flash of movement. One or more of the ALF-46s were climbing upwards. So as Cat arrived on the third floor, she turned to the right and pulled the fire door open. That allowed her to enter a long, sterile-looking hallway. Doors opened onto a row of conference rooms.

Cat chose the one labeled CONFERENCE ROOM C, entered a dimly lit chamber, and set off for the door on the opposite side. But the dress slowed her down so she paused to rip the side slits open even more. Having granted herself more freedom of movement, Cat approached the door, which slid out of the way.

A sign that read LOBBY pointed to the right. She paused for a second, wondered how many synths were waiting in the lobby, and decided to chance it. As she sprinted down the hall toward a waist-high barrier, Cat heard a burst of gunfire and knew that at least one of the robots was behind her. What sounded like a swarm of angry bees buzzed past, and a glass chandelier exploded as she was forced to stop. The atrium was three stories high, and she could see a synth on the floor below looking up at her.

That was the moment when a camera operator spotted her. He was miles away, "flying" his vidcam from the comfort of a chair, when he spotted Lady Catherine Carletto on the top floor of the atrium and produced a whoop of joy. Then, using a small joystick, he sent his unit up to capture a close-up. Was *she* responsible for the exploding light fixture? Probably, not that it mattered, so long as he got the shot.

A synth was firing on Cat from behind and another was racing up an escalator to intercept her. What happened next was more the result of an impulse than careful planning. Cat was a gymnast. Or had been prior to college. And she was desperate. So she vaulted over the waist-high wall and fell into the void.

Her timing was good. She hit the rising vidcam hard, wrapped her arms around the shiny ball, and felt it sink toward the floor. The synth that had been chasing her arrived at the waist-high wall and sprayed the lobby with bullets. Lamps exploded, plants were shredded, and a guest took a round between the shoulder blades as he tried to escape the destruction.

Cat let go of the vidcam and dropped to the floor. She felt a stabbing pain as something penetrated her right foot. But there was no time to stop and examine the wound, so she hobbled forward. The ALF-46 on the third floor was changing magazines by then, but the synth on the escalator had opened fire, and a line of bullets chased Cat toward the formal entry. A blast of humid, ozone-tainted air hit her in the face as the door slid out of the way, and she ran into traffic. Horns blared, tires screeched, and there was a loud crash as a semitransparent taxicab hit the rear end of an automated delivery truck.

A synth stepped out onto the sidewalk and opened fire as Cat dodged around the front end of a passenger car. Bullets rattled as they hit both sheet metal and the driver, causing him to jerk spastically and slump over the wheel. Then the robot's line of fire was blocked as a bus hit the pileup and propelled a limo into an intersection, where a powered unicycle slammed into it.

Cat had left the street by then and was about to limp into the half-lit passageway between two buildings, when there was a crack of artificial thunder. She turned in time to see multiple tongues of fire belch out of the tower's fifth-floor windows. Then, as tons of debris rained down onto the street, she witnessed a series of lesser explosions. That was when Cat realized something important. Esparto's governor had been appointed to her position by Emperor Alfred. Which meant that just about all of her guests could be counted among his supporters. So the synths had been ordered to kill *all* of them. Not just her. She was little more than a detail in a much larger plan.

The knowledge brought little comfort as sirens began to wail, and Cat turned away. Tears ran down her cheeks as she limped through a shadowy passageway to the street beyond. North–south traffic was still flowing there. So Cat stepped between a couple of cars and raised a hand. Two cabs passed her by, but the third stopped. The rear door hissed open, and Cat slid inside. The cab was semitransparent, but she knew her features would be little more than a shadow to people outside.

"Where to?" the driver inquired, as he eyed her in the rearview mirror. He was wearing dreadlocks, light-enhancing goggles, and had a stim stick dangling from one corner of his mouth. If he was aware of the explosion, there was no sign of it.

Outside of the rarefied world she lived in, Cat knew very little about Elysium. But she'd heard of an area called the darkside. A sprawling neighborhood, by all accounts, where many members of the working class lived. In other words, the last place a socialite was likely to go. "Drop me in the darkside."

The driver frowned. "Are you sure?"

"I'm sure."

A fire truck had been forced to stop behind the cab. The man at the wheel hit the siren, and the cabbie flipped him off before accelerating away.

Cat gave a sigh of relief and allowed herself to lean back against the seat. The next problem was how to pay the fare. And Uncle Rex was correct. The moment she used a credit card, the synths would know where she'd been. She checked and her clutch was still there—held in place by a gold cord that ran crosswise across her body. After poking around inside it she came up with a half dozen coins intended for use as tips. Would they be sufficient? Cat hoped so as the driver made a series of turns, and the skyscrapers gradually shrunk into five-and ten-story buildings. Garish signs battled each other for dominance as clothing stores, bars, restaurants, nightclubs, tattoo parlors, and bakeries fought for customers.

And there were lots of people on the streets. Most were human, although Cat spotted an exoskeleton-clad Dweller, some colorful Prithians exiting a bar, and a pair of Ramanthians. None were citizens of the human empire. But all three races had something in common, and that was the need for trade, and a common fear of the marauding Hudathans. "Okay," the driver said. "Where should I drop you off?"

"The next corner is fine," Cat said as she eyed the fare on the screen in front of her. The total fell just below the amount of money she had. And the rest would go to a small tip. A stupid indulgence given her circumstances. But that was how she'd been raised. "With wealth comes obligations," her father used to say.

The taxi coasted to a stop. Cat gave over her money, the door hissed open, and she stepped into a puddle of filthy water. The experience was not only unpleasant but served to remind Cat of the cut on her foot, which hurt and was open to infection.

But there were other problems to cope with. The ripped evening gown and bare feet were already beginning to attract attention as Cat made her way down the street. So the first priority was to buy clothes that would allow her to fade into the background. But with what?

Cat conducted a mental inventory. She was wearing a diamond on a chain around her neck, a small ruby on her left ring finger, and her lipstick dispenser was made of gold. Taken together, they were worth at least ten thousand credits. The knowledge made her feel better, as did a large sign that read PAWNSHOP half a block farther on. But getting there seemed to take forever. There was a group of men standing outside a bar. One of them whistled, and another said, "Hey baby... How 'bout a ride?"

Then a street vendor carrying a tray of veg wraps approached her, quickly followed by a preteen beggar and a dull-eyed woman who wanted to save her from a life of sin.

So it was a relief to enter the brightly lit pawnshop. Racks of musical instruments hung from the walls. Used power tools were piled on a table just inside the door. And a manikin wearing a suit of space armor stood guard by the entrance.

To reach the cash register located at the back of the room, Cat had to pass between glass display cases filled with jewelry, alien artifacts, and various types of weapons. It was tempting to purchase a pistol. But Cat knew she'd have to submit ID in order to buy a weapon, and that would almost certainly bring the synths down on her.

The proprietor was a middle-aged man with a halo of gray hair, a chubby face, and the manner of a person who had seen everything. His eyes flicked down her frame and back up. In less than two seconds she had been weighed and evaluated. "Good evening, young lady. What can I do for you?"

"I have this," Cat said, lifting the chain up over her head. "Plus *this*, and *this*."

The man selected the diamond, eyed it through a loupe, and put it down. The ring and lipstick received a similar scrutiny. "So," he said, having completed his evaluation, "what do you have in mind? Do you want to sell this stuff? Or pawn it?"

The diamond had been a birthday present from her parents. But Cat was desperate for money. "I want to sell it."

"Okay," the man said evenly. "I'll give you five hundred for the lot."

"They're worth thousands!" Cat objected. "The diamond alone is worth six or seven."

"Not to me," the pawnbroker replied. "I have to sell what I buy—and there isn't much of a market for diamond pendants around here. Maybe you should take it uptown. A regular jewelry store would give you a better price."

Cat knew that was true. But she couldn't go back. Not with the synths looking for her. "Point taken. But five hundred credits is too low, and you know it. I want a thousand."

"Six hundred."

"Nine hundred."

"Six-fifty, and that's final."

Cat looked around, saw a row of used suitcases sitting against a wall, and pointed to the nicest one. "Six-fifty plus that."

The man grinned. He had a silver tooth. "You're a lot tougher than you look. It's a deal."

Cat left a few minutes later with cash hidden in her bra and her new suitcase in tow. Rather than ask the pawnbroker about used-clothing stores, and provide him with information that could be shared with others, Cat was determined to find one on her own. A quick conversation with the owner of a fruit stand got the information she needed.

Walking briskly so as to discourage interference, Cat made her way to the end of the block and took a right. The store, which was called Rewear, was directly ahead. There was no front door. Just a mesh gate that could be pulled down to protect the shop.

Cat strolled in, cruised the aisles, looking for clothing in her size, and cautioned herself to forget about fashion. Twenty minutes later, she had three basic outfits including some new underwear, socks, and a knit cap. A pair of high-topped lace-up boots completed her wardrobe.

Cat was filthy but elected to change into a "new" outfit anyway because the ripped evening gown was attracting attention, and she wanted to protect her feet. So when Cat emerged from Rewear, she was clad in the cap, which effectively hid her blond hair, a waist-length leather jacket that had plenty of mileage on it, and a pair of military-style trousers. They were baggy and cinched at the ankles. Scuffed boots completed the outfit. The rest of her wardrobe was stashed in the black suitcase that rattled along behind her.

A short walk took Cat to a convenience store, where she purchased a first-aid kit, disinfectant, and some toiletries. By the time she left the store, Cat realized she was hungry. *Very* hungry. A stop at a food cart took care of that. The wrap was hot, greasy, and surprisingly good. She wolfed it down.

At that point the only thing Cat wanted was a place where she could enjoy a hot shower, take care of the cut, and get some sleep. There were hotels. Lots of them. And no way to know what they were like. So with no information to go on, Cat chose the Get Away Hotel. A name that was certainly consistent with her circumstances.

No bellbot came forward to help with her bag. The front door opened onto a seedy lobby that was furnished with a threadbare carpet, tired-looking furniture, and a pair of drooping plants.

A fortresslike reception desk ran along the back wall. Only one of the two check-in windows was staffed. The desk clerk had thick black hair and a five o'clock shadow. He was perched on a stool, and there was something slimy about the way he eyed her. "Good evening, miss. What can I do for you?"

A vid set was visible on the shelf behind him. Judging from the pictures, the fire on the fifth floor of the Imperial Tower had been put out. Had there been shots of her? Cat hoped not. "I need a room."

The man was wearing a sweat-stained tank top. And according to the name tag resting on the counter in front of him, his name was Fing Jat. "Of course," Jat said. "Our singles cost one hundred credits per night. We take all major credit cards."

"I plan to pay with cash."

"Then I'll need a deposit."

"Fine," Cat replied as she brought her roll of cash out and counted some bills onto the table. The stash was made up of small bills so it looked more impressive than it actually was. "Here's two hundred. I'd like a receipt please."

"This is a tough neighborhood," Jat said judiciously. "Be careful where you flash your cash. And your name?"

The first name that came to mind was that of a friend back home. "Harmon. Sissy Harmon."

"Okay, Miss Harmon, here's your receipt, and a keycard. You're in 808. The elevator is to your right."

Cat said, "Thank you," and felt the full weight of Jat's stare as she entered the elevator lobby. The lift made a sustained groaning noise as it carried her upwards. A man and a woman were waiting when the doors parted. They stepped to one side so she could pass.

Cat took a right, made her way down the hall to 808, and slid the keycard into the slot. A light glowed green followed by an audible *click*. Cat entered a small room that reeked of stim-stick smoke. There was barely enough space to accommodate a full-sized bed, a nightstand, and a dresser. An attempt to activate the vidset on top of it failed.

She could have requested a different room but was too tired to go through the hassle. Not yet anyway. So Cat lifted a blind and found herself looking down into a dimly lit alley. It wasn't much of a view, but she didn't need one.

After opening the suitcase and depositing her toiletries in the tiny bathroom, she shed her clothes. The next step was to try to change her appearance by hacking fistfuls of long blond hair off with a pair of scissors from the convenience store. It was, in addition to her wealth and pretty face, the single attribute most frequently used to describe her. So to part with it was to part with some of her significance. And it was difficult to hold back the tears. But when she looked in the mirror, the spiky-haired girl looked very different from the one at the governor's ball. And that was a good thing.

There was no tub in the bathroom. Just a shower. But it was reasonably clean. She stepped in, turned the water on, and was rewarded with a stiff flow of hot water. Having ducked under the spray, Cat allowed the water to break over her head and run the length of her body. Then, wrapped in the comfort of the liquid warmth, the tears came, and her body shuddered uncontrollably as wave after wave of sorrow overwhelmed her. Her mother, father, and all of the family's retainers were gone. Along with friends, friends of friends, and people who had the bad fortune to be in the wrong place at the wrong time.

The weight of it drove her down until she lay curled up on the floor of the shower, as the water continued to pound her flesh. And what made it worse was the knowledge that she had survived while the rest of them hadn't. *Why?* It was so wrong. Outside of college, most of her life had been spent finding new ways to have fun.

It was then, with her face just inches from the point where the water entered the drain, that Cat found a purpose. A reason to exist. And that was to bring Empress Ophelia to her knees. But *how*? She didn't have the faintest idea. But the notion gave her life meaning—and the motivation to stand up.

Having wrapped herself in a scratchy towel, Cat left the bathroom and sat on the creaky bed. The perfect spot to examine her foot. The cut was clean now. But she dabbed disinfectant onto it anyway, winced, and applied a self-sealing bandage.

She was physically and emotionally drained by then. So

she slipped into some new underwear, got into bed, and was about to fall asleep when she heard the mumble of voices from the next room. That was followed by distorted laughter and a *thump* as something hit the wall behind her head. Then came the rhythmic squeaking sound that the couple's bed made as they had sex. A siren could be heard off in the distance, a door slammed somewhere, and it wasn't long before Cat fell asleep.

Morning brought a gradual return to consciousness along with the vague memory of bad dreams and a sense of urgency. What was going on? What did the news nets have to say? Curiosity plus the fact that Cat was hungry drove her to get up, get dressed, and head out.

Cat dreaded running into Jat. But he was busy talking to a middle-aged woman. That was sufficient to lift her spirits as she exited through the front door. The sun was up. And as it warmed the streets, the combined odors of uncollected garbage, urine, and ozone grew stronger. But in spite of the smell and the run-down buildings all around, there was a sense of energy on the street. As if the locals were down but not out, and determined to accomplish something with their new day.

Rather than have breakfast in a sit-down restaurant, Cat chose to purchase a news tab from a street vendor, join the short line that led to one of the food wagons, and buy what was advertised as a "stir-up." The disposable container contained a mix of chopped ham, eggs, and potatoes. All drenched with hot sauce. It was delicious.

Cat took the food plus a large cup of caf over to the ledge that ran around a dry fountain. Because it was filled with weeds and garbage, she turned her back to it. And it was there, while spooning the stir-up into her mouth, that Cat read about the horrible "accident" that had taken place the night before. The explosion had been caused by a gas leak according to one public-works official, and had been responsible for the tragic deaths of the governor, her husband, and nearly all of their guests. A police officer blamed the tragedy on a bomb planted by antigovernment terrorists. Both agreed that there had been an altercation in the street out front. An investigation was under way.

That was bad enough, but according to the tabloid's editor, even worse news had arrived from Earth. It seemed that Emperor Alfred Ordanus had committed suicide two weeks earlier. Fortunately, Princess, now Empress, Ordanus had been able to step in to prevent the empire from spiraling into chaos.

According to Imperial spokesperson Tarch Othar, a firm hand would be required to root out the members of a conspiracy bent on seizing power in the wake of the emperor's death. A plot which, based on preliminary findings, had been led by none other than Cyntarch Dor Carletto. He and his wife had been killed during a raid on his home.

And, the article continued, Lady Catherine Carletto was on Esparto, and had been present at the governor's ball, but her body hadn't been found. Was she connected with the explosion in some way?

The implied answer was "yes." Cat thumbed her name, and the image that appeared was a picture of herself looking directly into the camera. The caption beneath the photo read, "Wanted dead or alive. A reward of fifty thousand credits will be paid to anyone who can apprehend Lady Catherine Carletto or prove that they killed her."

Cat paused to take a furtive look around. Her hair was shorter now. And she wasn't wearing makeup. But that wouldn't prevent a cop or a bounty hunter from recognizing her face. Fortunately, none of the people seated around the dry fountain were paying attention to her.

Cat's appetite had disappeared. She rose, threw the remains of the breakfast into a trash can, and carried both the caf and the tabloid back to her room. How many people had seen images of her face? *Millions?* Yes, since it seemed reasonable to suppose that the vidnets had been flooded with her pictures, too.

But once in her room, Cat was faced with the hopelessness of the situation she found herself in. Even though she hadn't been spotted yet, it was only a matter of time before she was. What she needed was a long-term plan. A way to hide, and remain hidden, until she could figure out a way to take Ophelia down. Eventually, having considered and rejected at least a dozen strategies, Cat fell asleep. And that's where she was, stretched out on her bed, when something woke her. A noise? She thought so but wasn't certain.

As Cat rolled off the bed she peeked out the window. What she saw came as a shock. A couple of synths were standing in the alley below! And Mr. Jat was there, pointing up at her room. It seemed that he had recognized her and was trying to collect the reward.

Then came the telltale thrumming sound as a transport took off from the hotel's roof and Cat knew what had awakened her. She said, "Shit, shit, shit," as she grabbed her hat and pulled it down over her hair. Then she put the leather jacket on and took a quick look around. Should she pack? No, there wasn't time. Plus the suitcase would be an encumbrance.

So Cat crammed her money, ID, and credit cards into her pockets and made use of a complimentary stim-stick lighter to start a fire in her trash can. Having blocked the door open with a bath towel, Cat ran down the corridor. It was a simple matter to pull the first fire alarm she came to. A bleating sound could be heard as the fire door opened, and a synth appeared.

Cat skidded to a halt and considered going back but knew it wouldn't work. So with no other options she did the last thing the android would expect and ran toward it. The machine raised its pistol, but it was too late. Her shoulder struck the robot, and the unexpected impact was enough to tip it over.

Cat landed on top of the synth, and the battle should have ended there, since the machine was at least twenty times stronger than she was. But being her father's daughter, Cat knew something most people didn't. Even though humans had created androids and programmed them to kill under certain circumstances, they were afraid of the machines as well. So various safeguards had been put in place to protect so-called soft bodies. They ranged from a planetwide shutdown of *all* ALFs, to the pistol-shaped synth stunners issued to police officers, and the last chance "kill switches" located at the base of each robot's neck. They were intentionally hard to access but gave humans some sort of chance should they be forced to grapple with a malfunctioning ALF. So Cat wrapped her arms around the machine's neck, felt for the kill switch, and succeeded in thumbing the protective cover out of the way.

But that was all Cat accomplished before the synth let go of the machine pistol in order to throw her off. The fire alarm continued to bleat, and the hallway was filling with smoke, as other guests sought to escape the building. And, not wanting to get involved in the fight, a couple began to edge past as Cat made it to her feet. That was their mistake.

Cat was able to grab the woman and jerk her off her feet. That led to a momentary tangle as the man, woman, and synth worked to sort themselves out. Cat took advantage of the confusion to reach in and flip the kill switch. The result was both dramatic and instantaneous. The ALF-46 gave a violent jerk, went limp, and collapsed.

Cat, who knew better than to take the machine pistol, saw that the android was carrying a nightstick and confiscated it instead. And no sooner had she freed the weapon than Cat had a reason to use it as the man took a wild swing at her. There was a cracking sound as the baton hit his wrist, and he screamed.

That was her cue to open the exit door and dash downstairs. Other guests were doing likewise and, as Cat fell in line, it seemed as though she would be able to follow them outside. But as she looked down through the center of the stairwell, she could see a synth waiting on the fourth-floor landing.

So Cat was forced to open the door on the fifth floor and enter the hallway. Maybe she could make her way to the south end of the building and use that set of stairs instead. There wasn't much smoke, but Jat was blocking the way. And he was armed with a wicked-looking knife. "Hold it right there," Jat said, ominously. "Or I'll deliver you in slices." And, judging from his expression, he was looking forward to the process.

The knife blade glittered as Jat carved giant X's into the air— and Cat held the baton with both hands. The path to freedom was *through* Jat, and she was determined to get there.

As the distance between them closed, Cat took a swing. The club missed hitting Jat's knife arm by a fraction of an inch. And she felt a searing pain as the razor-sharp blade cut a diagonal line down from a point just above her right eye onto her left cheek. She was half-blinded by a curtain of blood. Cat gave a cry of pain and backed away.

Jat grinned sadistically as he continued to advance. "You aren't so pretty now, rich bitch… And that's just the beginning."

Cat knew time was passing. And if she didn't deal with Jat quickly, the synths would arrive to help him. That left her with no choice but to take another run at the desk clerk. But this time she managed to block the falling knife with the baton and execute the only defensive move she knew.

Jat produced a grunt of pain as Cat's knee came up to make contact with his testicles. The knife fell to the floor as he sought to grab what hurt—and Cat took advantage of the moment to bring the club down on his head. Then she hit him *again*, felt his skull cave in, and ran. That was when the sprinkler system came on.

The sudden deluge of cold water served to wash some of the blood off Cat's face, and she made use of her free hand to tug the cap down over the top end of the laceration. Once in the stairwell, she took the stairs two at a time until forced to pause by a mother and her two children. One was a baby and the other was a toddler.

So Cat dropped the baton and scooped the older child into her arms. The foursome arrived on the ground floor less than a minute later. A fireman stood outside the door shouting, "Out! Out! Out!" An ALF-46 was standing right next to him.

By holding the child up in front of her face, Cat was able to keep the synth from getting a close look. And because the machine was on the lookout for a single human rather than a group of four, the strategy worked.

Having made it past the synth, Cat returned the toddler to his mother, who insisted on giving Cat a clean diaper to press against the laceration. Which was a good thing because Cat could tell that the cut was deep enough to require stitches.

First, she needed to put some distance between herself and the hotel, which she hurried to accomplish by setting a brisk pace and taking random turns. And that was fine. But she couldn't walk down the street holding a bloodied bandage to her face without attracting attention.

And now that the adrenaline had worn off, the wound hurt like hell. Cat was starting to feel light-headed when a kindly looking woman took hold of her elbow. "Come with me, honey," she insisted. "The free clinic is half a block away. They will take care of you."

Cat needed help and knew it. So she allowed the woman to steer her into a mazelike shopping arcade, and from there into a storefront with a sign that read FREE CLINIC hanging in the window. The door was propped open, and they walked inside. "There," the woman said as she helped Cat to a chair. "I'll let them know you're here."

Half a dozen people were seated in the shabby waiting room. But Cat was the only one who was bleeding. So it was just a matter of thirty seconds or so before a nurse and orderly arrived to escort Cat through a pair of swinging doors into a plain but well-organized treatment room. The air smelled of disinfectant. A slender woman in OR scrubs appeared moments later. She had short, bowl-cut gray hair, bright green eyes, and high cheekbones. "Hello… I'm Dr. McKee. What happened?"

Cat couldn't tell the truth, so she lied. "I tripped and fell down."

McKee gave a snort of derision as she took the bloodstained bandage and dropped it into a roll-around bucket. "Too bad you fell on a knife. We see two or three of these every day. Looks like you have a bleeder there. We'll cauterize it and stitch you up."

"Thank you."

"You're welcome," the doctor replied, as the nurse helped Cat up onto a table. "But there's something you need to know. There's going to be a scar. And a prominent one at that. But you're a pretty thing, so I'll use lots of tiny stitches. Later on, you can have the scar removed. A good biosculptor should be able to minimize the damage to the point where light makeup will cover it over."

Cat's head was spinning as the nurse started to swab her face with some sort of cold disinfectant. Her wealth had been snatched away the day before. Then it was her hair. And now she was disfigured as well. Cat remembered the nasty things she'd said about less attractive girls and wondered if she was being punished.

There was a series of pinpricks as Dr. McKee injected small quantities of a local anesthetic into the area around the wound, followed by the occasional buzz of a cautery, and the distinctive odor of singed tissue. Then came a long series of push-pull-tugs as the stitches went in. Cat counted thirty-six altogether.

"You can expect some bruising and swelling," McKee said, once all of the sutures were in place. "The stitches are self-absorbing and will disappear within the next week or so. But if you have any problems, come see me right away. And stay away from the person with the knife. Promise?"

Cat remembered the way Jat's skull had collapsed and knew he was dead. "I promise."

Once the dressing was in place, Cat was released into the waiting room, where she gave the clerk a fictional name, address, and com number plus a twenty-five-credit donation from her quickly dwindling store of cash. It wasn't smart, but it felt like the right thing to do.

With a bottle of pain pills in her pocket, Cat stepped out of the clinic into the flow of foot traffic. She let it pull her toward a clothing store a few doors down, where she went inside to examine her face in one of the mirrors. The bruising and the full extent of the diagonal dressing came as a shock. Cat experienced a wave of profound self-pity followed by a sudden realization. The bandage made her look different. *Very* different. And given the nature of her circumstances, that was a plus.

It wasn't much, but enough to lift Cat's spirits as she left the store and reentered the mall. It seemed natural to take a right turn, which led her past the Andromeda Travel Agency. She stopped and stood for a moment, looking at the exotic destinations advertised in the window. One of the holos showed a woman lounging on a beach with two suns shining above. Did Cat have enough money to reach a different city, never mind another planet? She knew the answer was no.

She was walking along, slowly, trying to come up with a plan, when an animated arrow appeared on the sidewalk in front of her. It zigzagged through the crowd to the far side of the passageway, where the image of a female legionnaire appeared.

The soldier had Cat's features, bandage and all, but was dressed in a white kepi and a spotless uniform. And, judging from the way the legionnaire was staring into space, she could see things that mere mortals couldn't. It seemed the Legion was using hidden cameras hooked to a computer to pick up possible recruits from the passing foot traffic. And the image brought Cat to a full stop.

Uncle Rex had been in the Legion. And told her all about it. So Cat knew that the image projected on the window was false. Because, like the original French Foreign Legion, the modern-day version was full of eccentrics, people on the run, and convicted criminals. *And that,* Cat thought to herself, *makes the Legion a possibility.*

That thought was enough to draw her across the passageway and into the recruiting station on the other side. The sparsely furnished interior had a makeshift feel. As if the office might be closed on short notice. The walls were covered with posters of legionnaires on leave in exotic locales, on parade, or in the field. All of them looked like professional models. Two desks faced the door. One was occupied by a noncom with a lot of stripes on his arms, and the other was home to a younger man, who was talking to a pimply faced youth of eighteen or so.

A possible recruit? Yes, Cat thought so, as the senior NCO stood. He had a high forehead, and his hair was so short that he appeared to be bald. Dark, heavily bracketed eyes peered out at Cat from fleshy caves, and a no-nonsense nose presided over what Uncle Rex might have referred to as "a shit-eating grin."

"Good afternoon," the legionnaire said as he shoved a giant paw in her direction. "I'm Staff Sergeant Boad. And you are?"

Cat *had* to give a false name, and based on what her uncle had told her, that wasn't unusual. The use of a *nom de guerre* was an accepted practice in the Legion. And had been for hundreds of years. So Cat gave him the first name that came to mind. "Andromeda McKee."

"It's a pleasure to meet you," Boad said as he crushed her hand. "Please have a seat."

The plastic chair made a rattling noise as McKee pulled it

closer to the desk and sat down. "So," Boad said as he eyed her bandage, "what's the other guy look like?"

"I left him facedown," McKee answered truthfully.

Boad looked surprised. "You're serious?"

"He attacked me."

"Well, that's what we're looking for," the NCO said. "People who aren't afraid to fight. Plus we need specialists. Com techs, mechanics, you name it. What kind of training are you interested in?"

McKee thought about Empress Ophelia. "I want to learn how to kill people."

Boad's eyebrows rose, and he nodded slowly. "Well, young lady... If that's what you want—we'll sure as hell teach you. Welcome to the Legion."

3

IMPERIAL PLANET EARTH

Everyone agreed. In the wake of Emperor Alfred's unfortunate death, the Imperial government had been transformed from a reactive bureaucracy to an engine of change. Initiatives that had been on hold were approved. A number of Alfred's pet projects were canceled, including his plan to provide the citizenry with affordable cyberbodies. So as Tarch (Duke) Hanno emerged from his air car, and was escorted through security, he could feel the energy crackling all around him. And it was intoxicating.

But there was something else in the air as well. A sense of caution that hadn't been there before. Which was to be expected. Because all of Alfred's senior officials, key associates, and friends had disappeared. A lucky few had been allowed to slip into retirement, but most had been assassinated by Ophelia's army of synths. That was a secret, but not much of one, because only a naïve fool would believe that thousands of prominent people would all suffer accidental deaths in such a short period of time.

So even though Ophelia's supporters had survived the purge, and were enjoying their sudden rise to power, they knew what could happen to anyone who fell under suspicion. And because Hanno had been summoned to the castle, what felt like a lead weight was riding the pit of his stomach. He couldn't let his fear show, however, since Empress O had eyes everywhere, and it would be a mistake to reveal any sign of weakness.

As a page led him through the busy hallways, Hanno responded to each greeting with a stiff smile as he compiled a mental list of the individuals he encountered. Because each person who greeted him could be an ally or an enemy during the days ahead. Assuming he survived that long.

Two minutes later, Hanno passed between a pair of watchful synth guards and was ushered into one of three ornate waiting rooms, each accessed via a different hallway. The idea was to keep visitors separated, so they weren't aware of each other. A precaution as old as monarchies themselves.

There was nothing for Hanno to do in the waiting room except sit in a high-backed chair, drum his fingers on worn gilt, and examine the retro decorations that Ophelia's grandfather favored. He was the man responsible for establishing the present empire. It was modeled on those of the seventeenth and eighteenth centuries and had proven to be much more effective than the democracy that preceded it. Until Alfred took over, and the governmental machine slowed down.

Hanno's thoughts were interrupted as a door opened, and Ophelia's secretary appeared. His name was Veneto. And in spite of his humble origins, everyone knew he was a player. A person who had Ophelia's ear every day *and* every night if the rumors were true.

So as Hanno stood, and the men exchanged courtesies, the nobleman was careful to match the depth of Veneto's bow. There were many stories about the fates suffered by aristocrats foolish enough to slight Veneto, and Hanno had no desire to test the extent of the secretary's influence.

Veneto had thick, curly hair, a bladelike nose, and a sensuous mouth. His lips smiled, but the look in his gold-flecked eyes remained the same. "Tarch Hanno! Welcome to the palace.

Please step this way. Her Highness is looking forward to meeting with you."

Hanno had his doubts about that but took comfort from Veneto's lighthearted tone and felt the lump in his stomach start to dissipate. As the two men entered the audience chamber, Ophelia was on her feet, speaking with an admiral. Having received his orders, the officer bowed and backed away. When Ophelia turned in his direction, Hanno was struck by both her beauty and the cold clarity in her eyes. She was a very different person from her brother—and a very dangerous one. He bowed.

"Good morning, Tarch Hanno," Ophelia said. "And thank you for coming on such short notice. Please have a seat."

Four chairs circled a table. Ophelia took the one that was lit in a way that would accentuate her beauty. Hanno chose the seat directly across from the empress and waited for her to sit down before doing the same. "So," Ophelia said as she settled into her chair, "you're wondering why you were summoned. And given how busy we are, I'll cut to the chase. I need someone with your talents to run a new department. One that will help shape the empire during the coming years."

Hanno felt his heart beat faster. Here was what he'd been hoping for. A position of real power. "I am honored, Highness. How can I be of service?"

"I would like you to become Director of the Bureau of Missing Persons," Ophelia replied.

Hanno felt his spirits plummet. The empress laughed. "You should see the expression on your face!" she exclaimed. "Never fear, Tarch Hanno... I'm not asking you to track down runaway teenagers. Far from it. No, the Bureau of Missing Persons will be in charge of locating individuals who represent a threat to the empire, but for one reason or another, have not been found. Not so far, anyway. Although I'm sure that you and the forces I will place under your command will be able to find most, if not all of them, and do so expeditiously."

Hanno's mind was racing. If he understood Ophelia correctly, she was asking him to complete the purge. An unpleasant task, perhaps, but a necessary one, lest someone try to overthrow the new government. It was the sort of task that would enable him to strengthen the Hanno family's ties to the empress and line their pockets at the same time. "I see," he said gravely. "And how many missing persons are there?"

"Three thousand, two hundred, and thirty-six," Ophelia replied. "Scattered across more than two dozen planets. That's a large area I know... But I can provide you with twenty-five human case officers and five hundred synth trackers."

"And when we find a missing person?"

"They're missing," the empress said with a smile. "Make sure they stay that way."

IMPERIAL PLANET ESPARTO

The one-story building designated as Receiving Facility 7654 (RF-7654) was located adjacent to Elysium's largest spaceport so that Cat—no, McKee; she had to start thinking of herself as McKee—and the 289 provisional recruits, or PRs, housed inside had to listen to the barely muted roar of engines at all hours of the day and night.

A third of what the PRs called the tank was devoted to rows of bunk beds, which were divided by gender and a yellow line painted onto polished duracrete. Tables and chairs, all of which were bolted to the floor, occupied the center of the space. An open assembly area was located adjacent to that. When not engaged in some sort of official activity, there was no discipline to speak of, and that allowed the strong to prey on the weak. Something they did primarily for the fun of it since all of their personal belongings had been confiscated and nobody had anything to steal other than Legion-issue toiletries, a scratchy towel, and two sets of olive drab fatigues.

The lack of military discipline struck McKee as strange until she noticed all the cameras mounted around the enormous room. Was their purpose to monitor the mayhem and ensure that it didn't get out of hand? Or were the PRs being tracked and evaluated via some sort of behavioral software?

She would have put money on the second possibility, but it raised more questions. If the PRs were being evaluated using a personality matrix, what sort of behaviors were considered *good*?

Teamwork was an important part of any military enterprise—so maybe the Legion was looking for the kind of individuals who could get along with others.

On the other hand it would be logical to suppose that the Legion placed a high value on aggressiveness. And by watching people interact with each other in the tank, the staff might be able to identify the PRs most likely to lead a charge up a hill. Or follow someone else up a hill. Then there was the possibility that the command structure wanted to recruit and retain a blend of personality types.

There were so many variables that McKee knew she wouldn't be able to game that part of the system and turned her attention to what she *could* influence, which were the tests that the PRs took each day. Some were physical in nature, and it didn't require a genius to know that the Legion was looking for recruits who were in good condition.

So McKee strove to deliver every push-up, every sit-up, and every jumping jack required of her. She couldn't, of course, since she hadn't been working out much, and the targets were set high. But she *tried.* And if McKee was right about the cameras and their purpose, then someone knew that. And was aware of the extra push-ups she was doing as well.

Unlike the measures of physical fitness, the electronically administered personality and aptitude tests could be gamed. Or so she assumed. And having completed a degree in cybernetics before setting out on the grand tour, she was an expert at taking tests. The key to success lay in simple multiple-choice questions such as, "Would you prefer to: (a) carry a stretcher, (b) operate a com set, or (c) perform maintenance on a crew-served weapon."

None of those choices got at what McKee *really* wanted to do, which was learn to fight. But it was a pretty safe bet that those assigned to operate crew-served weapons had to maintain them as well, so by choosing *C*, McKee was indicating a preference for a combat specialty, and the training that went with it. Wherever she could, she skewed her answers accordingly.

Once the tests were over, the PRs were left with a significant amount of unstructured time. Roughly half of each day was spent napping, shooting the shit, or playing improvised games.

One of which was called slave. It involved throwing a pair of dice that someone had smuggled in. Rather than wager money they didn't have, the players could bet five-minute periods of time during which the loser, or "slave," was required to do whatever the winner, or "master," wanted.

Did the people in charge of the tank know about "slave"? They had all of the necessary camera shots at their disposal. But for reasons unknown, the activity was tolerated. And that wasn't a problem for the most part because the demands put forward by most masters involved personal errands, silly antics, or slave contests. One of the favorites was who could eat the most rock-hard fruit bars in the shortest period of time.

But occasionally a master would insist on something darker. And such was the case one afternoon as she and the rest of the PRs finished their lunches. As usual, McKee was sitting by herself, worrying. There hadn't been any sign of the synths so far. But the medics had taken blood more than a week earlier. That meant the Legion had her DNA. Would they share it with the new government? Or would the Legion's stubborn insularity protect her from a cross match? The Legion was full of people who were on the lam, and if the organization ceased to be a place of refuge, the supply of volunteers would dry up.

Such were McKee's thoughts as a PR named Larkin won a series of throws thereby enslaving a young woman named Melissa Reese. And rather than order Reese to duckwalk around the room, or something similar, Larkin told her to strip. And when Reese refused to comply, he ordered his toadies to grab her. They obeyed, and Larkin had just ripped Reese's shirt open when McKee hit him in the back of the head with a metal lunch tray.

Larkin staggered, swore, and turned. He was angry. *Very* angry. Partly due to the pain. But mostly because of the way the incident might impact his social standing. Larkin's power, such as it was, lay in his ability to control other people through the use of his fists. So an attack, especially by a female, couldn't be tolerated.

For her part, McKee knew she was in real trouble. Not only did Larkin outweigh her by at least sixty pounds, he was in excellent shape, and proud of a criminal background that involved breaking bones for a loan shark. She wanted to run, but there was no place to run to, so she stood her ground.

Larkin took a roundhouse swing at McKee, and she ducked. And as his fist passed over her head, a whistle was heard. That was the signal for all of the PRs to line up in alpha order. And people who failed to obey such a summons had a tendency to disappear within a matter of hours.

So rather than continue the fight, Larkin grabbed a fistful of McKee's shirt and jerked her in close. His face was only inches from hers. "This isn't over, Scarface. I'll be watching you, and when you least expect it, *pow!* It will be payback time."

Larkin let go of her as the PRs hurried to line up. Once they were in formation, the NCOIC (noncommissioned officer in charge) made some routine announcements. There was no mention of Larkin's assault on Reese or McKee's attack on him. Had the assembly been called in order to prevent further violence? Or was it a coincidence? Either was possible. But one thing was for sure. McKee had an additional enemy now—and would have to be careful.

As the day wore on, McKee made an interesting discovery. She had never been popular thanks to her foreboding appearance and standoffish ways. But no one liked her now. Not even Melissa Reese. Partly because Larkin and his buddies were busy dissing her—but also because those who weren't members of the bully's group feared retribution.

In a strange sort of way, the social isolation was useful, however, because it gave McKee an opportunity to think about her previous life. A strange existence that had been lonely in spite of all the advantages. Or was it *because* of them? It had always been difficult to sort out those who wanted her body, wealth, or influence from those who actually cared about her. Assuming there had been any. So things were largely unchanged. She'd been alone before and still was.

Viewed from that perspective, she had lost less than she first thought. And when she went into the bathroom and looked in the mirror, she no longer felt the desire to flinch. True to the *real* McKee's prediction, the sutures had disappeared, leaving a pink line that would probably turn white with time. And just as her beauty had been an advantage in her previous existence, the scar was an asset now. It was both a disguise and an emblem.

So what did she want? Friends? That would be nice, she reflected. But would such a relationship be fair to them? What if Ophelia's assassins found her? Would they be satisfied with killing her? Or would the synths eliminate everyone she was close to? Those were difficult questions and remained unanswered as she went to bed.

The most obvious time for Larkin to attack her was during the night when she was asleep. So she arranged to trade her lower bunk for a rack located directly below one of the cameras. The idea was that if Larkin tried to reach her, he would have to climb up the framework, thereby shaking the stack and providing a few seconds of warning. Then, whatever took place would be visible to the people monitoring the cameras. Assuming they cared.

In spite of those precautions, McKee woke up frequently during the night and got very little sleep. And adding insult to injury, the morning whistle sounded an hour earlier than usual. That triggered all sorts of rumors, one of which was that the evaluation process was over.

The suspense continued to increase as the PRs ate breakfast, retrieved their trays, and fell in for morning roll call. Except the process was different this time. "Pay attention!" a corporal bawled. "The following people will assemble to my left. Allen, Cassie, Atkins, Phil, Banu, Beri…" and so forth until roughly a third of the PRs had been accounted for.

It looked as though the individuals in one group were going to be accepted while those in the other would be cut. And since McKee's name hadn't been called she was in group two. Was that good or bad?

All of the PRs wondered the same thing as an actual officer appeared. The first such creature they had seen so far. He was a captain and wore two rows of ribbons on his chest. After taking his place in front of the PRs, he stood at parade rest. His blue eyes swept both groups like lasers. "Good morning. My name is Captain Dawkins. I would like to thank the members of group one for applying to become members of the Legion—and to congratulate group two for being accepted."

That triggered a ragged cheer from group two and a mutual groan of disappointment from all the rest. And McKee might have added her voice to the celebration except for one thing: Larkin was in group two as well. And that didn't bode well.

The rest of the morning passed quickly as the PRs who hadn't made the cut were taken away, and the rest were given military-style buzz cuts. Once that process was complete, it was time for Dawkins to address them again. "You are," he said, "about to become members of the best fighting force that the human empire has. The Legion was founded on March 10, 1831. It was, and is, an elite unit, which is why we choose our members with care. That may sound strange to those of you who are familiar with the Legion's reputation as a refuge for people who want a fresh start. But, as one of our generals put it, 'We want the best of the worst.'"

It was a joke and generated plenty of laughter. "But regardless of what others may think," Dawkins continued, "we aren't outcasts. We have each other. Our motto is '*Legio Patria Nostra*,' which means 'The Legion Is Our Country.' That's how it was, is, and how it will always be. A lot of governments have come and gone over the last 875 years, but we're still here. That's because we fight for each other rather than a creed. Some say it is our greatest flaw. I say it is our primary virtue."

The officer's words had special meaning for McKee because it seemed as though Dawkins was sending all the recruits a message: "The Legion takes care of its own." Hopefully, that meant her DNA was safe from the government.

"Once you are sworn in," Dawkins continued, "some of the most difficult days of your lives will begin. From Esparto you will be sent to Drang for basic training. Those of you who survive the process will go from there to Adobe or other planets for additional instruction."

Having heard the phrase "those of you who survive," McKee scanned Dawkins's face for any trace of humor. There wasn't any. And though well traveled, she had never heard of a planet named Drang. One of her mother's favorite sayings came to mind: "Be careful what you ask for. You might get it."

Then it was time to raise their hands and swear an oath.

Not to the empire but to the Legion. Suddenly, everything changed. Requests became orders. The recruits were told to address noncoms as "sir" or "ma'am" until they graduated from boot camp. What seemed like picky details suddenly took on tremendous importance. Infractions were punished with push-ups. And there were lots of infractions as the recruits broke rules they didn't know about.

Finally, having stripped their bunks, cleaned the lavatories, and buffed the floors, the recruits were taken outside and loaded onto buses, which transported them to the spaceport. That was where three reentry-scarred shuttles were crouched waiting to take them up to the transport *Eta Tauri*.

Rather than exit the buses, the recruits were required to sit and wait. The reason for the delay wasn't clear. But as McKee watched a distant ship blast off, her thoughts turned to Earth and all that had been lost to her. The relationship with her parents had been rather poor during the months prior to her departure. Her father wanted her to join the family business, with an eye toward her running it one day—and her mother had been hoping for grandchildren. The problem was that neither possibility appealed to her.

Now, waiting to leave for Drang, she missed both of them so much that it made her chest hurt. And it was too late to please either one of them. She knew that. *But,* McKee told herself, *there is one thing I can give them. And that's revenge.*

That notion was comforting in a hard, cold sort of way, and she felt better as she and her companions were told to exit the bus. Then came a good deal of swearing reinforced by a kick or two as the NCOs herded their charges into a column of twos. "This ain't a column of threes, idiot," one of them said as a hapless recruit tried to line up next to a couple of his friends. "Get your ass to the back of the line. Goddamn it to hell, you people are stupid."

Then, having wasted time sitting on the bus, the recruits were required to run across the tarmac to one of the waiting shuttles and thunder up a ramp. Once inside the utilitarian ship, they were ordered to sit on fold-down seats and, in the words of one burly sergeant, "prepare to barf." But in spite of the initial urgency, nothing happened for another fifteen minutes. A pattern that McKee was coming to expect.

Finally, with barf bags at the ready, the ramp came up, and the shuttle lifted off. There were no viewports. All the recruits could do was stare at the people on the other side of the aisle or close their eyes as the additional gees pushed them down into thinly padded seats and the hull began to shake.

McKee had been through the experience many times before albeit on much more luxurious vessels. So she was prepared for the occasionally violent motion as the shuttle battled its way up through Esparto's gravity well and the sudden weightlessness that followed.

But most of her fellow recruits were entering space for the first time. About half threw up into the barf bags, much to the amusement of the free-floating NCOs. And she couldn't help but take pleasure in the fact that one of the people who came in for some ribbing was none other than Desmond Larkin.

Fortunately, most of the vomit went into the bags. But a few brownish globules managed to escape custody, and there was no defense against the odor that threatened to make McKee sick with all the rest of them. So she was thankful as the shuttle entered the *Tauri*'s landing bay and came under the influence of the larger vessel's powerful argrav generators.

There was a solid *thump* as the shuttle touched down. But those who hoped to escape both the ship and the smell were in for a major disappointment. It seemed that the *Eta Tauri*'s crew was engaged in a training exercise that required them to leave the landing bay open and unpressurized until what one corporal referred to as "the navy's circle jerk" was over. A full half hour passed before the bay was closed off, an atmosphere was pumped in, and the recruits were allowed to exit.

Then it was time to form up and listen to an orientation lecture from Chief Petty Officer Nambo. She had a hard face, a beefy body, and a prosthetic arm. It produced a high-pitched whining sound whenever its owner moved it. The chief had to raise her voice in order to be heard over the rattle of a power wrench and the nonstop flow of announcements from the PA system.

"Listen up," Nambo bawled as she eyed the faces in front

of her. "This is the combat supply vessel *Eta Tauri*. She is more than two miles long, she can carry 3 million tons of cargo plus a fleet of seventy-five shuttles like the ones you came up on. Approximately sixteen hundred men, women, and robots are required to run and defend the ship. Your job will be to stay out of their way and keep your pieholes shut. Someday, assuming that you graduate from basic, you will have both skills and a purpose. Until that fine day, you are cargo. And worthless cargo at that.

"Once you reach your quarters, you will be assigned to a lifeboat. If the captain orders us to abandon ship, report to that lifeboat, and *only* that lifeboat. The people assigned to other boats don't have to accept you and won't. So when the *Tauri* falls into the local sun, you'll be along for the ride.

"Last but not least, we will be watching you… Steal something, assault someone, or pass gas without obtaining permission first and we will put your worthless ass in the brig. Do you read me?"

The response consisted of a ragged chorus of "Yes"es.

A sergeant named Hasker took a step forward. If looks could kill, every single one of the recruits would have been dead. "Chief Nambo asked you a question, pukes… The appropriate answer is either 'Yes, ma'am,' or 'No, ma'am,' realizing that if you say, 'No, ma'am,' I will put my boot up your ass."

Having turned to Nambo, he said, "Sorry, Chief. Please try again."

Nambo grinned. "Do you read me?"

McKee joined with all the rest to shout, "YES, MA'AM!"

"That's better," Hasker allowed. "Now that you know everything you need to know about the *Eta Tauri*, it's time to get organized." At that point the recruits were divided into companies and platoons before being led through a maze of corridors and passageways to D deck, which was down in the belly of the ship.

The space assigned to the second platoon of Bravo Company was equipped with stacks of bunks along both sides of the compartment, tiny lockers, and a narrow table that ran down the center of the bay. Training began with a lesson on how to make up a bunk complete with hospital corners. Then the recruits were issued bedding and ordered to use their newly acquired skills.

McKee couldn't remember making a bed before. She tried, failed, and wound up doing a lot of push-ups before finally getting it right. Fortunately, Larkin had been assigned to the first platoon and wasn't present to witness her difficulties.

Eventually, after all of the recruits successfully passed inspection, they were taken to the mess deck and fed. Though a far cry from what she had been accustomed to, the food was better than the crap served in the tank, and she was hungry.

Some of the people around McKee tried to engage her in conversation. But being unsure of whom she could trust, she provided little more than monosyllabic responses and was soon left alone.

Once the meal was over, two platoons from Alpha Company were detailed to enter the hot, steamy galley and perform all of the cleanup work. The rest of the recruits, McKee included, were released to "free time." Assuming there was some after they had memorized the Legion's chain of command, washed their "number twos," and polished their boots.

McKee completed the first task in a matter of minutes but was a good deal slower where the other two were concerned. But by imitating those around her, she managed to carry out all of the tasks assigned to her before climbing into her bunk. Then, with the privacy curtain pulled, she fell into a dreamless sleep.

It seemed to be only moments later when Sergeant Hasker entered the compartment and began to yell at people. "It's time to rise and shine, boys and girls... You have thirty minutes to prepare for inspection."

The announcement triggered a race as all of the recruits bailed out of their bunks and made for what the navy referred to as the "heads." The compartments were of equal size, but due to the fact that there were fewer females, there was less competition for sinks and showers. So the women were among the first to exit and make their bunks. Then it was time to put on the clean uniforms and the boots they had worked so hard to polish the "night" before. As the half hour expired, the recruits were ordered to "stand to."

McKee watched out of the corner of her eye as Hasker and a stern-looking corporal came down the line, ripping poorly made bunks apart, pointing out flaws in the way uniforms had been pressed, and intentionally scuffing any boot that wasn't shiny enough.

Then it was her turn, and she braced herself for the worst, as Hasker stopped in front of her. His closely shaven face was only inches away, and she could see his furrowed brow and smell his aftershave. The NCO's flinty eyes scanned her face, her uniform, and fell to her mirror-bright boots.

Meanwhile, the corporal was eyeballing McKee's rack. But rather than rip it apart, he took a step back. That left Hasker to deliver his judgment alone. "You ain't no legionnaire, McKee. Not yet. But at least you look like one."

That was high praise coming from Hasker. And McKee felt an unexpected flush of pleasure. Because of all the thousands of compliments she had received during her life, she knew this one was real. And that meant a lot.

After breakfast, the "boots" began a full day of training. The *Tauri* had broken orbit during the "night" and entered hyperspace a few hours later. That made it impossible to launch small craft, so the noncoms were able to take the recruits out onto the blast-scarred flight deck for a strenuous workout followed by an attempt to march. A seemingly outdated skill, but one that taught teamwork and still played a role in building *esprit de corps*.

It was an often-comical affair, which Hasker referred to as "a complete fuck-up," although neither he nor the other NCOs seemed to be particularly surprised. Probably because they had seen the whole thing many times before and knew that a lot of practice would be required to get it right.

Then it was off to lunch, followed by a history lesson in the ship's auditorium. The holo presentation began with the Legion's birth and went on to document the early days in North Africa, Spain, and the Crimean War. All of which led up to the famous battle of Camerone, in which Captain Danjou and sixty-two legionnaires took on a much larger force at a village called Camerone. Finally, after Danjou had fallen, and with only four able-bodied legionnaires left, Sous-lieutenant Maudet ordered his men to level their bayonets and charge the more than two thousand Mexican soldiers who faced them.

Maudet was killed almost immediately, as was a legionnaire named Catteau, who was shot nineteen times as he tried to protect the fallen officer. At that point, the survivors were called upon to surrender, and agreed to do so on the condition that they would be allowed to keep their weapons, and their wounded would be cared for.

There would be thousands of battles to follow both on Earth and other planets, but none that meant so much. And it was then that she began to more fully understand the grim, inward-focused pride that people like Hasker felt for their organization.

Classes continued through the afternoon. They covered a wide variety of subjects, including basic hygiene, the Imperial code of military justice, and the way the Legion was organized. The latter was of special interest to McKee, who knew that if she were to succeed in the Legion, it would be necessary to understand it.

Then it was dinnertime, and as her platoon prepared to leave for chow, Hasker made the announcement that McKee's platoon had been dreading. "You people have KP tonight, so remain on the mess deck when you finish eating. Petty Officer Chan will collect you at 1700 hours. Do what he says—and don't screw up. Do you read me?"

The response was automatic by then. "Sir! Yes, sir."

It was, McKee decided, a pain in the ass. But one that had to be dealt with. So the best thing to do was work hard and get the chore over with.

Chan was right on time, and instead of being the hard-ass that McKee had imagined, the petty officer was an affable man with broad cheekbones, a ready smile, and a slight paunch. In marked contrast to the Legion's noncoms, the navy PO had little interest in turning the boots into effective soldiers and delivered his orders in a calm, laid-back manner.

Rather than be assigned to clean the galley, as she thought she would, McKee found herself working in a storage compartment adjacent to the kitchen. The task was to open the cases of food that had been brought up from one of the ship's holds and load them onto what Chan referred to as "the ready racks." That way, they would be secure if the argrav generators failed yet readily available to the cooks.

The job involved some lifting, but it was simple enough, and McKee enjoyed working alone. So she had been on the task for about thirty minutes, and was more than halfway through it, when she heard the hatch open and close behind her. Chan probably—come to check on her.

But when McKee turned, she realized that the visitor wasn't Chan. It was Desmond Larkin. And two of his toadies. All three of whom had finished their work in the galley. "Well, well," Larkin said. "Look what we have here. Scarface is all alone, with no big bad NCOs to protect her."

McKee looked left and right, hoping for some sort of weapon or escape route. But there wasn't any. Larkin chuckled. "That's right, bitch. You're mine. I told you it was coming—and here it is. You're real brave when a person's back is turned. Let's see how you do face-to-face."

McKee knew she couldn't win but was determined to go down fighting. So she threw a box of baking soda at Larkin's face. And when the bully raised his hands to deflect the object she launched a kick. Unfortunately, he was able to deflect it with the turn of a hip.

Then they swarmed her. Fists struck from every direction. McKee fell, curled up into a ball, and had the breath knocked out of her as a boot slammed into her ribs. Then came a blow to the head, the sound of distant laughter, and a long fall into darkness.

4

*Kill a man and you are an assassin. Kill millions of men and you are a
conqueror. Kill everyone and you are a god.*
CLERGYMAN BEILBY PORTEUS
Standard year circa 1761

IMPERIAL PLANET ESPARTO
Hans Simek hated robots. Especially robots made to look and
act like humans because most thought themselves superior to
the beings who created them. But due to the influence of a well-
placed relative on Earth, as well as a horrible twist of fate, Simek
had been named Case Officer Nine in the newly created Bureau
of Missing Persons (BMP) and placed in charge of creatures that
were theoretically incorruptible, willing to work around the
clock, and could be destroyed if necessary.

Now, sitting in his newly refurbished office on the seventy-
third floor of the Imperial Tower, Simek had no choice but to put
his bias aside and interact with a thing named Fyth. The killing
machine's head had a sleek, streamlined look; it was wearing
the colors of the Imperial Security Service and standing at
parade rest. Although all of the experts swore that robots didn't
have individual identities, most were willing to concede that
because androids had to operate in a semiautonomous manner,

they inevitably acquired experiences unique to them. That led to preferences and generalized behaviors that could be perceived as individual personalities but weren't. Not technically.

All of which was a load of crap from Simek's perspective, because he *knew* that Fyth had a personality, and an obnoxious one at that. But unless he wanted to go out and kill people himself, he had no choice but to use the machines placed under his control to get the job done. "So," Simek said, "give me your report."

"It was sent to you electronically," came the inflectionless response.

Simek swore under his breath. "You will provide an oral report now, or I will have you recycled."

Simek figured that a nonsentient machine shouldn't care about being wiped. But in his experience, most of the higher-functioning androids did. That was because certain subprograms encouraged the robots to survive. Just as an inborn survival instinct served to protect human beings. So if Fyth wanted to "live," it would comply. And it did. "I was ordered to find and terminate subject 1012."

Simek tapped the number into a keypad. A three-dimensional likeness of an elderly man appeared in front of him. A cloud of white hair seemed to float around his head, a caste mark could be seen on his forehead, and deep lines creased his face. The image began to rotate. "Continue."

"His daughter was on Worber's World," the machine said tonelessly. "So I went to the city where her house is located and placed it under surveillance. The subject arrived twelve days later, collected his grandchildren, and departed. I followed."

"And then?"

"The subject took the children to a wooded area," Fyth said. "There was a stream. He had fishing poles for the children. As they dropped lines into the water, I emerged from cover."

Simek raised a hand, tapped some keys, and seconds later he was looking at 1012, the children, and the wooded setting through Fyth's "eyes." Sunlight sparkled on the water, and it rippled as it flowed past, broke against a rock, and came back together again.

Ten-twelve had his back to Fyth, but must have heard

something because he turned. There was a look of surprise on his face, followed by what might have been resignation. His voice was matter-of-fact. "Ophelia sent you."

"The government sent me."

Ten-twelve laughed bitterly. "There is no government. Not anymore. Just Ophelia. Please spare the children. They know nothing."

"Grandpa!" came a high-pitched voice. "I got one. Come help."

Simek watched a pistol come up, and saw the crosshairs appear, as a blue-edged hole replaced the caste mark at the center of the old man's forehead. Ten-twelve fell over backwards, a child screamed, and the background began to blur as the reticle sought the source of the sound.

Simek stabbed a key, and the holo imploded. He had grandchildren of his own. Three of them. And there was no need to witness the murders that followed. "And their parents?" he inquired.

"Dead."

"And the cover story?"

"The pistol used to kill 1012 and the children was found clutched in their father's hand. Police theorize that he followed his father-in-law to the stream, where he killed 1012 and the children. Then he returned home and turned the weapon on his wife. And himself. A suicide note was found next to his body."

"Nice and tidy. I like it."

"Of course you do," Fyth replied smugly.

Simek felt a flash of anger. "You will refrain from gratuitous speech."

Rather than reply by saying, "Yes, sir," the android was silent. Was that a sign of obedience? Or defiance? Simek clenched and unclenched his jaw. "I have a new assignment for you," he grated. "Lady Catherine Carletto is, or was, the daughter of Dor and Carolyn Carletto. They were neutralized during phase one of the succession process. Lady Catherine, or subject 2999 if you prefer, was here in Esparto Prime at the time."

Simek tapped a couple of keys, and the likeness of a young woman blossomed over the desk. As he spoke, the disembodied head began to rotate. "During the lead-up to the explosion on the fifth floor of this building, she was called away. Unfortunately, all of the people who knew why she was called away are dead. However, there's reason to believe that someone warned 2999. Because when she reentered the ballroom, and spotted some of your kind, she was visibly alarmed. Then a synth named Varth took a shot at her and missed. You might be interested to know that the unit was wiped and recycled. Perhaps it will be reborn as a dozen garbage cans."

If Fyth was troubled by Varth's ignominious fate, there was no sign of it on his smooth, nearly featureless countenance.

"That was just the beginning," Simek said grimly. "Half a dozen of your mechanical brethren went after 2999, and she managed to elude them all. A society girl, for God's sake! But a resourceful one. She ran, bought new clothes, and was hiding in a third-rate hotel when a desk clerk saw her image on a vidnet and turned her in.

"*More* synths were dispatched, and she not only disabled one of them but acquired a weapon in the process. A nightstick, which she used to kill the hotel clerk. We know because her prints were on the handle.

"Are you seeing a pattern here?" Simek inquired rhetorically as he caused Catherine Carletto to disappear. "The score is something like society girl ten, machines zero. But you don't feel any shame, do you? Because at the end of the day, you're a *thing*. Well, *thing*, see if you can succeed where the rest of your kind didn't. Twenty-nine-ninety-nine was wounded during her escape from the hotel. And, judging from the amount of blood she left behind, the cut went deep. A defensive wound most likely. So even if she's wearing a disguise, there could be one or more partially healed lacerations on her hands or arms.

"But first you'll have to find her," Simek added. "And that won't be easy. Because after fleeing the hotel, the bitch disappeared. So either she's here on Esparto, or she found a way to get off-planet. Maybe she sold some jewelry, or sold herself, and is hiding out on some shit-hole rim world by now. That's *my* theory.

"There is another possibility, however, and *you're* going to check it out. After sifting through 150 terabytes of data, an AI employed by the local security service noticed that the Legion processed a draft of recruits during the days immediately after 2999's disappearance. That raises the possibility that she enlisted, and they shipped her to Drang for basic training.

"So get an oil change or whatever it is that you do between assignments and go to Drang. If she's there, take care of it. If not, we'll focus on the rim worlds. Do you have any questions?"

"Just one," Fyth replied. "If she *is* on Drang, what about the rest of the soldiers?"

It was a reasonable question and a tricky one. Because while it was one thing to scrub 1012 and his family, Tarch Hanno might object to Fyth taking out an entire contingent of legionnaires. Assuming he could, which would be difficult unless Simek brought the navy in and authorized them to attack the Legion base from space. But then there would be an investigation plus a shipload of navy personnel to eliminate, and that would create even more problems. So Simek delivered his answer. "If you find 2999, leave the rest of them alone. But bring some of her DNA back for verification."

"Yes, sir."

"And Fyth…"

"Sir?"

"Don't screw up. You'll wind up as scrap metal if you do."

ABOARD THE IMPERIAL TRANSPORT *ETA TAURI*, IN HYPERSPACE

McKee was working on a spider form with her father, and he was talking. Telling her something important. But try as she might, she couldn't understand him even though she knew it was vitally important to do so. Then the scene began to fade, the drone of his voice started to recede, and someone pushed one of her eyelids open. A bright light flicked back and forth. "She's back," a female voice announced.

McKee saw two hazy-looking blobs, blinked them into focus, and found herself looking up at Sergeant Hasker and a medical officer she'd never seen before. She tried to sit up, but the pain hit, and she was forced to let her head fall back against the pillow. *Everything* hurt. Her face, her torso, even her legs were sore. One eye was swollen shut, and she winced as she reached up to touch it. "Take it easy," Hasker advised. "Nothing was broken, but somebody kicked your ass."

"I'll get something for the pain," the woman said, and disappeared.

Hasker looked away and back. "So, McKee, who beat the crap out of you? Give me a name. I'll have their ass for dinner."

McKee wanted to give him a name. *Wanted* to see Larkin and his toadies go down. But as she looked up into the noncom's eyes, she saw sympathy combined with something else. Curiosity? Yes. Hasker was waiting to see what she would do. To rat or not to rat. During the last week, she and her fellow recruits had been required to learn all sorts of rules. Some directly and some indirectly. And even though no one had said as much, McKee knew that legionnaires didn't rat on legionnaires. Problems, especially interpersonal problems, were handled without going up the chain of command. It was a far different world than the one she had grown up in. One in which she'd *never* been struck. Not once. When she spoke, her voice was little more than a croak. "I don't know who attacked me, sir. They came from behind."

McKee saw disbelief in Hasker's eyes. But respect, too. And the complete lack of follow-up questions served to reinforce her decision. "That's too bad," the noncom responded. "The doc tells me you'll be up and around by tomorrow. I'll put you on light duty for a cycle, and we'll see how you feel after that."

"Sir. Yes, sir."

Hasker said, "Get some rest," and disappeared.

The doctor returned, gave McKee a couple of pills and a glass of water. "Take these. You'll feel better. And you'll look better in a couple of days. All except for the nose, that is. It might be a little flatter than before."

McKee managed to prop herself up, put the capsules in her mouth, and take a sip. Some of the liquid went down the wrong way and caused her to cough. That hurt, and it felt good to lie down again. The lights dimmed, the pain began to recede, and sleep pulled her down. She went looking for her father but couldn't find him.

* * *

Two "days" had passed since the beating and, while still sore in places, McKee had returned to full duty. That included two sessions of PT per day, an hour of marching, and a couple of classes. Some had to do with the Legion, but most were focused on a swampy planet named Drang. It was inhabited by a race of primitive amphibians that lived in beehive-shaped mud huts and steadfastly refused to do any of the things that a succession of interplanetary governments demanded of them. Like paying taxes and obeying Imperial laws. The result was an often-violent stalemate.

Such were the facts. But what McKee couldn't understand was *why*. The orientation materials made no mention of exploitable natural resources, geopolitical strategy, or other factors that would explain why the Legion was required to occupy a worthless rock.

So as a session on Drang's often-dangerous wildlife came to a conclusion, and the usual Q & A period began, she raised a hand. Hasker, who was standing at the front of the auditorium, aimed a laser pointer at her. A red dot wobbled across her forehead. "McKee, go."

"Given that the locals hate us, and there has been no mention of a strategic objective where Drang is concerned, why station troops there?"

Hasker smiled grimly. "Well I'll be damned. One of you pukes has a brain! Well, I ain't no general, but here's my take. First, Drang is pretty close to a jump point our Hudathan friends would like to own.

"Second, even though the people who run things like to use the Legion for a variety of purposes, they're scared of it, too. Because any organization with a motto like ours could be dangerous. So they figure it makes sense to keep us busy on puss-ball planets like Drang and Algeron.

"Third, there ain't no better way to learn how to fight than to spend some quality time with the frogs. Those water-sucking bastards are tough, and if you survive basic, you'll be a combat veteran. So pay attention, people. What you learn here could save your life."

Class was dismissed after that, and McKee was in the mob of

recruits headed for the mess deck, when someone shouldered her aside. It was Larkin. "Hey, watch where you're going, bitch... Or do you want another ass kicking?"

Then the bully was gone as he pushed his way toward the front of what would soon become the chow line. McKee felt a sudden surge of anger and battled to tamp it down. She couldn't take Larkin head-on. She knew that. *But I will take him*, McKee thought to herself. *It's just a matter of time.*

IMPERIAL PLANET DRANG

Thunder-and-lightning storms were common, and the shuttle shook like a thing possessed as it dropped into Drang's troposphere and entered its final approach. There was less airsickness this time, but half a dozen recruits had been forced to barf into their helmets and looked up in surprise as Hasker announced that "The ship's about to land—so put those brain buckets back on."

That got a big laugh from all the recruits who hadn't thrown up. But their moment of joy was short-lived as the shuttle fell into an air pocket and lost one hundred feet of altitude before lurching forward again. After another three minutes of flight, the pilot said, "Hang on to your panties," and the skids hit hard. As the repellers shut down, McKee heard the sound of rain drumming on the hull and knew it was going to be miserable outside.

"Welcome to Fire Base Charlie-Four," Hasker said cheerfully. "Or what will be FBC-4 once you pukes build it. Because right now, it ain't nothing but a clearing in the jungle. Release your harnesses and follow me."

McKee saw a rectangle of light appear as the noncom clomped down the stern ramp into the pouring rain. He was wearing a bush hat, a poncho, and jungle boots. An assault rifle and a wicked-looking bush knife completed the outfit. Humid air flooded the cargo compartment, and the mutter of distant thunder was heard as Corporal Anders hollered, "What the hell are you waiting for? An engraved invitation? Get your asses out there."

McKee felt the rain pelt her hat and poncho as she followed

the first group of recruits out onto soggy ground. What she saw was depressing to say the least. FBC-4 was nothing more than a landing pad and a pile of cargo modules sitting on a patch of high ground. And as far as she could tell, the "high ground" wasn't all that high—being only ten or fifteen feet above the dirty-looking swamp water that lapped all around it.

Heavy equipment had been used to strip all of the vegetation off the roughly circular plot of land, an electrified fence had been installed around the perimeter, and the soft glow of pole-mounted lights could be seen through the gloom. And of special interest, to McKee at least, were the Carletto Industries Trooper Is that could be seen patrolling just inside the fence.

Each cyborg was eight feet tall and weighed half a ton. And, because the war forms were intended to be intimidating, they had ovoid heads with smooth faces. Their bulky wedge-shaped torsos were designed to take lots of punishment, and their hydraulically operated limbs were thick and sturdy. A Trooper I could run at speeds up to thirty-five miles per hour for sustained periods of time and operate in a variety of other environments, including vacuum and Class I through Class IX gas atmospheres. Plus, each cyborg could carry a bio bod on his or her back.

McKee wanted to go over and inspect one of the cyborgs up close but was forced to put that desire on hold, as Hasker and his fellow NCOs began to holler orders. Anders pointed at a large stack of cargo containers at the center of the compound. "Unload those mothers or sleep in the mud. The choice is up to you."

Thus began a grueling sixteen-hour battle that McKee would never forget. The containers were numbered, and there were four powered exoskeletons in unit 001, three of which turned out to be operational. The loaders had civilian equivalents, so some of the recruits knew how to operate them, and it wasn't long before the eight-foot-tall machines were hard at work moving materials from place to place.

Once the exoskeletons had been put to work, it was time to open container 002, which held the first of four metal frameworks that needed to be bolted together. Unfortunately, the power wrenches that came with the kits weren't waterproof and had a tendency to short out. That forced the recruits to tighten a lot of fasteners by hand and torque them down.

About three hours into the construction process, dozens of three-foot-long blood worms came wriggling up out of the water-saturated soil and went on the attack. It wasn't clear whether they had been disturbed or *always* came up out of the ground at that time of day. Not that it made much difference. McKee swore as one of the fleshy horrors attacked her left boot. She hit it with a crowbar.

That put the creature down as Hasker and the other NCOs strolled about shooting the worms with short bursts of auto fire. "Pile 'em up!" Hasker ordered. "We'll cook the bastards for dinner."

So McKee forced herself to pick up her worm and carry it over to a quickly growing pile. "That's the ticket," Corporal Anders said approvingly as he began to gut one of the creatures. "They might be ugly, but they taste a lot better than MREs."

After that, it was time to put the roof panels in place and screw them down before starting on the siding. Each four-foot-by-eight-foot sheet of metal was equipped with what one recruit recognized as a bullet-resistant liner. That prompted McKee to ask the obvious question when Hasker passed by. "Sir, what's this stuff for? According to the orientation materials, the locals are Class Five indigs."

Class Five civilizations were almost always preindustrial, which meant that firearms if any were produced by hand and, therefore, in short supply. Hasker grinned. "Good one, McKee. The frogs *are* Class Five. Only trouble is that gunrunners can slip past the single ship that the navy keeps in orbit, put down in the bush, and trade cheap weapons for bales of sneeze. That stuff grows wild here—and a single hit can cost as much as a hundred credits on Earth."

McKee knew that was true because she had tried some of the drug while in college. "So they use the guns to shoot at us?"

"Every chance they get," Hasker answered cheerfully. "And that makes it real hard to sleep sometimes."

He might have said more except that a Klaxon sounded. Two or three blocks of F-1 had been placed on a piece of sheet metal and lit. The bricks continued to burn in spite of the rain that fell on them. A makeshift grill had been set up over the fire, and it was crowded with steaming worm carcasses. The smell was heavenly, and like all the recruits, McKee was hungry.

So even though she had some misgivings about eating worms, McKee took a foot-long section of the smoking meat. It was served on a freshly cut stick. The skin was crispy, and the flesh was firm, with a taste reminiscent of pork. She surprised herself by eating the whole thing and washed it down with swigs of bottled water.

Then it was back to work as the rest of the siding went onto the buildings, floors were laid, and the plumbing was installed. Floodlights bloomed as the sun went down and the surrounding swamps came alive with the sounds produced by a small army of nocturnal creatures. There were croaks, grunts, and what sounded like some very human screams.

Occasional bursts of gunfire were heard as the T-1s sought to keep the worst of the local fauna away from the fence, and there were occasional flashes of light as night wings attempted to land on the electrified fence and burst into flame.

Finally, after what seemed like a week of struggle, the exhausted recruits were allowed to lie down on their recently installed bunks with their muddy uniforms still on. McKee had never been so tired. Something screamed out in the swamp and was answered from half a mile away. Light could be seen through gaps in the siding as a computer-controlled beam swept across the compound, and another woman began to snore. Boot camp was under way.

The rain had stopped, and occasional rays of sunlight were touching down here and there, as the NCOs began to pound on the metal siding with their rifle butts. "Up and at it, people... Inspection in thirty minutes. That includes you *and* your shed. So turn to."

All of the females were housed in building three. And all of them were as filthy as the interior of their shed. So the first step was to place their gear on the top racks and wash the place down. A process made possible by the presence of hoses, plenty of hot water, and drain holes in the floor.

Working under the supervision of the so-called HPIC (Head Puke In-Charge) the women went about the process of scrubbing the decks. Once the dirt had been loosened, it was time to spray the place down.

The HPIC for building three was a beefy woman named Nora Pachek. She had tattoos all over her face, neck, and arms. She was buff, *very* buff, and had already served a tour with the marines. Why Pachek left the green machine for the Legion was a mystery and likely to remain so because none of the other recruits had the guts to ask her about it.

Though not a member of Pachek's all-female posse, McKee liked her straight-ahead style and had been careful not to complain when she drew various shit details. Maybe that was why Pachek assigned her to scrubber duty. It was hard work. But once the job was done, the scrubbers could hit the showers, and the first ones in were the first ones out. That meant they would have more time to prepare for inspection. And one of the many things that she had learned over the last few days was that little things could make a big difference.

So she was able to enjoy a hot, if somewhat brief, shower before putting on the uniform of the day, which consisted of a tank top, shorts, and barracks boots. The latter was for show and, as one wag put it, "to piss us off."

After that, it was time to go outside and line up. The sun was out, a swirling mist hung over the swamp, and the day feeders were in full cry as the inspection began. The cacophony of hoots, howls, and gibbering sounds was a constant reminder of the fact that FBC-4 was a very small island in the middle of a very large swamp.

Most of the recruits, McKee included, were found wanting where their boots were concerned and assigned to shit details that would eat up some if not all of their free time that evening. Once the inspection process was over, Hasker laid out the agenda for the day. "After chow, you're going to build an obstacle course. Not inside the fence, where everything is all snuggly, but *outside* the wire, where the creepy crawlies live.

The T-1s will try to keep the frogs away, but one or two of the slippery bastards could still get through, so stay sharp. If you see something suspicious, let us know.

"Ideally, you would be packing heat," Hasker continued. "But with the exception of Pachek and a couple of others, most of you pukes wouldn't know a rocket launcher from a mop. So right after lunch, I'm going to introduce you to your new best friend—and that's the L-40 Assault Weapon."

Breakfast consisted of a boxed MRE (Meals Ready to Excrete). Then it was time to switch their barracks boots for jungle boots. They were equipped with steel shims designed to protect the wearer from the spikelike pogi sticks the frogs liked to plant in the shallows near game trails.

Then it was time to pass through a gate, wade into the surprisingly cold water, and start work. Tall stakes marked the points where the various obstacles were to go. So it was a matter of hauling raw materials out and bolting, binding, or in one case welding them together. The result was a circular course that included a high wall, a rope challenge, a zip line, and more. All supervised by NCOs who weren't required to get their feet wet thanks to the fact that they were high and dry on cyborgs.

Lunch came next, followed by the distribution of weapons, all of which showed signs of heavy use. Pachek tore hers down and put it back together in a matter of minutes. "This piece of crap is more like a shotgun than a rifle," she complained. "Where's the rifling?" It was a rhetorical question. But having heard it, McKee made a note to find out what rifling was and why she should care about it.

The empty shipping containers had been stacked to form bleachers by that time. So the boots had a place to sit as Corporal Anders stood on a module repurposed as a stage. A holo projector had been placed on top of the box and quickly came to life. The weapon had a boxy look. The image was a bit thin due to the sunlight streaming down from above, but still viewable. And Anders, who clearly relished the role of instructor, was in top form.

"Listen up, maggots," Anders said, "and listen good. The weapon in your hands is called the Axer Arms L-40 Assault

Weapon—often referred to as the 'AXE' for short. Do not under any circumstances refer to the L-40 as a 'gun.' Because a gun is a crew-served weapon like a howitzer—and there ain't none of you pissants big enough to carry a cannon.

"Now that we got that straight, let's get to it. There will be a fucking test, and the people who flunk will wind up dead. Every time the L-40 fires a cartridge, it is fed down into the rotary breech from a magazine located on top of the barrel. Each 4.7mm caseless round is *square* in order to reduce friction and to maximize the number of rounds that can be loaded into a magazine.

"The cylinder rotates clockwise, bringing the cartridge into alignment with the barrel. When you squeeze the trigger, the firing pin will set off the round, and gas pressure will be used to feed a new cartridge into the chamber. By now you blockheads have noticed that all of the L-40's moving parts are sealed inside a protective housing. That means you can submerge the AXE in water, march through a sandstorm, or go belly down in the mud, and it will continue to fire.

"Now take a look at the grip. It is located near the vertical gravity axis, which makes the L-40 easy to use. The grip includes the trigger, the safety, and the fire selector switch. That allows you to choose between single-fire, burst, and full auto. You can expect to put out six hundred rounds per minute in the sustained-fire mode—and two thousand rounds per minute in the three-round-burst mode. Finally, we have a carrying handle up top, complete with a variable optical sight that can be used in low-light situations.

"So the next time you run into an Imperial taxpayer, you should go up to him or her and thank that taxpayer for providing you with the finest assault rifle in the whole fucking galaxy. Is that clear?"

The answer came back. "Sir! Yes, sir!"

"Good. It's nice to have people agree with me. From this point forward, you will carry your AXE to chow, you will carry your AXE into the showers, and you will carry your AXE when you take a shit. Because this planet is not a safe place to be, and there ain't no place to hide. Okay. Let's go down to the water and see if you can fire those weapons without killing each other."

The next couple of hours were spent loading magazines, learning how to insert them, and taking turns shooting at nothing in particular. Partly because the range hadn't been set up yet—and partly as a way to familiarize the boots with their weapons before worrying about accuracy. And as McKee sprayed the swamp with bullets, she couldn't help but think about Empress Ophelia and wonder what it would be like to kill her.

The sunny weather was too good to last. And by the time the recruits rose the next morning and lined up for inspection, a gentle rain was falling. Thousands of overlapping circles covered the surface of the muddy water as McKee followed a boot named Laraby into the obstacle course. The AXE was on a sling, and it felt heavy, but she was happy to have the weapon since one of the T-1s had nailed a frog during the night. And there it was, out in the middle of the O-course, with a sharp stick up its ass. The point was protruding from between the creature's shoulder blades, and its head was hanging to one side. A warning, Hasker said, which would help keep other indigs away.

McKee wasn't so sure about that since it seemed as though the impalement could easily attract trouble as well. But such considerations were above her pay grade. So rather than worry about the right and wrong of it, she took the opportunity to eyeball the creature from about ten feet away.

The indig had a snakelike head, a skinny body, and mottled skin. The warrior's arms ended in three-fingered hands that lacked opposable thumbs but had skin-covered bone spurs that served the same purpose. The individual in front of her had long, muscular legs that led to webbed feet. The latter was the only aspect of its physiology that was reminiscent of a frog. McKee felt sorry for it, tried to convince herself that it was stupid to do so, and failed. It was a victim of the empire, and *she* was a victim of the empire, which meant they had something in common.

The obstacle course was tough. But as McKee's upper-body strength continued to increase, she was getting better at physical training and managed to get through with only one boost from a fellow recruit. He took the opportunity to squeeze her butt cheeks as he pushed her up over the highest wall. She looked back over her shoulder and swore at him. And when he laughed, she saw that the offender was none other than a mud-smeared Larkin. The incident served as a reminder, and a timely one, because McKee knew she would have to deal with the bully eventually.

After completing the O-course, it was off to the recently completed firing range. It consisted of a level spot just outside the fence, a dozen pieces of metal siding to lie on, and two ranks of targets out in the swamp. There were ten of them at three hundred yards, and ten more at five hundred yards, with the second row being higher than the first.

Fortunately, there was no need to go out and retrieve targets, or to put more up, because the fabric through which the bullets passed was not only self-healing but designed to record the exact location of every hit. Data that was transmitted to a portable reader board set up on the beach.

Rather than use their own weapons, which, as Pachek put it, "are pieces of shit," the recruits were given new L-40s to fire. Both rows of targets could pop up and down, forcing the shooters to switch back and forth between them. Each boot was entitled to forty shots. Twenty-five hits were required to pass, thirty hits were required to earn a sharpshooter's badge, and thirty-eight hits were required to qualify as an expert. No small task with a short-barreled weapon.

Twenty shots had to be taken from a prone position, ten while kneeling, and ten using only their arms to support and control the L-40. McKee had excellent eyesight, as well as good eye-hand coordination, and managed to score twenty-six hits the first time on the firing line, a performance that earned a "Not bad," from Anders. High praise indeed.

By the time dinner rolled around, McKee felt fairly good about her performance for that particular day. She was sitting on a crate, working her way through an MRE, when a familiar roar was heard. She had a good view as a reentry-scarred shuttle lowered itself through the overcast and settled onto the huge X at the center of the compound. Such arrivals weren't unusual.

And as the transport's ramp made contact with the ground, McKee wondered who would be chosen to go aboard and hump supplies. Then, as a lone figure appeared at the top of the ramp, McKee felt something akin to ice water trickle into her veins. Because the silhouette looked very familiar. Frighteningly so.

She reached for the AXE, checked to make sure that the safety was on, and brought the weapon up. A quick look through the telescopic sight was sufficient to confirm her worst fears. A synth! On Drang. *Why?*

Suddenly, her appetite disappeared, and she felt a little bit dizzy as Hasker went over to speak with the android. The call went out over the PA system a few moments later. All of the recruits were to fall in. No exceptions.

For one brief moment, McKee toyed with the idea of opening fire on the robot or making a run for it but knew she'd wind up dead either way. No, the smart thing to do was to keep her cool and hope for the best. Besides, the odds were that the synth was there for a reason that had nothing to do with her.

So she took her place in the front rank of the second platoon and was standing at attention as both Hasker and the visiting android took up positions in front of the company. McKee knew Hasker pretty well by then. They all did. And judging from the noncom's expression, he wasn't happy. "Listen up, people… This is Tracker Fyth. It's looking for a fugitive named Catherine Carletto. If you are Catherine Carletto, or know where Catherine Carletto is, speak up."

McKee felt as if she were going to faint. It took all of her resolve to keep her head up and look straight ahead. The situation was bad. *Very* bad. Ophelia's security apparatus was looking for her on Drang. But McKee knew she had a couple of things going for her. One of which was the Legion's closed culture.

"All right," Hasker said after five seconds of silence. "Tracker Fyth has requested permission to inspect the ranks. You will remain at attention."

McKee watched out of the corner of her eye as the android started with the first platoon and inspected the recruits one by one. The process seemed to last for hours. But in all truth, less than ten minutes had elapsed by the time Fyth sidestepped into a position directly in front of her. And as McKee stared into the robot's red eyes, she knew it was comparing her features to those stored in its onboard computer. Everything was at stake—and time seemed to stop.

5

Humans have many weaknesses, not the least of which is their extensive reliance on cyborgs and robots. No good will come of it.

HAK HAKNA
Ramanthian xenoanthropologist
Standard year 1972

IMPERIAL PLANET DRANG

As the android made its way along the ranks of legionnaires, he could "hear" the Trooper Is talking to each other on the squad-level push. The cyborgs were heavily armed. And Fyth knew that if he found his target, he would have to be very cautious. The cyborgs might destroy him if he put a bullet in her head. Because humans were prone to act on emotion rather than logic, and the fact that they were wearing electromechanical bodies wouldn't make any difference. So the best strategy would be to arrest Lady Carletto, take her off-planet, and shoot her somewhere else.

Making the situation even more difficult was the fact that while the noncommissioned officer named Hasker was acting in a compliant manner, his face was devoid of expression. That raised the possibility that he was concealing negative emotions, a behavior that would be consistent with the Legion's tendency to protect its soldiers from civil authorities.

Fyth had registered two possible "hits" during the last few minutes but neither one held up under more intense scrutiny. So as the search continued the android kept a picture of Lady Carletto up where it could "see" it. Another face appeared as Fyth sidestepped into position directly in front of a female recruit. The Carletto image contracted to more closely match the size of the woman's closely cropped head. At that point the android experienced a pleasant buzzing sensation while text slid sideways cross the bottom of its electronic "vision."

"Subject is a 58.2 percent match to target 2999. Investigate."

So Fyth focused its attention on the superimposed images. There was a definite resemblance. The subject's hairline, eyes, and lips were a perfect match. But the recruit's nose was flatter, her face was thinner, and she had a pronounced scar that ran from just over her right eye down onto her left cheek.

That observation prompted Fyth's processor to replay part of the conversation with Simek. "Judging from the amount of blood she left behind, the cut went deep. A defensive wound most likely. So even if she's wearing a disguise, there could be one or more partially healed lacerations on her hands or arms." Could the facial scar have been received on Esparto?

"What's your name?" Fyth demanded.

The recruit looked at Hasker, saw him nod, and brought her eyes back to Fyth. "McKee... Andromeda McKee."

"Where are you from?"

The recruit opened her mouth to reply but Hasker spoke on her behalf. "McKee was sworn in on Worber's World."

Fyth "saw" the possibility of a match drop to 46.1 percent. "Let me see your arms."

The recruit was wearing a T-shirt. When she extended her arms, the android saw that they were free of scars. Fyth lost interest. The next recruit was male and way too tall. The search continued. When it was over, the android was left with nothing to show for its effort. A human might have felt a sense of disappointment. But not Fyth. It didn't have emotions as such. Just a continuing desire to complete its mission.

So Fyth boarded the shuttle, strapped itself in, and began to "think" about the rim worlds. Maybe Simek was correct. Maybe subject 2999 was hiding out along the very edge of human-controlled space. Fyth would find out.

McKee felt a profound sense of relief as the shuttle's repellers flared, and the ship began to rise. She was safe. For the moment at least. Thanks to Hasker. Thanks to the Legion. *Legio Patria Nostra*. It was true.

The troops had been dismissed, and she was about to leave the assembly area when Hasker motioned her over. The expression on his face was serious. "McKee..."

"Sir?"

"I don't know why the synths are looking for you, and I don't care. But watch your six... Maybe this is over, and maybe it ain't. You read me?"

"Sir, yes sir."

"Good. Report to your MOS group."

There was a great deal to learn before the recruits could graduate from basic training and join one of the regiments. Not just *any* regiment, but the one that Hasker and the other instructors deemed to be most in keeping with a recruit's test scores, skills, and apparent aptitudes.

The possibilities included aviation, supply, medical, the pioneers, infantry, airborne, and cavalry. The latter was of considerable interest to McKee because it would allow her to work with the cybernetic "forms" designed and manufactured by Carletto Industries. And because members of the cavalry were considered to be part of an elite organization that appealed to her as well. So when Hasker asked if any of the recruits wanted to learn more about the T-1s, her hand shot up. "You'll be sorry," Pachek predicted. "*Never volunteer for anything*. That's the second commandment."

McKee grinned. "And the first?"

"Pee when you can."

McKee laughed. "I have that one covered. How 'bout you? What specialty are you interested in?"

"Airborne," Pachek replied. "Why walk if you can fly?"

* * *

Corporal Anders was teaching the class on T-1 maintenance and ticked names off a list on his hand comp as McKee and a dozen other recruits gathered around a hulking T-1. "Okay," Anders said. "Let's get something straight right from the get-go. Private Fox isn't a machine. She's a person just like you. The difference being that you have biological bodies, and she is wearing a war form. So when you interact with her, keep that in mind.

"Now let's talk about what a Trooper I can do. Trooper Is are eight feet tall and weigh half a ton. They are equipped with three-fingered pincer hands, or shovel hands, as the occasion demands. A Trooper I can run at speeds up to thirty-five miles per hour for sustained periods of time while carrying a bio bod. And they can do fifty in a sprint.

"Now, no insult to Fox here, but the greatest weakness of a T-1 is that they are only as smart as the human beings installed in them. In most cases, a Trooper I has his or her name stenciled on his or her right chest plate, a unit insignia on its left arm, and some choose to wear artwork in place of the tattoos that bio bods are allowed to wear.

"If you look closely, you'll see that each cyborg has twelve small inspection plates located at various points on their bodies. They provide readouts for power, coolant, lubricant, life support, com systems, and so forth. Primary responsibility for checking the readouts rests with the bio bod assigned to each Trooper I, secondary responsibility rests with the platoon's cyber techs, and tertiary responsibility rests with the squad leader.

"*Every* bio bod is expected to carry out daily maintenance tasks and service their cyborg's weapons. And, if worst comes to worst, it will be your responsibility to pull your T-1's brain box. At that point, the cyborg is rendered unconscious but can survive for up to twelve hours. Then they have to be hooked to a 'rack' for external life support, or they will die.

"So," Anders finished, "if you've had some prior experience with electronics, hydraulics, and or life-support technologies, that would be very helpful. Okay, enough talk. Let's start with basic maintenance."

McKee was pleased to discover that she knew more about

the inner workings of T-1s than Corporal Anders did. And that made sense since her family manufactured war forms, and she had a degree in cybernetics. But it soon became clear that he knew a lot of things that she didn't, including which parts were substandard and how to carry out field repairs, that would have left her father shaking his head in amazement.

As the orientation session came to an end, and the light started to fade, the recruits lined up to get their MREs. Then it was time for a final roll call and some words from Hasker. "Get all the sleep you can, boys and girls. We're going for a stroll in frog country tomorrow, and this ain't no training exercise.

"It seems the gunrunners have been putting down about fifteen miles southwest of here. So we're going to lay an ambush for the bastards. And if that don't work, we'll booby-trap the LZ before we leave. Load up for three days. That includes ten mags each. No more and no less. Reveille is at 0400. We'll wade out at 0500. Sweet dreams, shitheads."

After more than two hours of tossing and turning, McKee had finally fallen asleep. And when the lights came on, and the noncoms began to beat on the sheds, she had a sense of having been somewhere better, although she couldn't remember where.

There was no time to waste as the women rolled out of their racks and lined up to take five-minute showers, before returning to the main bay. After putting her jungle-style camos and boots on, McKee ducked under her poncho-style body armor and poked her head up through the hole. The bullet-resistant liner and ballistic inserts were heavy in and of themselves. And with full ammo pouches, a combat knife, first-aid kit, entrenching tool, and two canteens of water, the rig weighed more than forty pounds. Her weapon plus a small pack brought the total up to something like fifty-five pounds. She was stronger now, thanks to all the physical conditioning, but was she strong enough to carry half her body weight all day long? She would know by nightfall.

There were attempts at levity as the recruits ate their rations, but the jokes fell flat, and there was tension in the air as the noncoms ordered the recruits to form up for an inspection. Not the kind they had experienced before, but a more casual affair, in which Hasker and Anders went over each recruit's kit, checking to make sure they had all the required gear and that their body armor was properly secured.

Once that process was complete, Hasker spoke to them over the company push. McKee could hear his voice via the speakers in her helmet. "Listen up... Anders and Chu will be on point followed by the first platoon and the second platoon. Fox and I will walk drag. Do your best to maintain visual contact with the person ahead of you but don't bunch up. Because if you do, a single grenade could cause a lot of damage.

"If we take fire, don't shoot back unless you can see a target—or a noncom calls for suppressive fire. And if that happens, be careful what you shoot at. If you hit me, and I survive, you'll wish I hadn't.

"Finally, keep those brain buckets on. Your HUD (Heads-Up Display) will show where you are relative to the rest of the unit and to Fire Base Charlie-Four. And so long as you are wearing your helmets, Corporal Anders and I will be able to remind you of how stupid you are. That's what we get paid for."

After that, Chu carried Anders out into the swamp, and the first platoon followed along behind. The sun was only a dimly seen presence above the low-lying clouds, the normally green plants looked gray, and, with the exception of the icons on the inside surface of McKee's visor, the men and women of the first platoon seemed to fade from existence.

Then it was the second platoon's turn as Pachek led them into the cold water while an unseen bird produced what sounded like a sardonic laugh, and McKee battled the fear that lurked in the pit of her stomach. It was an ally, or could be, so long as she didn't allow it to control her. That's what she told herself anyway as the relative safety of Fire Base Charlie-Four was left behind. Each movement sent wavelets out across the water, something coughed in the canopy above, and Drang closed in around her.

Kr-Kak, son of U-Keni and father-to-be, sat high in a soul tree as the strangely attired star devils wound their way through the swamp below. It was difficult to understand how they could be intelligent enough to create such devastating kill things yet stupid enough to walk past a sinuous choke slither without seeing it. Fortunately for them, the constrictor had feasted the evening before and wasn't hungry. At least one of the off-worlders would have been killed otherwise.

That didn't apply to the huge death walkers, however. They were strong enough to kill a slither with their graspers, carried powerful boom weapons, and could "see" heat. So as one of the monsters splashed past fifty warrior lengths to the south below, Kr-Kak froze. There was a good possibility that the machine thing knew something was clinging to the tree above. But it couldn't tell the difference between a warrior and a parasitic tree slug of the same size.

Once the star things had passed, Kr-Kak stood with harpoon gun in hand, eyed the turgid water below, and dropped straight down. There were many pools. Some were shallow and some were deep. Kr-Kak knew the difference.

There was a small splash as he went in, followed by a delicious coolness as the liquid caressed his mottled skin. Then, with a surety that Kr-Kak took for granted, he swam toward the slight turbulence signaling one of the planet's many subsurface rivers and entered the flow. The current carried him downstream. The star devils were on the move—and Queen Mar-mi would want to know.

Gradually, as the clouds began to clear, and rays of sunshine slanted down into the jungle, the air grew warm and humid. That made the already unpleasant journey even worse. There were three modes of travel. The first involved wading across large bodies of mostly shallow water. There were hidden holes, however, and they were extremely dangerous, especially for a person burdened with fifty pounds of gear. Because if McKee was sucked down into a subsurface river, she would drown in a matter of minutes.

The second mode of travel, walking on solid ground, was better in some ways and worse in others. Because while she could see the ground ahead, the surrounding vegetation was home to a variety of creatures, including prunelike "crotch suckers," so named because of their predilection for dropping off branches and oozing through damp clothing to a victim's pubic area. The perfect place to tap into a femoral artery. And there were other pests as well, which found ways to colonize, feed on, or simply annoy the humans.

But the *worst* mode of travel to McKee's way of thinking was the so-called deep crossings, in which the recruits were required to half walk, half swim across murky lakes teeming with aquatic life. There was no way to know what was brushing up against one's leg, why there was a sudden disturbance in the water nearby, or when the bottom would suddenly drop away. And being only five-six, she found it difficult to keep her head above water at times.

It was on one such crossing that the company came across an abandoned village located near the center of a shallow lake. It wasn't clear whether the surrounding body of water served the frogs as a natural moat, a ready source of food, or both. Hasker and Fox were out front and approached the seemingly lifeless island very carefully, knowing that such places were often booby-trapped.

But after circling the village and inspecting the huts, Hasker pronounced the island safe. Two squads were ordered to guard the perimeter while the rest of the troops broke out MREs and ate lunch. The area smelled of rotting fish, but it was dry, and that made up for the stink.

McKee hurried to eat her meal so that she would have time to inspect one of the huts before taking her turn at guard duty. She was sitting slightly apart from Pachek and the rest of them with her back against a log and her legs crossed when a group of recruits approached from the right.

What happened next occurred quickly. One of the men threw something. The object was already twisting and turning in the air when McKee recognized Larkin and heard him laugh. The snakelike animal was about three feet long and weighed a couple of pounds. It landed on top of McKee's lunch, whipped around, and snapped at her unprotected face.

She scrambled to her feet, spilling both the MRE and the reptile to the ground as Larkin and his toadies laughed and exchanged high fives. Rather than slither toward the water as she expected, the snake-thing came straight at her. So she grabbed the L-40, brought it up, and fired. The slugs tore the reptile apart.

Like most fully automatic weapons, the AXE had a tendency to rise. But rather than take her finger off the trigger, or force the barrel down, McKee allowed the bullets to draw a line that led straight to Larkin before letting up. The last geyser of mud shot up an inch from the toe of Larkin's right boot. "Oops," she said. "That was close."

Pachek and half a dozen other members of the second platoon had witnessed the entire incident and laughed uproariously as Larkin's face turned beet red. He didn't say anything, *couldn't* say anything, as Hasker arrived on the scene, but the hatred in his eyes was clear to see. He had been humiliated. And that was something he couldn't bear. "What the hell were you shooting at?" Hasker demanded.

"A snake," McKee said calmly, with her eyes still on Larkin. "It came straight at me."

"Good shooting," Hasker observed approvingly as he toed the bloody corpse. "Don't forget to recharge that magazine. We wouldn't want to come up short, would we?

"All right, people... Enough sitting around. Get off your asses and relieve the folks on guard duty. Stay sharp now. There's more where the snake came from."

The afternoon was much like the morning, only warmer. Eventually, after wading across a shallow pond, Hasker and Fox led the recruits up a muddy bank and onto dry land. There were trees, but most of them were dead, as if from a blight. So there wasn't much foliage. Just a litter of fallen branches.

There was something spooky about walking through the maze of skeletal tree trunks. At first, McKee wasn't sure why it felt that way. Then she realized that the feeling had to do with the brooding silence that hung over the area. There were no trilling birdcalls, hooting noises, or any of the other sounds she was accustomed to.

On the other hand, it was a relief to be up out of the water, with clear visibility all around. So she was tired, but otherwise in reasonably good condition, as Hasker and Fox led the column along a game trail and into a clearing. And that was where both of them disappeared.

It took Pachek a moment to absorb what had occurred before alerting Anders. "Charlie-Twelve to Charlie-Two... Charlie-One and Charlie-Six fell into some sort of hole. Over."

That brought Anders and his T-1 forward at a run. When he arrived, it was to find that Pachek had already established a defensive perimeter. Having jumped to the ground, the noncom went over to inspect the trap. McKee was there, along with half a dozen other recruits, all of whom were wondering what to do.

Dead branches had been laid crosswise on top of each other to create a matlike structure, strong enough to support a two-or three-inch-thick layer of soil plus another hundred pounds or so. Anything heavier would break through the brittle branches and plunge down into the bottom of the pit. The trap was at least twelve feet deep, four feet wide, and six feet long. Carefully sharpened stakes pointed upwards from the bottom, and Fox was impaled on a couple of them.

Hasker, who was still strapped in place on the cyborg's back, appeared to be unhurt. The noncom was shaken, however, as was apparent from his uncharacteristic silence as he worked to free himself. "Hold on, Sarge," Anders cautioned. "Wait until we can drop a rope down to you. One wrong move, and you'll land on top of a stake. Fox, what's your status?"

"I took some damage," the T-1 replied. "But judging from my readouts I'll be able to walk. Assuming you can get me out of here, that is."

"Don't worry," Anders replied confidently. "We'll dig you out. It looks like the frogs were hoping to bag something big for dinner and got you instead."

McKee wasn't so sure about that but kept her reservations to herself as a rope was lowered to Hasker. Beyond the initial shock, the episode had a secondary effect as well. It served to underscore something that should have been obvious from the beginning. Hasker, Anders, and the T-1s were not the all-seeing, all-knowing gods she had initially believed them to be. They could and did make mistakes. Like walking on a game trail rather than parallel to it in this case.

McKee was still in the process of absorbing that lesson as they pulled Hasker up out of the pit. Then began the long, tedious process of digging a ramp that would allow Fox to escape the hole. Finally, when that moment came, it was obvious that the T-1 had a noticeable limp. The damage done to the cyborg's hydraulic musculature couldn't be repaired in the field. But, all things considered, the company had been lucky to escape the incident without suffering a fatality.

Darkness was falling by that time. So even though they were five miles short of their destination, the decision was made to bivouac in place and get an early start in the morning. And as McKee dug the fighting position (FP) that would become part of the company's 360-degree defensive perimeter, she was forced to consider the night ahead. Up until that point, she had intentionally isolated herself from the others lest some slip of the tongue or other misstep inadvertently reveal her true identity.

The net result was that now, as the gloom closed in around her, she had no one to watch her back. And that was dangerous with Larkin lurking about. The bully had directed numerous dirty looks her way during the course of the afternoon, and there was absolutely no doubt that he would seek revenge.

There wasn't anything that could be done, of course, since one could hardly strike up a friendship on a moment's notice. But for the first time in her life, McKee realized that she was going to need help to survive.

Such were her thoughts as she banked loose soil to protect her flanks and checked to make sure that she could back out of the FP if that became necessary. Then it was time to eat an MRE and put in an hour of sentry duty before returning to get some sleep. Fortunately, she remembered what the burly instructor called Hasker's Law, which was: "If something can crawl into your boots, jump into your pockets, or slither up your ass, it will."

With that in mind, McKee directed a blip of light into her FP and saw that a coil of human feces had been left right at the center of the depression. She sighed. It was going to be a long night.

* * *

The sun had just broken company with the eastern horizon as the noncoms made their rounds. One by the one, the recruits stood. And because of the fog that lay like a blanket on the ground, they looked like zombies rising from their graves.

Once she was awake, the next step was for McKee to brush her teeth while waiting for a heat tab to boil the water in her metal cup. Then she ate a fruit bar, washed it down with scalding-hot tea, and began to pack her gear. She was one of the first people to report to the assembly area at the center of the encampment.

Fifteen minutes later, the rest of the company was ready to leave. The dimly seen sun was still only three fingers off the eastern horizon as Anders and Chu led the recruits into a foot of murky water. What promised to be a long day had begun.

The march took the column across a shallow lake and through a mile and a half of thick jungle before delivering them into a clearing. From the look of things, fire had been used to clear a landing zone, but time had passed, and tendrils of green were pushing their way in from all sides. Within a month, the open area would disappear.

There was a hillock off to one side, topped by three four-foot-long metal stakes, and it didn't take a genius to figure out that they were crude grave markers. A crash site was visible beyond that. Had the gunrunners been killed during a particularly difficult landing? Or attacked by frogs while on the ground? Someone had survived, or so it seemed to McKee, since the indigs weren't likely to set up grave markers. So where were *they*? It was impossible to know. But the presence of a dilapidated shack perched on pilings suggested a rudimentary base of sorts. Perhaps the survivor or survivors had been rescued by another shuttle.

"This is as far as we go," Hasker said as Fox came to a stop well short of the clearing. "Do not, I repeat do not, enter the cleared area. It could be booby-trapped. And even if it isn't, our footprints would be visible from the air. We want to ambush the bastards, not chase them away.

"Corporal Anders and I will select positions for you. Once placed, you will maintain radio silence, restrict your movements, and wait. If we're lucky, the runners will put down in the middle of the LZ, and we'll take them out. Over."

What followed was interesting, to McKee, anyway, who was busy learning everything she could. The noncoms set up an L-shaped ambush that would put the gunrunners in a cross fire but minimize the chances of a friendly-fire incident. That part was easy. The more difficult challenge had to do with hiding so many heat signatures which, if spotted from above, would be a dead giveaway. With the emphasis on "dead" since an incoming shuttle could hose the entire clearing with cannon fire and kill most of the company in a single pass.

The key to avoiding such a disaster was thin pieces of high-tech material that the recruits could pull over themselves. They were called heat exchangers. Each "sheet" was equipped with a microprocessor that was woven into the fabric and capable of raising or lowering its surface temperature to match the air around it via thousands of tiny cell-like nanos.

Although these preparations were interesting, what followed wasn't. Time slowed to a crawl once she was belly down in her FP. Insects invaded her clothes and bit her. And as boredom took over, situational awareness suffered. She woke up and was shocked to discover that she'd been asleep. A group of large weed-eating herbivores entered the LZ, paused to look around, and waddled into the jungle. The sun arced across the sky. And as the light began to fade, Hasker gave up.

"This is Alpha-One... It looks like the bad guys took the day off. The first platoon will continue to play defense while the second eats. Then we'll switch off. The plan is to clear the area by 1600 hours local. We'll camp a couple of miles to the west. Over."

McKee produced an appreciative groan as she threw the heat exchanger off and stood. All sort of things hurt, but that was nothing compared to the need to pee. Once that problem was resolved, she hurried to break out an MRE, ate the scrambled eggs and ham cold, and was surprised by how hungry she was.

Twenty minutes later, it was the first platoon's turn to scratch what itched, slather antibacterial ointment on their insect bites, and go on crotch patrol. Many people, McKee included, preferred to handle that chore privately. But there were some, like Pachek and one of her friends, who paired off into teams.

Then it was time to go back the way they had come. But not *exactly*, so as to avoid any traps the frogs had put in place during the last eight hours or so. Darkness found them in a swampy area, where it was necessary to harvest reeds in order to have something to keep them up out of water. Hasker wanted to cut saplings and construct a defensive ring around the company's position, but he knew it wasn't realistic. The troops were simply too tired.

So the platoons were scheduled to sleep four on and four off with the T-1s patrolling the perimeter. Their sensors were set on max, and they had permission to "...grease anything that moves."

And because there were lots of nocturnal life-forms on Drang, they were kept busy all night. The noise generated by their fifties firing on full automatic was strangely comforting and helped McKee fall asleep.

A few hours later, she rose to find that she and her fellow recruits were surrounded by a sea of dead bodies. The T-1s had not only killed anything that came close but all of the larger creatures attracted by the buffet of dead flesh. There was nothing scientific about it. Just the raw application of firepower. But effective though the strategy was, the recruits couldn't rely on it for long. Not without a lot more ammo than they were carrying. McKee wondered if the frogs knew that.

All the humans could do was break camp and head for the firebase as quickly as possible. So as Chu waded out into the water with his fifty at the ready and Corporal Anders riding high on his back, the resulting waves caused dozens of dead bodies to roll from side to side and undulate. And as the second platoon followed, McKee was forced to go around the larger carcasses and let the others caress her legs as they slid past.

It was gruesome business, and McKee was about halfway across the pond, and passing under the branches of a tree, when the attack came. About 10 percent of the "dead" bodies suddenly came to life, frogs dropped from above, and two indigs arrived on the water-slicked backs of battle-trained herbivores. They made trumpeting sounds as they charged out of half-hidden grottoes and stomped some of the recruits to death.

The surprise attack resulted in a horrible chaos, in which

Hasker shouted orders that no one could take the time to decipher, frogs slit throats, and recruits fired wildly. "Aim, damn you, aim!" Hasker shouted as McKee blew a slick-skinned frog away and felt another land on her back.

Rather than battle the warrior, who was much stronger than she was, McKee brought the AXE up to her shoulder and pulled the trigger. The sound was nearly deafening even with the helmet on. But the arm that had been wrapped around her neck fell away, and there was a splash as the indig fell back into the water.

McKee saw Chu charge one of the giant herbivores. The T-1 was firing, but the bullets had no perceptible effect on the two-ton monster, which simply absorbed them.

There was a monumental clash as the cyborg attempted to club the monster with his weapon, but the swamp beast hooked the T-1 with its nose horn and tossed the legionnaire into the air. There was an explosion of water as Chu landed. The cyborg tried to recover, but couldn't, and as he sank below the surface, McKee realized that Anders was still on board and trapped beneath the war form.

She was pushing her way forward, intent on a rescue, when Chu exploded and blew the monster into bloody chunks. They splashed as they landed. It wasn't clear if the demo charges the cyborg had been carrying went off on their own or had been detonated.

Meanwhile, the frogs had been able to divide the company in two, with the first platoon gathered around Fox and Hasker. They were in relatively good shape but separated from the second platoon, which was spread over a large area and battling to survive. And it wasn't working. Bit by bit, the second was being whittled down.

McKee didn't think about what to do—she just did it. And was surprised to hear her voice on the radio. "This is Alpha-Two-Three... Rally around me. Form a square and face out."

McKee had seen the formation in the training vids they had been forced to watch and knew it had been used for thousands of years. Much to her surprise, the other recruits obeyed her order, and as they began to gather around, they brought the wounded with them. "Place them inside the square," McKee ordered. "Okay, defensive fire only, and stay with me."

The square was lopsided. It came apart, re-formed, and lost integrity again. But she was there to shout and cajole. She was towing a wounded recruit with one hand and firing bursts from her AXE with the other as a line of frogs surfaced and charged straight at them. The indigs were close, very close, but wavered like reeds in a stiff breeze as the hail of bullets struck them.

Then they were falling as McKee yelled, "Now! Left flank, march…" She was rewarded by something like a stampede as the surviving members of the platoon made the turn.

Another recruit was helping to support the wounded soldier by that time, but it wasn't until they were up out of the water that she saw who the recruit was. A two-foot-long section of spear was protruding from Larkin's left thigh, and his face was contorted with pain. "Leave me a weapon," he said. "I'll take some more of those bastards with me."

McKee frowned. "What? So you can win a medal? Bullshit. Hey, Peters, Mendez… Make a litter. Larkin needs a ride. And let's get some dressings on that leg. He's leaking."

It took fifteen minutes to prep the wounded and get organized. The frogs launched a number of feints during that time, but they had taken hundreds of casualties and lacked the numbers required for an overwhelming charge into machine-gun fire. Meanwhile, the second platoon had lost contact with the first platoon, which meant they were on their own.

Having assigned herself to the point position, McKee followed the map projected on her HUD back toward the firebase. The journey would have been only a few miles had they been able to travel in a straight line, but the need to stay out of deep water nearly doubled that, and the bloodred sun was sinking in the west by the time Hasker and the first platoon were able to rejoin them.

Hasker was riding Fox. He eyed the muddy faces, the improvised stretchers, and the way the men and women of the second held themselves. Their weapons were ready, they were properly spaced, and at least half of them had wounds of some sort. He nodded. "You are some tough troops. Welcome to the Legion."

6

*We must accept that the enemy will penetrate through and between
our forward formations and so we must be prepared to destroy him...
by the resolute use of mobile forces...*

FIELD MARSHAL SIR NIGEL BAGNALL
Commander in Chief, British Army of the Rhine
Standard year 1984

PLANET ADOBE

"If the empire has an asshole, this is it," Larkin said as McKee
and a detachment of sixty legionnaires clattered down a metal
ramp and onto Adobe's orange-red soil.

"No, that would be *you*," Pachek responded cheerfully. She
laughed, and Larkin glowered. The relationship between McKee
and Larkin had changed during the weeks since the battle on
Drang. Thanks to her efforts to get her fellow recruit out of the
swamp, and the swift medical treatment that followed, he'd
been back on his feet in a matter of days. And since she had
taken care of him, Larkin was determined to take care of her.

So even though McKee didn't care for Larkin's moody, hair-
trigger ways, he had her six. And by that time she had concluded
that having a weird friend was better than not having any at
all. "Where the hell is everyone?" a legionnaire named Wiley
inquired. His B-1 bag produced a puff of dust as it hit the ground.
The group was standing in the shuttle's oblong shadow, and the

nearest structures looked as if they were at least a quarter of a mile away.

"Something's coming this way," Choa said as he squinted into the glare. "Maybe they're coming to get us."

McKee looked to the north and saw that Choa was correct. A column of dust was spiraling up into the clear blue sky. And it wasn't long before a pair of 6 X 6 trucks arrived. They were painted with the Legion's desert camo pattern, wore the 13th DBLE's insignia, and rattled loudly as a sergeant opened the passenger side door of the lead vehicle and jumped to the ground. He was short and stocky. His white kepi, khakis, and desert boots were spotless.

McKee hoisted her B-1 off the ground and waited for the order to fall in. But there wasn't one. That was when she realized that she and her companions weren't considered to be recruits anymore. They were legionnaires, which meant their relationship with the Legion's noncoms had changed. And Pachek, who had served in the marines, knew that. "Hey, Sarge," she said. "You lookin' for draft 481? 'Cause if you are, that's us."

"Glad to hear it," he replied. "Welcome to Adobe. And yes, it's always this hot. Okay, split up. I want half of you in the first truck—and half in the second."

It took the better part of fifteen minutes to load the trucks, turn them around, and head for the distant cluster of buildings. Having boarded truck two and taken a place on one of the two bench-style seats that ran front to back, McKee found herself looking out across the seared landscape. Some hazy bluffs could be seen off to the east. But the rest of it was a flat, monochromatic plain.

She was struck by how surreal the situation was. It felt as if the original her had been left behind, the way a snake sheds its skin, so it could grow. Was that what she was doing? Growing? McKee hoped so, but maybe she was hiding and nothing more. Still, she had survived an all-out battle on Drang, and that was more than the previous her could claim.

Her thoughts were interrupted as the trucks slowed and came to a stop in front of an inflatable hab. The neatly stenciled sign out front read COMMAND AND SERVICES COMPANY, THE 13TH DBLE

(13TH DEMI-BRIGADE DE LEGION ETRANGER). McKee knew, or thought she knew, that she wouldn't be assigned to the 13th DBLE, but couldn't be sure. Her sights were set on becoming part of the famed 1st REC (1st Regiment Etranger de Cavalerie). It consisted of about five thousand legionnaires split fifty-fifty between bio bods and cyborgs.

But would her efforts to manipulate the legion's aptitude tests work? Sergeant Hasker's recommendation would mean a great deal, too—but she had no way of knowing what had been entered into her P-1 file. The result was a rising sense of tension. "All right," the sergeant bawled. "Everyone out. Line up in alpha order. Bring those B-1s and follow the yellow line."

What ensued was a long, tedious process as the incoming draft followed the faded yellow line into the hab and from station to station. There was a stop to update their P-1 files, a visit with a bored medic, and a two-minute session with a specially trained "sky pilot" who was available to provide instruction in eight different religions. The concept struck McKee as laughable, and judging from the comments she heard, her peers agreed.

But even if the check-in process was somewhat tedious, the hab was air-conditioned, and as Larkin put it, "I'd rather be in here than riding a T-1 all over the desert."

Larkin was standing behind McKee. She turned to face him. "You put in for the 1st REC?"

"Of course." Larkin's lopsided grin was the same one McKee had learned to hate back on Esparto. "Where you go, I go. That's how it is with us."

"But what if they put me in another unit?"

"They won't," Larkin said confidently. "Hasker not only recommended you for a cav unit but put you up for lance corporal. Everybody knows that."

McKee stared at him. "I don't."

Larkin looked smug. "Yeah, I know. Maybe you oughta talk to people a little more."

McKee turned back toward the front of the line. By then, she had learned that there were very few secrets in the Legion. Somehow, some way, word of what was going to happen always leaked out. The problem was that the "scan," as the legionnaires referred to it, was frequently flawed. So while the rumor that a particular unit was slated for a load-out might be true, the destination could be Algeron rather than Earth, and the two planets were *very* different.

In spite of what Larkin thought he knew, McKee's fate was anything but certain. And making a bad situation worse was the memory of Drang and the synth that had been sent to look for her. Was she being tracked? The suspense continued to build as the yellow line led her into an office labeled PERSONNEL.

The staff sergeant seated behind the desk was female and looked up from her terminal as McKee stopped in front of her. "McKee, Andromeda?"

"Yes, ma'am. I mean sergeant."

The noncom had short gray hair, an aquiline nose, and a no-nonsense mouth. The name tag on her desk read SSGT. A. TRAVERS. She made a steeple out of her fingers and frowned. "Sergeant Hasker rated you as outstanding. He even went so far as to recommend you for a medal. That's ridiculous, of course. We don't award medals to recruits. So forget that.

"However," Travers continued, "Hasker put you in for lance corporal. That's unusual, but not unheard of, and I see no reason to get in the way. Don't spend the extra thirty-two credits per month all in one place.

"That brings us to your MOS. You requested a cavalry slot, and you've got the necessary test scores, but the system flagged you for tech school. How 'bout it, McKee? The cyberschool is located on Earth. It's a helluva lot cooler there. And when you come back, you'll be a qualified gear head, a shoo-in for tech sergeant, and a very popular lady with all the 'borgs. Sound good?"

McKee was tempted for a second, but only a second. Earth was a very dangerous place for a member of the Carletto family to be. "No, thanks. I'd rather fight."

"All of us fight when the shit hits the fan," Travers responded dryly. "But I know what you mean. And we don't force people to attend tech schools. So take your orders, follow the yellow line out to the pickup zone, and look for a vehicle from the 1st REC."

There was a whirring noise as Travers touched a key, and a sheet of hard copy emerged from the printer on her desk.

"Good luck," the noncom said as she handed it over. "And congratulations on your promotion."

McKee felt slightly light-headed as she left the office. Not because of the promotion, which, though higher than private, barely meant anything in the military scheme of things. No, her sense of relief stemmed from surviving a contact with officialdom. Fortunately, there hadn't been any questions about her identity. And she was about to join the famed 1st REC! A regiment where the war forms manufactured by Carletto Industries would be all around her. McKee found that to be comforting, although she would have been hard-pressed to say why.

As she emerged from the hab, and the afternoon heat pressed in around her, she discovered that many of her peers had already been cycled through and taken away. Pachek was there, however, waiting for a truck from the 2nd REP (*2nd Regiment Etranger de Parachutistes*) to pick her up. The 2nd didn't use parachutes much anymore, preferring drop pods instead, but the idea was the same, and Pachek was happy.

So the two women were busy congratulating each other, and extolling the virtues of their respective regiments, when Larkin appeared. There was a scowl on his face.

"What's wrong?" McKee inquired. "Did they put you in the Pioneers or something?"

"No," Larkin replied. "I was assigned to the 1st REC. Just like you."

"So what's the problem?" Pachek wanted to know.

"Sergeant what's-her-name told me to polish my brass and said I was a disgrace to the Legion."

"Well, you *are* a disgrace to the Legion," Pachek said.

Larkin brightened. "I am, aren't I? Serves the bastards right!"

McKee and Pachek exchanged looks as a 4 X 4 bearing the 1st REC's oval-shaped emblem arrived, and a cheerful corporal rolled a window down. "McKee? Larkin? Throw your B-1s in the back. You can sit up here where the AC is."

The sun was resting on the edge of the western horizon and just starting to sink as the truck carrying McKee and Larkin paused in front of a gate. A bio bod mounted on a T-1 waved the vehicle through. The driver had reddish hair, lots of freckles, and liked to talk. "I'm going to take you to HQ, where the OOD can sign you in. She'll send you over to the transit barracks for the night. Then, come morning, they'll figure out what company to put you in. We're short of people—so there are lots of open slots. Here we are," the corporal said as he brought the truck to a stop in front of a long, low-slung hab. "Welcome to the 1st. I'll see you around."

True to the corporal's prediction, McKee and Larkin were logged in, sent to the transit barracks to drop off their B-1 bags, and released to chow. Most of the regiment's bio bods had eaten by then, but the line was still open, and the pair were able to slip through the facility before it closed.

They carried their trays to an empty table, sat down, and began to eat. "What a dump," Larkin said, with his mouth full. "I wonder what people do for fun around here."

McKee, who was eyeing the well-executed battle scenes painted on the walls, had other thoughts. "I don't know. But what I *do* know is that we've got a lot to learn. Like how to ride a T-1, fight from a T-1, and maintain a T-1. We can play later."

Larkin shook his head in mock despair. "You are such a straight-leg. I tried to beat some sense into you back on Esparto. But it didn't take."

"Thanks," she said sarcastically. "That was real nice of you. We'll probably wind up in different companies. You realize that."

"No," Larkin said serenely as he produced a loud belch. "I don't. You saved my ass. I'll save yours."

McKee sighed. "Lucky me."

In keeping with orders received the evening before, McKee and Larkin reported to regimental HQ immediately after breakfast, where they were greeted with bored indifference by a sergeant who had them thumb half a dozen screens. McKee didn't want to, knowing that her thumbprint could be linked to Catherine Carletto, but had no choice.

"All right," the sergeant said, once the formalities were completed. "The duty driver will take you to supply. After you draw your gear, report to the 2nd Battalion, where Sergeant Major Chora will assign you to company-level slots. Any questions? No? Then why are you still here?"

Having collected their B-1 bags from the transit barracks, McKee and Larkin tossed them into the back of a 4 X 4 which dropped them off in front of a half-buried hard-wall structure ten minutes later. The sign out front read SUPPLY & LOGISTICS, 1ST REC.

They entered the huge warehouse, where it took the better part of two hours to find the correct section, draw what seemed like a ton of gear, and exit. Fortunately, Larkin was able to "borrow" a pushcart, so they didn't have to hump their B-1s plus helmets, body armor, and field gear out into the harsh sunlight. Once outside, it was necessary to wait for transportation. And by the time the truck finally arrived, they were hot and miserable.

Despite the long wait, the trip to the 2nd Battalion's rectangular chunk of reddish orange desert took only five minutes. After piling their gear in a patch of shade, McKee and Larkin entered yet another inflatable hab, where they went in search of Command Sergeant Major Chora. She turned out to be a stocky no-nonsense sort with gun-barrel eyes and a horizontal slit for a mouth. Her sentences were short and clipped. "McKee... Larkin. You're slotted for Echo Company."

McKee saw the way Chora was looking at her and knew the noncom was thinking about her scar. It seemed as if women always stared longer. Or was that her imagination?

There was a smirk on Larkin's face as he directed a glance her way. She could practically hear him saying, "See? I told you we'd be in the same outfit."

"Captain Avery and his people will decide which squads and platoons are most likely to benefit from your complete lack of experience," Chora continued. It could have been a joke, but since Chora wasn't smiling, McKee didn't either.

"However," Chora said, "before we can send you over to play patty-cake with Echo Company—Monitor Snarr would like to have a word with you." There was something in Chora's eyes at that point. Something McKee couldn't read with certainty. Disapproval? Annoyance? She wasn't sure. Suddenly, servos were heard, and a synth appeared. McKee felt the bottom drop out of her stomach and fought the impulse to run as the machine came to a stop next to Chora. There was something birdlike about the way it looked from McKee to Larkin and back again. The robot's voice was flat and nearly inflectionless. "My name is Snarr. I was assigned to the 2nd Battalion to ensure that each and every legionnaire is a loyal member of the empire and stands ready to defend it."

"Which is a fancy way of saying that Snarr was sent to make sure we don't revolt," Chora put in pointedly. "Isn't that right, Snarr?"

"No," the robot replied pedantically. "I was assigned to…"

"Yeah, yeah," Chora replied impatiently. "You made your point. You can leave now."

Snarr remained where it was for a couple of seconds, turned, and left the office. "That's something new," Chora observed. "Every battalion has one. It would appear that someone had doubts regarding the Legion's loyalty. Be careful what you say and who you say it to. Especially when Snarr is around. Lord only knows who that thing reports to. Okay, enough of that… Let's get you over to Echo Company."

By midafternoon, the newcomers had checked in, stowed their gear in the lockers located at the foot of their beds, and were ready to begin the integration process. Both of them were placed in the first platoon. But while McKee was assigned to the second squad, Larkin wound up in the third, and that was a relief.

McKee's squad leader was a lanky man with a shaved head, quick brown eyes, and dark skin. His name was Hux, and once her gear was stowed, he took her on a quick tour. There were brief stops at the medical clinic, the armory, and the so-called morgue, where decommissioned war forms were stored. It was cool inside but kind of spooky, and she had no desire to linger.

Then it was time to return to the battalion's grinder to meet McKee's T-1. "His name is Rudy Weber," Hux said as they left a shaded walkway for the blistering parade ground. "He's a combat veteran. So when he speaks, be sure to listen. There he is… Weber is the one wearing the 300-Z series war form."

Two T-1s were facing each other and about to clash. One was

a 300-Z and the other was a newer 460-C. The differences were subtle but apparent to a trained eye. "So Weber is the one on the left," McKee said matter-of-factly.

"That's correct," Hux replied as he directed an approving glance her way. "You were paying attention in basic. I like that. Now watch what happens."

As far as McKee knew, the Hudathans didn't have any cyborgs. So the contest was a way for the legionnaires to stay sharp and make sure that their war forms were functioning properly rather than a preparation for hand-to-hand combat with enemy cyborgs.

There was a *thump* as the T-1s slammed into each other, a pause while both of them sought more leverage, and a clatter as the 460-C landed on the ground. Hux grinned. "A hip throw! Nice move. Hey, Weber," Hux said. "Meet your new bio bod. McKee's fresh from Drang, but she knows the difference between a 300-Z and a 460-C, so there's hope for her."

"That's a good start," Weber acknowledged. "And she's light. That's worth a couple of miles per hour."

"Glad you approve," Hux said. "Get her ready... The battalion has a field exercise slated for tomorrow morning. And it would be nice if she survived." And with that he left.

"So," Weber said, "have you ever ridden a war form before?"

The truth was that McKee had ridden dozens of cyborgs, starting when she was a little girl and continuing through college. But always in the context of her family's test facility. Yet she couldn't admit that and didn't. "No, I haven't."

"Well, circle around behind me and use the steps built into my legs to climb up into your fighting position. Once you're in place, secure the harness."

McKee did as she was told. Her feet went in the deep slots located on the back of the cyborg's legs, and the well-placed grab bars made the task that much easier. Once she was in position, with her head almost immediately behind the T-1's, it was time to fasten and adjust the safety harness. Normally, she would wear a helmet, but that was back in her locker. A headset was clipped to the metal in front of her, so she put it on. "Can you hear me?"

"Loud and clear," Weber replied. "Let's take a couple of laps around the parade ground. Remember to bend your knees to absorb some of the shock and keep your head on a swivel. My sensors are good, but they aren't perfect, and we're especially vulnerable from behind."

Weber began with a slow walk and took it up to a jog. "How are you doing?" he inquired.

Too much time had passed for McKee's previous experience to be of much value. It felt as if she were riding a jackhammer. "Just fine," she lied.

"Good. Let's try something faster." When Weber ran, the ride became a lot smoother, but it was difficult for McKee to assimilate what was going on around her at the higher speed. That was going to take some getting used to—and she was grateful when Weber slowed down.

The workout ended half an hour later, and it felt good to enter the barracks and lie on her rack. The sun was a warm glow beyond the fabric roof. She was a member of the 1st REC now—which meant her first objective had been achieved. She had a place to hide.

But she hadn't even begun to work toward her ultimate goal, which was to bring Princess Ophelia down. A notion so absurd, so silly, that it was ridiculous. Except the need to try burned so brightly inside her that no amount of internal dialogue would make it go away. So the only thing she could do was to take the next logical step: master the art of killing.

The new day dawned clear and bright. The air was still cool as the 2nd Battalion 1st REC left its compound and formed up around the trucks loaded with troops from the 6th REI (*6th Regiment Etranger D'Infanterie*). The first part of their mission was to accompany the motorized infantry east toward the hazy-looking hills. That's where the men and women of the 4th REI were dug in. They were playing the part of Hudathans, who had taken control of a strategically important objective called the castle, and were determined to hold it.

It wasn't a real castle, of course, but a natural rock formation that bore a resemblance to a castle, and was located at the end of a narrow valley. That meant that if the invaders went up the middle of the valley without neutralizing at least some of the enemy batteries on the hills to the right and left of them, they would be in a cross fire. But since all of them were aware of the danger, McKee assumed that her leaders had some sort of plan to counter the threat.

Echo Company's job was to parallel the infantry and screen the trucks from the possibility of an attack by Hudathan armor. And from her position high on Weber's back, McKee could see the full sweep of the assault. A wispy column of dust marked the progress of each vehicle or cyborg—some of which were little more than dots to the south. It was an amazing display of military might.

Meanwhile, by looking at the HUD displayed on the inside surface of her visor, and selecting one of many views, she could see how she was positioned relative to the rest of the squad. She could also access what Weber was "seeing" via his sensors, and the macro readouts for his electromechanical body.

According to the screen, Weber's life-support module was functioning at 98.4 percent efficiency, and with the exception of his left knee actuator, all of his primary systems were in the green. Unfortunately, the actuator had begun to overheat. Probably as the result of normal wear since the war form was designed to run for long periods of time and should be able to take it. Either way, it was something that would require her attention once the exercise was over.

And McKee could feel the pounding. Because in spite of her efforts to lean back and keep her knees slightly bent, each footstep sent a jolt up through her body.

McKee's thoughts were interrupted as Captain Avery spoke over the company push. She had been introduced to him the day before and been struck by both his manner and appearance. Rather than a Hasker-style hard-ass, Avery came across as thoughtful, and mild-mannered. He had thick brown hair, even features, and a slightly haunted look. Or so it seemed to McKee. The second or third son of a wealthy family perhaps? Forced to accept a military career because he wasn't slated to inherit? Yes,

McKee had gone to school with many young men who had to join the military, seek their fortunes on rim worlds, or serve as minor functionaries on Earth.

"This is Echo-Nine," Avery said. "On my command, the lead elements of the company will break left and follow the *north* side of the ridge in an easterly direction. The enemy has missile batteries on the top of the ridge. Fly-forms will engage them— but keep your eyes peeled. They're likely to get off a few rounds before they can be neutralized. Break left... Over."

McKee was mystified. It appeared that the infantry, along with most of the 2nd Battalion 1st REC, were headed straight up the valley and into a withering cross fire. Meanwhile, for reasons not clear, Echo Company would be moving parallel to the main force, but on the other side of a ridge. The same ridge that constituted the north side of the valley.

However, when she chinned a map onto her HUD, she saw the gap. It was located about five miles ahead on the right. The low saddlelike break offered an opportunity to cross over into the neighboring valley and attack the batteries clustered around the "castle."

But only if the enemy had been stupid enough to leave the gap undefended or their defenses had been neutralized somehow. Then there was no longer any time to think about the matter as the battle began.

Neither side was armed with actual weapons. But each soldier, vehicle, and cyborg could be "hit" electronically and scored as wounded or killed by a computer that had access to thousands of helmet cams plus satellites. Once hit, a person or unit would be ordered to stand down as the fight continued. Nor was the battle a sterile affair in which the two sides could go at each other with surgical precision. There were lots of electronic, visual, and auditory effects including electronic jamming, what looked like explosions, and artificially created gray smoke to simulate the fog of war.

Echo Company was jogging along the edge of a dry riverbed when preplanted smoke bombs went off all around them, and two T-1s were neutralized. "This is Echo-Three," Hux said over the squad-level push. "Keep moving. Take evasive action. Over."

McKee was thrown back and forth as Weber zigzagged between boulders and the "enemy" fired at them from the top of the ridge. "This is Nine," Avery said. "A squadron of fly-forms will hit the gap in two minutes. We'll pass through it sixty seconds later. Follow the path to the left. That will carry you up into the castle. Over."

McKee felt a wild sense of exultation as the fly-forms swooped in, dropped dozens of proxy bombs onto the gap, and were rewarded with clouds of billowing smoke. Then, as the airborne cyborgs disappeared, Avery led his company into the swirling grayness. McKee couldn't see, but Weber could, and they broke out of the fog and into the valley beyond moments later. A battle was raging there, but the assault was stalled, as the men and women of the 6th REI were forced to crouch behind whatever cover they could find.

"Now!" Avery shouted as he and his T-1 led Echo Company up a steep path. "Kill the bastards!"

Avery, the company sergeant major, Lieutenant Camacho, and their cyborgs were all "killed" within seconds and forced to step aside as Sergeant Boyce led the first squad past them. Hux, McKee, and the only other surviving member of the second squad came next. He was a T-1 with a "dead" bio bod strapped to his back.

Weber was firing his fifty as a solid phalanx of defenders came down to meet the invaders, and the fighting grew more intense. McKee triggered short bursts from her proxy AXE. Her primary responsibility was to prevent enemy soldiers from flanking Weber or attacking the cyborg from behind. She saw at least two "Hudathans" break off and head for the sidelines after she fired bursts into them.

All the while, they were climbing, and each stride took them closer to their objectives, which were the heavy weapons on the ledge above. The attackers were close, very close, and McKee thought they were going to make it when her HUD went dark to protect her from a flash of light, and a buzzer sounded in her helmet.

"You were killed by a rocket-propelled grenade," the synthesized voice said emotionlessly. "You will withdraw from the exercise and await further orders."

That suggested that Weber was dead, too, an assumption that was confirmed as the cyborg stepped off the trail, and the battle continued. There was very little left of the company by that time, and the last of them were "killed" just short of the ledge where the heavy weapons were. That part of the exercise came to an end soon thereafter, a reedy cheer went up from the "Hudathans," and both sides were ordered to stand down.

The next few hours were spent setting up encampments, complete with carefully placed defenses, in case of an attack. The sun was just starting to set as McKee collected her MRE and went looking for a quiet place to eat. She found it a couple of hundred yards from the company HQ just inside the company perimeter. A short climb took her to the top of a huge boulder, where she could eat and watch the sun go down.

Five minutes later, the self-heating entree was ready, and she was digging into it with a plastic spoon when the tell-tale crunch of gravel was heard. Then she heard a voice that she recognized as belonging to Captain Avery. "This is far enough... Now, what do you want? I have work to do."

McKee wondered if she should announce her presence, and was just about to do so, when a second person spoke. The voice was unmistakably that of the synth named Snarr. That changed everything, and she decided to remain silent. "I think you will appreciate my discretion once you learn what I have to say," the android answered.

"All right, say your piece."

"It's about your brother," Snarr said. "Recently, while at a party in old New York, he made comments that were critical of the empress. Then he questioned the circumstances surrounding her brother's death. He even went so far as to suggest that the emperor could have been murdered."

Avery's voice was tight. "So this is what things have come to. Every word we say is monitored."

"Not *every* word," Snarr replied. "But the government has an obligation to protect itself."

"Knowing George, he was probably drunk."

"That may be," the robot acknowledged. "But humans have a tendency to tell the truth when they are under the influence of alcohol—so such statements cannot be ignored."

McKee was uncomfortable by that time. But afraid to move lest she make a sound or send a pebble rolling down, revealing her presence.

"Okay," Avery said. "Why are you telling me this?"

"Because as a loyal member of the empire's armed forces, I thought you would want to know," Snarr replied. "Think of it as an example of something you want to avoid. More than that, consider your responsibilities as an officer. You are in a position to observe your legionnaires every day. They are, as I'm sure you will agree, trash swept up off the streets of a dozen planets. Almost all of whom are hiding from something. However, the people I work for couldn't care less about their various crimes. What they *do* care about is loyalty. Watch them, Captain Avery— watch them carefully. And if you observe anything suspicious, report it to me. Understood?"

"Understood," Avery grated.

McKee couldn't see them. But the clatter of loose rocks told its own story as Snarr and Avery departed. She allowed herself to exhale and was surprised to discover that she'd been holding her breath. It was terrifying to realize that Snarr was not only on the lookout for people like Catherine Carletto—but busy trying to establish a network of informers who might turn her in. People like Captain Avery.

McKee felt sorry for him. Judging from what she'd heard, his brother George was an ongoing source of trouble for the family. Still, it was comforting to know that there were those who shared her views regarding Empress O and the succession. And that raised an interesting possibility. What about Captain Avery? Could she enlist him in the effort to take the empire back? No, that was absurd. As a lance corporal, she couldn't even talk to the man unless it was to say, "Yes, sir." The best thing she could do was keep her head down, learn how to be a soldier, and wait for an opportunity. The sun was about to disappear, and when she took her first bite of food, it was stone cold.

7

The Legion is, it pains me to say, a necessary evil.
EMPRESS OPHELIA ORDANUS
Standard year 2706

PLANET ADOBE

It was Camerone Day, and as General Winton climbed a flight
of stairs and made his way out onto the speaker's platform,
thousands of legionnaires were waiting. The bio bods stood in
neat ranks, their white kepis gleaming in the sun, weapons at
parade rest.

Behind them were row upon row of Trooper Is, each standing
eight feet tall and packing enough firepower to grease an infantry
platoon. The cyborgs didn't need uniforms, but many had
been awarded medals for valor and wore them on ceremonial
harnesses designed for such occasions.

And all the way to the rear, towering above the rest, were the
new forms commonly referred to as Quads because each had
four fully articulated legs. The big walkers could function as
armored personnel carriers, tanks, or antiaircraft batteries.

All of them were assembled because on this day, in the spring
of 1863, a battle had been fought in what was still known as

Mexico on Earth. And now, as Winton took his place, it was time to honor the men who had fallen there. A voice boomed through the PA system. "Atten-HUT!"

Thousands of legionnaires crashed to attention, and Lance Corporal Andromeda McKee was one of them. It was just past 1300 hours, and she could feel the heat on her shoulders as the battalion's sergeant major bellowed the order, "Parade, REST."

The formation had originally been scheduled for 0800 but had been pushed into the afternoon. There were various theories, but according to the most popular scan, a message torp had arrived from Earth, and a whole lot of troops were about to load out. Maybe that was true, and maybe it wasn't, but one thing was for sure: The command structure had been caught off guard—and were playing catch-up.

Winton took a moment to survey the troops, then gave what might have been a nod of approval. "Good morning. As you know, we are gathered here today to celebrate the most famous battle in the Legion's much-storied history.

"The French had laid siege to the town of Puebla about 150 miles inland from the Gulf of Mexico, and five thousand feet above sea level. So to strengthen their forces, and overwhelm Puebla, a supply convoy was sent into the highlands. It consisted of sixty horse-drawn wagons loaded with guns, food, and gold."

McKee could imagine the dust, the horses, and the clatter of their hooves as the column followed a dirt road upwards. There would have been brightly colored uniforms as well, proud flags, and hundreds of hot, sweaty soldiers.

"Two days later, a spy brought some disturbing news. The convoy would be ambushed by several battalions of infantry, cavalry, and local guerrillas. Hoping to avert disaster, the Legion's commanding officer, a colonel named Pierre Jeanningros, sent a company down the road to warn the convoy, or make contact with the enemy. He chose the 3rd company of the 1st Battalion, which, due to illness, had no officers well enough to go.

"That's why Captain Jean Danjou, a member of the headquarters staff, volunteered to lead the patrol. Two subalterns agreed to join him. Out of a normal complement of 120 men only 62 were fit for duty.

"The company left before first light on April 30 and marched toward the coast. They made good time during the hours of darkness and reached a post manned by the battalion's grenadiers before dawn. After coffee and some black bread, the march resumed.

"Danjou took his men out just before dawn, which was just as well since it was going to be an extremely hot day."

McKee was sweating by then. The air seemed to shimmer, Winton was slightly out of focus, and her throat was dry. How long was the story going to take? Legionnaires had been known to pass out during such formations. She was determined to stay upright.

"They passed through a number of settlements during the next few hours," Winton said. "One such settlement was a run-down collection of shacks called Camerone.

"Danjou, a veteran of the Crimean War, led the column. Had someone been watching, they would have noticed that his left hand was missing—it had been lost in an accident—and replaced with a hand-carved wooden replica. The substitution did nothing to slow him down. Fortunately, thanks to science, the Legion can offer us new bodies now... And that's an improvement. Wouldn't you agree?"

The cyborgs produced a roar of approval, and Winton nodded knowingly.

"The legionnaires entered Palo Verde about 7:00 a.m. The village was empty. The men had brewed some coffee, and were in the process of drinking it, when Danjou saw a dust cloud in the distance. The cloud could mean only one thing—horsemen, and lots of them.

"'*Aux armes!*' Danjou shouted.

"The company was terribly exposed, so they fell back toward Camerone and looked for a place to make a stand. A shot rang out, and one of the legionnaires fell. They charged a hacienda, but the sniper had vanished by then.

"So Danjou gathered his men and was just about to lead them to an adjacent village when a squadron of Mexican cavalry galloped into sight. Danjou waved his sword in the air. 'Form a square! Prepare to fire!'

"The Mexicans split their force in half and approached at a walk. And then, when they were two hundred feet away, they spurred their mounts and charged.

"Danjou ordered his men to fire, and thirty rounds hit the tightly packed horsemen. A second volley rang out. At least a dozen cavalrymen fell. Then, as the Mexicans prepared for another charge, Danjou led his men into a deserted hacienda."

McKee felt dizzy. Out of the corner of her eye she saw a bio bod go down. There was a meaty *thump* as the body hit the grinder. If Winton was aware of the casualty, he gave no sign of it. And no one moved to help the unfortunate man.

"During the subsequent confusion, the pack animals were lost, along with most of the legionnaires' food, water, and ammunition," Winton said. "Sixteen men were killed. Danjou's force had been reduced to two officers and forty-six men.

"In the meantime, the Mexican cavalry had been reinforced by local guerrilla fighters who fired on Danjou and his men—even as a sergeant named Morzycki climbed up onto the stable's roof. He reported that they were surrounded by 'hundreds of Mexicans.'

"The ensuing battle was an on-again, off-again affair in which periods of relative quiet were interrupted by sneak attacks and sniper fire. Meanwhile, about an hour's march away, three battalions of Mexican infantry received word of the fight and headed for Camerone.

"At about nine-thirty, a Mexican lieutenant approached under a flag of truce and offered the legionnaires an honorable surrender. 'There are,' he said, 'two thousand of us.'

"'We have enough ammunition,' Danjou responded. 'No surrender.'

"Shortly thereafter, Danjou spoke to his troops, asked each to fight to the death, and received their promises to do so. Danjou was shot and killed two hours later."

McKee swayed, took an involuntary step forward, and caught herself. Then, determined to hold her position, she returned to parade rest. The legionnaire who had fallen still lay crumpled on the ground. Medics would tend to him—but not until the full story of Camerone had been told.

"Second Lieutenant Napoleon Villain assumed command," Winton said.

"By noon, the youngest members of the company, Jean Timmermans and Johan Reuss, were dead. A bugle sounded, and Morzycki announced that approximately a thousand additional soldiers had arrived, each of whom was armed with an American carbine.

"The Mexicans called for the legionnaires to surrender and were refused once again.

"At about 2 p.m., a bullet hit Villain between the eyes and killed him instantly.

"As time passed, the legionnaires died one by one. The fatalities included Sergeant Major Henri Tonel, Sergeant Jean Germays, Corporal Adolfi Delcaretto, Legionnaire Dubois, and an Englishman named Peter Dicken.

"When evening came, the Mexicans piled dry straw against the outside wall and tried to burn them out. Smoke billowed, and, unable to see, the legionnaires fired at shadows. By five o'clock, only nine legionnaires remained alive. And the Mexicans had suffered hundreds of casualties.

"Another surrender was called for and summarily refused, after which fresh troops assaulted the hacienda, and hundreds of rounds were fired at the legionnaires.

"Sergeant Morzycki fell along with three others. Now there were only five men left. They included Second Lieutenant Maudet, Corporal Maine, and Legionnaires Catteau, Constantin, and Wenzel. Each had a single bullet left.

"Maudet led the charge. Catteau tried to protect his officer and fell with nineteen bullets in his body. Maudet was hit and gravely wounded, but Maine, Constantin, and Wenzel remained untouched. They stood perfectly still. A colonel named Cambas stepped forward.

"'You will surrender now,' he said.

"'Only if you allow us to keep our weapons and treat Lieutenant Maudet,' Maine replied.

"'One refuses nothing to men such as you,' Cambas answered.

"They were presented to Colonel Milan shortly thereafter. He looked at an aide. 'Are you telling me that these are the only survivors?'

"'Yes, sir.'

"'*Pero, non son hombres, son demonios!*' ('Truly, these are not men, but devils!')

"Days passed before the bodies were buried, and during that time a rancher named Langlais found Danjou's wooden hand, and eventually sold it to General Bazaine for fifty piastres. That hand can be seen at Fort Camerone on Algeron. It is symbolic of what we are."

Winton was silent for a moment. Then he spoke. "A great deal has changed since then. But our purpose remains the same. Many of you are about to receive orders. Prepare yourselves, and above all else, remember Camerone."

A sergeant major said, "Atten-HUT!"

The legionnaires crashed to attention. "What did the General say?"

"CAMERONE!"

McKee mouthed the word, and was just about to faint when someone stepped in to support her. "Oh no you don't," Larkin said as the formation was dismissed. "What you need is a beer... And this is the one day of the year when it's free! Come on, let's drink a toast to that Dan-jo guy." McKee had been saved.

The next few days were extremely busy as the 1st REC, along with elements of the 6th REI and the 13th DBLE (*13th Demi-Brigade de Legion Etranger*) worked to prepare thousands of men, women, and cyborgs for combat on a world called Orlo II. An agricultural planet that McKee had never been to but that was, according to the briefing from the battalion's S-2, a backwater world where nothing ever happened.

Or that's how things were until Princess Ophelia took over, raised Imperial taxes by 12 percent, and threatened to cut off imports if the inhabitants refused to pay. And that would hurt since the citizens of Orlo II were dependent on trade for a wide range of manufactured goods.

There were protests, but the Marine Corps put them down with brutal efficiency. That sparked a civil war, with loyalists on one side and secessionists on the other. And if there was anything that the new empress wasn't going to tolerate, it was secession.

The Marine Corps didn't have enough boots on the ground to impose Ophelia's will on anything more than a few cities, however—so the Legion had been ordered to land on Orlo II and help restore order. But first there were what seemed like a thousand things to do, starting with McKee's responsibility to Weber.

The official load-out for the 1st REC included a full complement of by-the-book spare parts for the regiment's cyborgs, vehicles, and weapons. The problem was that by-the-book wear and actual wear were two different things. So some components were certain to wear out faster than they were supposed to, leaving the regiment in short supply. Something McKee's father would have hurried to correct had he been aware of it. But Dor Carletto was dead.

All McKee could do was take a look at the T-1's maintenance records for the last year, note down the parts that wore out the fastest, and take steps to lay in her own supply of them. A strategy that wasn't as simple as it sounded because hoarding supplies was illegal, she was in competition with other bio bods who hoped to accomplish the same thing, and the supply people knew what the scroungers were up to. That meant all of the hard-to-find parts were under lock and key.

But necessity is the mother of invention. So after giving the matter some thought, she came up with a plan. She would need help though—and that was where Larkin came in. The whole notion of planning for future eventualities was foreign to him, but stealing things came naturally, and he never refused a request from McKee.

So she devised a raid. Not on the supply warehouse, which was well guarded, but on the so-called morgue, where scrapped T-1s were stored until they could be shipped back to Earth for recycling. Because even though the "empties" had been taken off-line, they still had parts that could be used in a shortage. Although McKee knew that, once installed, some of the previously used components would burn out in a matter of hours. And if that occurred during combat, the results could be fatal. That was why legionnaires weren't supposed to install anything other than new or reconditioned parts. But McKee felt it was her responsibility to do *something*—even if it was risky.

The most obvious course of action was to carry out the raid at night, when fewer people were on duty. But given all of the activity associated with the load-out, McKee figured that the resulting confusion could offer as much protection as the hours of darkness would. The problem was finding the time required since Lieutenant Camacho kept the platoon busy.

Finally, however, McKee and Larkin were able to slip away during the two-hour period of time allotted for lunch and a physical-hygiene lecture. Sergeants Hux and Fanta would almost certainly make note of their absences and go through the motions of chewing them out, but that was a small price to pay for some spare parts.

Rather than break into the morgue, as originally planned, McKee had conceived a better strategy, which was to bullshit their way in. A task made considerably easier by all of the activity associated with a major load-out.

So with Larkin in tow, and an official-looking data pad tucked under one arm, McKee simply walked into the office marked BAT-SUP and requested the pass code for the morgue. A harried-looking corporal was seated behind the counter. She had a buzz cut, slightly protuberant eyes, and plenty of attitude. "Why do you need access? And who sent you?"

"Sorry, Corp," McKee replied. "It's just part of the fun. Some O-3 on the regimental staff wants us to count the empties before we lift. He doesn't trust the manifest."

"Sounds like he's covering his ass," the corporal replied darkly. "In case a war form disappears after the battalion pulls out."

"Yup," McKee agreed. "That's my read."

"I'll write the code down and kill the alarm system," the noncom said. "Let me know when you're done, so I can change the code. What's your name?"

"Peters," McKee lied. "Lance Corporal Peters." Then she remembered that the name McKee was printed on her shirt and prepared herself for the trouble that was sure to follow.

But the corporal didn't think to look as she gave McKee a slip of paper. "Okay, here you go."

McKee said thanks, turned, and led Larkin out into the stifling heat. "Damn!" he said admiringly. "I didn't know you had it in you."

"Nor did I," McKee replied. "Maybe it's your influence."

"That makes sense," Larkin said proudly. "Now what?"

"We get our tools and go to work," McKee replied. Having stashed a duffel bag and a couple of omnitools behind an airconditioning unit, all they had to do was retrieve them and walk a short distance to the morgue. It wasn't called that, of course. The sign on the steel door read BAT WAR FORM STORAGE. AUTHORIZED PERSONNEL ONLY.

McKee was not only unauthorized, but extremely nervous, so she fumbled the first attempt to enter the code. The second effort was successful, however, and a rush of cool air met the legionnaires as they entered the long, narrow room. There was a solid thud as the door swung closed, and the overhead lights flickered momentarily as they came on. There weren't very many of them, so the overall level of illumination was low.

There were two ranks of T-1s. They stood upright, like old-fashioned suits of armor, with their backs to the walls, staring at each other across a four-foot-wide corridor. The empties weren't people and never had been, but they had been invested with life at one time, and evidence of that was stenciled onto their chests. Names like Franco, Chu, and Antov. Had her father touched any of them? On the assembly line perhaps? During one of his walkabouts?

McKee forced herself to ignore her emotions and focus on the job in front of her. The first task was to choose which machines to cannibalize. But as she made her way down the central aisle, there was no way to tell which war forms were in the best shape simply by looking at them. "Okay," she said. "You know what we're looking for. But be sure to run a diagnostic check before you pull any parts. Otherwise, you'll wind up stealing worn-out components."

"Yes, Mother," Larkin said impatiently. "What? You think I'm stupid?"

McKee thought it best to ignore the question, paused in front of a war form with the name Chavez on its battle-scarred chest, and thumbed an inspection panel. It popped open to reveal a glowing screen. Each one of the war form's primary systems could be seen. And as she scrolled down the list, she was disappointed to see that two of her high-priority targets were in the red.

So she closed the panel, moved to the next T-1, and had better luck there. Both of that unit's arm servos were shot, but the war form's knee actuators were listed as 80 percent, and its all-important com module was green as well.

A high-pitched mosquito-like whine announced the fact that Larkin was already at work as he made use of a flashlight-sized omnitool to go after a knee coupler. "Remember," McKee said as she began work. "Clean up after yourself. Don't leave any evidence."

"Relax already," Larkin replied, as a retainer clip popped out of the T-1's actuator housing and flew across the room. "I've got it under control."

But McKee *couldn't* relax because the clock was running, and there was the constant risk of discovery. The pressure caused her normally nimble fingers to feel clumsy, and it seemed as if everything took twice as long as it should have. But item by item, she was filling her wish list. And, according to intermittent reports from Larkin, so was he.

So McKee was beginning to feel more confident when the door opened, and two people entered the room. If it hadn't been for the noise generated by her omnitool, she might have heard them in time to hide everything. But that wasn't the case, so all she could do was kick the duffel bag of parts into the shadows and pocket the tool. Her heart was beating like a trip-hammer by that time, and there was an open place where the bottom of her stomach should have been.

Rather than legionnaires, McKee found herself looking at a pair of civilians. The woman had a sunburned middle-aged face, and was dressed in neatly pressed khakis, with half-moon perspiration stains under her arms. She smiled. "Hello there... My name's Maggie Cooper. Sorry to barge in. Sig and I work for Carletto Industries. We're here to take these forms off your hands."

McKee had never seen either one of the civilians before, so

there was no way to know if they were longtime employees or had been hired since the company had been expropriated. She scanned their faces, looking for signs of recognition, but there weren't any. She forced a smile. "Glad to meet you, ma'am. We were sent over to carry out some routine maintenance, and were about to leave."

If Cooper wondered why the Legion would perform maintenance on empties, she gave no sign of it. "Right... Well, by this time tomorrow, the building will be empty. That will be one less thing for you to do."

"Roger that, ma'am," McKee replied. "Come on, Hawkins... Let's get some chow."

Larkin frowned, and McKee was afraid that he was going to correct her when he said, "Right. If you want to call that slop 'chow.'"

The civilians chuckled and stood to one side as McKee lugged the bagful of parts out into the broiling heat. "I have an idea," Larkin said. "Rather than keep these parts, we could sell them to hard-charging suck-ups like you! Then, next time we get a chance, we'll party."

"You do that," McKee replied. "And I'll make sure your 'borg hears about it."

"God, you're a pain in the ass," Larkin complained. "Why do I put up with you?"

"You shouldn't," McKee replied. "Let's call it quits here and now."

"Oh, no you don't," Larkin objected. "We're like two halves of the same thing."

"Two halves of *what* thing?" McKee inquired.

"You know," Larkin said mysteriously. "Us."

The raid was over.

ABOARD THE TRANSPORT *RHEA*, IN ORBIT AROUND PLANET ORLO II

The better part of three weeks had passed since the outfit had been loaded aboard the *Rhea* and packed into a multiplicity of cabins, compartments, and bays. The latter being where the T-1s were quartered. So, with less than six hours left until a small fleet of shuttles took the first elements of the battalion dirtside, McKee was busy running one last check on Weber's systems when Sergeant Hux appeared. He had to shout to make himself heard over the sound of conversation, the whine of omnitools, and the latest announcement on the PA system. "Follow me, McKee... The loot wants to see you."

Any summons by a person with authority caused a stab of fear. Was this it? The moment when her past caught up with her? *No,* McKee told herself, *get a grip. It's a routine matter of some sort. Nothing more.*

She stood and turned to face Hux. "Sure, Sarge... What's up?"

"I'll let the loot explain," Hux said. "But one piece of advice."

McKee felt a sinking sensation. It wasn't routine then. "Yes?"

Hux smiled. "Lie like hell."

And that was all the noncom would say as he led her out of the bay and down a gleaming passageway, to the tiny cabin that Camacho shared with Lieutenant Sarr. A varnished knock block was mounted next to the steel hatch. Hux came to attention and rapped three times. "Sergeant Hux, and Lance Corporal McKee, reporting as ordered, *sir!*"

McKee heard a male voice say, "Come," and followed Hux inside. Lieutenant Sarr was nowhere to be seen. With his troops probably—getting ready for the drop. Camacho was young and good-looking in a brooding sort of way. He had black hair, dark brows, and very intense eyes, both of which were fastened on McKee. "I must say, I'm disappointed," the officer said. "I had you down as one of the good ones. A shoo-in for corporal. Now, based on what I've been told, it looks like you're a thief."

McKee felt her skin prickle and began to sweat. The statement was just that, a statement, so she remained silent.

"I am referring to the theft of parts from the morgue on Adobe," Camacho continued. "According to a civilian contractor named Cooper, you, or a person matching your description, were in the morgue when she and an associate entered two days prior to liftoff. A person who could have been Private Larkin was present, too.

"Later, once Cooper and her team began to prepare the

empties for transport to Earth, it became clear that more than two dozen parts were missing. A message torp was waiting when we dropped into orbit, and there, along with a shitload of stuff for the colonel, was a report addressed to Captain Avery. He passed it on to me. What, if anything, do you have to say for yourself?"

McKee thought about how the accusation had been phrased and took comfort from the words "or a person matching your description." That seemed to indicate that they weren't entirely sure. And she had Sergeant Hux's advice to go on as well. Her eyes were focused on a spot directly above Camacho's head. "Nothing, sir… I didn't do it."

Camacho's left eyebrow rose slightly. "Really?" he said skeptically. "Fortunately for you, this unit is no longer on Adobe. So citizen Cooper isn't here to call you a liar. You are one, however. And that's why Sergeant Hux is going to give you and your partner in crime some extra duty. Now get the hell out of my cabin."

Both legionnaires said, "Yes, sir!" and performed a neat about-face. Moments later, McKee was out in the corridor walking next to Hux. "Sorry, Sarge."

Hux grinned. "Don't worry… The loot knows the score… And since you were scrounging parts for *his* cyborgs, he's not going to poop on your parade."

McKee was surprised. "Really?"

"You've still got your stripe, don't you? And nobody ordered me to search your gear. But," Hux added, "don't do it again. And if I catch you or Larkin selling any of those parts, you will be pulling shit details until I make general."

"What about the extra duty?"

"That's for real," Hux replied. "Camacho is sending you the same message I did."

"So I'll be digging latrines on Orlo II?"

"Worse than that," Hux said darkly. "While the rest of the outfit is strutting around Hoodsport, looking important, you're going to babysit some brass. Good luck, McKee… You're going to need it."

* * *

Colonel George Rylund had been in the Legion for more than twenty years, and he was, according to the scan, a good if somewhat eccentric officer. One of his eccentricities jutted out from between clenched teeth and emitted regular puffs of cherry-flavored smoke. That in spite of the NO SMOKING signs posted on the battered bulkheads around him. He was dressed in camos, seated on an ammo crate rather than a drop seat, and engrossed in whatever was on his data pad. Intel reports? Probably, or so McKee assumed, as she eyed the officer from twenty feet away. The assault boat shook violently as it passed through a jet stream high in the atmosphere and continued to lose altitude.

McKee, along with Weber, Larkin, and his T-1, were on temporary assigned duty to Rylund's bodyguard. It was a relatively small force of eight people led by a no-nonsense staff sergeant named Sharma. He and the rest of his squad were members of the 2nd REP (2nd Foreign Parachute Regiment) and wore berets rather than helmets, thereby putting pride before safety. It was a questionable trade-off in her opinion.

The T-1s and their bio bods had been sent along because they could "throw a lot of lead," as Sergeant Hux put it. Something that would be important if the enemy attacked during what Hux referred to as "the upcoming circle jerk."

Of course, the two bio bods were being punished as well, because while they were glued to Rylund's six, the rest of the company would be taking part in what everyone expected to be an unopposed landing near the loyalist town of Hoodsport. A community which, according to some highly questionable scan, would insist on providing the battalion with free sex, beer, and food.

McKee would have preferred to be with the rest of the company but was somewhat philosophical about the chore, knowing it could have been much worse. Larkin, on the other hand, was absolutely furious because he was about to be denied the only thing worth fighting for. And that was a full-fledged bacchanal.

But like it or not, they were part of the security detail, and McKee was determined to learn what she could from the experience. So as the assault boat came in for a landing, and

Sharma issued his orders, she was ready to go. "The T-1s will de-ass the boat first," Sharma said, "and scan the LZ for hostiles. Unless something has gone very wrong, there will be friendlies in the area. Try not to shoot them. Once the area is secure, the rest of the security team will exit, followed by Topper-One and his staff. Do you read me?"

A flurry of double clicks confirmed that they did. McKee was already mounted on Weber by then, and the cyborg was positioned in front of the main hatch as it was lowered to the ground and transformed into a ramp. They didn't expect trouble, but she was nervous anyway and took comfort from Weber's professionalism as he clanked down onto solid ground. His voice boomed through her headset. "This is Echo-Four-Five... I have three bio bods inside the zone—and all of them appear to be friendlies. There are numerous heat signatures farther out, but they are consistent with Imperial vehicles of various types, and none of them are lasing us. Over."

Weber broke right, as Larkin's T-1 turned left, so that they were positioned to defend the hatch. "Roger that," Sharma replied. "Stand by... We're on the way. Over."

The security team exited the boat at that point, split, and took up positions around the T-1s. Then, as if out for a stroll, Colonel Rylund clomped down the ramp. Except for his pipe, and a swagger stick, he was unarmed. Which, according to the stories McKee had heard, was the way he typically entered battle.

A phalanx of officers followed along behind, including the battalion S-2 (Intelligence), the S-4 (Logistics), and the S-6 (Communications). All of whom would want to confer with their counterparts in the navy and Marine Corps as the three branches came together to agree on a course of action. Because while Empress Ophelia had given orders to pacify Orlo II, she hadn't said how. That was up to Vice Admiral Jonathan Poe. He, and two of his senior officers, were waiting to greet Rylund.

The colonel made use of his pipe to salute Poe, who, if offended, gave no sign of it. In marked contrast to the camo-clad men and women around him, Poe was wearing a crisp white uniform, and looked as if he were about to attend a tea party. The admiral was a tall, thin man who was known for his intelligence in a branch where scientific expertise was critical.

There was a flurry of handshakes as the security team moved forward with a T-1 on each flank. That was when it started to rain. Two umbrellas appeared over the admiral, and Rylund was left to get wet as the group left the LZ for the line of trees beyond.

After passing through the trees and a defensive position manned by some bored-looking marines, the group arrived at the center of a temporary HQ, where they took shelter under a large tent. It was equipped with weatherproof walls, which were rolled up to let the muggy air circulate. A female officer was waiting to greet Rylund, and McKee had the impression of a stocky woman with a plain face.

As the rain continued to fall, McKee, Weber, and the rest of the detail stood with their backs to the tent ready to defend Poe and his subordinates should the secessionists launch a surprise attack. Standing guard was a drag, but she could hear most of what was being said, and couldn't resist the opportunity to learn what she could. "All right," Poe said, "Hoodsport is ours. So we have a secure beachhead. And, if it hadn't been for the idiot who shot himself in the foot, our casualty rate would be zero.

"But taking the city of Riversplit won't be so easy. According to all of the Intel reports, the rebels are not only dug in, they have hundreds of black-market surface-to-air missiles (SAMs) in hardened launchers. So we won't have air superiority in that area."

"Then let's nuke it," a female voice said.

McKee couldn't see because her back was turned, but since the voice didn't belong to Rylund, she knew that Colonel Mara McKinney had weighed in. The Marine Corps officer's name had been mentioned during the predrop briefing, but McKee didn't know anything about her.

"That would save us a whole lot of trouble," Poe admitted, "but it could cause a lot of backlash and even more unrest. The empress sent us here to pacify Orlo II—not to glass it."

"Exactly," Rylund said mildly. "So we'll have to take Riversplit the old-fashioned way. Over the ground."

"Suits me," McKinney put in. "We'll follow Route 3 right up the Sarvo Valley to Riversplit. As we advance, we'll torch everything within five miles of the highway. That will destroy a lot of crops, put the rebel supporters on short rations, and sap their morale."

"I have something different in mind," Rylund countered. "I would suggest *two* columns. And rather than use Route 3, which is what the rebs would expect us to do, let's use secondary farm roads *here* and *here*. That will allow us to attack from two directions and split their forces."

McKee couldn't see, but imagined the officers standing around a 3-D map table, which was updated every ten seconds based on data gathered in orbit. "Furthermore," Rylund continued, "I think the scorched-earth strategy is likely to alienate even more citizens, making our task more difficult."

McKinney produced a snort of derision. "Who cares? If they get too pissy, we'll carpet bomb them."

There was a long pause while Admiral Poe considered both plans. Finally, after what McKee assumed was thoughtful deliberation, he spoke. "We will attack Riversplit from two directions. Colonel Rylund will be in command of all ground forces."

McKee felt the first stirrings of fear. Soon, within a matter of days, she was going to war.

8

Creating an empire is difficult. But governing one can be nearly impossible.

LIN PO LEE

Philosopher Emeritus, The League of Planets

Standard year 2168

PLANET ORLO II

War was rather pleasant. Or so it seemed to McKee as the 3rd Combined Cavalry Battalion followed Route 367 along the left bank of the Green River, toward the rebel-held city of Riversplit, which lay roughly ninety miles to the north. More than a week had passed since Admiral Poe and Colonels Rylund and McKinney had met and agreed upon a common strategy. Now it was time to implement the plan.

The column consisted of two armored cars contributed by the Marine Corps, two companies of legionnaires, and a loyalist outfit called the Gray Scouts. The latter were keen to see some action, but as green as grass and therefore relegated to the rear guard.

Air cover, such as it was, consisted of a single fly-form. Her task was to scout ahead and monitor both flanks in an effort to prevent the battalion from being ambushed. But there hadn't been any signs of enemy activity other than bursts of scrambled radio traffic and the occasional glint of reflected light as secessionist scouts spied on the column from the safety of distant hilltops. So with no immediate threat in the offing, McKee was content to lean back and let Weber carry her north.

Lieutenant Camacho and his T-1 were in the lead, followed by the first and second squads. And that included McKee. The sun was high in the sky, but a cool breeze kept the air from being too hot as huge cloud-shaped shadows caressed the land.

Neatly planted fields stretched off to the left, with a house beyond, and McKee was glad that Rylund had prevailed. He was right. Burning farms was no way to win the hearts and minds of the local populace.

The view on the right was equally spectacular. In spite of its name, the slow-moving river wasn't green. A heavy load of silt made it brown. Three six-legged herbivores could be seen on the far side of the river. They were standing knee-deep in a thick bed of reeds as they chewed big mouthfuls of dripping vegetation. If they were aware of the column, there was no sign of it. The two-ton monsters were armed with wicked-looking horns, but according to the scan, the animals were quite docile except during mating season.

Over the next twenty minutes or so, the ground on the left side of the road began to rise as a series of overlapping hills pushed it over toward the river. And as that occurred, a steep cliff rose next to them. Huge boulders lined the foot of the embankment, and judging from appearances, landslides were common. McKee didn't like the feel of it, and neither did Camacho, who sought to contact the fly-form circling above. "Echo-One to Sky-Eye. Give me a sitrep. Over."

"This is Sky-Eye," came the reply. "I see no signs of enemy activity in the area. Over."

"Well, look again," Camacho replied. "It has been a long time since a vehicle passed us going the other way. Maybe that's a coincidence, and maybe it isn't."

"Ignore that order," a third voice said. "What part of 'no' don't you understand, Lieutenant? Alpha-One out."

McKee knew that Alpha-One was the battalion's CO. A militia officer named Lieutenant Colonel Jack Spurlock. Though technically in command, Spurlock was supposed to take counsel from Captain John Avery, who was somewhere to the rear. All because Admiral Poe wanted it to look as if the loyalists were in charge. A rather transparent ploy in McKee's opinion.

A dark shadow fell across the highway as the column entered a blind curve. The platoon's channel was separate from the battalion push. So when Camacho spoke, Spurlock couldn't hear what he said. "Heads up, people... Sky-Eye is probably correct, but you never know."

The words were barely out of Camacho's mouth when a powerful charge went off, part of the cliff above them came loose, and tons of debris fell onto the road. The landslide buried a squad of legionnaires and cut the column in half.

There was mass confusion as all sorts of conflicting orders were issued, someone began to scream over the company push, and a cloud of dust enveloped the lead units. Then two additional explosions were heard. One at the head of the column and one at the end of it. "Shit! We're sealed in!" someone exclaimed, and it was true.

"This is Sky-Eye" the fly-form said. "The rebs took the cover off an artillery piece just to the east of you. Over."

That was followed by a shout of "Incoming!" from one of the T-1s, and the shells began to land moments later. The explosions threw columns of pavement and dirt high into the air, and McKee heard the debris rattle on her helmet.

"Echo-One is down," Hux said grimly. "Track the incoming shells and kill those bastards."

One T-1 in each squad was equipped with a launcher. Those cyborgs that could send surface-to-surface missiles arcing up into the air. The weapons were equipped with sensors that had no difficulty locating the artillery and homing in on it. The howitzer ceased to exist a few seconds later.

Meanwhile, a half dozen well-sited and formerly well-camouflaged crew-served machine guns had opened up on what was left of the column from the other side of the river. That was when Sergeant Hux disappeared from the diagram on McKee's HUD.

What happened next was more the result of the rage she felt

rather than anything else as she spoke into her mike. "This is Echo-Four-One. The river isn't very deep. Follow me!"

It wasn't until the words were already out of her mouth that McKee realized she should have spoken with Weber before committing him to a suicidal charge. But if the T-1 objected to her plan, there was no sign of it as the cyborg turned toward the enemy, raised the big fifty, and opened fire. Then, after a series of well-coordinated jumps, Weber landed in two feet of water.

That was followed by a moment of complete madness as the T-1 waded out into the current. Machine-gun bullets pinged his armor, threw up geysers of water all around, and buzzed past McKee's head. Someone shouted "Camerone!" over the radio, and when McKee checked the display on her HUD, she was gratified to see that a half dozen T-1s had followed her into the river.

The water felt cold as it rose around her, and McKee experienced a moment of gut-churning fear as she realized that her initial impression might be wrong. What if the river was deeper than she believed it to be? The cyborgs could operate under the surface if necessary—but what about the bio bods? They could drown.

Fortunately, her fears proved to be groundless as the water rose chin high, but no farther, as Weber pressed forward. Progress had slowed because of the current and the rocky bottom. Fortunately, the legionnaires were only partially visible at that point, and water robbed the incoming projectiles of their force.

Still, McKee could see the flashes on the opposite bank as the machine guns fired, and saw a symbol vanish from her HUD as a bio bod was killed and left to hang rag-doll-like in his harness. And since they were mostly underwater, the T-1s couldn't raise their weapons high enough to make effective use of them.

Then someone shouted "Grenades!" and at least a dozen black dots sailed out over the river to fall in among the helpless legionnaires. The resulting explosions sent gouts of water up into the air and killed a T-1. She fell over, took her struggling bio bod with her, and disappeared under the surface.

Meanwhile, the bottom had started to shelve upwards, the water fell away, and Weber was able to employ his LF-Storm machine gun. He fired the underbarrel grenade launcher first, scored a direct hit on a machine-gun emplacement, and was rewarded with a series of explosions as a crateful of grenades cooked off.

Then Weber began to fire short three-round bursts as he lurched up out of the river and stood on dry land. McKee saw movement off to the right as a trio of secessionists tried to flank the legionnaires. A long burst from her L-40 assault weapon knocked them down. They weren't people at that moment, they were targets, and she felt nothing more than a sense of satisfaction as they fell.

After that, it was shoot, move, and communicate as the avenging cyborgs destroyed each machine-gun nest in turn. The soldiers in the last emplacement tried to surrender, but Larkin and his T-1 were there to cut them down. The rebels jerked spastically and fell in a heap.

The firing had stopped as McKee confronted Larkin. "Why did you do that? They were trying to surrender."

She couldn't see Larkin's expression through his visor but recognized the aggrieved tone. "Why not? They tried to kill us."

"Because they wanted to *surrender*," McKee replied tightly. "And the S-2 might have been able to get some valuable information out of them."

"Screw the S-2," Larkin replied. "What the hell's wrong with you? You're starting to sound like a frigging sergeant."

McKee gave up on Larkin, dismounted, and began the grisly business of checking bodies for documents, data chips, and anything else that the Intel people might be interested in. And that was when the reality of it hit her. People were dead because of a decision she had made. People on both sides. And it hadn't been her desire to kill anyone. Not the indigs on Drang nor the rebels on Orlo II. No, that wasn't true. She *wanted* to kill the people who killed her parents. And she was learning how.

Her thoughts were interrupted when Camacho appeared. His helmet was off and dangling from its chin strap. The officer smiled grimly and held it up for her to look at. A sizable dent could be seen where a piece of shrapnel had struck it. "Always wear your brain bucket. I speak from experience."

McKee pushed her visor up out of the way. "I'm glad you're okay, sir. How's Sergeant Hux?"

Camacho's expression darkened. "He didn't make it."

A sense of loss hit her. She liked Hux. And knew he had a family on Earth. "They should have listened to you, sir. We walked right into it."

Camacho shrugged. "Sky-Eye didn't see 'em the first time. Odds are she wouldn't have seen the bastards on a second circuit either."

McKee knew Camacho couldn't and wouldn't say anything disrespectful about Lieutenant Colonel Spurlock. So she let the matter drop. "Sir, yes sir."

"You did a good job," Camacho said. "Leading that assault took clarity, initiative, and courage. I'm bumping you up to corporal and placing you in charge of the second squad until we can get a replacement for Hux. Captain Avery will have to confirm your promotion, but I'm sure he will."

McKee had mixed emotions about replacing Hux, even on a temporary basis. She fought back the tears and managed to swallow the lump in her throat. "Thank you, sir."

Camacho forced a smile. "We'll see if you still want to thank me after you've been a squad leader for a while. Right now, we need to pull everyone together, get them back across the river, and establish a defensive position north of the landslide area. It's going to take the rest of the day to clear the road and bury our dead. Odds are we'll be spending the night. Let your people know."

"Yes, sir."

Camacho's prediction proved true. It took the rest of the day and part of the evening to reconstitute the battalion, bury the casualties where the graves-registration androids could find them, and prepare for the next day.

The ceremony took place in the quickly gathering dusk, and when it was over, twenty-six names had been added to the thousands of graves the Legion had left behind on Earth, Algeron, and a dozen other planets. Some Grays had been killed, but since most of the casualties were legionnaires, it was up to Captain Avery to read the words written by a man named Rudyard Kipling:

> *The tumult and the shouting dies;*
> *The Captains and the Kings depart:*
> *Still stands Thine ancient sacrifice,*
> *An humble and a contrite heart.*
> *Lord God of Hosts, be with us yet,*
> *Lest we forget—lest we forget!*

I won't, McKee thought to herself as she stood with head bowed. *I won't forget.*

It took the battalion the better part of a day to reach the southern suburbs of Riversplit, where they joined a confusing mishmash of other units, all making ready for the upcoming attack on the rebel-held city. As McKee sat on an ammo box and ate her noon ration, she could look out over the cratered no-man's-land that separated the loyalists from their objective. And it didn't take a military genius to see that Riversplit would be a tough nut to crack.

Like many ancient cities on Earth, the city had been built on a hill. Not to protect it from marauding armies but because the early colonists wanted to look out over the surrounding countryside. But the result was the same. The secessionists would have the advantage of height. And thanks to thickets of SAMs, Admiral Poe's aerospace fighters were going to run into a lot of resistance. Camacho's voice came from behind her, and she turned to look. "McKee? There you are. Sorry to interrupt your lunch, but Captain Avery sent for us."

McKee felt the stab of fear that always accompanied such a summons. "'Us,' sir?"

Camacho smiled. "Don't worry. You're not in trouble. The captain confirmed your new rank by the way. That's why you were invited. They've got a special mission laid on for us—and I need a good squad leader."

McKee thought about the other NCOs, all of whom had years

of experience, and wondered why Camacho had chosen her. The doubts must have been visible on her face. "You can think on your feet," Camacho said. "And people do what you say. Not because they have to... But because they *want* to. Come on. The brass are waiting for us."

McKee accompanied Camacho through a maze of tents, habs, and parked vehicles to the plain-looking one-story building where Colonel Rylund and his staff were headquartered. It had been a primary school prior to the hostilities, and children's drawings could still be seen on both sides of the corridor that led to room 103. Two legionnaires were posted outside the door, and they snapped to attention as Camacho approached them. "At ease, men. We're here for a meeting. I'm Lieutenant Camacho. This is Corporal McKee."

The shorter of the two bio bods consulted a list and nodded. "Yes, sir. Go right in. They're expecting you."

McKee felt nervous as she followed the officer into the classroom. The windows were blacked out, an effort had been made to furnish the space with adult-sized furniture, and the odor of cherry-flavored tobacco hung in the air. Colonel Rylund was present, as was Lieutenant Colonel Spurlock, and something that made her blood run cold: the synth named Monitor Snarr. McKee had seen the android on numerous occasions ever since the first day she met it on Adobe. But always at a distance. And now, as the machine's sensors scanned her face, she felt a terrible emptiness in her stomach.

But the robot remained silent as Captain Avery came forward to greet her. What had become of Avery's brother? she wondered. And Avery himself, for that matter? Had he been forced to do Snarr's bidding? Or managed to maintain his independence? There was no way to know as they shook hands. "Congratulations on your promotion, McKee. You already know Command Sergeant Major Chora and Monitor Snarr. But I'm not sure that you've met our S-2, Lieutenant Oxby. Grab a chair. The lieutenant is about to amaze us with his grasp of what's going on inside Riversplit. Isn't that right, Oxby?"

The Intel officer was young, slightly chubby, and good-natured. He smiled. "Yes, sir. I have a guide to all of the best restaurants, a copy of a children's book about the zoo, and a secessionist poster entitled, 'Why the empress should take her tax and shove it.' All of which will be critical to our success."

Everyone chuckled except for Snarr, who had no sense of humor, and McKee, who was far too frightened. As it turned out, Oxby knew quite a bit about what was going on inside the rebel city thanks to orbital surveillance, recon missions by unmanned drones, and interviews that had been conducted with secessionist POWs, refugees, and paid informants. McKee listened attentively as Oxby described a city that was heavily fortified, well provisioned, and home to Governor Naoto Jones. The man most people considered to be responsible for the rebellion. "But," Oxby continued, "the purpose of *this* raid is to locate an Imperial official and rescue her."

"That's right," Rylund said as he emptied the bowl of his pipe into a makeshift ashtray. "Her name is Samantha Frood. She was sent to Orlo II about a year ago with orders to put a lid on the simmering trade issues. Then, when the empress raised the tax, and hostilities broke out, the rebs took her hostage. My fear is that they will use Frood as a human shield when we attack Riversplit. That wouldn't stop us, of course. But I feel we owe it to Representative Frood to extract her if that's possible."

"Quite so," Spurlock put in sanctimoniously. "It's the right thing to do."

"Yes, sir," Oxby said expressionlessly. "Fortunately, we have a good lead on where Representative Frood may be. So the mission is to enter the city, go to that location, and pull her out."

"We'll launch a feint at the same time," Rylund put in, as he held an old-fashioned match to his pipe. "That plus an air raid will give the rebels something to think about as you sneak in."

Avery eyed Camacho and McKee. "The team will be led by Lieutenant Camacho. It will consist of a civilian guide, Monitor Snarr, and a squad led by McKee here. That's six T-1s, including Lieutenant Camacho's cyborg, and a spare for Representative Frood. So the group will have plenty of firepower if it runs into trouble. Questions?"

Camacho had lots of questions. Good ones. But as McKee listened, she was thinking about the question the platoon leader couldn't ask. Why was Snarr coming along? No obvious answer came to mind. But whatever it was, McKee figured she wouldn't like it.

The rescue mission was scheduled for that night. Just twenty-four hours before the all-out attack on Riversplit was to begin. That left McKee with only a short period of time in which to prepare the second squad for combat. The process began with readiness checks on each T-1, including Marco, a cyborg on loan from the first squad. It was going to be his job to carry the guide into the city and take Representative Frood out. A risky proposition since neither bio bod would be of any use in a firefight.

There were some maintenance issues, just as she figured there would be, but none that couldn't be fixed. Especially with Camacho on hand to motivate the company's cyber techs. No, the real difficulty was legionnaire Tim Nayer, a bio bod who had been in the Legion for three years without rising above the rank of private. There were reasons for that, of course, including the fact that he was obstinate, lazy, and somewhat slow-witted. All of which were problems that previous NCOs had done their best to deal with.

But Nayer was in perpetual denial and insisted on believing that his lack of advancement was caused by misfortune, happenstance, and willfully incompetent officers. So when Sergeant Hux was killed in action, and McKee was promoted to Corporal, Nayer was incensed. And since he couldn't punish Camacho for what he saw as a gross miscarriage of justice, Nayer took his anger out on her. Not via direct insubordination. He wasn't that stupid. But in more subtle ways. And without Larkin there to watch her six, McKee knew she would have to be very careful. Would Nayer shoot her in the back if he got the chance? She didn't think so but couldn't be sure. And that added even more risk to an already dangerous mission.

It was dark by the time all the preparations were complete. The city of Riversplit was blacked out. Both sides were firing on each other with artillery. The shells rumbled like freight trains as they took to the air and shrieked like banshees on the way down. Red-eyed explosions winked as the rounds went off, and the earth shook.

But it was a pro forma exchange for the most part, since the tubes they were using had a maximum range of nine miles. That meant most of the shells landed in the no-man's-land between the two sides. Still, Camacho's team would have to risk fire from *both* sides as they passed through the pitch-black moonscape on their way into the city.

With only thirty minutes left before departure, McKee checked the squad one last time. That gave Nayer another opportunity to needle her. He was a scrawny man of indeterminate age. He pushed his visor up to reveal a beaklike nose and two beady eyes. They were filled with hostility. "Don't you ever get tired of playing general?" he sneered. "What are you going to do now? Check to see if I should take a dump?"

"There's no need to check," McKee replied evenly. "Everyone knows you're full of shit."

That elicited laughs from those close enough to hear and put a scowl on Nayer's ratlike face. "You're Camacho's bitch today," he said, dropping his voice so only she could hear. "But you'll be mine soon."

"Be careful what you ask for," McKee replied, as she shoved the barrel of her pistol into Nayer's crotch. "I'd say my dick is bigger than yours. Now fasten that chin strap and mount up."

Nayer opened his mouth to say something but closed it as Camacho materialized out of the surrounding gloom. "Mount up, Corporal. Colonel Rylund's feint will start soon, and I want to take full advantage of it."

McKee's pistol was down along her right leg by that time. "Yes, sir. Private Nayer was just about to climb aboard. Isn't that right, Nayer?"

Nayer mumbled something incomprehensible and turned toward his T-1. Camacho watched him go. The light was uncertain—but McKee could see the crooked smile on the officer's lips. "Don't shoot yourself in the foot, Corporal... I need you." And with that he walked away.

McKee felt foolish as she slid the pistol back into her shoulder holster and secured it there. The fact that she'd been forced to use a weapon in order to get compliance from a member of her squad didn't speak well of her abilities as an NCO—and it seemed safe to assume that Camacho was disappointed in her. Had there been time, she would have asked that someone else take over.

The feint began with a loyalist rocket barrage and air raid. McKee was barely aware of the fireworks as the civilian guide and Marco led the rest of the team through a checkpoint and out into the ocean of darkness beyond. Camacho and his cyborg came next, followed by Snarr, who preferred to run rather than ride. The fact that the android could keep up with a group of T-1s traveling at 20 mph impressed and frightened McKee. Because it meant that if it ever came to a footrace with a synth, she was going to lose.

The team couldn't use any lights, not without the risk of being targeted, but didn't need to. The T-1s could "see" via their infrared sensors, as could Snarr, and had no difficulty threading their way through cratered streets. And, thanks to directions from their guide, they were able to maintain a steady pace.

Meanwhile, bombs exploded, long strings of red tracer explored the night sky, and infantry companies grappled with each other deep inside no-man's-land. Dozens of flares, some launched by soldiers, some by mortars, cast their ghostly light on the proceedings as they drifted ever lower before being consumed by the inky blackness below.

There were moments when the team came perilously close to the fighting. But in spite of some close calls, they always managed to slip away. A series of twists and turns took them down into a dry sluiceway. They followed it to a point where, thanks to the night-vision technology built into her helmet, McKee could see the green circle and the vertical lines that marked the entrance to a dark hole. Marco came to a halt, causing the rest of them to do so as well.

The civilian spoke over the squad-level push. His name was Billy Balbo, or so he claimed, although McKee suspected it was one of many. Not that it mattered so long as Balbo kept his word and guided the team into Riversplit undetected.

"Pay attention," Balbo said tersely. "We're at the foot of a large storm drain. During the rainy season, it's full of water, which flows into the sluiceway and from there to the river. We're going to blow the gate and walk uphill into the city. Then, if all goes well, you'll leave the same way."

The plan was for Balbo to remain inside the city once Frood had been rescued, and McKee wasn't sure how she felt about that. On the one hand, it would feel good to get rid of the civilian. But that meant making their way back without a guide. And that could be dicey. "What about sentries?" Camacho wanted to know.

"There aren't any," Balbo responded. "That's why I chose this route."

That meant the rebs were stupid, careless, or both. McKee found that hard to believe. But such considerations were above her pay grade, so all she could do was go along as Singh placed a charge and blew a hole in the gate designed to keep people and animals out.

Because McKee was second-in-command, she and Weber had to wait for the rest of the team to start up the steep slope before they could follow. If the column was cut in two, both sections would have leadership. That was the theory—and she prayed it wouldn't come to that. First, because of the casualties such a calamity would produce, and because of her own inadequacies. Deep inside she knew that Nayer was right. She *wasn't* qualified to lead a squad. And the people under her command deserved better.

The team could use lights once they were inside the storm drain. Beams from the T-1s slid over the walls, threw shadows, and glinted off the trickle of water that ran down the pipe. McKee figured it was about twelve feet in diameter.

Smaller drains came in from the left and right at regular intervals. "Smaller" being a relative term since most were large enough for her to stand in. Some were dry, but most produced at least a trickle of water that dripped down to join the flow, which splashed away from the cyborgs' podlike feet. And there were vertical access tubes as well. When she aimed her helmet light up into them, she could see metal rungs.

Meanwhile, as the last bio bod in the column, it was McKee's job to watch the team's six. But the harness made it difficult to turn back, and the light from her helmet couldn't penetrate very far. She could "see" heat, however, thanks to the technology in her helmet. And on two different occasions she spotted what looked like green blobs. But then, after a second or two, they disappeared, leaving her to wonder if the sightings were real or if her night-vision gear was on the fritz.

So she looked forward again. But as the minutes passed, McKee couldn't shake the feeling that something wasn't right. Finally, she chinned her mike. "This is Echo-Four." That had been Sergeant Hux's call sign, but was hers now, and would be so long as she was squad leader. "I'm about to light off a flare. Over."

"Roger that," Camacho answered. "Over."

She withdrew a flare from a pouch on her combat vest, thumbed the igniter, and threw it into the darkness. The sudden flash of light caused her visor to darken, and there, exposed by the glare, was a silvery patrol drone! It was flying about three feet off the bottom of the pipe—and had been for who knows how long. It had the capacity to attack, but hadn't. Why?

The question was left unanswered as McKee yelled, "Contact!" and opened fire. The burst from her AXE had the desired effect. Light strobed the pipe as the drone exploded and peppered her with small pieces of shrapnel. Her body armor was proof against most of the flying debris, but there were stings, as fragments of metal bit into her unprotected arms and legs.

But that wasn't the end of it as *more* drones sped out of the darkness firing energy cannons as they came. Weber swore as he took a hit, triggered his grenade launcher, and blew one of the machines into a thousand pieces. McKee was protected by the T-1's bulk at that point, so none of the shrapnel hit her.

She fired over Weber's left shoulder as bolts of blue energy blipped past her head. The rest of the team was taking fire, too, but the T-1s were too big to fight side by side in such a confined space and couldn't use their weapons without hitting McKee and Weber.

So that meant that the two of them were battling the drones alone until Snarr appeared next to them. The android was significantly smaller than a cyborg and had a pistol clutched in each hand. Snarr fired a dozen well-aimed shots, and another drone blew up. And when Weber nailed the last one, the fight was over. The success of the rescue attempt depended upon secrecy. And the rebs knew that an effort to infiltrate the city was under way. Surely Rylund wouldn't blame Camacho if he decided to abort the mission. So what would he do?

Apparently, Monitor Snarr was wondering the same thing because he spoke before Camacho could make his intentions known. And there was nothing subtle about the words he chose. "It is my duty to remind the team that we are engaged in a mission of critical importance. The empress is counting on us to do our duty. Over."

"This is Echo-One," Camacho said. "With all due respect, no one in my platoon needs to be lectured regarding his or her duty," he said tightly. "That being said, it's my opinion we can pull this thing off. Let's move."

The upward journey continued for five minutes. Then, as Marco arrived at the point where three pipes came in to join the main line, Camacho called a halt. The junction was so large that four of the T-1s could gather while two stood guard. "Okay," Camacho said. "The bio bods will dismount. That includes you, Mr. Balbo."

"Why stop here?" the civilian demanded. "We haven't reached the top yet."

Camacho was standing next to his T-1 by then. His headlamp was aimed up at Balbo. "We're stopping here because the rebels will be waiting for us up top. Something you're aware of—since you sold us out."

"I did no such thing!" Balbo insisted stoutly. "I'm taking the same chances you are."

"I don't think so," Camacho countered. "It's my belief that the drones would have attacked us earlier if it hadn't been for your presence. Fortunately, McKee spotted them. Now get down off that T-1. Or should I ask Monitor Snarr to remove you?"

Balbo was clearly afraid of the android and hurried to dismount. "Good," Camacho said. "Marco will lift each bio bod up into the vertical maintenance tube above us. I will go first.

Nayer, Chiba, and Singh will follow. Then it will be your turn, Mr. Balbo... And never fear. Monitor Snarr will be there to assist you. Corporal McKee will bring up the rear."

Camacho looked at his wrist term and back up again. "Echo-One-Two will be in command here." McKee knew that Lance Corporal Zikey, AKA Echo-One-Two, was Camacho's T-1. A role some cyborgs coveted and others tried to avoid.

"We will try to return here," Camacho said as he eyed the cyborgs. "But if you haven't seen us by 2400 hours, then you're to withdraw and return to base. In the meantime, be sure to post guards both above and below the junction. Because of the size of the pipe, the rebs will have to attack two or three abreast if they come. But keep an eye on those incoming pipes. Copy?"

"Sir, yes sir," Zikey replied formally.

"Good. We'll see you shortly."

It took five minutes for Marco to boost the bio bods and the android up into the maintenance tube. As McKee followed Snarr upwards, she gave momentary consideration to shooting the robot. But there would be no doubt as to who was responsible—and Snarr's body would fall on her. But maybe, just maybe, there would be an opportunity later on.

Boots rang on metal, Snarr's servos whined softly, and McKee could hear the blood pounding in her ears. For that moment in time there was no past or future. Just the present. And a determination to survive.

9

What soldier relishes the sight of a civilian flourishing a sword?
PHILIP GUEDALLA
Wellington
Standard year 1931

PLANET ORLO II

As the legionnaires continued to climb, the blobs of white light projected from their helmets slid back and forth across the inside surface of the access tube. McKee heard a grating sound as her AXE made contact with the wall behind her.

She felt it was her duty to pause occasionally and look down between her boots even though she couldn't see beyond twenty feet or so. There was some comfort in the knowledge that attack drones couldn't enter the bottom end of the tube so long as the T-1s were there. But there was nothing to prevent the robots from accessing the shaft via horizontal ducts that had been excavated by machines for machines.

However, there were no signs of pursuit as Camacho arrived at the top of the ladder, braced himself, and pushed the circular lid up out of the way. As cool night air flooded the shaft, McKee could hear the persistent *thump, thump, thump* of antiaircraft fire and the occasional *BOOM* generated by incoming artillery rounds. Maybe Rylund had been able to push some of his batteries forward, thereby bringing the hill within range, or maybe some bigger tubes had arrived on the scene and were pounding the rebs from twelve miles away.

As McKee followed Snarr up out of the tube, she saw flames in the distance, as one of Riversplit's buildings burned, and heard a sonic boom as an aerospace fighter passed above. The team was so small that Camacho saw no need to use call signs. "All right, Mr. Balbo... Lead us to the house where Representative Frood is being held. And don't make any mistakes. You'll be sorry if you do. Nayer, take the point. Mr. Balbo and Monitor Snarr will be right behind you, and McKee will guard our six. Okay, let's go."

The fact that Riversplit was blacked out and under attack was helpful to the legionnaires as they followed Balbo up a series of winding streets. Darkened buildings loomed all around. There were places where light was visible along the edges of windows or below doors. But for the most part, McKee and the rest relied on night-vision technology to find their way.

Camacho kept the team out of the streets, and on sidewalks to the extent that he could, and a good thing, too. Five or six vehicles passed them, and McKee's heart very nearly stopped when a column of soldiers appeared out of the gloom and double-timed down the road toward the ramparts at the foot of the hill. The rebs were so close that she could hear the rattle of equipment, the *thump* of their boots, and a burp of static. Then they were gone.

Minutes later, the team came to a halt as Nayer whispered over the radio. "Contact... The house is just ahead. There's a wall and four rebs out front. Over."

"Chiba," Camacho said softly, "go high. Find a spot where you can look down into that courtyard. And give me a sitrep as soon as you can. Over."

Chiba was not only known for his ability to climb—but was arguably the best shot in the platoon. That's why he was armed with a sniper's rifle rather than an AXE. He clicked his mike twice by way of a reply and faded into the darkness.

From what McKee could see, which was damned little, they were in a neighborhood of large homes. Most were at least two or three stories tall and were surrounded by high walls. And that included the one Frood was being held in. Four green blobs were visible. So if an equal number of guards were posted on the other three sides, that would mean sixteen in all. But what about the people *inside* the walls? Hopefully, Chiba would be able to tell them.

Five minutes ticked by. They seemed like hours as artillery rumbled in the distance, a series of flares popped high above, and tracers cut the night sky into abstract shapes. After what seemed like an eternity, Chiba spoke. "I'm on the roof of the building directly behind you. There are so many gutters, decorations, and balconies that even Singh could climb up here."

McKee knew there was a friendly rivalry between the two men and smiled as a pair of aerospace fighters screamed overhead, leaving trails of decoy flares behind them. The rebs launched an SLM and it took off after the nearest source of heat. The resulting flash of light lit the top of the hill. "I can see into the courtyard on the other side of the wall," Chiba said. "The rebs have an autocannon set up in front of the house. It's pointed at the gate. Three people are clustered around the gun and two more are standing off to the right. That's five altogether. Over."

"It's imperative that we enter the house and reach Representative Frood," Snarr put in.

"All of us are aware of your desire to rescue Miss Frood," Camacho said carefully. "Please refrain from unnecessary radio transmissions.

"Now," Camacho continued, "here's the plan. Thanks to Mr. Balbo, the rebs are expecting a force of T-1s. That's why they placed an autocannon in the front yard. Chiba will neutralize that threat by killing the crew. His fire will serve as our signal to open up on the sentries. Remember... There are bound to be more. So wait for them to appear before crossing the street. Meanwhile, Private Chiba will rejoin us. That will be the signal for Singh to blow the gate. Questions?"

"Yes, sir," McKee said. "What about security?"

"Normally, we would leave people outside," Camacho acknowledged. "But I've been on the radio with Captain Avery—and they're going to send a fly-form to take us off the roof."

McKee looked up, saw that the house on the far side of the street had a flat roof, and realized she should have noticed that. What else had she missed? The question continued to dog her as Camacho issued the final order. "Kill the gun crew, Chiba. And let me know when they're down. Over."

It was a good plan, or so it seemed to McKee. And it might have worked if Balbo hadn't broken free of Snarr—and run out into the street. "They're here!" he shouted. "Kill them!"

Camacho triggered the burst that cut Balbo down. The guards fired in response, and all hell broke loose. McKee had taken cover behind a concrete planter and was firing short bursts as Chiba opened up from above. The sniper announced success thirty seconds later. "The gun crew is down. Over."

"Then get down here," Camacho ordered. "All right, let's move!"

By that time, all of the sentries had been killed. But there were more, just as Camacho had said there would be, and the sound of gunfire brought them around to the front of the house. There was a melee as the two groups collided and fired at each other from only yards away.

That was when McKee's AXE ran dry. She hit the release, and was in the process of seating a new magazine, when a reb took aim at her. McKee saw him grin and knew she was going to die when Nayer backed in between them. He'd been firing at one of the guards and momentarily lost his situational awareness.

As half a dozen rounds hit Nayer, he staggered, turned a full circle, and collapsed. McKee's AXE was in position by then and the reb's smile turned to a look of surprise as she fired a burst into his chest. He crumpled as she ran forward to kneel next to Nayer. A flare went off high above and the light was reflected in his eyes. "Shit," he said. "I took a hit. For you."

McKee eyed his torso. His body armor had protected him from some of the enemy projectiles but not all. One of them had ripped through his throat and he was bleeding profusely. She slapped a self-adhesive battle dressing onto the wound but knew it wasn't going to make much difference. "Yes," she said. "You did."

Nayer frowned. The blood in his throat made it sound as if he was gargling when he spoke. "I didn't mean to."

"I know."

"You're not good enough to be a squad leader."

McKee nodded soberly. "I agree."

A look of satisfaction appeared on Nayer's face. "Good. That's settled then."

Suddenly, as the light faded from Nayer's eyes, McKee heard an explosion, and Camacho yelled at her. "Is he alive?"

"No."

"Then let's go. Our bird is inbound, and we have work to do."

McKee removed the dead man's tag plus two magazines before following Camacho through the shattered gate and past a sprawl of bodies. All victims of Chiba's marksmanship. The cannon sat unused, with a dead reb slumped in the gunner's seat. The rest of the squad was waiting on the porch.

Snarr nodded, put four rounds into the door lock, and there was a spill of light as he kicked it open. A burst of automatic fire passed over the robot's head and stopped as the android fired both pistols. Camacho led the way, and McKee had to step over a dead officer in order to follow her platoon leader up a spiral staircase. She got the impression of a glittering chandelier, dark wood, and beautifully framed landscapes. It was a look very similar to what she'd grown up with.

Fire lashed down from above, Camacho paused to return fire, and a body fell past her to land somewhere below. "According to Balbo, Representative Frood is being held on the top floor," the officer said grimly as they arrived on a landing. "One more to go."

Boots thundered on the stairs as the legionnaires continued to climb. But as they rounded a curve, glass shattered, and an attack drone nosed into the stairwell with its gun firing. McKee turned to look as the railing exploded into splinters. The robot was vaguely cylindrical in shape and equipped with bladelike vanes that protruded from its sides.

There was no need to yell "Contact!" but McKee did, as she fired from fifteen feet away. The machine was well armored, however, and it took a combined effort by the entire team to damage the drone. The robot seemed to stagger in midair, slammed into a wall, and blew up.

McKee felt what must have been a sizable piece of shrapnel strike her body armor. The impact knocked her off her feet and saved her life, as a second machine entered through the broken window. It fired on the spot where she had been and was destroyed by Camacho, Snarr, and Chiba.

At that point, she half expected to see a *third* drone appear and was relieved when it didn't. "Okay," Camacho said. "Rebel troops will arrive soon. Let's get this thing done."

Once the team arrived on the third floor, it was only a matter of seconds before they located the table and chair where a guard had been stationed. He or she was absent now, and McKee was reminded of the body that had fallen past her earlier.

Snarr tried the door, but it was secured, and McKee could see that a heavy-duty lock had been installed. Camacho turned to Singh. "Open it."

Singh grinned through his black beard. He was well over six feet tall and very muscular. So when his boot hit the door, wood splintered. A second kick finished the job.

Then, as the door swung open, McKee saw a sparsely furnished bedroom with a woman standing in a corner. She had gray hair and was clearly terrified. "Representative Frood?" Camacho inquired. "We won't hurt you. We're here to get you out."

Frood looked hopeful. "Really? Thank God!"

And that was when Snarr raised a pistol and shot her between the eyes. Frood's head jerked as the bullet hit, her face lost all expression, and she slid to the floor.

Camacho was the first to react. His weapon was coming to bear on Snarr when the android shot him as well. Twice.

McKee watched in disbelief as her platoon leader went down with two bullets in his brain. After months of training, her reaction was as natural as breathing. The AXE seemed to fire itself. Snarr took dozens of hits but was seemingly impervious to bullets as he continued to turn in her direction. But finally the 4.7mm rounds ate through his armor, found something vital, and destroyed it. The android jerked spastically, lost motor control, and crashed to the floor. That was when Chiba put a final bullet into the robot's head. "And stay down, you piece of shit."

A heavy silence followed. Singh was the first to break it.

"Damn," he said wonderingly. "What happened?"

"It looks like Snarr had orders to kill Frood," McKee said darkly. "And used us to get at her."

"But *why*?" Chiba wanted to know.

McKee knew the answer. Or thought she did. Chances were that Frood had been sent to Orlo II by Ophelia's brother. And having any sort of relationship with the dead emperor was a crime against the state. So Snarr had been ordered to kill Frood by someone who was willing to sacrifice the android if necessary. But she couldn't say that. Not without revealing information about herself. "Who knows?" McKee said. "But one thing's for sure... If we're smart, we'll stay well clear of whatever it is."

Singh looked worried. "How can we do that?"

"We'll tell the same story when they run us through the after-action hot wash. The drone killed Camacho and Snarr as we fought our way up the stairs. The door to Frood's room was open and she was dead when we found her. Stick to those points. Don't add details and don't drop anything. Keep it simple."

"This is Lifter-Five to Echo-One," a female voice said over the platoon push. "I'm thirty out. Drop some flares."

McKee chinned her mike. "This is Echo-Four. I read you. We're headed for the roof. Over."

She looked from face to face. "So how 'bout it? Are we on the same page?"

Singh answered for both of them. "What you say makes sense. I never liked that frigging machine—and I don't think the loot did either. And there's more of the bastards. All linked in with the government somehow. So we need to stay clear of it. Right, Chiba?"

Chiba nodded. "That's, right. Plus McKee's our squad leader... So what she says goes."

That was acceptance of a sort, and McKee felt a momentary flush of pleasure as she ordered the other two to find a way up to the roof. Then she bent over to collect Camacho's ID tag and wished there was time to perform a cybernetic autopsy on Snarr. But there wasn't. So all she could do was pull the pin on a thermite grenade, drop it next to Snarr's body, and leave. Hopefully, the heat would destroy the android and burn the house down, making a forensic investigation impossible. Because a battle was coming, and if the loyalists won, the people who sent Snarr might go looking for its remains.

The next few minutes were taken up by the mad scramble to reach the roof, lay out the necessary flares, and wait out the final seconds as the fly-form swooped in for a landing. Then, once all three of them were aboard, the cyborg took off. It wasn't until they were speeding away that McKee had an opportunity to react. Snarr was dead, but so was Camacho, and the horrible reality of that continued to sink in. She could run—it was impossible to hide.

McKee awoke with a start as a bright light probed her eyes. "Rise and shine, Corporal," a male voice said. "They're waiting for you."

The choice to turn off the glow strip and lie down on the concrete floor had been hers, and now McKee was paying for it as she sat up. She felt cold, stiff, and sore. A questionable trade-off for an hour's worth of sleep. "I need to pee," she said thickly as she stood.

"Okay," the other legionnaire said, standing to one side. "But make it quick. The little girl's room is on the right—two doors down."

McKee nodded as she stepped out into the school's main hallway. It was a lot busier than it had been the previous day. People in all sorts of uniforms were coming, going, or standing around. Was the all-out assault coming up soon? Judging from all the activity, it seemed likely. Her thoughts went to Weber and the other cyborgs. They had returned safely according to what she'd been told, and for that she was thankful.

Having pushed her way in through a swinging door, McKee discovered that it really was a little girl's room—complete with small commodes and low sinks. Filtered daylight came in via three frosted windows, and a sign instructed her to WASH YOUR HANDS.

Having taken care of the most pressing need, she went over to a washbasin. The face in the mirror looked tired and worried. And the scar was still a shock. Had Singh and Chiba been through the hot wash? And if so, what had they said? There was no way to know, so all she could do was stick to the story and hope for the best. Because the truth wouldn't set her free. Far from it. Though officers like Rylund wouldn't like what Snarr had done, they weren't going to take on Empress Ophelia, not for a lieutenant, never mind a corporal.

The same legionnaire was waiting for McKee when she emerged from the restroom. He wasn't a guard in the normal sense but had clearly been assigned to make sure that she didn't discuss the mission with her squad. That was SOP, and nothing to be concerned about under normal circumstances, but the situation wasn't normal. Far from it.

McKee steeled herself for what was to come as the legionnaire led her into what had been the teacher's lounge. And there, seated around a table were Captain Avery, Lieutenant Oxby, and Monitor Snarr. The very sight of the robot was enough to open an empty place at the pit of her stomach. The machine was dead... It had to be.

Then, as Avery stood to greet her, McKee realized that the android in front of her *wasn't* Snarr. Even though its appearance was identical to that of the "dead" robot. "You met the lieutenant earlier," Avery said. "And this is Monitor Jivv. We know this is a difficult time for you—but it's important to get everything down while the details are fresh in your mind. Please... Have a seat."

McKee took some comfort from the concern in Avery's eyes—but it felt as if Jivv's sensors were looking right through her. One thing was for sure... It might be hard to replace Sergeant Hux, or Lieutenant Camacho, but there were plenty of synths to go around.

The first part of the debriefing was easy. All she had to do was tell the truth. But then, as she described the attack on the house, it was necessary for her to be extremely careful. Details could be her undoing if they varied from what the others said. But Jivv called her on it right away. The timbre of its voice was slightly different from Snarr's. As if some irregularity in the production process had caused it to be lower. "Please be more precise, Corporal. We are interested in the details of what occurred."

"Yes, sir," McKee replied. "Sorry, sir, but there was a lot

going on. Like I said, a drone smashed through a window in the stairway and fired on us. We returned fire and destroyed it. I wasn't aware that the lieutenant had been hit until I turned back toward the stairs. Both he and Monitor Snarr were down. Both of them were dead. So I took Lieutenant Camacho's tag and put it in my pocket."

"Which placed you in command," Avery said.

"Yes, sir. I knew Representative Frood was supposed to be on the third floor. So we went looking for her. The room where they were keeping her was unlocked, and she was dead. It looked as though she had been executed."

None of the interrogators looked surprised. And that meant they had heard the story before. "The rebs shot her," Oxby said evenly.

"Yes, sir," McKee said. "That was the way it appeared."

"So you left," Avery said.

"Yes, sir," McKee responded, hoping to bring the session to a speedy conclusion. "Lieutenant Camacho had requested that a fly-form pick us up on the roof."

"And that's all?" Jivv demanded. "You have nothing to add?"

The android was after something. But what? McKee was so tired it was difficult to think. Then it came to her. "There was one other thing, sir… I smelled smoke as we left. There could have been a fire. I'm not sure."

Jivv nodded as if satisfied. "Aerial photographs became available early this morning. The rebels had a lot of fires to fight last night. The house where Frood was being held, plus three neighboring dwellings, burned to the ground."

Avery's eyes met hers. McKee got the feeling that the officer was trying to ignore Jivv. "It's no secret that we will attack Riversplit sometime soon," Avery said. "The odds of getting a replacement for Camacho before then are slim to none. So I'm going to take command of your platoon. I know last night was difficult. Can I count on you to lead the second squad?"

There it was. A chance to say no. But judging from the way her story had been accepted, it was clear that she had support from Chiba and Singh. And if they believed in her, then maybe she should, too. "Sir, yes sir."

Avery nodded. "Good. Get some sleep."

McKee said, "Thank you, sir," stood, and turned to go.

She was halfway to the door when Jivv spoke. "Corporal…"

McKee stopped and turned. "Yes?"

"According to the squad-level load-out checklist for last night's mission, you were carrying a thermite grenade. But you made no mention of using it—and there was no mention of the grenade on the list of ordnance that was turned in. What happened to it?"

McKee felt something cold trickle into her bloodstream. Jivv was on a fishing expedition. Or did he suspect foul play? She made an effort to keep what she was feeling off her face. "I lost it."

Avery frowned and looked at the robot for the first time since McKee had entered the room. "If you believe that Corporal McKee violated regulations, or was remiss in the performance of her duties, then say so. Otherwise, keep your mouth shut."

Oxby looked uncomfortable and clearly wanted to be somewhere else. Jivv opened its mouth as if to reply, apparently thought better of it, and remained silent.

Avery returned his gaze to McKee. He was furious, judging from the expression on his face. "Dismissed."

McKee said, "Yes, sir," and left the room. Then it was time to grab a sandwich in the makeshift chow hall that occupied the gymnasium, return to the company area, and collapse on her cot. Sleep came quickly—and Nayer was there to greet her.

Twelve hours had passed since McKee had been debriefed. Six had been spent sleeping, five had been spent getting her squad ready for combat, and one had been spent waiting for the briefing to begin. That pissed her off because there were so many other things that she could have been doing. Although the Legion's official motto was *Legio Patria Nostra* (The Legion Is Our Country), it might as well have been "Hurry Up and Wait."

But, finally, Captain Avery and Lieutenant Oxby entered the classroom where Echo Company's officers and noncoms were assembled. "Sorry about the delay," Avery began. "But the battalion briefer ran over. The good news is that we finally have a time. The assault on Riversplit will begin at 0500 hours in the morning. The 6th REI will go in first, with support from the Grays.

"We will be in the second wave. Our task is to seek out the enemy's cavalry and neutralize it. Thanks to some HUMINT, we have images to share with you. Lieutenant Oxby—if you would be so kind."

McKee was surprised to hear that the rebs had cavalry, as were the men and women around her, since T-1s, quads, and fly-forms were unique to the Legion insofar as she knew. But the picture that appeared on the wall screen was something very different from the sort of cavalry she was used to. So much so that the image provoked laughter and comments like "You've got to be kidding," "We'll cream them," and "Get serious."

McKee remained silent, but she could see why the others were so contemptuous. The video had been shot from a distance. It jiggled from time to time and showed a human encased in a nine-foot-tall exoskeleton. The same sort of machine used to load and unload cargo vessels. The reb was running an obstacle course or trying to. But his machine hadn't been designed to high-step through rows of tires, and she wasn't surprised when he tripped and fell. That triggered gales of laughter, which Avery cut short. "Atten-HUT."

The talking stopped, those who had been seated stood, and everyone came to attention. "So you think the guy in the exoskeleton is funny?" Avery demanded as he glared at them. "Well laugh at this… The rebs call them Rippers. And for good reason. They're slower than a T-1, and less agile, but a good deal more powerful. And that could be very important in an urban setting, where combat can get up close and personal.

"Plus, the rebs have armed their machines with heatseeking fire-and-forget missiles (SLMs). Two tubes per Ripper. And that's in addition to the .50-caliber machine guns mounted on both sides of the operators' cages. All of which is to say that you'd better take these things seriously. Do you read me?"

The answer was in unison. "Yes, sir!"

"Good. As you were. Lieutenant Oxby—you may proceed."

McKee listened carefully and took notes, knowing it was her

responsibility to pass the information on to her squad. Oxby's briefing came to a conclusion ten minutes later. Avery offered a closing comment. "Remember... The infantry is counting on us. Two Rippers could decimate a company of ground pounders. And the enemy may have as many as fifty of them. Be ready at 0400, have your people in the assembly area by 0430, and keep radio traffic to a minimum. The sergeant major will be kicking ass and taking names. I'll see you there. Dismissed."

She left with all the others, returned to her hooch, and found Larkin sitting on her cot. He had a shit-eating grin on his face. "So, *Corporal*," he said, with unnecessary emphasis on the word "Corporal." "Where should I put my gear?"

McKee frowned. "You don't mean..."

"I sure as hell do!" Larkin said triumphantly. "I put in a request for the second squad—and Sergeant Fanta signed the chit!"

McKee could imagine how thrilled Fanta had been. Nobody wanted Larkin, and the chance to get rid of him had been too good to pass up. Even if it left Fanta one bio bod short.

But while Larkin was a burden in many ways, McKee knew that she could count on the troublemaker even if no one else could. And with Jivv around, it would be nice to have somebody to watch her six. She forced a smile. "That's wonderful news. As it happens, I have a slot for a crazy, undisciplined pain in the ass like yourself. You'll replace Nayer. Go find his T-1 and get acquainted. And run every diagnostic there is. We're going to visit Riversplit tomorrow."

Larkin grinned and came to his feet. "Got it."

"And Larkin..."

"Yeah?"

"Don't make me sorry."

If the rebels were wondering when the attack would come, the question was answered at 0430 hours when the artillery and rocket barrage began. Hits were marked by red-orange explosions that lived for a second or two before being swallowed up by the predawn darkness. Meanwhile, Echo Company was assembled behind the Grays and stood ready to follow them into no-man's-land, where the first clash was expected to take place. If Rylund's forces were successful on the flat ground, they would have the dubious privilege of assaulting the hill beyond.

McKee had checked her squad twice by that time and knew there was no point in doing so again. Weber was fidgety and kept shifting his weight from foot to foot, which meant she had to compensate for it. It was annoying and an act of will was required to refrain from saying something to him.

Everyone was nervous, and that included Avery, who was making the rounds and talking to soldiers in each squad. He *looked* calm enough, but his words came more quickly than usual, and he was telling jokes. Something he never did under normal circumstances and wasn't very good at.

In fact, the only person who didn't seem concerned was Larkin. He was doing what he always did, which was to complain about everything from what he considered to be a substandard breakfast to the constipation that would surely result. McKee smiled when Singh told Larkin to "shut the hell up."

Finally, after what seemed like an eternity of waiting, the artillery barrage stopped, at least two dozen flares went off over no-man's-land, and the infantry began to advance. Avery's voice sounded unnaturally loud in her helmet. "Echo Company will advance on my command. Remember... Keep those intervals right, watch for enemy cavalry units, and maintain your situational awareness. It could get real complicated out there, and it would be easy to wind up shooting at each other."

The order came moments later. "Echo Company will advance in extended order."

Someone yelled, "Camerone!" and other legionnaires did likewise. Sergeant Major Essex snapped at them for violating radio protocol, but everyone knew he didn't mean it.

A gentle slope led down over broken ground into the warscape beyond. The sun had risen by then, and McKee could see the miles of bombed-out houses, buildings, and rubble-littered streets through which the invaders would have to pass before reaching the hill.

The Grays and elements of the 6th REI were already in the maze and feeling their way forward under the direction of officers who could "see" the terrain ahead via drones and real-time images on their HUDs.

Then, as Weber arrived at the bottom of the slope and followed Avery into what had been a major thoroughfare, McKee's line of sight was greatly reduced. As a squad leader, she could access the drone feeds, but she knew that if she did, it might be a distraction rather than a help. No, she decided. It was better to let Avery worry about the big picture while she focused on the area around her squad.

The lead elements of the infantry had made contact by then, and the rattle of automatic weapons together with the steady *crump* of mortars signaled a brisk firefight. But there hadn't been any reports of Rippers, so Avery was compelled to reduce the rate of advance or risk overrunning the ground pounders. And that could be disastrous. Because lethal though the T-1s were, the cyborgs weren't ideal for urban combat—a situation in which their size made them excellent targets for rocket-propelled grenades, obstructions kept them from using their speed, and massed infantry attacks were a constant threat.

As Echo Company slowed, McKee was conscious of the fact that one of her jobs was to protect Weber's six. That meant keeping her head on a swivel even as she monitored the three units under her command. Larkin's 'borg, a male named Hower, had a tendency to walk right down the middle of the street as if daring the rebs to shoot at him. And if Larkin was aware of the problem, he showed no signs of doing anything about it. So as they came within range of the enemy's artillery, she told Hower, "Stay out of the street and use cover."

And it was then, while she was focused on the tactical situation, that the big picture changed. "This is Echo-Nine," Avery said. "The first platoon will close up and prepare for a left turn at the next intersection. Some Rippers were hiding in an underground parking garage, and now they're coming out to play. The first platoon will follow me. The second and third will continue to advance. Over."

And with that, Avery's cyborg began to jog. The rest of the company did likewise, as twelve T-1s snaked around a corner and threaded their way through an obstacle course that consisted of shot-up vehicles. Shoulder-launched missiles wouldn't be very useful in an urban environment, so all of the 'borgs carried bio bods instead.

McKee could hear frenzied firing by then as well as desperate radio calls on the battalion push. All semblance of proper radio procedure had fallen by the wayside as a company of Grays battled to survive. "Behind you, Mac!" "It's got Kowalsi..." "Medic! We need a medic here."

All of that and more was flooding the push even as a voice that McKee recognized as belonging to Lieutenant Colonel Spurlock ordered his people to get off the battalion frequency. Then the platoon rounded a corner, and she could see the mayhem firsthand. A shopping mall had been transformed into a battlefield. And judging from the bodies that lay strewn about, the Rippers were stalking the Grays with near impunity, jerking them out of their hiding places and systematically dismembering them. A woman uttered a long, piercing scream as an exoskeleton-clad rebel plucked her off the ground and ripped her right leg off.

McKee felt anger flood in to replace whatever fear she'd been feeling. The rebs were clearly enjoying themselves and killing for killing's sake as they painted the mall red. And it was clear that Avery felt as she did. "This is Nine... Choose your targets and take the bastards down! No prisoners. Over."

Theoretically, cyborgs were supposed to do what bio bods told them to do. A practice that reflected the extent to which people at the highest levels of the Legion continued to be frightened of their new weapons. But in combat, that was rarely the case because the time consumed in a two-way conversation could mean the difference between life and death. Weber took the lead by heading straight at a rampaging Ripper. And because the reb was so engrossed in swinging a noncom around by his ankles, he failed to see the danger until it was too late.

Weber fired his grenade launcher and scored a direct hit. One of the exoskeleton's legs collapsed, dumping the machine onto the pavement. A long burst from the fifty finished the job. Unfortunately, the Gray had been released to sail through the air and hit the side of a building headfirst. His body crumpled to the ground.

The first Ripper's death elicited an amplified roar of outrage from another reb, who charged across the plaza at Weber. It happened so quickly that the cyborg wasn't able to get off more than a three-shot burst before the tooth-rattling collision.

Then the battle was hand-to-hand, or grasper-to-grasper, as McKee looked over Weber's shoulder and into what she could see of the rebel's face. Only his eyes were visible thanks to the makeshift armor that protected him. Servos whined, and the air was filled with the acrid odor of ozone as the giants grappled with each other.

McKee had seen Weber throw other T-1s during training sessions, but not only was the Ripper more powerful than he was, it was heavier, too. So she aimed the AXE at the enemy pilot and fired a sequence of short bursts. But because of the thickness of the reb armor, plus violent movements by both machines, she wasn't able to score a hit.

So McKee released her harness and dropped to the ground. Then, as she circled the machines that loomed above her, she fired short bursts. Sparks flew where her bullets struck. But the 4.7mm rounds had no noticeable effect on the Ripper. It had a lock on Weber's head and was trying to twist it off.

More out of desperation than anything else, McKee let the AXE dangle from its sling as she launched herself at the Ripper from behind. Then she pulled herself up to the point where she was directly behind the pilot. He was protected by an improvised cage. But it wasn't perfect, and a small gap offered the opportunity she needed.

Noncoms carried pistols, and that included corporals, even if McKee hadn't had a chance to fire hers yet. As Weber struggled to escape the exoskeleton's grip, she held on with one hand and pulled the weapon with the other. McKee felt proud of herself as she remembered to release the safety before shoving the barrel into the hole. The pistol's magazine held thirty rounds and she fired fifteen of them into the control compartment.

There was no way to know if she hit the reb directly or via a ricochet. And it didn't matter. Suddenly, the Ripper went limp,

Weber was able to regain his freedom, and the exoskeleton collapsed. McKee rode it down, was thrown free by the impact, and rolled to her feet with pistol raised.

Avery, who was still aboard his cyborg, was there to greet her. "I saw what you did, Corporal... And Sergeant Hux would have been proud. No wonder they call you the Steel Bitch."

McKee hadn't been aware of the nickname until then and didn't like it. But she knew that once given, such things were impossible to get rid of. "Thank you, sir. I think."

Avery grinned. "We beat 'em, McKee. We beat 'em good." And as McKee looked around, she saw that the officer was correct. A couple of T-1s were down, but at least six Rippers had been destroyed, one of which was little more than a smoking wreck. That meant the Grays were free to enter the meat grinder up ahead.

"Mount up," Avery ordered. "And collect your squad. With any luck at all, we'll eat our rations on the hill tonight."

As it turned out, Echo Company didn't get to eat dinner in the city of Riversplit. The rebs were too tough for that. But they did have breakfast near the top of the hill. A spot from which it was possible to look out over the devastated landscape and watch the sun come up. Not *her* sun, but an alien sun, which, like the planet itself, belonged to Empress Ophelia. *And I helped her take it back*, McKee mused. *How ironic is that?*

But her belly was full, her tea was hot, and she felt strangely happy. A battle had been won, her squad had survived, and that was sufficient.

10

PLANET ORLO II

Echo Company was bivouacked in the ruins of a machine shop on the east side of the city. McKee had removed Weber's head and was replacing the rotator bearing in the cyborg's neck when Singh stopped by. "Jeez, McKee, shouldn't you call in Hosker for a repair like that? What if you can't put him back together?"

McKee would have preferred to have a tech do the work, but she'd seen some of the shoddy repairs that Hosker made. And wasn't about to let him work on Weber. But if she said that, Singh might tell Hosker, who would report her for carrying out repairs she wasn't qualified to make. And the charge would stick. "Hosker's busy right now," McKee said evasively, "given all the battle damage he has to repair. So I figured I'd take care of it myself. And Weber doesn't mind. Do you, Web?"

The cyborg's head was sitting on a beat-up table and was connected to his body via an armored umbilical. "Hell, no," Weber responded. "McKee has the touch. She can work on me anytime."

"Okay, if you say so," Singh replied doubtfully. "I've got a message from the PL. She wants to see all of the squad leaders at 1000 hours."

Lieutenant Cally Kaylor had been sent to replace Camacho. According to the scan, she was a jacker, meaning an officer who had risen through the ranks, and a stickler for regulations. McKee had been introduced to the officer but hadn't spent any time with her. She frowned. "So what's up?"

Singh shrugged. "Beats me. The loot didn't say."

"Whatever it is won't be good," Weber predicted darkly.

"Quit being so pessimistic," McKee said, although deep down she agreed with him. "Maybe we're getting a pay raise."

That was sufficient to elicit a laugh from both legionnaires, and as Singh left, McKee returned to work.

At 1000 hours she reported to the small parking lot that served as Echo Company's HQ. It consisted of an inflatable hab, tarps stretched over a crude framework made from salvaged lumber, and lines of four-man tents. Captain Avery was nowhere to be seen, but Kaylor was seated under a large sheet of plastic along with squad leaders Boyce and Fanta. As McKee came to attention, Kaylor waved the formality off. "As you were. No need for that when the four of us get together. Grab a chair."

Kaylor had white sidewalls, a blond crew cut that stood straight up, and a square face. Her eyes were green and an army of freckles marched cheek to cheek across an unremarkable nose. The officer's mouth was so straight it looked as if it had been issued to her.

"All right," Kaylor said as McKee took her seat. "Let's get to it. Captain Avery and Echo Company's platoon leaders were required to attend a briefing this morning and here's the download. Governor Jones led the rebellion so the brass want to get their hands on him. But for political reasons, the locals insisted on arresting him themselves.

"Our troops were ordered to stand down while the Grays took him into custody. But while they were getting their act together, the governor took off. The Intel people don't know where the bastard is, but have a pretty good idea of which way he went, so a mixed battalion is going to track him down. And

Echo Company will be part of that battalion. Don't tell me—let me guess. You have questions." The last comment was delivered with a smile.

McKee was impressed by Kaylor's direct no-nonsense manner and figured that was at least partly the result of having worked her way up from private. She had questions, but Boyce beat her to it. He had black hair, dark skin, and intense eyes. "Yes, ma'am. Did you say 'mixed battalion'?"

Kaylor made a face. "Yes, I did. Although one might question whether it's going to be a small battalion or a reinforced company. But, since Lieutenant Colonel Spurlock says it's a battalion, I guess it is. The force will include Echo Company, a platoon of Grays, and two squads of marines. That way, everyone will be able to take credit once we capture the governor."

McKee was reminded of the march north and the way in which Sergeant Hux and twenty-five others had paid for Spurlock's incompetence. A hole opened up in the pit of her stomach as Fanta entered the discussion. He'd been on that march, too, and clearly had reservations. "Spurlock? You must be joking."

Kaylor frowned. And for the first time, McKee got a glimpse of the strict disciplinarian that she'd heard about. "Be careful, Sergeant. That comment could be construed as mutinous. But I'll assume that it was simply a poor choice of words. It isn't for us to judge who commands the battalion. Our job is to run the first platoon. The members of which look to noncoms such as yourself to set the appropriate tone. Do we understand each other?"

McKee felt sorry for Fanta because it had been clear from the beginning that Kaylor had misgivings about the battalion, and his question had been consistent with that. But it seemed as if Fanta had stepped over an invisible line and paid the price. All of which was being absorbed and filed away as a chastened Fanta said, "Yes, ma'am."

"Good. Colonel Spurlock wants to get an early start tomorrow. So have your people assembled and ready to go at 0500. Monitor Jivv will deliver a briefing for officers and noncoms. Once that's out of the way, we'll head out. You and your troops have the rest of the day to perform maintenance and load up for what could be a long march."

McKee felt a sense of alarm at the very mention of Jivv's name and cursed her luck. No matter where she went, it seemed as if a synth was always nearby. Kaylor's voice interrupted her thoughts. "Corporal McKee? Please stay after the others leave. I'd like to have a word with you."

It was a clear dismissal for Boyce and Fanta, who stood and hurried to extricate themselves from what had become an uncomfortable meeting. At that point, McKee's already flagging spirits sank even further. Was she in trouble? It appeared that way judging from the expression on Kaylor's face.

"So," the officer said once the other noncoms were gone, "tell me about your relationship with Private Larkin."

Suddenly, McKee understood. Having heard that the two of them were inseparable, and that Larkin had engineered a transfer to the second squad, Kaylor jumped to the obvious conclusion: The legionnaires were having an affair. The thought caused McKee to laugh, and when Kaylor frowned, she hurried to explain. Once Kaylor heard about the battle in the swamp, followed by Larkin's almost-doglike devotion, she was amused rather than critical.

"Well, it takes all kinds, I guess, but you can see how people could get the wrong idea. And now that you're a squad leader, you've got to guard against any perception of favoritism. So make sure Larkin gets his share of shit details."

"Yes, ma'am."

"Plus," Kaylor continued, "you're on something of a roll. Captain Avery thinks very highly of you. He can't promote you until you have some time in grade. But if you stay on the straight and narrow, the bump will come. Meanwhile, he forgot to request a sergeant to fill your slot. That's a gift, McKee. Don't screw it up."

"Yes, ma'am. I mean no, ma'am."

"Okay, get back to work. I'll see you in the morning."

It was raining as the dimly seen sun began to rise. Not hard, but steadily, as if determined to wash all of the blood off the streets of Riversplit. McKee had to turn up the collar of her slicker to prevent the cold water from trickling down her neck and into her clothes. So thanks to the weather, and the brooding hostility projected by the locals as the column of legionnaires clanked, whined, and strutted past them, the mood was anything but upbeat as Echo Company made its way to a park filled with temporary graves. Rebs mostly, and civilians, who had been killed during the battle for Riversplit.

As soon as they arrived, the officers and noncoms were required to assemble a few hundred yards away from the rest of the battalion. Monitor Jivv was waiting for them in front of a wall inscribed with the names of the first colonists to land on Orlo II.

As the officers and noncoms arrived, an order was given to form a single rank. McKee saw a *second* robot. The machine was shaped like a globe, about three feet in diameter, and hummed softly as it floated next to the android's left shoulder. "Good morning," Jivv said as rivulets of rain ran down his alloy body. "As you know, we've been tasked with pursuing the traitor Naoto Jones and apprehending him before he and his followers can cause more strife or escape from the planet."

McKee remembered Snarr and the way Frood had been executed. Would Jones suffer a similar fate once he was caught? Yes, it seemed likely. And, just as before, she would be partially responsible.

"The unit next to me is called a fugitive-tracking device or FTD," Jivv continued. "It can see microscopic evidence, detect even the faintest odors, and perform a variety of forensic tests under field conditions. For example, if one of you were a wanted criminal, and the government had a sample of your DNA on file, this device could take a specimen, analyze it, and make a match. All in a matter of seconds."

McKee felt a chill run down her spine. Jivv had been looking at her as it spoke. Or was that her imagination? One thing was for sure, however. The government almost certainly had DNA taken from her parents. So if the FTD ran a check on her, it would come up positive.

"Because the FTD is going to accompany us, I want it to be familiar with all of those who may need to give it orders," Jivv said. "So please state your name and remain stationary as the FTD carries out some routine scans."

They weren't standing at attention, so McKee was free to turn her head and watch as the FTD sailed over to Colonel Spurlock and hovered in front of him. Then, person by person, the robot worked its way down the line until it was directly in front of her. She could hear the humming sound it made, smell the ozone it produced, and feel the warmth that the machine gave off. Her heart was beating like a trip-hammer by then, she felt light-headed, and feared that she might faint as the FTD began its inspection. It took all of her powers of concentration to say her name.

There was no way to know for sure, but McKee assumed the robot was recording photographic images of her, scanning her retinas, and mapping her heat signature. The question, and a life-and-death one at that, was whether it would take a sample for DNA extraction. She hadn't seen it do that with anyone else, but her knees felt weak as a servo whirred, and the robot extruded a flexible probe. Some sort of sensor was mounted on the end of it, and she heard a sniffing sound as the instrument probed the air around her face and neck. Then, having completed its task, the FTD moved on. She had survived.

McKee's inner clothing was soaked with sweat by then, and as the moisture started to cool, she started to shiver. The FTD had to be destroyed. The only question was when and how.

Governor Naoto Jones had fled south. That was what loyalist informers claimed, and it made sense because there were lots of reb sympathizers to the south, not to mention the Big Green, a vast track of unsettled land where Jones could hide.

Admiral Poe's drones had flown dozens of missions over the Big Green looking for the fugitive and would continue to do so during the days ahead. But it was, as Lieutenant Oxby put it, "like looking for a needle in a haystack." Vehicles would be easy to spot if they were out in the open, but it was difficult if not impossible for the drones to "see" through the forest canopy, and their infrared sensors were of little assistance because Orlo II was home to a race of sentients called the Droi. And the indigs lived in the Big Green, as did their herds of partially domesticated P-Yani, plus thousands of forest-dwelling animals. So there were countless man-sized heat signatures to choose from and no way to know which ones to focus on.

All of which had to do with why the battalion had been sent south. The hope was that people on the ground would find the governor's trail and catch up with him. McKee was the exception, however, because she was a reb sympathizer at heart and secretly hoped that Jones would escape.

But regardless of McKee's desires, there was a lot of soldiering to do. Not for the benefit of politicians good and bad but for her comrades in arms. And with the possibility of an ambush around every corner, there were lots of things to worry about. Including the fact that Kaylor had a sharp eye for details and was quick to criticize her squad leaders if their 'borgs were too slow, or a bio bod was dozing in his or her harness.

And when the first platoon was on point, as they were at the moment, it seemed as if Kaylor was extravigilant. McKee didn't know if that was due to the constant threat of an attack—or the fact that Spurlock's open command car was behind the lead platoon.

Two of the Marine Corps' Scorpion armored cars were next in line, followed by four 8 X 8 trucks, each loaded with supplies and a squad of Grays. A fuel tanker occupied the eight slot, followed by a rear guard consisting of T-1s.

It wasn't fair, everyone knew that, since the arrangement meant that the Legion was always on point and drag. The most dangerous slots in any column. But Spurlock justified the practice by pointing out that the T-1s were best able to protect themselves and the rest of the vehicles were the battalion to be attacked. And even McKee had to acknowledge that.

So the rain fell, Echo Company's platoons rotated every hour, and the column followed Route 36 south at a steady 40 mph. Spurlock's goal was to cover at least three hundred miles per day.

Eventually, the well-cultivated farms gave way to scrubland and what looked like miniature fortresses all owned by agro companies. The fortifications were a necessity according to Oxby—since the Droi were none too happy with the way in which the gigantic farms were eating into the Big Green. And, because the conglomerates were aligned with Empress Ophelia's government, the Droi were allied with the rebs.

Dwellings became few and far between as the paved road turned into a muddy track, and the column's speed fell to 20 mph. A sure sign that Spurlock was going to fall well short of his three-hundred-mile-per-day goal.

And slowing progress even more was the need to stop for lunch, which they did right at the point where a poorly maintained track led off into a tangle of vegetation and disappeared. The Grays were ordered to establish a defensive perimeter, and rations were issued.

That was when Oxby, Jivv, the FTD, and three bio bods from the Echo Company's third platoon followed the parallel ruts back into the bush. They were looking for Intel, but McKee figured it was going to be a waste of time, and said as much to Larkin.

Fifteen minutes later, she was forced to eat her words as the party returned with a wizened-looking human in tow. His head was surrounded by a halo of frizzy gray hair, and he was dressed in bush clothing. The man carried a scope-mounted rifle, suggesting that he was one of the hunters who eked out a living along the margins of the Big Green.

McKee wasn't privy to the conversation that ensued between the local, Spurlock, Jivv, Oxby, and a gaggle of officers that included Captain Avery. But once the session was over, she saw Oxby give the hunter a case of rations, which he hoisted onto a shoulder and carried into the bush. "He'll be sorry," Chiba predicted, and the others laughed.

Later, as the scan percolated down through the ranks, McKee learned that a convoy consisting of four fancy off-road vehicles had passed through two and a half days earlier. The group didn't stop, so the hunter hadn't spoken to them, but there wasn't much doubt as to who the "city folks" were. It appeared the battalion was on the right track.

The afternoon was a long, slow affair. But eventually the rain stopped, the sun came out, and McKee removed her slicker. That made the trek more pleasant, as did the knowledge that the battalion would be forced to stop pretty soon. Although it wasn't until the orange-red sun was resting on the very edge of the western horizon that Spurlock finally called a halt next to a small stream.

But before anyone could plop down next to the stream and eat dinner, it was first necessary to establish a defensive perimeter. That was accomplished by using the trucks, the Scorpions, and the command car to create a laager. The Grays were ordered to dig defensive firing positions two hundred feet out from the vehicles, and with T-1s patrolling the area beyond, the battalion was ready for the night.

Thanks to the luck of the draw, McKee's squad wasn't due to walk the perimeter until 0300, which meant they could grab about six hours of uninterrupted sleep. Not ideal, but better than the poor slobs on the 1100 to 0100 watch, who would have to get up and pull a couple of hours of guard duty before hitting the sack.

So McKee crawled into her tent as soon as she could, got into the sleep sack with most of her clothes on, and checked to make sure that the AXE was within reach. Then she lay there for a minute or two, wondering if the screech produced by a cyber tech's power wrench was going to be a problem, only to wake up five and a half hours later to the gentle *beep, beep, beep* of her wrist chrono. Then it was time to brush her teeth, take a pee at the female latrine, and grab a cup of glutinous coffee from the pot in the mess tent.

With those things accomplished, McKee walked over to the point where the squad was supposed to assemble, discovered that Larkin was MIA, and was forced to go looking for him. He was none too pleased when she pulled him away from a card game in the supply sergeant's tent—and even less so when she informed him that he would be digging shit holes that evening.

After relieving a squad from the second platoon, McKee led her people out into the surrounding darkness. Their job was to detect potential enemies *before* they could attack the battalion, neutralize them or, failing that, slow them down.

She ordered the T-1s to crank their sensors up to max and began what promised to be a boring watch. Her squad had responsibility for half of the perimeter. That meant they ran into their counterparts occasionally. But with that exception, the next hour passed uneventfully. Then, as the second hour began, Chiba's T-1 spotted something. "This is Echo-Four-Seven. I have three heat sigs north of my position at approximately two o'clock. Over."

McKee had been daydreaming and felt guilty about it as the transmission cleared her mind. "Roger that… Hold your position and continue to track them."

The call sign for the bat command post was Papa-Eight. So when she relayed the information, it was to whatever officer had the duty at that moment. "Echo-Four to Papa-Eight. We have three heat sigs in the northwest quadrant of the perimeter. Request permission to investigate. Over."

It was Captain Avery's voice that answered. "This is Papa-Eight… Permission granted. I'll give you some light. Over."

The flares shot up into the inky blackness, popped, and threw dark shadows as they drifted down. McKee felt her heart pound as Weber followed Chiba and his T-1 into the bush. Branches whipped past her shoulders, and she was forced to duck lest some low-hanging limb smash into her visor. "This is Echo-Four-Seven. The heat signatures are fading. Wait a minute… What's *this*?"

As McKee rode Weber into the small clearing where Chiba and his cyborg were standing, she could see what they saw, thanks to the wash of light from the flares and helmets. A sapling had been cut off shoulder high so that the human head could be placed on it. There was no mistaking the halo of gray hair or the leathery face. McKee was looking at the hunter who had spoken to Spurlock, Oxby, and Jivv the day before. The sight turned her stomach.

Suddenly, Avery and his T-1 were there to add even more illumination to the scene. "So somebody's watching us," Avery said reflectively. "The question is who? The rebs or the Droi?"

The FTD was summoned. It sniffed the head, scanned the ground, and took minute samples. But when the process was over, the machine wasn't able to tell the humans anything they didn't already know.

As the sun rose, the head was given a burial next to the road, a metal marker was driven into the ground, and the battalion departed. The marching order was the same, it was a nice day, and it wasn't long before McKee had adjusted to the now-familiar rhythm of Weber's movements.

Because there were some false alarms during the first few hours, everyone was on edge. But the fears began to fade as miles passed and the sun rose higher in the sky. Drones passed over occasionally but had nothing of substance to report.

Then, after a brief stop for lunch, the battalion ran into the first problem of the day. A river designated as 6452 flowed west to east, was at least three feet deep, and running along at a very good clip. That was the bad news. The good news was that a sturdy-looking wooden bridge offered an easy way to cross it. But was it safe to do so? The battalion came to a halt as the brass discussed the situation. The first platoon was on point again, which meant McKee was close enough to hear some of the conversation.

Spurlock was in favor of sending a Scorpion over. Then, if it survived, the rest of the battalion would follow. Avery thought the plan was too risky and pointed out that if they lost an armored car, they would be losing its offensive/defensive capabilities as well, making the entire unit more vulnerable. McKee had the feeling that Spurlock would have rolled right over him had the legionnaire been a Gray. But the militia officer knew Colonel Rylund was likely to side with one of his own—so he let Avery have his way. Even if the decision was delivered with a grudging, "All right get on with it then... But remember. Time is of the essence."

A few moments later Kaylor and her T-1 appeared at McKee's side. The platoon leader's visor was raised, and she was smiling. "Can you swim?"

"Yes, ma'am."

"Good. Captain Avery thinks it would be a good idea to take a look at the underside of the bridge before we cross it. And I told him that you were expendable. Keep an eye out for explosives—and watch the current. Oh, and one other thing, Captain Avery will be riding shotgun via your helmet cam."

Why us? McKee wondered. The expendable thing was a joke.

Or so she assumed. Had Avery requested her? Or had the choice been Kaylor's? She would never know. All she could do was say, "Yes, ma'am."

Weber gave his fifty to another 'borg in order to keep his graspers free. The T-1 followed a gently sloping beach down to the fast-flowing river. The water broke white around the beams that held the bridge up. And as Weber waded out into the flow, McKee stared up into a maze of crisscrossing supports. Captain Avery's voice sounded in her helmet. "Be on the lookout for command-detonated explosives, a mine hooked to a pressure plate on the bridge deck, or something more primitive. Like partially sawed through timbers for example. Stay sharp. Over."

"Roger that, sir. Nothing so far."

The next voice she heard was Weber's. He was speaking over their intercom rather than the squad push. "The current is pretty strong. Be ready to bail if I go down."

The water was up to McKee's knees by then, and it was *cold*. Weber was correct. It wouldn't feel very good if the cyborg fell on top of her. But the alternative wasn't all that attractive either. Once free of the harness, and in the frigid water, she would be swept downstream into the rock garden below. "Thanks, but no thanks," McKee replied. "Stay vertical please."

They were out in the middle of the river by then, with Weber leaning into the current, as McKee studied the beams above. They were clear insofar as she could see—but what about the topmost surfaces? They were invisible. She chinned her mike. "Echo-Four to Echo-Nine... Over."

Avery was quick to respond. "This is Nine. Go. Over."

"I know the FTD wasn't designed to provide surveillance," McKee replied, "but maybe you could use it to get a topdown look at those beams. Over."

There was a pause, as if Avery and the other officers were discussing the idea, followed by a burp of static. "This is Nine. Good idea. Over."

McKee felt a momentary sense of pleasure, but it was short-lived as Weber put his left foot into the crevice between two rocks and fell sideways. She had her hand on the harness release when the T-1 slammed into a vertical support. Fortunately, he was able to grab hold of it and keep from falling farther. Then, when he had regained his footing, they were able to continue.

Meanwhile, the FTD was flying above them and darting in and out as Avery and the others monitored what it "saw." Five minutes later, McKee and Weber emerged from the river and made their way up onto the south bank. She knew people could see her but felt obliged to make a final report. "This is Echo-Four. I saw no explosives or signs of sabotage. Over."

McKee heard a *click*, as if Avery had opened his mike with Spurlock talking in the background. "I hope you're satisfied, Captain. We would be ten or fifteen miles down the road by now if it weren't for this nonsense."

Then Avery spoke. His voice was empty of emotion. "This is Nine. Copy that Four. Over."

McKee felt sorry for Avery. Checking the bridge had been the right thing to do. She felt certain of it. But Spurlock was in command, so it was *his* opinion that mattered.

It was only a matter of minutes before the first platoon crossed the bridge, followed by the command car, and the first Scorpion. Then, with no warning other than a muted *crump*, the second armored car took a direct hit and blew up. Fortunately, the intervals were such that the vehicles ahead of and behind the Scorpion suffered only minor damage.

McKee was still trying to understand it, still wondering how she had missed seeing the explosive charge, when Kaylor shouted "Mortar!" over the platoon push, and Avery called for counterfire. Each cyborg was equipped with a variety of sensors plus an onboard computer that could be networked with all the rest. So what one of their processors knew, *all* of them knew. Lightning-fast calculations took place, targeting data was uploaded to four shoulder-mounted SLMs, and the rockets sleeted into the air a few seconds later.

The explosions overlapped each other to create a muted roar, smoke billowed up into the sky about half a mile to the south, and the incoming fire stopped as suddenly as it had begun. But the damage had been done. A Scorpion had been destroyed, four marines were dead, and one was wounded. McKee watched with a heavy heart as the second armored car pushed what remained of the first off the bridge so that the rest of the battalion could get through.

"The bastards had the bridge preregistered," Kaylor said bitterly as she and her cyborg stopped next to McKee and Weber. "All they had to do was wait for a juicy target. And, so long as there were only two or three of them, the drones wouldn't be able to pick their heat signatures out from the surrounding clutter." McKee, who was still learning tactics and strategy, took the comment for what it was: a lesson.

There were questions, however, including who had fired the mortar, and why. The answers came half an hour later when the FTD returned from the point where the SLMs had landed to report that human remains were scattered about the site. The robot estimated that there had been three of them—but wasn't absolutely sure given the extent of the carnage.

That suggested that, after Naoto Jones passed through, a trap had been laid for the purpose of delaying any pursuit. And it worked. Because by the time the marines were buried, and some minor repairs were made to the bridge, half a day had been lost.

The good news, if any, was that Avery had been correct about the bridge. Not the exact nature of the threat. But right nevertheless. That was cold comfort, however.

The rest of the day went well until one of the trucks broke down. After some diagnostic work, the techs announced that they could fix the problem in two hours. But having been subject to so much delay, Spurlock refused to wait. So Avery was forced to leave the third squad, second platoon, to defend the truck while the rest of the battalion continued south. "Well, we ducked that shit detail," Weber said as the first platoon fell in behind the last truck.

"Yeah," McKee agreed. "Now we get to walk drag. We're the lucky ones."

Weber made a rumbling sound that McKee knew to be laughter.

As the march continued, the winding ribbon of road carried the battalion up and over a succession of vegetation-clad hills. A few hours later, the sky grew cloudy, flashes of lightning could be seen off in the distance, and the air felt increasingly humid.

McKee was debating the merits of putting on her rain slicker when Kaylor's voice invaded her helmet. "The second squad will fall out and stand by... I have a job for you."

Weber groaned. "I knew it was too good to last."

The battalion continued down the road as McKee and her legionnaires broke formation and made their way over to the spot where Kaylor was waiting. A case of MREs was sitting on the ground next to her cyborg's feet. "Okay, people, here's the situation. A navy drone spotted some wreckage about three miles east of here. According to the report, the crash must be fairly recent because there was a fire, and the surrounding foliage hasn't had time to grow back. Trouble is that we aren't missing any aircraft—and the loyalists aren't either. That means it could be a reb aircraft of some sort. And who knows? Maybe the governor was on it.

"So we're sending you out for a look-see. Once you arrive on the site, scope things out, collect any Intel you can, and report in." Kaylor paused to look up at the sky. She blinked as the first raindrops hit her face. "The weather is deteriorating—and you'll have to stay the night. Be careful out there. McKee will divvy up the MREs, then you can get going. The coordinates have been downloaded by now."

McKee felt a strange combination of fear and excitement as she released her harness and jumped to the ground. The fear had to do with the amount of responsibility involved. Was she up to the task? The anticipation stemmed from the opportunity to break away from the column and operate on her own. "Oh, and one more thing," Kaylor added. "We're sending the FTD along to examine the crash site. Any questions?"

The robot arrived right on cue and hovered next to Kaylor. McKee kept her face blank as she looked up at Kaylor. "No, ma'am. No questions."

Kaylor offered a jaunty wave as her cyborg turned and took off. The T-1 would have to run in order to catch up with the battalion. Suddenly, there was a clap of thunder, the skies opened up, and a deluge of rain fell. McKee was on her own.

11

A patrol leader can take his men a mile into the jungle, hide there, and return with any report he fancies.

SIR WILLIAM SLIM
Defeat into Victory
Standard year 1956

PLANET ORLO II

Raindrops landed on the leaves over McKee's head, where they coalesced into fat globules and fell like miniature bombs exploding on her helmet and shoulders. Taken together, they produced a soft roar that was almost enough to drown out the rhythmic whine of Weber's servos.

There was no trail, so all Weber could do was follow the FTD between the forest giants that towered hundreds of feet above. It wasn't that the globe-shaped robot was determined to lead the way. It was homing in on the coordinates downloaded from the navy—and seemingly intent on reaching the crash site regardless of what happened to the legionnaires.

McKee and Weber were on point, followed by Chiba on Poto, Singh on Kinza, and Larkin on Hower. Their sensors were on max as lightning flashed above, thunder rolled across the land, and rain lashed the foliage around them. Powerful though the cyborgs were, she knew they could be overwhelmed by a massed attack. But she figured that an ambush was unlikely since they weren't on an established trail.

Eventually, the FTD led them out of the forest and into a clearing. The remains of some thatched huts occupied the center of the open space, surrounded by what might have been gardens but were now thick with weeds. A Droi settlement? Abandoned months or even a year earlier? McKee assumed so as Weber crossed to the other side and reentered the forest.

Branches brushed past, wetting her slicker in the process, as Weber splashed through a fast-flowing creek and up a low bank. Then they headed uphill, past a mist-shrouded rock formation and onto a scree-covered slope that made for uncertain footing. The cyborgs struggled to stay upright as the pieces of wet shale slip-slid downhill and threatened to take them along.

Finally, having achieved the summit, McKee called a halt and ordered Weber to check their position. The FTD was probably correct—but what if it wasn't? Rather than take that chance, she thought it best to double-check. And as Weber verified their location via a satellite, the FTD kept going. Moments later, it disappeared. That was annoying, but there wasn't anything she could do about it other than contact the robot by radio and request that it return. But when she did so, there was no reply. Was there some sort of com problem to blame? Or did the robot have the capacity to ignore her? McKee didn't know.

After the two-minute break, it was time to make their way down the other side of the hill. That process proved to be as difficult as climbing up it had been. Only this time it was necessary to contend with mud rather than shale. Weber swore as he lost his footing and was forced to execute a series of leaps in order to maintain his equilibrium. All she could do was hang on to the grab bar and bend her knees to absorb a quick succession of shocks.

The others had similar difficulties, and it was a miracle that none of them took a serious spill. Once on the forest floor, Weber led the squad through head-high thickets of vegetation that reminded McKee of bamboo. And that was when she heard a clap of thunder followed by what might have been a distant rifle shot. Except that the two sounds came so close together it was hard to tell if there was a difference.

Weber turned into a small stream after that. It served as a highway for a while until they had to bear right in order to stay on course. Then they entered a blight-ravaged area where the trees had been stripped of foliage. Now they stood like jagged splinters against the gray sky, shoulder to shoulder in a spooky wasteland. And that was where they found the FTD. Weber gave the alert over the squad push. "Echo-Four-Five to Four-Four. I have a fix on the FTD. It's about four feet off the ground at two o'clock. Over."

McKee held up a hand to slow the others and peered through the gathering gloom. As they closed on the object, she could see that Weber was correct. The FTD was hovering just above the ground, waiting for them. Or that was how it appeared until they were ten feet away. Then she realized that the robot was impaled on a stick. The hunter's decapitated head came to mind as she said, "This is Four-Four. Look sharp everybody... We've got company. Over."

As the squad took up defensive positions all around, she freed herself from the harness and dropped to the ground. Then, mindful of the need to record what she saw, McKee activated her helmet cam. Once they got back, she would have to file another after-action report, and a picture was worth a thousand words. Meanwhile, she knew it was important to look for trip wires or any other indication that the FTD had been booby-trapped.

There was no response when McKee spoke to the machine, and the reasons for that quickly became obvious. A hole could be seen where a large-caliber bullet had penetrated the robot, and an equally sizable exit wound was visible on the opposite side of its body. And that was to say nothing of the sharpened stake upon which the FTD was impaled.

McKee felt a prickly sensation between her shoulder blades as she did a slow 360. They were being watched, she felt certain of that, even if the rain was interfering with the accuracy of the team's infrared sensors by cooling everything down. "So what now?" Larkin demanded. "This place is spooky."

"Four-Two will use proper radio procedure," McKee said as all sorts of thoughts flickered through her mind. What, if anything, had the FTD "seen" prior to being hit? Maybe it was still there, resident in the robot's memory, waiting to be accessed. The mere possibility of that meant it was her duty to pull the machine's CPU and take the device with her.

But what sort of information had the FTD acquired since the battalion departed Riversplit? Data about her perhaps? Gathered at Jivv's request? Or just gathered. Because that was what the robot was designed to do. The decision seemed to make itself. "This thing is too big to carry, and we can't leave tech laying around, so Echo-Four-One will destroy it. Then we're out of here. Over."

That was the moment when McKee feared one of her team members would suggest that she jerk the CPU, but none of them did, and she felt a sense of relief as Singh attached a small charge to the robot. Then, once they were a safe distance away, he thumbed a remote. There was a flash of light followed by a loud bang. The FTD and whatever it knew was history.

"Okay," McKee said, "keep your heads on a swivel. And max those sensors. Over."

There was a series of double clicks by way of a response as Weber led the others into the forest. McKee had more reason to worry about the possibility of an ambush at that point because the enemy knew they were present and could guess where they were headed. It would be easy to calculate a line of march and lie in wait for the legionnaires. But by moving quickly, she hoped to reach the crash site before the opposition could get organized.

Unfortunately, what light there was had begun to fade, adding even more urgency to the situation. They were going to spend the night, and that meant she'd have to find a spot that the squad could defend. A task best carried out during the day when one could see the surrounding territory.

Thick brush gave way and was forced to surrender as Weber smashed through it. Eventually, after five minutes of concerted effort, the cyborg broke free of the foliage and entered an area blackened by fire. And there, with its nose half-buried in the ground, was a spaceship. It was too large to be an air car of the sort Governor Jones might have access to—but about right for a scout or small transport. But that was all she could discern without inspecting the wreckage more closely. "This is Four-Four... That thing could be empty or full of bad guys," McKee said. "So be careful. And watch for trip wires, land mines, and IEDs."

Step by step, the squad advanced over broken ground until the dark hull loomed above them. "Does anyone know what kind of ship this is?" McKee inquired. "Over."

"This is Four-Three," Chiba replied. "I'm no expert. But it doesn't look human to me. I think it's military, though. See the bulge on the side of the hull? And the tube that's sticking out? That looks like an energy cannon. Over."

That set McKee's mind to churning as she led the team counterclockwise around the wreck. Not human? Military? If so, the wreck was a real wake-up call. Something the brass would be very interested in. But before she sought to make radio contact with the battalion, McKee wanted to learn more. And find a place where the squad could hole up for the night.

The ship had thrown up a berm of soil as it hit and dug in. And the dirt was turning to mud as the rain continued to fall. Big clumps of it stuck to the legionnaires' foot pods and made it difficult for them to walk as they circled around the hull to the point where a ramp led up into the ship. And that was very interesting since it suggested that at least one crew member had survived the crash. But where were they? Out in the forest, shooting FTDs? Or inside the ship waiting to blast anyone stupid enough to enter? There was only one way to find out.

"This is Four-Four," McKee said. "The bio bods will dismount while the cyborgs take up defensive positions around the ramp. Execute. Over."

Once the T-1s were in place, with their backs to the ship, McKee led the rest of the squad up the ramp, with her AXE at the ready. The white blob projected from her helmet swung back and forth across the cargo hold as she turned her head. Crates and cargo modules were secured to the deck, and most if not all of them had been opened and ransacked. So they weren't the first ones to enter the wreck. Far from it.

Having established that fact, she forced herself to pay attention to the sort of details that might provide a clue as to what race the ship belonged to. The first thing she noticed was that what looked like control panels were higher off the deck than they would be on a human ship, a fold-down set was much bigger, and the handles on a storage box were *huge*. And there was the alien script associated with what might have been access panels, fire extinguishers, and other mundane items. All of which suggested a possibility that Chiba put into words before she could. "This is Four-Three. I think the ship is Hudathan. Over."

McKee was aware of the Hudathans, of course, but only vaguely. They were *big*, she knew that, and very warlike. And some said paranoid because they regarded every sentient race as a potential threat no matter how peaceful it might be. As the empire continued to expand, there had been more and more contacts with the Hudathans as well as raids on human-occupied rim worlds in recent years. "Roger that," McKee replied, as they arrived in front of a steel bulkhead. A hatch was centered in the middle of the barrier but refused to budge when Larkin tried the handle.

Clearly, they would have to break in. But that would have to wait. McKee felt reasonably sure that the wreck was deserted—and would be more defensible than a makeshift encampment would be. So she ordered the other bio bods to search for Intel while she returned to the ramp.

It was dark by then, and McKee was glad the team had a secure place to hole up as she ordered Kinza and Hower inside. Their electromechanical bodies didn't require rest, but their brains did, and two cybernetic sentries would be sufficient. The T-1s left a trail of mud on alien steel as they tromped up the ramp, went off to one side, and locked their joints. The cybernetic equivalent of lying down.

Then it was time to plug into one of Hower's jack panels so she could access a radio powerful enough to reach the battalion. It took two tries to raise one of the outfit's com techs and request a link to Lieutenant Kaylor. What she got was a hookup with Captain Avery, who had clearly been waiting for a report. "This is Echo-Nine. Go. Over."

What McKee delivered was modeled on the sort of report she'd heard Sergeant Hux give. It was short and to the point. The team had traveled cross-country, been separated from the

FTD, and been forced to destroy it later on. Presently, they were inside a ship that might or might not be Hudathan. No mention was made of lightning, thunder, or any of the other difficulties they had been forced to overcome.

After listening to McKee, Avery said, "Well done, Four-Four. Break into the control compartment if you can and bring us every memory module, data pad, and scrap of paper you can lay your hands on. Assuming it is a Hudathan ship, Admiral Poe is going to be very interested. Over."

McKee acknowledged the order and signed off. Her first report from the field had gone well as far as she could tell—and it felt good to have it behind her. But there was no opportunity to enjoy the small victory as she went back to work.

Upon returning to the cargo compartment, McKee discovered that the other bio bods had hung glow strips here and there and assembled a small treasure trove of items that might or might not be of value to the Intel people. But like Avery, she felt that the *real* finds, if any, were waiting behind the locked hatch. And that would give them something to do during the evening.

But first it was time for the bio bods to heat up some water, pour it into their favorite MRE, and mix the two together. Once the resulting meals were ready, the personal condiments came out. Larkin was partial to garlic, Chiba favored hot sauce, and Singh sprinkled curry powder onto his chicken and rice. That made McKee the only person to consume her meal without adding anything to it—and once the legionnaire was finished, she couldn't remember what had been in the glutinous mixture.

With dinner taken care of, it was time to confront the hatch. The first and most obvious way to tackle the problem was to place a charge over the lock and blow it. So McKee ordered Singh to take his best shot.

After fifteen minutes of careful preparation, the legionnaire declared himself to be ready, and once everyone had pulled back to the ramp, Singh thumbed the remote. There was a brilliant flash of light followed by an explosion that shook the ship's hull. Smoke billowed and gradually began to dissipate as McKee went forward to inspect the damage. As her helmet light played across the bulkhead, she saw that, while the hatch was warped and pushed inwards, it remained intact.

Singh shook his head. "The problem is that this bad boy was built to be airtight. It's my guess that lock bars extend from the central control mechanism out into the surrounding frame. Kind of like a bank vault." What Singh *didn't* say was why he knew so much about breaking into bank vaults. But McKee wasn't the only one who was hiding in the Legion, and she knew better than to ask.

After giving the matter some thought, she called Kinza forward. She pointed at the obstruction. "It looks like the charge did some damage. Let's see if you can kick it in."

The T-1 took a look, backed away, and positioned himself. Then, like a cop busting through a door, Kinza delivered a powerful kick. His foot pod hit, something gave, and a three-inch space appeared between the hatch and the surrounding frame. Two additional blows were required to push the steel door back far enough so that a bio bod could slip through.

McKee nodded approvingly. "Nice work, Private. Go back and get some rest." Kinza uttered a grunt of acknowledgment and clanked away.

McKee drew her pistol before slipping through the gap into the darkness beyond. There was no need. What appeared to be a small lounge was empty, as were the bunks beyond, what the swabbies would call a "head," and a two-person cockpit. There was something that looked like dried blood, however. *Lots* of it. And she could see why. When the ship hit the ground, it appeared that a piece of metal had been driven through the control panel and into the pilot's body. Or was that the copilot's chair? Not that it made any difference.

Then, after the crash, the surviving crew member had removed the corpse. For burial? Most likely. That was the point when McKee remembered the need to record everything she saw. So she put her helmet on and instructed the other bio bods to do the same.

The next hour was spent taking the cockpit apart trying to find any- and everything that might have memory or a CPU. Some of the modules were hard to remove, and McKee was afraid that damage was being done, but it couldn't be helped.

Once the cockpit had been stripped, it was time to shut off the cameras, rotate the cyborgs, and place two bio bods on sentry duty as well. McKee and Chiba took the first stint in what turned out to be an uneventful watch.

Finally, when McKee was free to enter her sleep sack, she was so tired that she fell into a dreamless sleep. And when she awoke it was to find that Larkin was crouched next to her. "Hey, McKee... Time to rise and shine."

McKee felt a sense of alarm as she looked at her chrono and realized that it was 0500. That meant she had slept through her second watch. She sat up and began to shove the sleep sack down off her legs. "Why didn't someone wake me up? I was supposed to stand watch with Kinza."

"That was my fault," Larkin said evenly. "I forgot."

McKee looked around, saw Singh grin, and knew it was a plot. The whole squad was in on the plan to give her some extra sleep. It was, as far as the very privileged Catherine Carletto could remember, the finest gift she had ever received. She said, "Thank you, guys... But don't ever do that again. You'll be busting ass in the jungle if you do."

That got a chuckle as McKee laced up her boots, grabbed the AXE, and went outside to take a pee. The rain had stopped, the sun was rising, and a thick blanket of mist covered the ground. Then, as McKee stood and hurried to pull up her pants, she heard Weber's voice over the radio that was slotted into her body armor. "This is Four-Five... We've got company. *Lots* of it. Over."

McKee made her way over to the ramp, where she took up a position between Weber and Poto. "This is Four-Four. Gear up everybody... And be ready."

McKee saw the Droi materialize out of the mist. There were dozens, no *hundreds* of them, all standing shoulder to shoulder. Larkin spoke from his position at the top of the ramp. "They're like sitting ducks. Let's grease 'em."

"*No*," McKee replied firmly. "Not unless I give the order." Then, having placed her AXE on the ground, she went out to meet the indigs with hands up and palms out. A light breeze blew the remaining wisps of mist away to reveal an individual who stood about six feet tall and was armed with a *huge* assault rifle. From the ship? Yes, McKee thought so, as the indig bent to place his weapon on the ground.

The Droi's head was covered with iridescent scales that flowed down the back of its neck to merge with the mantle that covered its upper torso. It was dressed in a pair of cross belts, a short skirt made of leather, and a pair of sturdy sandals.

When the Droi straightened up, McKee found herself looking into a face dominated by two slitted cat eyes, a series of bony ridges where a human nose would have been, and a thin-lipped mouth. "My name is Insa," the Droi said simply. The standard was a pleasant surprise—but made sense since McKee knew that the rebs had been trading with the locals for many years.

"And I'm McKee," she replied.

"McKee," Insa said slowly, as if testing the name. "Come, we have tea."

"I'm sorry," McKee replied, "but I can't leave my squad."

"Not far," Insa replied, and pointed.

McKee saw that a small fire was burning in a ceramic bowl about twenty feet away—and as she watched mats were placed on either side of it. Though no expert in xenoanthropology, she didn't need to be in order to understand the situation. Insa was inviting her to take part in some sort of ceremony and, given how many of its people were in attendance, McKee figured the right answer was, "Thank you."

What ensued took a full twenty minutes as they knelt on the mats, water was heated to a boil, leaves were added, and Insa said what might have been a prayer in its native language. Then it was time to strain the leaves out and rinse two small containers with water, before pouring the fragrant liquid into the exquisitely crafted cups.

At that point, McKee was careful to watch and mimic Insa as it offered the cup of tea to the sky before bringing it down to the point where its snakelike tongue could sample the air around the steaming liquid. Then, with the reverence of a priest performing a sacred ritual, it took a sip.

McKee, who was determined to get the brew down no matter what it tasted like, did likewise. She was pleased to discover that it was sweet and minty. "It's good," she said politely. "Very good."

Insa offered a slight inclination of its head. "We are pleased that you like. Talk now."

McKee took a second sip, heard her stomach growl, and remembered that she hadn't had breakfast. "Good. What shall we talk about?"

"War," Insa answered grimly. What followed was more like a speech than a two-way conversation. The way Insa told the story, the Droi welcomed the first human colonists and had been grateful of the opportunity to trade for items they wouldn't have been able to obtain otherwise. Yes, there had been friction when the humans tried to carve farms out of the Big Green. But that conflict had been resolved by an agreement negotiated with Emperor Ordanus's government in which the Big Green had been ceded to the Droi in perpetuity.

Then the emperor died, his sister assumed the throne, and the agreement had been vacated by a royal decree. That was when employees of the big off-world companies began to invade the Big Green, searching for valuable minerals, cutting trees down, and staking out what were to become huge farms. This, Insa explained, was why the Droi were aligned with the rebels. That and the fact that the humans who had been born and raised on Orlo II were generally respectful of the Droi and acknowledged their right to the Big Green.

McKee took advantage of a momentary pause to speak. "What you say is interesting, but I'm a low-ranking soldier and have no say in such matters."

Insa was in no way dissuaded. "You come for ship, yes? We talk ship." That was when the Droi launched into another diatribe, this one being focused on what it called "the second threat." Namely the possibility of an invasion by the Hudathans. There had been a number of landings since the last planting and, according to Insa, it was only a matter of time before the Hudathans arrived in force. Something that would threaten everyone.

"I see your point," McKee replied carefully. "And I will tell my superiors what you said."

"You tell," Insa agreed. "And give present."

McKee frowned. "A present?"

"Yes. Present." Insa raised a hand, and that was when four Droi led a Hudathan out into the clearing. Ropes were attached to the leather collar around his neck, his wrists were secured to a thick pole that rested on his massive shoulders, and chains rattled as he shuffled forward. All of which served to emphasize the extent of the alien's considerable strength.

And he was *big*, at least three hundred pounds, and maybe more. The alien had a humanoid head, the vestige of a dorsal fin that ran front to back along the top of his skull, froglike ears, and bony lips. His temperature-sensitive skin was gray at the moment. But what impressed McKee the most were the Hudathan's small and rather malevolent-looking eyes. She saw no signs of fear in them, just hate, as the Droi jerked their prisoner to a halt. "He yours," Insa said. "You take. Make talk. Stop war."

McKee's head was spinning by then. What had begun as a reasonably straightforward mission was suddenly very complicated. But she knew that the Hudathan was a high-value prisoner—and Avery would expect her to bring him in. "Yes," she said. "I will do as you say. Can I ask a question?"

Insa inclined its head. "Ask."

"There was a machine... A flying machine. We found it impaled on a stake."

"We kill," Insa said unapologetically. "It attack Thua."

The FTD wasn't armed insofar as McKee knew, and that led her to believe that the robot had detected the person named Thua and headed straight for it with plans to perform a scan. And, feeling threatened, Thua or one of Thua's companions put a bullet through the machine.

In any case, what could she do? Tell Insa not to shoot any more FTDs? It seemed best to let the matter go, so she changed the subject. "With your permission, I'm going to request that an aircraft land and take the Hudathan away."

Insa looked up as if the shuttle might appear at any moment. "Yes. That okay."

It took the better part of six hours to contact Avery, explain the situation, and get a navy shuttle on the ground. No easy task since the LZ was extremely tight. But things went quickly after that, as six heavily armed swabbies herded the Hudathan aboard, soon followed by the T-1s and bio bods.

Twenty minutes later, the ship put down next to the clearing in which the battalion was camped. It paused just long enough for McKee's squad to disembark before taking off again.

Lieutenant Kaylor came out to meet them. She stood with hands on hips. "Your uniforms are filthy! A disgrace to the Legion." Then she grinned. "Welcome home—such as it is. You did a helluva job. And that's from the captain. He would have come himself except for the governor and all."

McKee frowned. "The governor?"

"Oh, right," Kaylor said. "You wouldn't know. We caught the bastard! They're interrogating him now. Come on… I'll show you where Echo Company is quartered." McKee followed the officer toward a crude palisade and the encampment beyond. The governor had been captured. It seemed anticlimactic.

Thanks to the fact that the brass were busy with the governor, McKee was spared the sort of hot wash she had endured after the effort to rescue Frood. That meant she was free to eat, spend five minutes in a jury-rigged shower, and hit the sack. She awoke feeling rested, went about the process of getting ready for the day, and was eating her breakfast next to the first platoon's all-purpose fire when Kaylor appeared. McKee started to rise. But Kaylor said, "As you were," and took a seat on a crate of MREs. The officer had a mug with her and took a sip from it. "How are you feeling?"

"A little sore," McKee admitted. "Jungle busting is a bitch. But otherwise fine."

"Good," Kaylor replied. "I'm sorry to do this to you—but we have some female prisoners including the governor's wife and niece. And since there are three men for every woman in Echo Company, we're short of female guards. So I was forced to put you into the rotation."

It wasn't good news, but it was typical of the way things worked, and there was no point in complaining. Especially to Kaylor, who had seen and done it all. "Yes, ma'am. What time?"

"Twenty-four hundred to oh-three-hundred hours."

"I'll be there. Can I ask a question?"

"Shoot."

"How did we catch the governor?"

"An armed drone spotted his convoy as it left the forest and began to cross a large open space. Two vehicles were destroyed, and a third was damaged. The rebs were trying to repair it when the third platoon caught up with them."

McKee had been hoping that the governor would escape, but she forced a smile and nodded. "Sounds like good teamwork. Was Monitor Jivv with the third?"

"No," Kaylor responded as she emptied her mug. "Why do you ask?"

"Just curious, that's all," she replied. "When are we going to pull out?"

Kaylor stood. "I thought the swabbies would swoop in and take custody of the governor this morning. But I hear Monitor Jivv is opposed to that. I'll let you know when things come together."

Kaylor walked away, and as McKee ate the last of her breakfast, she was thinking. Why would Jivv stall? Because he had orders to kill Governor Jones, but wasn't supposed to do so in front of witnesses? That seemed like a pretty good guess. Not that she could do anything about it. Taking care of herself was difficult enough.

After a day spent cleaning her gear, performing maintenance on Weber, and looking after the squad, McKee reported to the tent set up for the female prisoners. It was large enough to house twelve Grays—and had, prior to being appropriated. There was one entrance guarded by two legionnaires, one of whom was a sergeant. He gave her the job of patrolling the back side of the tent.

McKee was happy with the assignment since it meant she would be by herself and wouldn't have to take responsibility for whatever comings and goings took place. The tent was lit from within, and McKee could see shadows moving about as she patrolled back and forth. It was a very boring activity, so the minutes seemed to crawl by, and it was difficult to stay alert.

Then, with roughly an hour to go, there was an altercation

out front. McKee could hear voices as a loud argument began. She was tempted to go check it out. But that would mean leaving her post. So she stayed, and that was when she noticed a dark shadow, and realized that one of the prisoners was right up against the back wall of the tent. Moments later something sharp penetrated the fabric and McKee heard a ripping sound.

There were a number of things McKee could have done, including let the escape play itself out, or call for backup and put a stop to it. But she did neither. Instead, she took up a position directly in front of the newly created aperture, aimed her flashlight, and turned it on. There was a gasp of surprise followed by a look of fear on the part of the face she could see.

Then it was her turn to feel a sense of shock as she realized she was looking at Marcy Tanaka. One of her best friends in college. "Marcy? It's me, Cat." McKee hadn't used her real name in months and immediately wished she hadn't.

The eye McKee could see registered surprise. "*Cat?* I heard you were killed in a bombing. And your face…"

"Think of it as a beauty mark," McKee said dryly. "What are you doing here?"

"Governor Jones is my uncle… You remember that."

McKee didn't remember that. All of Cat's friends had important relatives. And she had made very little effort to keep track of them. "We've got to escape," Marcy continued. "There's a synth. A robot named Jivv. He's going to kill us."

McKee swore. It was just as she feared. The knife seemed to leave its sheath of its own accord. The tent fabric parted, and as McKee waved Marcy out, a middle-aged woman appeared. "This is my aunt Cia," Marcy whispered, and McKee knew that she was looking at the governor's wife.

"You've got to save my husband," Cia Jones said desperately. "He's in a tent over there." And that was when McKee realized how stupid she'd been. With one careless stroke of her knife she had compromised her identity, betrayed her comrades, and committed herself to a hopeless cause. The world she had built for herself was about to collapse.

12

I have learned to hate all traitors, and there is no disease that I spit on more than treachery.

GREEK POET AESCHYLUS
Standard year circa 451 B.C.

PLANET ORLO II

In a matter of seconds, McKee had been transformed from a noncommissioned officer into a deserter and, in the eyes of many, a traitor. But to allow herself to consider the ramifications of that would be to plunge into despair. And there were others to worry about. Marcy and Cia were waiting for her to take action. Meanwhile, the argument heard earlier was still under way out front. A female with a shrill voice was clearly unhappy about something. "The woman," McKee said. "Who is she? And how long do we have?"

"She's my maid," Cia replied. "She's too old to run. This was her idea."

McKee was about to say, "They'll kill her," but it was clear from the look on Cia's face that she knew that. "Follow me," McKee said. "And move quietly."

All of the shelters faced the center of the compound. The entire battalion was asleep except for the guards. And as McKee came closer, she could see that a sentry had been posted at the rear of the governor's tent as well. He was a Gray, which was just as well, since she didn't want to blindside a legionnaire. "Wait here," McKee whispered, and pointed to a dark shadow.

Then, with the nonchalant manner of an NCO making her rounds, McKee approached the guard. Her AXE was in her right hand rather than on its sling. The Gray nodded politely and was opening his mouth to speak when the rifle butt struck the side of his head. There was a solid *thunk* followed by a *thump* as the soldier hit the ground. McKee took all of the soldier's ammo before turning her attention to the tent.

McKee figured the same technique she had used before would work now. The knife penetrated the fabric with ease, and the sharp blade made a ripping sound as it sliced to the ground. She half expected the governor to appear at that point, but he didn't. And when she looked in through the slit, McKee saw why.

A single glow strip dangled from one of the tent poles. Two folding chairs occupied the center of the space and were positioned to face each other. A human was bound to one—and a Droi to the other. That squared with what McKee had heard. An indig leader had been captured with Jones.

As McKee entered, she could see that both prisoners had been beaten. Jivv's work? Most likely. The air reeked of sweat and urine. The Droi was awake, head up, watching her. But the governor appeared to be unconscious and was slumped against the ropes that held him in place.

McKee held her left index finger to her lips in what she hoped was the universal sign for "keep quiet." The Droi nodded as she went to work with the knife. Her plan was to free the indig first in hopes that it would help with Jones.

She felt a stab of fear as male voices were heard. Had Marcy and Cia been missed? And what time was it anyway? The guards were due to be relieved at 0300. A quick glance at her chrono revealed that it was 0246.

The conversation faded as the participants walked away— and McKee allowed herself a sigh of relief. As she made a final cut, she spoke to the Droi. "I'll need your help to get the governor out of here. Understood?"

The Droi nodded as the ropes fell away. "Understood."

"Good. We have five minutes. Then we'll have to run."

The Droi spoke to Jones in low tones as McKee cut him free. The governor's head came up, and his eyes blinked. "Water."

But there wasn't enough time to give Jones water as McKee and the indig hoisted him off the chair and guided him toward the back of the tent. Seconds later, they were outside the fetid enclosure and stumbling away. The Droi took over as Marcy and Cia appeared out of the shadows. "I lead," it said decisively, and McKee allowed it to do so.

Because most of the battalion was sleeping, and no alarm had been given, the five of them were able to slip from shadow to shadow. Jones had difficulty walking at first, but the farther they went, the more his mobility improved, and that was good because the defensive perimeter lay directly ahead.

McKee's already pounding heart felt as if it was going to beat its way out of her chest as the sound of shouting was heard—and a flare went off high above. "Get down!" she said. "And don't run until I tell you to."

A ditch fronted by stacked logs lay directly in front of them, and she ran straight at it. "The prisoners are escaping!" she shouted. "Over there! Get them!"

The legionnaires assigned to defensive position were already looking her way because of the noise and the flare. So when they saw the familiar silhouette of a helmet and gear, they took off in the direction she was pointing. She waved the others forward. "*Now!* Run."

The edge of the forest was only a hundred feet away, but it seemed like miles as McKee supported one of the governor's arms and the Droi took the other. Marcy and Cia were up ahead and glanced back occasionally to make sure the others were there.

Then all hell broke loose as somebody spotted the fugitives and opened fire. Bullets threw geysers of dirt into the air as McKee let go of Jones and skidded to a halt. A projectile whined past her head as she turned and brought the AXE up at the same time. The burst was high and had the desired effect. A legionnaire dived for cover—and that bought time for the fugitives to reach the tree line.

As McKee entered the protection of the trees, she discovered that the indig was waiting for her. *More* flares had been fired by then, and some of the harsh light made it through the foliage. The Droi looked a lot like Insa, but had wrinkly skin, which she assumed to be a sign of age. "My name is Anslo. You?"

"McKee." She gave the same name that she had given Insa.

"McKee follow." And with that, Anslo took the governor's left arm and turned east.

McKee gave herself the task of walking drag, and hadn't gone more than a hundred feet when *more* Droi materialized around her. At that point she realized that the indigs had been present all along, watching the battalion and waiting for a chance. Now they were filling in behind the fugitives and... McKee had a horrible thought and hurried to catch up with Anslo. Once she was alongside the Droi, it was difficult to jog and speak at the same time. "T-1s... The Legion will send T-1s... And we can't outrun them."

"No worry," Anslo replied. "The P-Yani block."

Block? How the hell could the Droi block a T-1? The answer arrived moments later and was headed in the opposite direction. The P-Yani were about the size of a small horse, with warthoglike tusks and big, three-toed feet. And there were *hundreds* of them, all thundering west. Normally the P-Yani were a source of nutrient-rich blood, meat, and leather for the Droi. Now they were an army.

The governor's party was forced to take shelter behind one of the forest giants as the P-Yani flowed around them. Gunfire could be heard in the distance as the animals came into contact with the Legion. McKee could imagine the T-1s trying to move forward but being pushed back by a tidal wave of flesh and bone. Some would open fire on the animals. Others would wait them out. They were blocked either way.

"Come!" Anslo said, and waved the party forward. Most of the herd had already streamed past, but it was necessary to dodge stragglers as the group headed east. Rather than beat obstacles down the way the T-1s had on the trip to the wreck, the Droi seemed to slip *between* them, like water through a streambed.

Because McKee was still wearing her helmet, she could

"see" the distance traveled on her HUD and knew they were making good time. So by the time the sun rose in the east, and sunlight pooled on the forest floor, the fugitives were deep inside the Big Green.

Drones passed over on two different occasions, prompting McKee to turn her helmet off lest the navy home in on the tracking signal it produced. That meant she was cutting herself off from her new family—and it was as difficult as giving up her former identity had been. But all she could do was grit her teeth and keep going.

McKee had seen the remains of a Droi village on the way to the wreck—so as they entered the forest encampment she recognized it as a temporary affair. At least two hundred Droi were present, and they were armed with a hodgepodge of weapons. There were no fires other than those used to make tea, and they produced very little smoke. Shelters consisted of leather tarps strung up between smaller trees—or draped over vines that stretched from trunk to trunk.

Anslo was welcomed in a fashion that suggested considerable respect, as was Governor Jones, and to a lesser degree the rest of his party, including McKee. Not long thereafter, Anslo and Jones were asked to participate in a meeting. That left McKee sitting at the foot of a tree and feeling lost until Marcy brought her a pot of tea. The next hour was spent catching up.

McKee told Marcy about her adventures since that fateful day on Esparto. And Marcy gave an account of what had occurred since the initial purge. Like McKee's parents, thousands of other people had been systematically executed by Tarch Hanno and the newly created Bureau of Missing Persons. And that was why Marcy had been sent to Orlo II—in the hope that she would be safe there.

But, according to Marcy, it wasn't safe *anywhere*. And the only reason she hadn't been killed was the heavy security that surrounded her uncle and the manner in which the rebellion acted to screen her from synths like Jivv. But now that the uprising had been crushed, her only hope was to escape from Orlo II. "There are smugglers," she explained. "People who live out on the rim, where Ophelia is nothing more than a dirty word. They trade with the Droi and Uncle Naoto says we might be able to book passage with one of them. If we do, I'll make sure he takes you along. He owes you... We all do."

The conversation ended shortly thereafter as Marcy left to return the teapot and cups to their owner. And for the first time since deserting, McKee had a moment to think about her future. The plan to get off Orlo II and travel to a safe place made sense except for one thing. McKee wanted to bring Ophelia down. And more than that, to kill her. However unrealistic such an ambition might be. Could she accomplish that out on the rim? It was something to think about.

McKee found a mossy nook to lie down in and fell asleep with the AXE clutched in her arms. Dreams came and went. None were good. So when Marcy woke her, McKee was happy to escape wherever she'd been.

The sun had arced across the treetops by then and was settling into the west. McKee sat up and wished that she could brush her teeth. "Sorry to bother you," Marcy said. "But a rebel leader named Howard Trask arrived an hour ago. He's going to meet with Anslo and my uncle. You're invited."

McKee said, "Thanks," and scrambled to her feet. Her uniform was a mess, but she did the best she could to brush it off. How was she going to get civilian clothes? Or anything else, for that matter. What little bit of money she had was back with the battalion.

Such problems would have to wait, however, as she followed Marcy to a grove of trees where Anslo, Jones, and a man she'd never seen before were seated on the ground. Food, all heaped on large leaves, sat in front of them. McKee's stomach growled at the sight of it.

"There you are!" Jones said cheerfully as he came to his feet. The governor had a black eye as well as various cuts and bruises on his face. An indication of the treatment McKee could expect if she was captured. "Please have a seat," he said. "You're the guest of honor."

McKee didn't *feel* like the guest of honor as Anslo welcomed her to the circle, and she was introduced to Howard Trask. He was a short man, with a barrel-shaped chest, and thick arms.

He had white hair cut short, twinkling blue eyes, and a two-day growth of beard. A huge paw swallowed McKee's hand. "It's a pleasure, little lady! Thank God you were there. Odds are the governor and his family would be dead otherwise. You were very brave."

McKee couldn't accept such praise. Especially since part of her regretted taking the action she had. So she mumbled something by way of a reply, accepted the invitation to eat, and loaded a leaf with strips of spicy meat, sliced fruit, and a tangy concoction that reminded her of sauerkraut. Meanwhile, the strategy session got under way.

McKee was only half listening at first since the others were discussing people and events that she knew little to nothing about. But then, as talk turned to the battalion, she began to pay more attention. "This is a wonderful opportunity," Trask was saying. "Spurlock is an idiot. His so-called battalion is so far from Riversplit that Rylund can't reinforce him, and for reasons we're not sure of, the navy isn't as active as it was earlier, so he won't get much help from above. Spurlock put his neck on the chopping block. The least we can do is chop it off for him."

"I agree," Jones added grimly. "Let's teach the loyalists a lesson. Once the battalion has been destroyed, they'll think twice before they send more troops into the Big Green."

Not too surprisingly, Anslo had a similar view. As McKee listened to the Droi, she could imagine a scene in which thousands of warriors attacked the battalion at once. Echo Company would give a good account of itself, but even they could be overrun. That was a horrible thought. So she listened carefully, hoping to hear a date and time. But no mention of that was made, leaving her to wonder as the light continued to fade, and the meeting came to a conclusion.

A Droi led her to a lean-to, where a neatly folded trade blanket and a gourd full of water were waiting. After brushing her teeth with a finger, she lay down and wrapped the blanket around her body. But try as she might, sleep wouldn't come. Not while her friends were at risk. Yet what could she do? Leave the Droi encampment and warn them? That would amount to a double betrayal. First the Legion, then those who opposed Ophelia's corrupt government.

And what if she was able to alert the battalion? What then? Jivv would kill her. But maybe that was okay if it would save her unit. More than that, maybe she deserved to die given what she'd done.

At some point the roiling thoughts gave way to an uneasy sleep. But not for long. When McKee awoke, it was still dark, and much to her surprise, she knew what to do. It wasn't right, not by a long shot, but a decision had been made.

McKee unwound the blanket, sat up, and began to consider her options. Ideally, she would take the blanket, the AXE, and the helmet with her. It was going to be a difficult trip through the forest, and all three items would come in handy.

But if she took them Anslo, Jones, and Trask would know what she was up to and attempt to track her down. Whereas if she left such important items behind, it would appear that she had gotten up in the middle of the night, wandered off to take a pee, and gotten lost in the darkness. Yes, they would still search for her, but not in the same way. And if they did manage to find her, she could use the story, and they would believe her. That made sense, so the decision was made.

But while McKee planned to leave the blanket, AXE, and helmet behind, she still had her body armor, knife, pistol, and lots of ammo. Because the assault rifle and the handgun were chambered for the same 4.7mm rounds. That, plus the compass function built into her chrono, would see her through.

McKee used quick blips from her flashlight to scan the ground for any other items, spotted the water gourd, and wished she could take it. But that wouldn't make sense. Not for someone who had gotten up to go relieve herself. She could take a drink from it, however, and did.

She feared that leaving the encampment would be difficult but quickly discovered that the Droi were a good deal more lax than the Legion was, having placed their sentries hundreds of feet apart. That allowed her to slip between two of them and follow a gully downhill. Two of Orlo II's moons were up. The trees blocked most of the silvery light—but some of it found its way to the forest floor. And luminescent insects darted here and there. Each was like a flying jewel—and they were comforting somehow.

McKee paused every now and then to listen. But all she heard were the usual night sounds and the gentle rasp of her own breathing. Eventually, the gully opened into a small stream that led west. The Droi were good trackers, but even *they* couldn't follow her through running water.

Roughly half a mile later, McKee was forced to leave the stream when it turned north. At that point she figured it was safe to probe the area ahead using occasional blips from her flashlight. Doing so not only kept her from colliding with obstacles but provided a measure of psychological comfort as well.

And there were things to be afraid of in the darkness. Every ecosystem has predators. She knew next to nothing about the creatures that lived in the Big Green except for the fact that some of them were noisy. She was reminded of boot camp on Drang as something screeched—and was answered from a long way off.

Such sounds were frightening, and caused her to put a hand on her pistol more than once. However, if the days spent on Drang had taught her anything, it was that the most dangerous animals were frequently silent. Especially when stalking their prey.

But there was nothing she could do except stay alert and keep going. The idea was to get well outside the area the Droi would search by the time the sun came up. Such were McKee's thoughts as she felt the first stomach cramp.

It came out of nowhere, caused her to double up in pain, and was followed by a bout of nausea. Then, after a minute or so, she felt fine. McKee remembered the food heaped on leaves—and the water in the gourd. It seemed that one or more of the dishes she had consumed didn't agree with her or was spoiled. *Great,* McKee thought to herself as she climbed over a half-rotten log. *That's just what I need.*

The nausea returned two minutes later. Then the food came up. She heaved, and continued to do so even after there was nothing left to throw up. It felt as if she would be turned inside out. But maybe that was good. Maybe she would feel better once the bad stuff had been purged from her body. That was her hope. But it wasn't the case. The dry heaves were followed by more stomach cramps. And they were so painful that she could barely walk as she sought a place to curl up and die.

McKee turned the flashlight on and kept it on long enough to spot an overgrown stump and what looked like a hole between two enormous roots. It would have to do. She was staggering forward when she felt a pressing need to defecate.

The thought of shitting her pants, and doing so in a place where it would be almost impossible to get them clean, drove her to clamp down long enough to get her pants down. Having no toilet paper, she had to use handfuls of moss instead.

Then came the need to put some distance between the scat and herself lest the odor attract animal attention. Thus began a painful trek as McKee forced herself to keep walking. Eventually, the beam from her flashlight swept across a jumble of rocks. As she came closer, she saw a hole between two of them.

With one hand clutched to her stomach, she fell to her knees in front of the opening and began to crawl inside. That was stupid, of course, since there was a very real possibility that the cavelike space was occupied. If so, an animal might come charging toward her at any moment. And as McKee entered, there *was* evidence of habitation including tufts of fur, a scattering of well-gnawed bones, and a desiccated corpse about the size of a raccoon. The previous owner? Yes, she thought so, but felt so sick that she didn't care who or what shared the cave with her.

McKee turned the flashlight off in order to conserve power, curled up into the fetal position, and allowed herself to cry. The pain began to abate after a while, and nothingness took her in. Later, when she awoke, it was to see rays of sunshine streaming down through small holes above. She was thirsty. *Very* thirsty. *So get some water,* she told herself. But when she attempted to do so, the effort was too much, and she collapsed. The cave began to spin, she felt dizzy, and a whirlpool pulled her down.

It seemed like years later when thunder rolled and a drop of water hit her right eyelid. McKee blinked and blinked again as another droplet splashed against her face. Only a small effort was required to reposition herself so that the liquid landed in her mouth. The rainwater tasted sweet as it hit her tongue. But there wasn't enough of it. She forced herself to flip over and crawl outside. The downpour soaked her back within a matter of seconds. But then, as she rolled over, the full force of the rain hit her face. She drank it in coughing, swallowing, and opening her mouth for more.

Bit by bit, McKee felt strength return to her body. It wasn't long before she was up collecting large leaves to use as bowls. And as water collected in them, she went from leaf to leaf, drinking her fill.

Then, unable to consume another drop, McKee retreated to the cave. There were leaks, but she could dodge the worst of them by leaning against the back wall. That was when she noticed the dry twigs that had been part of the previous occupant's nest. After scooping the detritus into a pile, and throwing the body of the dead animal on top, she lit a fire with her lighter.

The twigs caught, crackled, and sent flames up under the desiccated corpse. Soon it was burning, too, and McKee had a fire. Smoke billowed, found its way up through cracks, and disappeared. She held her hands out, took in the warmth, and wished she had something to eat. Even an MRE would have been welcome.

Then she remembered the battalion, the mission she had set for herself, and the importance of time. A quick look at the chrono confirmed her worst fears. More than a day had passed since she'd left the encampment. When were the Droi going to attack? She didn't know. All she could do was dry out, wait for the rain to ease, and start walking.

The rain stopped half an hour later, the sun appeared, and McKee left the cave. The combination of heat and moisture turned the forest into a steam bath. And that made the hike uncomfortable. There were other things to worry about, however, including the need to stay on course and the persistent feeling that someone or something was following her. But was that really the case? Or was the crawling sensation between her shoulder blades the product of an overactive imagination?

McKee paused frequently to look around yet saw nothing. So she climbed a tree in order to spot her pursuer and returned to the ground with no more than some additional scrapes and scratches as a reward for her effort. And as she resumed her march, the crawling sensation went away.

But not for long. Fifteen minutes later, it returned and McKee was beginning to wonder. Was a lack of food affecting her mind? In an effort to solve the mystery once and for all, she doubled back, searched for the trail she had left, and followed it. Her spoor consisted of broken twigs, a bare spot where a patch of moss had been dislodged from a log, and a boot print next to a stream. And there, partially obscuring the impression she had left, was a *second* print.

The creature that was following her had widely splayed toes, and judging from the depth of the print, it was *big*. The realization sent a chill down her spine as she straightened up and took a long, slow look around. But there was nothing to see other than the rays of sunlight that were slanting down from above, the insects that darted from one place to another, and the lush greenery all around.

McKee continued to walk until the sun was only a dimly seen presence and the evening gloom started to close in on her. She knew it was important to find a place to spend the night and to do so while there was light to see by. At least half a dozen potential hidey-holes were considered and rejected during the next half hour, and she was more than a little worried by the time she spotted the trees.

There were three of them all clustered together so that their branches intersected. And at one point, which she estimated to be about twelve feet off the ground, there was a spot where she could create a serviceable sleeping platform by laying saplings across some intersecting limbs.

Conscious of the fading light and the fact that she was unlikely to find anything better, McKee went out to harvest what she needed. She came across a cluster of what looked like melons, except they had woody shells that reminded her of coconuts, and grew on the ground instead of up in trees.

The mere thought of food set her stomach to rumbling—and she dropped the armful of freshly cut sticks to inspect her find. She had to stab one of the globes in order to penetrate the outer surface. Then it was possible to make a continuous cut and divide the object in half. Five rather large seeds were clustered at the center of each hemisphere and surrounded by relatively soft, apricot-colored flesh. It smelled familiar, and a taste confirmed her suspicion. Here was some of the same fruit that had been served in the Droi encampment! Did that mean it was safe to eat? Or was it the cause of her stomach cramps? Consuming it would constitute a roll of the dice. But McKee knew she was going to chance it. Had to chance it or grow increasingly weak.

The platform had to come first, however. Then, if she became sick, she would be up off the ground and well out of reach. As darkness fell, McKee was up on the platform trying to make herself comfortable, an activity that turned out to be a waste of time.

So she turned her attention to the melons. After opening one of them she tried a seed. It was too bitter to eat, so she spit it out. That left the fruit. Her plan was to eat a small portion and wait for an hour. Then, if she hadn't suffered any adverse effects, she would consume the rest of it.

So McKee forced herself to chew slowly as she ate six chunks of fruit. There was lots of sweet juice, which she allowed to trickle down the back of her throat. Having consumed the allotment, she checked her chrono and allowed her back to rest on the centermost tree trunk. A howl came from very nearby and caught her by surprise. As McKee pulled the pistol out of its shoulder holster, the first cry was echoed by a second. There were at least two of them!

A metallic *click* was heard as the flashlight mated with fittings on top of the pistol. Then, having turned the light on, McKee directed the beam down. What happened next came as a complete shock as a large animal jumped upwards, crashed through a couple of branches, and looked at her. It had big yellow eyes, and for one brief moment, they locked with hers before falling out of sight.

The whole thing was so unexpected that McKee failed to get a shot off. She realized that the sleeping platform was too low. It should have been twenty feet off the ground. But it was too late to correct that, so all she could do was hold the handgun in the approved two-handed grip and wait for the next attack. It came seconds later as a big head struck the bottom of the platform and nearly knocked her off.

As the animal dropped to the ground, McKee fired down through the floor and had the satisfaction of hearing a roar of outrage from below. That was her signal to holster the weapon and start climbing. There were plenty of branches, and in a matter of seconds she was able to put an additional six feet between herself and the platform.

Having found a new perch, McKee directed the flashlight downwards, quartered the area below, and spotted two yellow eyes looking up at her. She knew that there were twenty-five shots left in the magazine. She managed to get ten of them off before the predator jumped sideways and out of the light. Most if not all of her bullets had hit the monster. But the puny 4.7mm ammo lacked enough punch to kill the beast. Not unless she could score some good head shots.

That was what McKee was thinking when the predator hit one of the trees. All three of them shook, but she held on and was ready when the monster jumped up at her. This time she fired *before* the carnivore could reach apogee. And because the light was on it, she could see the hits as at least five of six rounds punched their way down through the top of the animal's triangular skull and into its brain.

The predator fell, hit hard, and lay sprawled below. As McKee's light passed over the creature, she saw that it was larger than she had first imagined. It had shimmery skin, powerful hindquarters, and a hooked claw at the end of each forearm.

Suddenly, the second predator appeared at the very edge of the flashlight's reach and snarled menacingly. McKee had to tip the light up and away in order to reload. This time she would aim for the head first. But there was no need as the newcomer uttered a grunt of what might have been satisfaction and began to rip bloody chunks of meat off the stillwarm body.

McKee felt a tremendous sense of relief as she removed the flashlight from the pistol and restored the weapon to its holster. She wanted to return to the sleeping platform, or what was left of it, in order to get the melons, but thought it prudent to let a full ten minutes pass before doing so. Then, careful to make as little noise as possible, she descended branch by branch while pausing occasionally to make sure that the predator wasn't paying attention to her.

Once on the platform, she played the light across the floor until she spotted a melon. The rest had fallen through the hole the first monster made and were somewhere below. But this one remained. And as McKee edged her way over to it, she remembered how good the sample had been—and realized that her stomach felt fine! Perhaps the meat had been to blame for the cramps. Or the sauerkraut-like stuff. It didn't matter. She had food!

Five minutes later, McKee had climbed higher in the tree, settled into the crotch between two large branches, and opened the surviving melon. And as she gorged herself on fruit, the beast below continued to growl and gobble gobbets of raw meat. It was the most memorable meal of her life.

After consuming the entire melon, and with her stomach full for the first time in two days, McKee slept sitting up. She woke frequently, once to hear the crunching of bones, before drifting off again. It made for a long night. But eventually she opened her eyes to discover that the sun was up, though just barely, as filtered light found the forest floor.

McKee felt stiff as she knelt on the platform and peeked over the side. The second predator had departed. In its place were at least a dozen scaly meat eaters who were busy stripping the carcass. The scavengers scattered as McKee threw pieces of melon husk at them, but they didn't go far. Dozens of beady eyes were on her as she lowered herself to within four feet of the ground and dropped the rest of the way.

The smell associated with the carcass was horrible. So McKee did the best she could to breathe through her mouth as she recovered a melon and drew her pistol. Then, weapon at the ready, she began to move toward two of the weasel-like animals. They scurried out of the way. Once she was at what they considered to be a safe distance, the animals returned to their feast.

Having checked the compass function on her chrono, McKee began to walk west. With light to see by and perfect weather, she made good time. And after an hour or so, she decided that the melon was something of an encumbrance and paused long enough to eat most of it. Then she was off again.

Half an hour later, McKee entered a section of the forest that had been blackened by fire. Her first thought was that the Big Green was subject to the occasional burn-off just as any forest would be. But this fire was recent. So much so that the charred remains of spiky trees were still smoking. And a strange smell hung in the air. A distinctive odor that she knew to be fuel.

Then McKee saw the first charred body, realized that she was looking at a dead Droi, and began to run. Each time one of her boots landed, it sent a cloud of gray ash into the air. Bodies lay everywhere, some whole, some in pieces—all blackened by the blanket of aerosolized fuel that had been sprayed over the forest and ignited.

McKee tripped, fell, and struggled to her feet. Now she understood. She was late. Way too late. The attack had taken place. And in order to defend the battalion from what must have been thousands of Droi, Spurlock had called for an air strike and been granted one.

Tears were streaming down McKee's cheeks as she ran. And there, at the center of an area untouched by the fuel-fed fire, was the skeleton of a burned-out truck. Farther on, the wreckage of a Scorpion could be seen. Judging from the look of it, the armored car had taken a direct hit from a shoulder-launched missile. But that wasn't the worst of it. There were metal grave markers. Rows of them. And beyond the makeshift graveyard the remains of a T-1 were visible.

The cyborg was sitting with its back against a rock and its head slumped forward. One of its arms was missing, its body was riddled with shell holes, but it was too big to bury. McKee knelt in front of it, ran a wet thumb over the block printing on the T-1's chest, and read its name: Weber. Deep sobs racked her body as McKee said, "I'm sorry... So sorry. I should have died with you." Contrails clawed the sky, a series of sonic booms chased each other across the land, and a blanket of silence settled over the battlefield.

13

To continue on when there is no reason to hope... That is heroism.

HIVE MOTHER TRAL HEBA

Ramanthian Book of Guidance

Standard year 1721

PLANET ORLO II

Having cried all the tears there were to cry, McKee stood. Then, after one last look at the desolation that surrounded her, she began to walk north toward Riversplit. She couldn't survive in the Big Green, not for long, so there was nowhere else to go.

What then? she wondered. *I'll be on an Imperial planet, in a loyalist city, with no money or connections. And both the synths and the Legion will be looking for me. Maybe I should save everyone the trouble and shoot myself.*

But McKee *didn't* shoot herself. She remembered what her uncle Rex had said. "When the going gets tough—the tough get going." The saying was trite, but true all the same. Plus, she had a purpose, and that was to bring Ophelia down.

So she put one boot in front of the other and kept walking. And thinking. The trail was easy to follow. The battalion had left tire tracks, pod prints, and occasional pieces of litter in its wake. Where were they going? Riversplit most likely. Just like she was.

But when had they left? A day ago? Or earlier that morning? It would pay to be careful lest she round a curve and run into the rear guard.

But the danger, if any, wouldn't last for long. Assuming the battalion was traveling at a steady 20–30 mph, it would soon leave her in the dust. Could she hitch a ride somehow? No, that wouldn't be wise so long as she was in uniform. The Legion would put the word out, and people would be looking for a female deserter.

Such were McKee's thoughts as she followed the dirt track through the overarching jungle, between a couple of rocky hills, and up a rise. She paused at the top to survey the land ahead. But without binoculars, the chances of spotting the battalion were slim to none. So she made her way down the other side of the rise to a spot where a small stream cut across the road. Rays of bright sunshine poured through a large opening in the jungle canopy to flood the area with light.

With no canteen, it was important to drink when she could. McKee knelt next to the brook, cupped her hands, and drank her fill. She was splashing water onto her face when a shadow slipped over her head and fled north. She looked up, expecting to see a bird. But the drone *wasn't* a bird. Not in the conventional sense anyway. There was a hollow sensation in the pit of her stomach as the machine banked and began to turn back. The aircraft had a smooth, nearly featureless fuselage and the long wings that enabled it to fly low and slow.

All McKee could do was stand, turn, and run. The drone passed over her seconds later. It fired a machine gun, and bullets kicked up puffs of dust ahead of her. And she knew it could launch missiles, too. The message was clear: Stop running or die.

McKee considered pulling the pistol and firing at the aircraft but knew the 4.7mm rounds wouldn't bring it down. So she came to a reluctant stop and was forced to stand in the middle of the road as the vulturelike drone circled above. She knew it was sending real-time video of her to someone. But to whom? A navy ship in orbit? And then to the battalion? Yes. That made sense, and the hypothesis was confirmed when a cloud of dust appeared to the north, and a Scorpion armored car arrived minutes later.

As the vehicle skidded to a stop, McKee placed the handgun on the ground, took three steps back, and locked her hands behind her neck. Doors opened, and three marines got out. Two of them pointed weapons at her while a sergeant bent to retrieve the pistol. The noncom knew his stuff as evidenced by the way he stayed out of the line of fire. "Corporal McKee?"

"Yes."

"Remain as you are while I pat you down."

The marine was thorough but didn't try to cop a feel like so many men would have, and McKee was grateful for that. Having found no weapons other than her knife, which the sergeant confiscated, he ordered her to put her hands behind her back. A plastic tie was used to bind her wrists. "Okay," he said. "Get in the vehicle."

McKee did as she was told. Sitting with her hands behind her was uncomfortable as the Scorpion bucked its way through a series of potholes and the marine reported in. His head was turned toward her, which meant that whoever the sergeant was talking to could see her face via his helmet cam. "Yes, sir, it's Corporal McKee all right. No, sir. Yes, sir. About ten minutes, sir. Over."

It seemed as if only five minutes had passed as the Scorpion passed through a checkpoint manned by a squad of bio bods and a T-1. Then, as the vehicle bumped over a crude bridge, McKee realized that she'd been wrong. The battalion *wasn't* on the run. It had been relocated to a more defensible position. A ditch had been dug all around the compound and was lined with sharpened stakes. An arrangement as old as the Roman Legions but effective nevertheless.

T-1s could be seen patrolling the perimeter, each corner was anchored by a log bunker, and a landing pad had been established in front of the command tent. At least a dozen people came out to meet the car, and McKee saw that most of them were Grays. One of the soldiers opened the door and another jerked her out. A bandage was wrapped around his head, and he was visibly angry. "Remember me, bitch? No? Well, I remember *you*."

McKee doubled over in pain as the soldier buried his fist in her stomach. As she threw up, she remembered hitting him in the head with her rifle butt. No wonder he was pissed. Then a familiar voice said, "We'll have none of that... Take that man's name! Bring McKee into the command tent. The colonel wants to speak with her."

Avery! Captain Avery! He was alive. That was good news. Although judging from the expression on the officer's face, he felt nothing but contempt for her.

Then McKee remembered Jivv. Where was the synth? Given the circumstances, she would have expected the robot to be front and center. Had it been killed during the battle with the Droi? The possibility gave her something to hope for as she was hustled into the command tent. Spurlock was there, seated behind a folding table, and there was a look of satisfaction on his face. He turned to look at Avery. "Here it is, Captain... Proof that criminals don't make good soldiers." There was nothing the legionnaire could do but remain silent.

Having turned his attention back to McKee, Spurlock frowned. "So, Corporal... I'm going to ask questions—and you're going to provide answers. Why did you help Governor Jones and his family escape?"

There hadn't been time to think. But McKee knew one thing for sure. She couldn't tell the truth without revealing her true identity. And insofar as she could tell, they didn't know. Not yet. So all she could do was keep her mouth shut and hope for a miracle. "I have nothing to say, sir."

Blood began to suffuse Spurlock's face as he came to his feet. "I don't think you understand the situation. Once we reach Riversplit, you will be charged with desertion and treason. That means the death penalty unless you cooperate. Then, if I were to speak on your behalf, you might receive a lighter sentence. Fifty years at hard labor perhaps. What are you? Twenty something? With luck, you'll be free someday. Now I'll ask again. *Why* did you help Governor Jones and his family to escape?"

McKee stood at attention with her eyes on a spot four inches over Spurlock's head. "I have nothing to say, sir."

"*Damn you!*" Spurlock said, and made a stylus jump as he brought his fist down on the metal tabletop. "Where are

Governor Jones and his family hiding?"

"I have nothing to say, sir."

Spurlock circled the table. When he stopped, his face was only inches from McKee's. His right hand came up to clutch her throat. "Tell me what I want to know or die right now."

McKee found it difficult to breathe. And that was when a gun barrel entered her field of vision. It was pressed against Spurlock's temple, and the voice was Avery's. "Please remove your hand from the corporal's throat. There are regulations regarding how military personnel are to be treated in situations like this one—and I won't be a party to violating them. *Sir.*" The last sounded like what it was. An afterthought.

Spurlock's expression registered surprise, followed by fear, and even more anger as the pistol was withdrawn. "Lieutenant! Place Captain Avery under arrest and find a place to confine him. And make sure his guards are Grays... Legionnaires can't be trusted."

Spurlock took a step backwards. "You can remove the corporal as well. I'll deal with her later. In the meantime, send for my platoon leaders so I can brief them on the situation."

Two Grays grabbed McKee's arms and hustled her out of the tent. There were moments when her boots didn't touch the ground as a sergeant led the way. People stopped whatever they were doing to stare. She scanned their faces, hoping to spot members of her squad, but didn't. She saw others though... Including Tacker from the third squad, first platoon, Blonski, from the first squad, second platoon, and a T-1 named Mishko. It was difficult to read their expressions, but a thumbs-up from Blonski was enough to give her heart. Most of her comrades had been up on charges at one time or another. So their sympathies generally lay with the accused rather than the accusers. Especially if the accuser was a Gray. "Put her in the bunker," the sergeant ordered.

McKee saw that a rectangular hole had been dug at the center of the compound and topped with logs and dirt. It was intended to be a place where troops could take cover in the case of a mortar attack, but it was about to become a cell.

McKee was stripped of her body armor before being thrown

inside. She fell, rolled, and wound up on her back. Tiny bits of blue sky were visible through holes in the cover above. But most of the light came in through the entrances located at each end of the bunker. She wondered about Avery. He was under arrest as well, and she felt badly about that.

Then the heat closed in around her, and McKee realized that the bunker was a solar oven. And, like any oven, it was going to cook her. Water. She needed water. Maybe they kept some in the bunker.

She got up, discovered that it was impossible to stand without bumping her head, and was forced to explore her cell while hunched over. Thirty seconds later she knew the truth. There was no water. Was that intentional? Or the result of an oversight? McKee thought the first possibility was the most likely and wasn't about to beg, not yet anyway.

All she could do was wait for evening, when the temperature would fall. McKee was reluctant to take off the outside layer of her clothing at first, knowing male soldiers could enter the bunker at any time. But it wasn't long before she surrendered to the stifling heat and removed everything except her sweat-soaked olive drab bra and her Legion-issue briefs.

Having done what she could to stay cool, McKee sat with her back against an earthen wall and took advantage of the opportunity to think. That was the plan, anyway, but she hadn't had much sleep the night before, and her thoughts morphed into strange dreams as she drifted in and out of consciousness.

Eventually, after what seemed like an eternity but was only a couple of hours, something hit McKee's leg and jarred her awake. She felt for the object, found the familiar outlines of a canteen, and hurried to unscrew the top. The water was warm, and slightly brackish, but it restored moisture to her mouth and took the edge off her thirst as it slid down her throat.

McKee wanted to drink half of it, and pour the rest over her head, but forced herself to replace the cap. How long would the water have to last? Three hours? Six? It made sense to assume the worst. And that was when she noticed the writing on the water bottle.

She crawled over to the point where a shaft of light entered the bunker and held the canteen up for inspection. It was a common practice for soldiers to print their names on their gear. The letters were all caps. "LARKIN."

McKee felt an unexpected surge of emotion as she sat in the shaft of light with the canteen clutched to her chest. The sobs came from deep inside, and she didn't want the Grays to know that she was crying, so she crawled back into the bunker. Catherine Carletto had been given many gifts, but none so precious. That included the water and the knowledge that Larkin was still alive.

The water seemed to revive McKee, but in some ways made her imprisonment worse, because in the absence of the all-consuming thirst, she had more capacity to think. And no matter what she chose to focus on, it was bad. All she could do was summon up happier times, try to ignore the fact that the most important people in her life were dead, and relive the past.

The hours crawled by, insects bit her, and eventually the air began to cool. So much so that McKee was compelled to put her clothes back on. She still had her chrono so she knew it was 18:33 when someone tossed an MRE in through the entrance on the north side.

Just the sight of the box was sufficient to remind her of how hungry she was. Once the container was open, she sought to make the meal last as long as possible. Each item became a course—and each bite was an experience. Not necessarily a *good* experience, but a distraction, and that was welcome.

Once darkness fell, McKee had nothing other than the glow from her chrono for illumination. The temperature continued to drop until she felt cold. All she could do was sit up with arms wrapped around knees and try to conserve body heat. Sleep came and went, as did a collage of dreams. Some from the past, some from the present, and some too strange to categorize. She was lost in a surreal landscape, searching for her face, when the Grays came for her.

There was no warning, no declaration of purpose, as the men entered the bunker from both ends at once. They grabbed McKee's arms, pulled her up onto her feet, and dragged her out into the early-morning light. A layer of mist hovered just above the ground and shivered as a light breeze nudged it. The first thing she noticed was that most of the battalion was present. They were lined up in ranks, with the legionnaires at the front. That was strange given the fact that they were in the field rather than on a parade ground.

And there, standing in front of the formation was a contraption made out of logs. It consisted of two uprights, each having one end buried in the ground, so as to from a large X. McKee didn't understand the purpose of the construct at first. Then she saw the noncom with the coiled whip, plus the smirk on Spurlock's face, and knew the truth: She was about to be flogged.

A voice shouted "Atten-HUT!" as the guards brought her to a halt. McKee saw that Avery was present as well. His wrists were cuffed in front of him, and he was under guard. His face remained expressionless, but it looked as though Spurlock was enjoying himself as he read from a piece of paper. "Military discipline is critical to unit cohesion—and unit cohesion is critical to operational success. For that reason, our superiors have seen fit to lay down a system of military law known as the Military Code of Conduct.

"And that system spells out the penalties associated with each possible offense. Some of these penalties are discretionary, meaning they can be imposed by a unit commander such as myself, while others fare judicial and require a formal court-martial. Owing to the nature of her crimes, Corporal McKee is subject to both."

Spurlock paused at that point as if to let his words sink in prior to continuing his speech. "Once the battalion returns to Riversplit, McKee will be tried for desertion and treason. But in the meantime, it is my responsibility to punish her for abandoning her post, striking a fellow soldier, and stealing government property. With those charges in mind, I hereby sentence her to ten lashes."

"I object," Avery said, in a loud clear voice. "McKee is a legionnaire—and the Legion doesn't permit flogging."

"Well the militia *does*," Spurlock responded sternly. "And I would like to remind those present that Captain Avery stands accused of assaulting a superior officer. If he speaks again, the master-at-arms will tape his mouth closed. Prepare the corporal for punishment."

McKee felt a combination of fear and embarrassment as a Gray stepped forward to rip her shirt open—and another proceeded to cut the fabric away. That left her topless with the exception of a bra. And once that was removed, her breasts were exposed.

The world seemed to close in on her at that moment as the men dragged her over to the X-shaped framework, where her arms and legs were bound to the uprights. McKee couldn't hear anything other than the twitter of birds and her own harsh breathing as the Grays completed their work.

"In accordance with UCMJ regulation 147.326, the subject is to receive ten lashes, each of equal force, all administered to her back," Spurlock proclaimed loudly. "You may proceed."

McKee didn't want to scream. Not in front of the Grays, much less her fellow legionnaires. But as she waited for the first blow to land she knew that she would. If not in response to the first strike then to the second or third.

Then there was a dull cracking sound as braided leather made contact with pale flesh. Her skin parted as if cut with a knife, and the force of the blow drove all of the air out of her lungs. The pain was excruciating, and the only reason she didn't scream was the fact that she lacked the air necessary to do so.

But even as all of that registered on her senses, she knew that the whip was being readied, and would soon strike again. She had no idea where the impulse came from, but welcomed it, and was ready when the leather smacked against her flesh. "CAMERONE!"

Her intent was to avoid a scream. But the word had an unexpected effect. Because her fellow legionnaires echoed the cry. "CAMERONE!"

"There will be silence!" Spurlock shouted. "The next person to speak will be whipped."

A sound similar to a pistol shot was heard as the snakelike whip sliced through the air, cut deep, and drew blood. McKee arched her back in pain. Her "Camerone" was weaker this time, but still audible, as was the thunderous response. *"CAMERONE!"*

Suddenly, Spurlock found himself in a trap of his own making.

He couldn't flog *all* of the legionnaires, and they knew it. More than that, with Captain Avery in cuffs, and one of their own being subjected to a punishment not permitted by the Legion, they were feeling rebellious. Something that could be dangerous since they not only outnumbered the Grays but included dozens of T-1s whose well-amplified voices could be heard over all the rest.

So even after the eighth blow landed, when McKee lost consciousness, the chant continued. And there was nothing Spurlock could do but fume. The first battle of Camerone had been lost. But, on a planet many light-years from Earth, the second had been won.

McKee awoke facedown on a cot. It wasn't the first time, but she couldn't remember the others all that well. By looking sideways, she could see the walls of a tent and some medical gear. Her back felt as if it were on fire, and she made a feeble effort to get up. Maybe she could find some water to pour on the pain. Maybe...

A gentle hand pushed her back down. The voice was female. "Where do you think you're going? Stay right there. I've got some stuff that will make you feel better."

McKee heard some rustling sounds followed by the hiss of a spray can. Then, as the analgesic mist made contact with her back, the pain started to abate. "Thank you," McKee said. "Can I get up?"

"You can try," the other woman said. "But take it slowly."

It was good advice. Even the slightest movement hurt, and it took twenty or thirty seconds for the pain to fade. So the process of getting up took the better part of ten minutes. During the interim, McKee had an opportunity to get acquainted with the medic. Her name was Corly, and even though she was a Gray, Corly disapproved of the punishment meted out to McKee. "I'm sorry," she said. "I really am. Colonel Spurlock didn't have to flog you. He *wanted* to."

"Yeah," McKee agreed, as she made it to her feet. "He sure as hell did. Have you got a mirror? I'd like to see my back."

Corly had light brown hair, which she wore in a knot at the

back of her head. She had a high forehead, intelligent eyes, and a lower lip that stuck out in what looked like a perpetual pout. "No, we don't haul mirrors out into the field. But I could show you a picture... If you really want to see it."

McKee made a face. "It's that bad?"

Corly shrugged. "Some of the cuts are superficial. Others required some stitches. But you're young and healthy, so the prognosis is good."

McKee got the feeling that the medic was trying to put a positive spin on the situation. "Please take a picture. I'd like to see it."

McKee was already half-naked. So all Corly had to do was aim the camera, record a few seconds of video, and play it back. What McKee saw was worse than she had imagined. Red welts crisscrossed her back, and in places where the leather had gone deep, sutures could be seen. First her face—now this. The self-pity was there, ready to surface, but McKee pushed it down. "How will the cuts look later?"

"Some will heal well," Corly said. "You'll barely notice them. As for the deeper lacerations, I'm not sure. You could have some keloid scarring."

"Meaning?"

Corly shrugged. "Meaning some raised scar tissue. A doctor could give you a better idea. And who knows? A biosculptor might be able to get rid of them."

McKee forced a smile. "So no backless cocktail dresses?"

Corly looked relieved. As if she'd been worried about the way her patient would take the news. "No, I guess not."

"Okay," McKee said. "Could I have something to wear please? No bra... Not yet."

Corly gave McKee one of her own shirts. McKee winced as the fabric came into contact with her lacerated back. "So what's the situation? Are guards waiting outside?"

Corly nodded. "Two of them."

"So it's back to the bunker?"

"I'm afraid so. I'd like to keep you here—but I haven't got enough room."

"No problem. I understand."

"Take this," Corly said, and gave McKee the can of spray-on anesthetic. "Plus these. Take the antibiotic twice a day— and no more than one pain pill every four hours. They're pretty potent."

McKee accepted the medications and put them in various pockets. "Thanks. A question before I go. Why is the battalion sitting here?"

Corly looked surprised. "You don't know? I guess you wouldn't. The Droi attacked two days ago."

McKee remembered the battlefield and what she'd seen there. "Yes, I know that much."

"Well, Monitor Jivv was using some very special ammo. Bullets that can be tracked electronically. So any indig who caught one of Jivv's slugs, and was carried away, could be followed. And that's where Jivv is now. Out tracking them down. Once he gets back, we'll pull out."

McKee felt sick to her stomach. The synth was alive! That was bad news. As was the fact that it was searching for the Droi. The indigs were sure to outnumber Jivv's party. So what would the machine do if it found them? Call in another air strike? She remembered the smoking bodies and felt a sense of foreboding.

The guards stepped into the spill of light from the tent as Corly led McKee out into the cool night air. "Don't touch her back, make sure she has plenty of water, and bring her back at 0900. Copy?"

One of the guards made a face. "Sure. Whatever."

"Be careful," Corly cautioned. "If something happened to your shot record, you'd have to get all of them again."

The second man laughed. "She's got you there, Pauley. Come on. Let's put the bitch in her box."

Five minutes later, McKee was back in the bunker. New amenities had been added to the makeshift cell, including a blanket. She lay facedown on it. Her back hurt, she was under arrest, and Jivv would return soon. If McKee had ever been more miserable, she couldn't remember when.

Thanks to the pain pills, McKee was able not only to fall asleep but to stay that way, until another MRE was thrown into the bunker. It was 0813 and raining outside, a fact made obvious by the water that had begun to drip from above.

Her back was sore, but not as bad as it had been the day before, and for that McKee was grateful as she opened the MRE. After sorting through the items within, she chose a small can of mixed fruit, crackers with jam, and a nut bar for her breakfast. It would have been nice to have a cup of tea, but she lacked a container to boil water in. She was still chewing the nut bar when she heard voices, and a Gray ducked into the bunker. "Get up and come with me. The colonel wants to see you."

McKee felt a stab of fear but was determined to hide it as she stood. "Good. He owes me an apology."

If the Gray thought the comment was funny, there was no sign of it on his face as he stepped to one side. McKee blinked and felt blood-warm raindrops hit her face as she emerged from the bunker. Troops were busy loading their gear onto trucks. It looked as though the battalion was preparing to pull out.

The Gray placed a hand on her back and gave her a shove. It sent her stumbling forward. The pain was so intense that she wanted to cry out. It required an act of will to resist the impulse to and keep going. Most of the shelters had been taken down, or were in the process of coming down, but the command tent remained in place. And as McKee crossed the compound, she heard someone yell, "Camerone," and knew that at least one of her fellow legionnaires was watching.

A private held the tent flap to one side so that McKee could enter. There wasn't much light, and most of the furniture had been removed, but the enclosure was far from empty. Spurlock was present, as were Jivv, Jones, Cia, and Marcy. It appeared as though Jivv's efforts to track the Droi down had been successful.

McKee could see that all three of the prisoners had been beaten. They were seated in a row, heads down, tied to folding chairs. "Ah," Spurlock said as she entered. "The last piece of the puzzle has arrived. Bring the bitch forward so that Governor Jones can see her."

Another shove propelled McKee forward. The pain made her feel dizzy. Jivv was positioned behind Jones. He took control of the human's head and tilted it upwards. "Look at her! She set you free. *Why?*"

McKee was shocked by what she saw. There was an empty

socket where one eye had been, the governor's nose was split open, and dried blood covered his chin. As she looked at him, McKee saw something flicker in his eyes. Determination? Yes, she thought so. His voice was hoarse, as if from endless talking and a lack of water. "Who is she? I've never seen her before."

"You're lying," Jivv said as he released the politician's head. "And that is very, very stupid."

McKee felt a rising sense of dread as the robot took up a position immediately behind Marcy. He grabbed a fistful of the woman's badly tangled hair to use as a handle. Marcy's eyes popped open as Jivv jerked her head back. Her face was black-and-blue from repeated beatings. But, judging from the question Jivv had put to Jones, none of the prisoners had revealed McKee's actual identity. That was truly amazing, and she felt a deep sense of admiration for all three of them.

The knife seemed to appear out of nowhere and Marcy whimpered as the razor-sharp blade drew blood. "Now," Jivv said as he made eye contact with Jones, "I will ask again. Why did Corporal McKee help you to escape?"

As Jones opened his mouth, McKee had no way to know what he would say. She spoke before he could. "Leave her alone. I'll tell you."

"Good," Jivv said expressionlessly. "Please do."

"My real name is Catherine Carletto."

"Ah," Jivv said. "Fugitive 2999."

Spurlock looked confused. "Fugitive 2999? What are you talking about?"

"That's classified," Jivv said as he drew the blade across Marcy's throat.

Marcy made a horrible choking sound as blood flooded her chest. McKee charged the robot, or tried to, but the guards had hold of her arms. "Our work is done here," Jivv said as he produced a pistol. "Once I tidy up, the battalion can get under way."

The weapon made a popping sound as Jivv shot Cia in the back of the head. Then, having turned to Jones, he fired again. The governor's head jerked and flopped sideways.

By that time the pistol was swinging around, coming to bear

on McKee, as Spurlock raised a hand in protest. "No! Stop! That's an order."

McKee knew Spurlock wasn't trying to protect her. He was shocked, confused, and trying to reassert his authority. There was a long moment of silence as Jivv continued to point the pistol at McKee. But three Grays were present in addition to those who were restraining McKee. And all of their weapons were aimed at Jivv. There was no way to know what the robot was thinking—although McKee could guess. Having killed three out of four targets, Jivv was willing to wait. The synth would get another chance during the journey to Riversplit. And that was when McKee would die.

"Yes," Jivv said as he lowered the weapon. "It shall be as you say. Now, if you'll excuse me, I will prepare for the trip." Servos whined as the robot left the tent. Fugitives 1018, 1019, and 1022 had been terminated. It was, all things considered, a good day.

14

The Legion is a lot of things… But it's never easy.
COMMAND SERGEANT MAJOR MARY MURDO
Twenty Years of War
Standard year 2617

PLANET ORLO II

The sky was gray and thunder muttered in the distance as McKee was escorted out into the compound. Dead. All of them were dead. Tears ran down her cheeks but were indistinguishable from the rain that soaked her hair and ran in rivulets down her face.

It was obvious that the battalion was preparing to leave as McKee was led to one of the huge 8 X 8 trucks and ordered to climb in. She winced as she pulled herself up into the transport and her shirt made contact with raw flesh. Rain pattered on the canopy over her head as a stone-faced Gray pointed toward the front of the vehicle.

In order to get there, McKee had to climb over cases of ammo and MREs. Rather than follow her forward, the guards sat opposite each other next to the fold-down tailgate. The perfect spot from which to look outside while they told each other largely fanciful war stories.

Because of the weather and the truck's canopy, the light was so dim that McKee didn't realize another person was present until she sat down. Avery smiled grimly. "Hello, Corporal. Fancy meeting you here. How's your back?"

"Better, sir," McKee said. "Thank you."

Avery frowned. "You were in the command tent. I saw the Grays take you there. What happened?"

Before she could answer, there was a muted explosion, and both of them turned to look out through the back of the truck. All that remained of the command tent were pieces of flaming fabric that drifted down through the air and were quickly extinguished by the rain. Larger bits and pieces fell into puddles or landed in the mud. Engines started, orders were given, and the truck jerked ahead. The journey to Riversplit had begun.

Avery swayed slightly as the truck lurched through a pothole. His voice was gentle but insistent. "What happened in the command tent, McKee? I need to know."

McKee remembered the look on Marcy's face as Jivv cut her throat. The tears began to flow again. "Jivv killed the governor, his wife and niece. He was going to kill me, but Colonel Spurlock stopped him."

"Why?" Avery demanded. "Why did you desert? And why would Jivv want to kill you?"

McKee looked at the guards and concluded that they were too far away to hear so long as she kept her voice down. She hadn't spoken to anyone about her situation before and for good reason. Doing so could get both people killed. But Avery knew more than most. His brother was under suspicion. And he was under arrest. So maybe she could trust him. And there wasn't any downside. Jivv knew her identity and was planning to kill her.

Avery listened as McKee told her story from beginning to end. There were moments when he looked surprised, like when she told him her real name, and others when he was clearly impressed. The fight in the hotel on Esparto being one example. And the true account of Camacho's death being another. But, with the exception of a prompt here and there, Avery remained silent until she was finished. Then, in what might have been an attempt to lighten the mood, he smiled. "So I have a celebrity in Echo Company."

"More like a troublemaker," McKee replied. "I'm sorry, sir. You wouldn't be under arrest if it wasn't for me. It took guts to do what you did, and I appreciate it."

Avery shrugged. "I was doing my duty. But you're welcome. I thought there was something different about Corporal McKee, and I was right."

"So what now?"

"All we can do is wait," Avery replied. "And hope for the best."

"I'm going down no matter what," McKee put in. "But once we reach Riversplit, and Colonel Rylund gets involved, you might catch a break. I find it hard to believe that he would support charges against an officer who intervened to protect a legionnaire."

"Maybe," Avery said grimly. "But there's something you don't know. Or I assume you don't know."

McKee frowned. "What's that?"

"Remember the Hudathan wreck? And the pilot that the Droi captured? Well, the ridge heads attacked Poe's fleet two days ago and broke through. And they have already started to land here and there. That's why the battalion hasn't been reinforced. So given everything that's going on, Rylund won't have time to worry about Captain Avery or Corporal McKee. Once the outfit arrives in Riversplit, we'll be thrown into cells—and our cases will be handed off to Lord knows who. We might even find ourselves in front of a court dominated by Grays."

McKee thought about that. What Avery said was true but likely to apply to his situation rather than hers since she would be dead by then. But there was no point in saying that so she didn't. The Hudathan landings were a surprise though—and they spent the next fifteen minutes speculating about how things would go.

Then the point came when neither one of them had anything to add, so they lapsed into silence for a while. Eventually, they spoke about other things, including their childhoods. Avery's had been similar to McKee's but different as well. She was an only child, but he had two brothers. There was Frank, who was in charge of the family's pharmaceutical company, and George. Avery described George as a lost soul, but he sounded like a slacker, who had been openly critical of Empress Ophelia, thereby placing the entire family in jeopardy. "You chose the Legion," McKee said once Avery had finished. "Why?"

Avery smiled. "There wasn't any place for me in the family business—and I was looking for adventure. That sounds silly now—but I was seventeen when I applied to the academy."

"I was kicked out of school when I was seventeen," McKee observed. "For the third time. They wanted me to go to classes."

Avery laughed. "And Corporal McKee is such a hard worker."

"Are you referring to the Steel Bitch?"

"Yes, I am. The Steel Bitch is a good noncom. She gets things done."

There were sporadic bouts of conversation after that, but even though McKee enjoyed talking to Avery, the reality of what lay ahead made it difficult to think about anything else. Meanwhile, the convoy continued to plow forward but slowly given the weather. The road hadn't been much to begin with, and the torrential rain quickly turned it to a soupy mess. As the T-1s moved forward, big clods of mud clung to their foot pods, and even the 8 X 8 trucks had a tendency to bog down in the muck, which brought the entire battalion to a stop until they were freed. The result was slow progress at best.

Except for short breaks to relieve themselves, the prisoners were kept on the truck. Eventually, tedium took over, and they managed to doze for periods of time in spite of the jolting ride. As the light began to fade, the column came to a stop and formed a laager. McKee wondered if she and Avery were going to spend the night in a tent—but it soon became obvious that the prisoners and their guards were to remain on the truck.

Four outposts were established a hundred yards out to warn the unit if it was about to be attacked—but that was the extent of the defenses that Spurlock put in place. "The man's an idiot," Avery said bitterly, and McKee knew he was thinking about Echo Company's safety. And the fact that he was willing to say as much to an enlisted person was a measure of something. But what? Trust? She hoped so.

In any case, Avery was correct. Spurlock's failure to put more defensive measures in place was unforgivable, because if the enemy was shadowing the battalion, the results could be catastrophic. But maybe, just maybe, McKee could take advantage of the situation.

The opportunity to do so had to do with the bulkhead that separated the driver's compartment from the cargo area where she was sitting. It was solid. But at the center of the divider, about a foot off the floor, a metal plate was visible. And it looked as though the panel could be removed so that personnel could move back and forth between the cab and the back of the truck should that be necessary.

Had the hatch been taken into consideration when the prisoners were ordered onto the truck? Or had the presence of the plate been overlooked? Because if it had, and McKee could access the cab, it would be relatively easy to slip out of the vehicle and vanish. The plan was chancy, to say the least, but she had nothing to lose.

But what about Avery? The charge against him was serious, and he could be court-martialed, but there was also the possibility that Rylund would refuse to prosecute one of his officers for defending a legionnaire. In that case, Avery might be better off staying behind. Or the officer could wind up in front of a hostile court. McKee figured it could break either way.

That was what she was thinking about when a couple of MREs were tossed toward the front of the cargo area. Avery was in the process of opening his when McKee spoke. "Sir, there's something I need to tell you."

What light there was emanated from a dangling glow strip. Avery looked up. "Shoot."

McKee pointed to the panel. "I plan to remove that, enter the cab, and bail out."

Avery frowned. "What if the driver is sleeping in the cab?"

"Then I'll be SOL."

Avery opened a container of mixed fruit and ate a spoonful. "Okay, count me in."

McKee looked at him in surprise. "Really?"

"Yes, really."

"I thought you were smarter than that. Sir."

Avery chuckled. "So much for that theory."

There was a companionable silence while they ate. Then, once they were finished, McKee explained her plan. Her voice was pitched low. "The guards will expect us to lie down. Once we do so, it will difficult for them to see what we're doing. That's when we'll open the panel. It shouldn't be difficult. Six toggle-style latches are holding it in place."

"Roger that," Avery said. "But let's wait until most of the battalion is asleep."

"Absolutely… I agree."

"Then what?" Avery wanted to know. "Let's say we make it into the forest. How will we survive?"

"I don't know," McKee admitted. "But at least we'll be free."

"All right. Let's get some sleep. We're going to need it."

She tried to sleep but couldn't. Fears about what would happen if the escape attempt failed kept her awake—as did the possibility that it would succeed. Because, in Avery's words, "Then what?"

Time seemed to crawl by, and she was grateful when 0100, a time when all but those who had guard duty would be asleep, finally arrived. Apparently Avery had been awake, too, because as she stirred, so did he. It was difficult to see what the guards were doing. But that cut both ways, or McKee hoped that was the case as she went to work on the latches. The first four turned easily. But the fifth refused to budge. Perhaps it had always been tighter than the rest—or maybe it was rusted in place. In either case, the latch refused to give.

Avery whispered, "Let me give it a try."

McKee squirmed out of the way so he could move in. The panel was free seconds later. Perhaps his fingers were stronger, or maybe it was simply a matter of luck, but whatever the reason, they were ready for the next step. And that was for Avery to press an ear against the plate and listen. McKee waited impatiently for his report.

Finally, after thirty seconds or so, Avery turned her way. "I can't hear anything," he whispered. "But that doesn't mean the cab is empty."

"True," McKee replied. "So we'll have to take a chance."

Avery nodded. And since he was already in position, he lifted the panel out of the way. There was a pause while they waited to see if there would be a reaction. But nothing happened. It appeared that the cab was empty.

"I'll go first," McKee said. "I'm smaller." That was true, but there was something else on her mind as well. Perhaps, if they caught her right away, Avery could escape blame. It wasn't much, but his predicament was her fault, and she owed him.

McKee wriggled through the hole without difficulty and emerged between the two high-backed seats. Her back hurt because of the contact with the top edge of the aperture—and it took some effort to maneuver around the floor shift and slide into the driver's seat. Rain rattled on the windshield, and it was almost pitch-black outside.

She heard a rustling sound and a muted swearword as Avery pushed his larger body into the cab and had to go through a number of contortions before taking his place in the passenger seat. It was tempting just to sit there for a while, savoring the moment and preparing for what lay ahead. But McKee knew time was of the essence. The guards in the back of the truck could check on them at any moment. So the sooner they slipped into the night, the better. She turned to Avery. "When we open the doors, the cab light will come on."

"Not now," Avery replied, as he reached up to flip a switch. "I'll come around and meet you on your side."

"Roger that. Let's do it."

The driver's-side door opened smoothly, and because the 8 X 8 had a lot of ground clearance, it was necessary to jump. Cold raindrops hit McKee's skin, water splashed away from her boots, and she could feel the adrenaline as it trickled into her bloodstream. Avery arrived moments later. "Ready? Let's move."

The officer took the lead, and McKee was happy to let him do so. There was no light to speak of. Just the glow from inside the mess tent, a momentary blip from a distant flashlight, and eerie blobs of phosphorescence that she knew to be nocturnal insects. So it was important to stay close as Avery pursued a zigzag path between vehicles and dimly seen shelters. McKee missed her helmet and the night-vision technology built into it. But any soldiers who happened to be in the area had theirs and could see the escaping prisoners if they were looking in the right direction. Luck, that's what they needed, and lots of it.

Such were McKee's thoughts as a beam of excruciatingly white light hit them, and an amplified voice said, "Hold it right there."

McKee said, "Larkin? Is that you?"

"Aw shit," came the reply. "Goddamn it, McKee... Why did you decide to run in *this* direction?"

The question was left unanswered as the escapees were forced to stop, *more* lights came on, and red targeting lasers explored their bodies. That was the good part. The bad part came moments later, when a squad of Grays took the legionnaires into custody and beat the crap out of them. Then, having imposed some rough-and-ready justice on the prisoners, the Grays loaded them back onto the truck. This time they were cuffed with their hands in front of them and their ankles bound. And, just to make sure that they didn't escape in spite of the restraints, a guard was stationed in the cab.

McKee's face hurt, her back was on fire, and it felt as if the rest of her body had been stomped by a T-1. But she could still see through one eye and Avery was looking at her. There was a cut on his left cheek, his lips were puffy, and a crust of dried blood was visible under his nose. *What's he thinking?* she wondered. *Does he hate me? I wouldn't blame him.*

Then Avery winked at her. And the sense of relief she felt was almost overwhelming. And frightening as well. Because ever since the point when Andromeda McKee parted company with Catherine Carletto, it had been her goal to be self-sufficient. And here, in the wave of emotion she felt, was evidence that she had failed.

Three and a half very uncomfortable hours followed. It was impossible to sleep sitting up, bound hand and foot, while almost every square inch of her body ached. Finally, at about 0400, the guards escorted the prisoners to the latrines. With that out of the way, they were herded back onto the truck, where they were allowed to eat while the battalion broke camp. "It looks like I was wrong," Avery observed. "The bastard got away with it."

McKee knew that the "bastard" was Spurlock, and that "it"

was the officer's failure to adequately fortify the encampment. "He got lucky," McKee replied. "We aren't clear of the Big Green yet."

The battalion got under way shortly thereafter. And, as if to emphasize how lucky Spurlock truly was, the rain stopped, and the sun appeared. It would take days for the mud to dry up, however, so the battle against the mud continued.

Once breakfast was over, McKee feared that her wrists and ankles would be secured once more—and was pleasantly surprised when they weren't. That meant she could position herself in a way that minimized the pain. Thanks to the beating received the night before she hurt *everywhere*, so her back felt better by comparison.

Thus began another day. There wasn't much McKee and Avery could say to each other, so they were mostly silent as the convoy pushed its way north at about 20 mph. And for the first couple of hours it seemed as if the battalion would be able to travel north completely unopposed. Then the sniper fire began.

Because she didn't have a radio, McKee was unaware of it at first. But then she heard the sound of outgoing gunfire followed by a loud *clang* as a bullet smacked into the side of the truck. Avery said, "Hit the floor!" and quickly followed his own advice.

As she landed next to him a projectile hit the canopy, passed through the cargo compartment, and exited through the other side. "What do you think?" she inquired. "Droi? Or the rebels?"

"It could be either one or both," Avery replied from inches away. "But they aren't serious. Not yet anyway."

McKee realized that Avery was correct. There had been no effort to block the convoy—and the incoming fire consisted of single shots. That suggested an effort to harass the battalion rather than stop it. Why? Because the people in the jungle lacked the means to engage such a heavily armored unit? Or were they shooting at the column in order to slow it down. And if so, what did they plan to do? Questions swirled through McKee's mind, none of which could be answered by anyone other than the enemy.

Then, as suddenly as it had begun, the firing stopped. Two minutes later, the prisoners were back on their seats. They had no way to know if the battalion had suffered casualties. Nor could they see anything other than the truck behind theirs and a patch of road on either side. Not knowing was a special sort of torture—and McKee longed to be back on Weber once again. Then she remembered his shot-up war form and had to fight back what would have been a flood of tears.

As the sun rose higher in the sky, and water-saturated ground gave up its moisture, the humidity soared. So it wasn't long before McKee, Avery, and the guards perched next to the tailgate were soaked with sweat. McKee, who hadn't had a shower in days, could smell herself. Or was that Avery? Not that it mattered.

Time passed, albeit slowly, and McKee was daydreaming when a bullet smacked into one of the Grays. The report was like an afterthought, and because she happened to be looking in that direction, she witnessed the moment when the body fell out of the truck and onto the road.

The soldier part of McKee's brain informed her that, because the bullet had passed through the canopy at an angle, it was unlikely that the sniper had been able to see his target. So the hit was more a matter of good luck rather than skill. As those calculations were going through her mind the next vehicle in line rolled over the dead man's corpse, and Avery pulled her down.

The harassing fire lasted for two or three minutes, and there was nothing the battalion could do about it. Because to stop and try to engage the snipers would not only be a waste of time but might be exactly what they wanted. So the trucks continued to roll as the T-1s fired on anything with a heat signature. It wouldn't make much difference, but it felt good.

Once they cleared the area, and the incoming fire stopped, the boredom returned. McKee sat, thoughts adrift, until an uneasy sleep pulled her down. The next thing she knew, Avery had hold of her arm. As she opened her eyes, his were waiting for her. "We're on the bridge."

The words were said with such intensity that she knew the message was important. But why? Then she remembered the wooden bridge, the effort to spot explosives from below, and the subsequent mortar attack. And a single glance out over the tailgate confirmed Avery's statement. They *were* on the bridge.

The frame shook, and tires made a rumbling sound, as the truck bumped across the span at a good 10 mph. It was as if Spurlock thought that safety lay in speed. And that was stupid.

A loud explosion served to punctuate her thoughts. It was followed by the roar of collapsing timbers and barely heard screams as the truck tilted backward and fell into a hole that hadn't existed moments before. As the 8 X 8 landed in the river, tons of cargo came loose and fell on the remaining guard. Thanks to their position just behind the cab, the prisoners landed on top of the boxes of ammo and rations.

The impact knocked the air out of McKee's lungs. And she was trying to suck air as the canopy surrendered to the river, and cold water flooded in around her. She told herself to stand, and was about to do so, when Avery scooped her up. That raised her head above the flow, which if it hadn't been for the wreck, would have swept both of them downstream.

Long bursts of automatic fire could be heard by then, and McKee knew this was it—the moment that the Droi and/or rebels had been waiting for. She reached up to grab onto one of the tubes that were supposed to support the canopy. "Thanks... I'm okay."

Avery let go, and she found herself standing waist-deep in the frigid flow. "Come on, Corporal... Let's get out of here." And with that, the officer led McKee out of the truck and into the rush of water beyond. Timbers from the collapsed bridge helped to moderate the force of the current and provided something to hang on to. Bit by bit they managed to work their way over to the north shore and a rock beach. And there, with weapons leveled at them, were three Droi. There was nothing McKee and Avery could do but raise their hands and allow themselves to be herded up toward the road.

Firing could still be heard. But it was sporadic and soon stopped altogether. The battalion, or what was left of it, had been captured. But how? Even if all of the bio bods were KIA or WIA, the T-1s could fight on. Unless the enemy had antitank weapons that is—but there had been no evidence of that.

The answer became clear as McKee and Avery arrived on the road. An enormous tree had been felled so that it lay across it.

Two vehicles sat empty in front of it. The first was a Scorpion, and the second was Spurlock's command car, although the officer was nowhere to be seen. Nor was there any sign of Jivv. But T-1s could be seen on both sides of the river. They stood frozen in place but appeared to be undamaged.

Had the legionnaires surrendered? No, that didn't seem likely, so what then? The answer was more intuitive than logical. Being her father's daughter, McKee was familiar with both the cyborgs' strengths *and* weaknesses, one of which was a susceptibility to electromagnetic pulses delivered over certain frequencies. When she left Earth, her father had been hard at work trying to develop better shielding. But somehow the Droi had acquired, or been given, at least one EMP bomb, which they had used to good effect.

As McKee took her place with the other survivors, she knew, or thought she knew, where the technology had come from. Because there, with a rifle slung over one shoulder, was Howard Trask. The same rebel she had been introduced to deep inside the Big Green. "Corporal McKee!" he exclaimed. "We looked everywhere. I'm glad you survived."

Then his expression darkened. "But what are you doing *here*? With the battalion?"

McKee was still in the process of deciding what to say when Avery jumped in. "She was a prisoner, on her way to a court-martial in Riversplit," he said.

Trask raised an eyebrow. "And you are?"

"Captain Avery. McKee got lost, stumbled across the road, and was captured. Our CO, Lieutenant Colonel Spurlock, placed her under arrest. *And* had her flogged."

"I see," Trask said sympathetically. "I would release you if I could… But the Droi are in charge here. And whatever happens next will be up to them."

"That true," one of the natives said as it took a step forward. "McKee… I see you."

McKee recognized Insa right away and felt the beginnings of hope. At least she knew the Droi, no matter how superficially. "And I see you, Insa."

"You deliver Hudathan?"

"Yes, just as I said I would."

"Too late. They here."

"I'm sorry. The Legion will fight them."

"The Legion *is* fighting them," Trask put in. "And getting its ass kicked. Poe's fleet was forced to withdraw. So the shovel heads are on the ground, and Rylund's forces are trapped in Riversplit."

"What about the rebels?" Avery wanted to know.

"We're sitting this one out," Trask replied. "What's the old saying? My enemy's enemy is my friend? Well, for the moment, the Hudathans are our friends."

"The Hudathans don't have any friends," Avery said grimly. "They see each and every sentient race as a potential threat that must be eliminated."

Trask shrugged. "I don't make policy. My role is to help the Droi resist the loyalists and Ophelia's thugs. And that means *you*."

McKee frowned. "Where did you get the EMP bomb?"

Trask grinned. "We built it. The goal was to use it during the battle for Riversplit, but the tech heads had a hard time identifying the right frequency. But finally, after trying *all* of the possible frequencies on a captured T-1, they found it. So when I requested a bomb, it was ready to go."

There was a hollow place where McKee's stomach should have been. The cyborgs were still alive, trapped in their war forms, and would remain so until their power ran out. That's when their life-support systems would shut down, and they would die. Her mind was racing, trying to find a way to save the 'borgs and what remained of Echo Company. McKee had an idea—but would Avery support it? She was about to find out. Her eyes locked with Insa's. "You heard Trask… The rebels plan to sit this one out. Is that *your* view? What if the Hudathans win? They hate *all* sentients. That includes the Droi. So your best bet is to fight them *now*. Before it's too late. We'll help you."

Trask laughed harshly. "Help them… With *what*? I see about twenty people here. Let's say there are ten on the other side of the river. What difference will thirty soldiers make?"

"Look again," McKee said steadfastly. "And you'll see that we have seventeen T-1s."

"Yes, but they're useless."

"No," McKee said, "they aren't. I can repair them."

Avery directed a questioning look at her. "You can?"

The truth was that she was far from certain. But if she were to admit that, the moment would be lost. "Yes, sir," she said. "I can."

It was a seemingly outrageous claim but Avery knew that the T-1s had been manufactured by the Carletto family and that she had a degree in cybernetics. He nodded. "If Corporal McKee says she can repair the T-1s, then I believe her. And I agree with the proposal. With support from our T-1s, the Droi could have a significant impact on the war against the Hudathans."

Trask shook his head but chose to remain silent. Insa hesitated but only for a moment. "McKee right. We fight."

ABOARD THE BATTLE CRUISER *GLORY OF HUDATHA*, OFF PLANET ORLO II

War Commander Tebu Ona-Ka stood in front of a huge portal and looked down on Orlo II. His job was to wipe the planet clean of sentient life so that his race could colonize it. Because their world was gradually dying—and the race would need new planets.

He was six and a half feet tall and weighed a little over three hundred pounds. That wasn't much by Hudathan standards—and explained the nickname that had been bestowed upon him at the age of ten: the Runt. A sobriquet that followed him into the military and was still used behind his back. But never to his face because Ona-Ka had fought seventeen duels, all with the same outcome. He was alive, and his enemies weren't.

Ona-Ka heard a polite cough and turned. Good manners dictated that one pause before entering a space occupied by another and give warning. To do otherwise was not only considered rude, but dangerous, since all Hudathans were armed. Ona-Ka saw that the first person to arrive was Vice Admiral Nola-Ba and waved him in. "Greetings, Admiral. Please have a seat."

The command center was oval in shape, with twelve niches set into the bulkheads, one for each member of Ona-Ka's staff.

And as Nola-Ba sat down, other officers filed in and took their seats. Once they were settled, Ona-Ka spoke. "You are to be congratulated. The first phase of the battle has gone well. But there's more work to do. Admiral Nola-Ba... Your report please."

Nola-Ba had a broad, craggy face. The vestige of a dorsal fin ran front to back along the top of his skull, one of his funnel-shaped ears had been sliced off in combat, and his temperature-sensitive skin was gray. A blue jewel glowed at the point where two leather belts crossed his chest. His voice sounded like a rockcrusher in low gear. "As you know, the human fleet was forced to withdraw and leave a substantial number of troops on the ground. There's no way to be certain of what the enemy will do next, but it is logical to assume that they will either return in force or pull back and reinforce worlds closer to Earth."

Nola-Ba paused at that point and his space-black eyes probed the faces around him. "*If* they return," he continued, "there's reason for concern. Especially if they are able to muster a force superior to our own. And there's a secondary threat as well. In order to stay and fight, we will have to maintain a long supply chain that's twice the length of theirs.

"But," Nola-Ba added, "in spite of those challenges, there are ample reasons for us to stay and complete the task before us. I believe that Lance Commander Horba-Sa is ready with the most recent intelligence summary."

Ona-Ka, who was still standing with his back to the portal, made eye contact with the officer in question. "Please proceed."

Horba-Sa had a reputation as a plotter and a schemer. Talents that made him ideal for the position he held. His eyes glittered. Opportunities to show War Commander Ona-Ka how smart he was didn't come along every day, and he planned to take full advantage of it. "As Admiral Nola-Ba suggested, we have some significant advantages, beginning with the nature of our adversaries. There are two races to contend with—the humans and the Droi.

"The humans who were brought in from off-world are equipped with weapons equivalent to ours but are relatively few in number and hold a single city. And since their fleet withdrew, they are vulnerable from the air."

"What about the local humans?" Ona-Ka inquired.

"There are a couple million of them spread out across the surface of the planet," Horba-Sa replied. "But they are in the midst of a civil war and therefore divided."

Ona-Ka nodded. "Go on."

"The Droi are more numerous," Horba-Sa continued, "but relatively primitive and lack a centralized command structure. Because of that, I believe we can ignore them for the moment and concentrate on eliminating the off-worlders first."

Commander Urlo-Ba was a tough, no-nonsense ground pounder with a reputation for getting things done. And having been a soldier for more than twenty years, he was no fool. He had been wounded in the throat years before, and his voice was permanently hoarse. "You say we should focus on the off-worlders. What do we know about them?"

Horba-Sa had a ready answer. "The Legion, as they call themselves, is comprised of murderers, thieves, and misfits. All sent here because they are considered to be expendable. We will crush them."

Ona-Ka cleared his throat. "Lance Commander Horba-Sa is factually correct. But there's someone I want you to meet. Once you have, I'll allow you to draw your own conclusions."

Horba-Sa didn't like the possibility that he was going to lose face in front of so many senior officers. But there was nothing he could do about it as the door to the command center whispered open and a human appeared. He was unshaven, dressed in a tattered uniform, and had clearly been beaten. A guard gave him a shove. He stumbled, caught himself, and looked around. "What a fucking freak show... You should charge admission."

The words were translated by a computer and played over the PA system. More than one officer rose in response to the insult, but Ona-Ka raised a hand. "Who are you?"

The legionnaire looked the Hudathan in the eye. "I'm Staff Sergeant Harvey Hill. Who the hell are *you*?"

"I'm in command here," Ona-Ka replied mildly. "Tell me something, Staff Sergeant Hill... What will your comrades do when we attack Riversplit?"

Hill grinned. His skin was dark, and his teeth were extremely white. "They'll rip your fucking heads off and piss down your throats."

"Because they are loyal to Empress Ophelia?"

"Shit no. We *like* to shoot freaks. Especially *big* ones. They're hard to miss."

Ona-Ka nodded and looked at a guard. "Eject him from a lock."

Having heard the translation, Hill took three running steps and dived through the air, his hands reaching for Ona-Ka's throat. The Hudathan stepped to one side as two stunner bolts hit the human. There was a *thump* as his body landed on the floor. Guards came forward to drag it away.

Once they were gone, Ona-Ka's eyes swept the room and came to rest on Horba-Sa. "Remember Sergeant Hill over the next few days. There are more where he came from. Dismissed."

15

There's nothing like a common enemy to create new alliances.

AUTHOR UNKNOWN

A Dweller folk saying

Standard year circa 2300

PLANET ORLO II

A lot of things had changed. The prisoners had been freed, and since Spurlock was MIA, Avery had assumed command. And, because of the many casualties the Grays had suffered, there was no one with sufficient authority to object.

The bridge was beyond repair, so Avery ordered what remained of the battalion to rig ropes enabling the bio bods stranded on the south side of the river to join those on the north bank. After consolidating his troops, it was time for Avery to salvage what he could. One of the 8 X 8s had been just short of the bridge deck when the span blew. So it was necessary to winch the truck across the river. A tedious process made even more so when legionnaires were forced to lever a couple of small boulders out of the way.

Meanwhile, the rest of the legionnaires were in the river, trying to salvage what they could from the wrecked vehicles. It was a very difficult task that involved wading waist- or even chest-deep through cold water, risking injury from jagged pieces of metal, and staggering ashore with heavy boxes. It was backbreaking work that left the participants exhausted. But thanks to their efforts, cases of food, ammo, and medical supplies were piling up on the shore. All of which were doubly precious given the fact that the unit was on its own.

Meanwhile, McKee and a tech named Forelli were on the south side of the river fighting a tense battle to save seventeen lives. Because if they couldn't get the T-1s up and running within the next nine hours and eleven minutes, the cyborgs would run out of emergency power, their life-support systems would shut down, and they would die. McKee tried not to think about that as she worked to find a solution.

They had chosen to work on Hower first. The T-1 stood frozen in place as McKee tried to reboot his distributed processing swarm (DPS). One of his inspection ports was open and she and Forelli were peering at a status display. It was unbearably hot, and McKee's clothes were soaked with sweat as she stared at the tiny screen. The onboard computing system was self-healing, or it was supposed to be, but the pulse from the EMP bomb had fried something. But what? The readout listed all of the T-1's critical components as REQUIRING MAINTENANCE. But McKee didn't believe that because she had spent the last hour isolating the subprocessors and testing them. And all of the subs were in the green.

So what remained? "I think we're dealing with a software glitch," McKee said. "If we can find and isolate it, the DPS will heal itself."

"Terrific," Tech Sergeant Forelli replied doubtfully. "But how are we going to do that?" Forelli had a plain face, a sturdy build, and a reputation as an above-average poker player. She was a good if unimaginative tech.

McKee wiped the sheen of sweat off her brow with the back of a forearm. "I think the problem is hiding between two computing swarms. So I'm going to write new code for the interface. We'll splice it in, and, voila, problem solved."

Forelli stared at her. "*Really?* You can do that?"

McKee thought she *might* be able to do that. But Hower was

listening, so it was important to be positive. "Sure… But I'll need to borrow your cybergloves."

Forelli removed a pair of field-programmable nanomesh gloves from her tool bag and handed them over. They were composed of nanomesh computing cores that could interpret microgestures as information and transmit it to any DPS. "You sure know a lot about T-1s for someone who never went to tech school."

"I used to work at a Carletto Industries factory," McKee said truthfully. "Okay… Let's see how much I remember."

The problem was that she hadn't hacked any code since graduating from college. So it took some doing to bring the necessary knowledge up, funnel it through her fingers, and send it streaming into Hower's DPS. The effort consumed more than ten minutes, and once she was done, McKee felt anything but confident as she gestured the last shapes into the hacked interface. Her eyes were fixed on the images rippling across the fabric in front of her. But rather than the result she hoped for, the words SYSTEM MALFUNCTION blinked on and off.

McKee swore softly and bit her lower lip. A glance at her chrono confirmed what she already knew. Time was melting away. "What now?" Forelli inquired.

"We try again," McKee replied, as she took a swig from her canteen. "I made a mistake, but I'll put it right. Then, once we have Hower up and running, we can transfer the same code onto the others." It *sounded* good, but bullshit isn't code. Still, all she could do was try, and keep trying, until she succeeded or Hower and the rest of them died.

So McKee tried again—and *again*. With each attempt, she inserted small changes that she hoped would do the job. But none of them worked.

Finally, with the sun going down and only two hours left to work with, McKee decided to take a shot at hacking the underlying protocol. Forelli held a flashlight as McKee went back to work. She was tired. Very tired. So much so that her mind seemed to be floating somewhere outside her body. But then, as she pushed ahead, the moment arrived when the code began to write itself. It was like music flowing from the fingertips of a pianist into her instrument.

But just because it *felt* good didn't mean that it was. So when McKee stopped twenty minutes later, she didn't know what she had. *Please,* she thought to herself as she paused before the final finger flex. *Please make it work.*

Her finger moved, boot-up symbols rippled across the video fabric in front of her, and Forelli uttered a whoop of joy. "You did it!"

Something was taking place. That much was certain. But what? McKee held her breath as the loading sequence ended. There was a pause that seemed to last forever. Then Hower stirred, and as he did, the readouts for his various systems began to morph from red to yellow. "The power's back on," Hower rumbled. "And I can move again!" Servos whined as he lifted an arm by way of proof. "Thanks, McKee. I owe you."

"Quick," McKee said as she palmed the program to a couple of data cubes. She put one of them in a pocket and gave the other to Forelli. "Load this into all of the T-1s on the south side of the river. I'll cross over and take care of the rest."

McKee returned Forelli's gloves, ran down to the river, and plunged in. The cold water was a shock, and rocks shifted under her boots. They gave unexpectedly, and would have dumped her into the current if it hadn't been for the hand rope. It held her up as she floundered forward. "It was a software problem!" she shouted. "We hacked it."

A beam of white light found McKee as Avery waded out to give her a hand. He helped her up onto the beach, and, together, they ran for the nearest T-1. "Hower is up and running," she told Avery, "and Forelli is loading the new code into the T-1s on the south side. But there isn't much time."

Having arrived in front of a cyborg, she opened an access panel, fumbled the memory cube into place, and touched a button. Avery looked on as code scrolled, the war form came back to life, and McKee hit the eject button. After recovering the cube, it was on to the next T-1, and so forth, until *all* the cyborgs were fully restored.

Even Trask was impressed. "You never cease to amaze me," he said as McKee took a place on the other side of a crackling fire. "To say that you're resourceful would be an understatement. Who are you anyway?"

"She's a corporal," Avery put in as he materialized out of the gloom. "And all of our corporals are outstanding individuals. Please stand. From this point forward, you will be treated as a POW."

As bio bods appeared next to him, Trask looked left and right but remained where he was. "That's where you're mistaken, Captain," he said confidently. "The Droi won't allow it."

Avery smiled thinly. "Tell us, Insa… Will the Droi allow it?"

The Droi stepped into the circle of firelight. His eyes were on Trask. "Sorry… But Avery right. Hudathans bad. We kill."

Trask stood. "I don't make policy," he said with a shrug. "The council does that. But, for whatever it's worth, I agree with you." The bio bods led him away.

McKee ate an MRE after that, then crawled into a shelter and one of the salvaged sleep sacks. She was asleep seconds later. No one had to wake her. Filtered sunlight and the pressure on her bladder took care of that. And as she lay there, looking up at the fabric above, McKee knew something was different. But what? Then she remembered. After days of captivity, she was free! Or as free as any legionnaire could be. And hungry.

McKee crawled out of the shelter to discover that the unit was much smaller than it had been. It consisted of the command car, a Scorpion, one 8 X 8 truck, and twenty-three bio bods. That was down from forty and reflected an overall casualty rate of roughly 50 percent. Much of which was due to Spurlock's poor leadership. That was how McKee saw it—although she knew she was biased.

In any case, the feeling was different, and in spite of the heavy casualties, morale was up. And if any of McKee's fellow legionnaires thought poorly of her because she had gone AWOL, there was no sign of it in the cheerful greetings that came her way. Perhaps that was due to her lifesaving efforts the night before—or maybe it had to do with the Legion's culture. Because with only a few exceptions, all of the legionnaires were guilty of something.

McKee was one of the last people to eat breakfast. While she was at it, Larkin arrived with an armful of gear and an extra AXE dangling from one shoulder. "Here's the smallest body armor I could find," he said. "Plus an L-40 and a helmet."

The two of them hadn't had a chance to talk previously, and as Larkin dumped the load onto the ground, McKee met his eyes. "I'll never forget the canteen… The one you tossed into the bunker that day."

Larkin shrugged. "You'd do the same for me. We're a team."

Then, having looked around as if to make sure that no one could hear, he lowered his voice. "Going AWOL was a good idea… But don't leave me behind next time. I'm ready when you are."

McKee sighed. "I'll keep that in mind. But, given the situation, I think we should stay. Echo Company needs us."

"Okay," Larkin said reluctantly. "But it's been a long time since I had a cold beer."

Once the company had broken camp and formed up on the road, it was time for *another* burial ceremony. All the Legion-issue markers had been used up by then, so pieces of scrap metal were employed instead. Given the demands of the war, McKee wondered if the graves-registration robots would make it to that lonely patch of road, or would the Big Green claim the bodies first?

The T-1s were at the back of the formation, towering over all the rest as Avery spoke. Most of his belongings were still at the bottom of the river, and that included the book by Kipling, so the words were his own. "These men and women were our comrades and friends. They died fighting for us and we will miss them greatly. And when *we* fall, they will be waiting for us beyond the gates of hell."

The message was harsh, like the Legion itself, and judging from the expression on Trask's face, different from what he had expected. But the legionnaires liked it and understood. Sergeant Boyce shouted, "Camerone!"

"CAMERONE," came the reply, and McKee emptied her lungs with all the rest. Then the troops were dismissed. A bio bod named Katica was the XO *and* the platoon leader by virtue of being the only lieutenant who had survived. Boyce was acting as company sergeant, and the T-1s had been divided into three squads. McKee was put in charge of the third. And as she climbed up onto a 'borg named Eason, she was reminded of Weber. She missed him and still felt guilty about being AWOL when he died.

Thanks to the way McKee had brought the T-1s back to life, she was very popular with the 'borgs, and Eason was no exception. His voice boomed over the speakers in her helmet. "Welcome aboard, Corp... I'll take good care of you."

McKee thanked him, leaned back into the harness, and was pleased to discover that there wasn't any pain. Her back had healed, but there was no telling what it looked like.

The company left shortly thereafter with a squad of T-1s out front followed by the command car, the Scorpion, and the truck that was carrying both the wounded and most of the company's remaining supplies. The second squad came next, followed by the third, which brought up the rear. It wasn't until they were under way that McKee realized that she didn't know where the company was going.

The relationship with Avery had been close when they were prisoners, but he was an officer, and more than that, her *commanding* officer, and not likely to consult corporals. That made sense even if it rankled a bit, and served to point out a strange irony.

The truth was that McKee had enjoyed the freedom she had experienced when she was AWOL—even if she had been on the run most of the time. The absurdity of that brought a wry smile to her lips as she swayed back and forth in the harness.

Old habits soon took over, and it wasn't long before she was putting her newly formed squad through the usual evolutions. Typically, they would march for a while, closed up behind the others, only to let the column get ahead. The best place to do that was around a blind curve, so that if they were being followed, the enemy would run into a trap.

And so it went until the sun was high in the sky and the column turned off the road onto a track just wide enough to accommodate the big 8 X 8 truck. Then, once the company was well within the jungle's humid embrace, Avery called a halt. Lookouts were posted and rotated so that everyone could eat.

The company got under way again half an hour later. McKee's

squad was on point this time, with Insa and a party of Droi riding in the command car. It was a sturdy vehicle, and had to be, since the legionnaire behind the wheel used it to knock saplings over, drove through streams, and sent the car up hillsides. They were headed west, but why? Avery still hadn't chosen to share that information. One thing was for sure, however—they couldn't go very far. Because the tanker had been destroyed. And if they ventured too far into the Big Green, the company would be stranded there.

True to McKee's prediction, the company arrived at its destination one hour later. The sprawling encampment was extremely large, and as the off-worlders arrived, hundreds of Droi came out to gape at the T-1s. The village was located in a canyon that, judging from the marks on the rock walls, had been home to a mighty river thousands of years before.

During that time, the force of the water had removed most of the softer material, leaving mushroom-shaped pillars that stood at least a hundred feet high and were festooned with greenery. There was a commotion as Avery told Insa what the unit needed, and the local issued a series of orders in his native tongue. A space was cleared under one of the umbrella-shaped towers, and as the company took up residence there, McKee was struck by the extent to which the formation would protect them from orbital surveillance. A good thing given that the Hudathans owned the sky.

The next couple of hours were spent getting settled. McKee made use of the time to run routine maintenance checks on all of her T-1s. She had just completed the last one when Private Caskin appeared. There was a white bandage wrapped around his head, and it made his hair stand up. Like so many legionnaires, his face was young and old at the same time. He nodded. "Hey, McKee, the old man wants to see you."

McKee wiped some grease off her hands with a rag. "Okay, where is he?"

"The Droi forgot to put up street signs," Caskin said. "I'll take you there."

McKee told Larkin and the rest of the squad to take a break and followed Caskin through a maze of shelters, cooking fires, and animal pens to the foot of a rock tower. They had attracted a retinue of juveniles by then. They stared at the off-worlders and chattered among themselves. "They're up top," Caskin said, and pointed.

McKee looked, saw that a spiral pathway had been hacked out of solid rock, and realized that the locals had been using the canyon for a long time. She said, "Thanks," and began to climb. The path was about two feet wide, and tool marks were still visible where material had been cut away. There was no handrail or rope. Just a sudden drop off to the right and tiny shelters below. She did her best to ignore that as she climbed steadily higher and emerged onto a flat area. It was covered with lush greenery, flowering plants, and a tangle of vines.

The garden was natural, or so it appeared, as McKee followed a footpath to a clearing where a thatched roof threw shade down onto Avery, Insa, and a pair of Droi she hadn't met before. They were seated in a circle and rose when she appeared.

Insa nodded. "I see you, McKee."

"And I you," she replied.

"We meet," the Droi explained. "This Ola and this Tran. They leaders."

McKee greeted each Droi in turn, and once the introductions were complete, she was invited to sit down. Avery spoke first. "The council and I have been discussing what to do next. The Droi could attack the Hudathans on their own," he said. "And that would be helpful. But all of us believe that a well-coordinated effort could inflict more damage. Unfortunately, the ridge heads are jamming the Legion's communications, so we've been unable to reach Rylund by radio."

There was nothing McKee could do but nod, and say, "Yes, sir."

"So we're going to send Rylund a message, letting him know about the alliance with the Droi," Avery continued. "I would prefer to handle that myself—but I owe it to Echo Company and the Droi to remain here. Even though we don't know what Rylund will ask us to do, this is the time to set up a chain of command and teach tactics."

McKee knew all of those things were important and knew what was coming next. Avery saw her expression and nodded.

"That's right… I'm sending you, a bio bod from your squad, and three T-1s."

McKee raised an eyebrow. "*Three* T-1s?"

"Me go, too," Insa put in. "Tell Rylund. He believe."

That made sense. A visit from a Droi leader would command attention that she couldn't. And Insa's knowledge of the terrain that lay between the encampment and Riversplit would be helpful as well. She nodded. "Copy that. When do we leave?"

"First thing in the morning," Avery replied. "So get ready. Which bio bod will you take?"

McKee thought about it for a moment. "Larkin."

Avery frowned. "Really? He's got a bad rep. What's to keep him from deserting once you arrive in Riversplit?"

"Me," McKee said flatly. "Sir."

Avery smiled. "Okay, Corporal… We'll leave it at that. Now let's go over the message."

McKee left the meeting an hour later and made her way down to the ground. With no one to guide her, she got lost among the maze of Droi campsites but eventually found her way back to the area where the company was camped. Then it was time to notify the T-1s chosen to go north and hand off responsibility for the rest of the squad to Sergeant Boyce.

With that accomplished, she went looking for Larkin and found him teaching poker to half a dozen Droi. All sorts of items were piled up in front of the legionnaire, including what looked like a handful of uncut gemstones. Just part of the mineral wealth hidden in the Big Green.

Larkin complained loudly as McKee ordered him to leave the game, but stopped once the city of Riversplit was mentioned. He was busy stuffing loot into his pockets when she grabbed a wrist. "Give it back. *Now*."

"Or *what*?" Larkin demanded hotly.

"Or I'll take someone else," McKee replied.

"Damn it, McKee… Why are you such a drag? First you go over the hill—then you get all uptight about a poker game. They're sheep, and sheep are meant to be sheared."

But he returned his winnings, promised the Droi that he would continue to mentor them once he returned, and followed

McKee back to the company area, grumbling all the way. "Load up on food and ammo for your 'borg," McKee said. "We're still a hundred miles from Riversplit, and according to what I was told earlier this afternoon, there are at least ten thousand Hudathans on the ground."

Larkin's face lit up. "We get to grease some freaks?"

"It would be best if we could avoid them, but yes, odds are that we'll have to grease some freaks."

"I like it," Larkin said enthusiastically. "I'll get ready."

It was dinnertime. So McKee took an MRE and went looking for a place to eat. And that, as it turned out, was a hundred yards away in a grove of trees. She saw signs that a shelter had been erected there in the recent past, but the spot was vacant at the moment and perfect for a peaceful dinner.

A few minutes later, McKee had settled in and was about to heat up her main course when she heard a rustling sound and drew her pistol. Avery saw the weapon and looked apologetic as he entered the tiny clearing. "Sorry about that… Can I join you? Boyce said you were headed in this direction."

McKee wondered what Boyce would make of Avery's looking for her with his MRE in hand and decided that she didn't care. The chance to spend time with the one person who knew her better than all the rest was too good to pass up. "Of course… Make yourself at home. Sorry about the mess. The maid quit."

Avery grinned and sat on the log next to her. "It's so hard to find good help these days. Are you ready to go?"

McKee nodded. "Pretty much. I'll run one last check on the 'borgs after dinner."

"That's good, real good," Avery said awkwardly. "I wish I could go with you."

"I know," McKee said sympathetically. "But you're right. Getting the Droi ready to fight is very important. And you're the only person qualified to do it."

"There's something else," Avery said. "Something I wanted to talk to you about alone. There is the distinct possibility that Spurlock and Jivv are in Riversplit by now. If so, you could run into some serious trouble. That's one of the reasons why I want

Insa to go along. Your relationship with the Droi will make it more difficult for Rylund to throw you in jail.

"Plus there's this," Avery said as he gave her a memory mod. "I recorded a full account of what took place—minus the Catherine Carletto stuff. So if you think my testimony might be helpful, please feel free to use it."

"Thank you," McKee said as she accepted the module. Jivv would shoot her on sight, but if the robot had been destroyed in the fighting, then Avery's account could be useful. More important, however, was the fact that he was trying to take care of her. That meant a lot.

Avery looked into her eyes as if trying to see through them to whatever lay within. "Catherine…"

"Cat."

"Cat… It isn't right, I know that, but there's something I want to say. A lot of things could happen over the next few weeks. Bad things. And well, if I don't say something now, it might not get said. And that would be too bad because I…"

Avery's words were cut off as she placed an index finger on his lips and used her other hand to pull him closer. As their lips met, something flowed between them. The giving and taking was both tender and exciting. And, had the circumstances been different, McKee knew that the kiss would have been little more than a beginning. But that couldn't be. Not a hundred yards away from Echo Company and their responsibilities.

And it was as if Avery knew that, too, because he made no attempt to follow up as their lips parted. "Wow," he said. "That was good."

McKee smiled. "What? You weren't sure?"

"No, I wasn't," Avery said lightly. "Just because you can lead, fight, and repair cyborgs doesn't mean you'd be any good in bed."

"And you think you could get me there?"

"I'd sure like to try," Avery said. "But not here. Not now."

"No," McKee agreed. "Not now."

Avery broke the ensuing silence. "Now I have even more riding on this mission. I want both of you back."

"Both?"

"Cat Carletto *and* Andromeda McKee."

"I'm hard to kill."

Avery nodded soberly. "But you aren't bulletproof. Watch your six, Corporal. I'll be waiting."

The legionnaires and the Droi emissary departed the canyon without fanfare at exactly 0600 the following morning. The sun sent shafts of light down through holes in the canopy to form pools of gold on the forest floor. Birds chittered, insects buzzed, and the T-1s generated a steady *whir-thump-whir* sound as they followed the track back toward the main road.

With no infantry or heavy vehicles to slow her down, McKee hoped to travel fifty miles on the first day. Then, depending on conditions, they would either push on during the hours of darkness or hole up while she went forward to scout the way. That was the worst part. Not knowing how the enemy was deployed. It seemed safe to assume that the Hudathans were primarily focused on Riversplit and keeping the Legion penned in.

Would that focus make it easier to sneak in? Maybe… Although once inside the fortified city, she and her party might have trouble getting out again. There were lots of questions and very few answers as Eason began to pick up speed.

Conscious of the fact that riding a T-1 took some getting used to, McKee looked back over her shoulder. The Droi was riding a 'borg named Noll. The only part of Insa that McKee could see was the Legion-issue helmet, which was bouncing up and down. She spoke to the native over the squad freq. "Hey, Insa… Are you okay?"

"Me fine," came the reply. "Bumpy but learn soon."

"Roger that. Let me know if you need a break." Thankfully, Insa was a quick study, and it wasn't long before his helmet steadied, and McKee could focus on other things. Primary among them was the need to prevent the group from being spotted from the air. Contrails could be seen through gaps in the trees, and unless the strategic situation had changed a great deal overnight, they belonged to Hudathan aircraft.

Fortunately, the enemy weren't looking for her group, not specifically anyway although that could change later on. But the Hudathans would certainly take action if they spotted the T-1s. So her responsibility was to make sure that they didn't. And with Insa to guide them, there was a very real chance that they could escape notice during the initial part of the journey.

So when the group came to the main road, she led them across it instead of taking a right. They continued west for a good two miles before veering north on what Insa said was an ancient trade route. Though not an actual road, it was wider than a trail. With the jungle canopy to protect them, the T-1s could stay under cover and make good progress.

Strange though it seemed given all that could go wrong, McKee took pleasure in the warm air, the dappled sunshine all around her, and the rhythm of Eason's movements. And while she told herself to stay sharp and keep her head on a swivel, there were times when her thoughts turned to Avery.

She knew he was very different from the man-boys that Cat Carletto had loved to toy with. Not as pretty for one thing, relatively poor, and not very hip. All of which meant that the previous her wouldn't have given him the time of day.

But the party girl had been transformed into a battle-scarred warrior and a person with very different values. Now the very things that would have struck her as boring in the past meant everything. Avery had a good mind, moral clarity, and ten times the courage of the sports-boys she had dallied with on Earth. Enough to stand by her even if it meant a court-martial and the possibility of imprisonment. How many men would do that?

And then there was the kiss. Cat Carletto had never been one to sleep around casually, but there had been lovers, some of whom wanted to marry her. Or said they did, although there was always the possibility that what they *really* hoped to marry was her family's money. In any case, some of them were very good in bed. And she'd enjoyed that.

But not once had there been a connection like the one she'd felt with Avery as they kissed. There was a physical attraction, a strong one, but something more, too. She didn't have the right word for it, although "completion" came close. And he wanted her in spite of the scars on her face and back. Proof that the attraction wasn't based solely on her appearance. All of which was very interesting.

Of course, there was danger, too... Because ever since she'd been forced to part company with Cat Carletto, she'd been very lonely. Maybe that was it. Perhaps she was so desperate for love and attention that she was willing to grab onto the first man who took an interest in her.

Her thoughts were interrupted as Eason spoke over the squad push. "I have a target. It's at twelve o'clock and coming..."

McKee saw the drone. The machine was so low that it had been hidden behind a rise, where Eason's sensors couldn't "see" it. Now it was flying straight at them, and there wasn't enough time to hide. So she said, "Kill it!" and Eason opened fire. There was a bright flash followed by a loud bang as the cylindrical robot exploded. Pieces of shrapnel flew in every direction—but Eason and McKee were unscathed.

"Nice shot," McKee said, her mind racing. She had never seen that type of drone before, which meant it was probably Hudathan. Why send it into the Big Green? Intelligence gathering probably. One of many such machines dispatched to spy on the Droi. That was her theory anyway.

But what to do? Odds were that the images captured by the drone had been streaming to some sort of ship. So the Hudathans had seen Eason and possibly the others as well. How would they react? McKee thought she knew. "Insa! The Hudathans know we're here—and can home in on our heat signatures. We could use a river to conceal them."

"No river," came the reply. "Small streams only. But lake nearby."

"Noll," McKee said, "take the point. Insa, guide him to the lake. And hurry! The Hudathans will be here soon."

Noll passed Eason, ran for a short distance, and took a hard left. The jungle was ripped asunder as the T-1 plunged into it, closely followed by the other 'borgs and their bio bods. "I've got an incoming aircraft," Eason warned. "It's two miles out and closing fast."

McKee wanted to say, "Damn, damn, damn," but knew leaders were supposed to be imperturbable. So she kept her mouth shut as limbs threatened to decapitate her and passing branches tried to rip her off Eason's back.

Then she heard Insa say something in its own language, and the trees parted to reveal a small lake. Noll plunged in, and Eason followed. Once in the water, the cyborg began to wade out to where it was deeper.

McKee felt the cold liquid invade her clothing and knew that while the T-1 could survive when completely submerged, she couldn't. So it was time to release the harness and hang on to the grab bar for as long as she could. The trick would be to keep everything but her head beneath the surface.

A quick look around revealed that the others were pursuing the same strategy, for which she was grateful. Then the Hudathan ship was upon them. The disk-shaped vessel was bigger than she had expected. So much so that the hull blocked out most of the sky. A loud, thrumming noise could be heard as the ship's repellers cut momentary grooves into the surface of the lake and steam rose all around. Then the Hudathans opened fire with large-caliber projectile weapons. Was it aimed? She didn't think so. It appeared as if the Hudathans were hoping for some lucky hits. And she figured they might get some as bullets churned the surface of the lake—sending thousands of miniature geysers shooting up into the air.

At that point, McKee did the only thing she could. Having let go of Eason, she forced her head down and dived for the bottom. It was a mistake. The combined weight of the helmet, body armor, and weapon pulled her down. Then she was at the bottom of the lake, struggling to release the helmet's chin strap as projectiles plunged around her. Her gear was like an anchor, her lungs were on fire, and she was going to drown. The last thing she saw before darkness closed in was a bed of flowering animals that lived on the bottom of the lake. The "blossoms" were red—and they were pretty.

16

Who dares, wins.

MOTTO OF THE BRITISH SPECIAL AIR SERVICE (SAS)
Formed standard year 1941

PLANET ORLO II

When McKee came to, she was coughing, spluttering, and hanging upside down. Larkin was peering at her from six inches away. "Okay," he said. "Her eyes are open, and she's breathing. Go ahead and put her down."

Once the bio bod had a grip on her, Eason let go of her ankles. There was an awkward moment when McKee nearly landed on her head. But disaster was averted at the last second, and she wound up lying on her back, staring up at the sky. She didn't realize the helmet was still on her head until Larkin removed it. "What happened?"

"You went diving, and Eason plucked you off the bottom," Larkin explained. "We thought you were dead."

"The ship," McKee said. "What happened to the ship?"

"The shovel heads got tired of wasting ammo and went away," Eason rumbled.

"They could come back," she said as she forced herself to sit up. "Where's my AXE? We need to get out of here."

"You can tell she's back to normal, she's bossing everyone around," Larkin observed.

McKee felt a moment of embarrassment as Larkin helped her to her feet. Both he and Insa had survived the ordeal without drowning. She was too stupid to be in charge, and if a realistic alternative had been available, she would have asked that individual to assume command. But there wasn't. So all she could do was accept the AXE that Insa handed her and climb onto Eason's back. The group was under way two minutes later.

Her mood was different now. She no longer saw the beauty around her—or allowed her thoughts to stray to Avery. The Hudathans had been a theoretical threat before, and they were real now. Very real.

The first thing they had to do was get off the trade route lest the enemy send more drones along it or, worse yet, an ambush. So, based on directives from Insa, they traveled west until they came across what was little more than a game trail. It was safer, but narrow, and had a tendency to wander. The net effect was to cut the T-1s' speed by half.

It couldn't be helped, however, and McKee felt safer on the little-used path with a canopy of green overhead. But as the day progressed, the protective vegetation began to thin. And at about 15:30 hours, they ran into the first sign of civilization. It consisted of row upon row of carefully planted trees, all carefully pruned, and spaced so that machines could roll down the corridors between them. As the cyborgs crossed the plantation, McKee knew that she and her charges were about to become a lot more vulnerable. Especially if the Hudathans *and* the rebels were gunning for them.

But as the light began to fade, and they pushed north, she realized that most if not all of the local civilian population had fled in order to escape from the alien invaders. And for good reason. Homes had been burned, farm animals had been slaughtered, and anything that remotely resembled civilian infrastructure had been destroyed. That included transmission towers, grain silos, and even the most insignificant of bridges.

And why not? The Hudathans didn't want to conquer

humans and enslave them; their objective was to obliterate what they saw as dangerous pests.

Insa's knowledge of the countryside had been invaluable up until that point. But the Droi had never been to Riversplit and knew nothing about the local area. McKee wondered if it would have been wise to bring Trask or one of the surviving Grays along but quickly rejected the notion, knowing that she wouldn't be able to trust them. So all she could do was proceed slowly, look for an opening, and seize it when it came.

It was dark by the time the group crossed a small river, passed the bloated corpses of some quadrupeds, and approached a cluster of buildings. Judging from appearances, the house had been fired on from above and caught fire. And the attack had been fairly recent because wisps of smoke could still be seen drifting away from the charred ruins.

Sheds had been destroyed as well, but the bullet-riddled barn was made of metal and remained standing. Having checked to make sure that the structure was empty, McKee ordered everyone inside. They needed to hole up for the night, and it was her hope that the residual warmth from the house fire would serve to cover their heat signatures.

Of course, a barn could attract humans looking for a place to hide. And, since the civil war had been under way *before* the Hudathans arrived, such individuals could be armed. That made it necessary for the cyborgs to dig fighting positions inside the building where they couldn't be seen. The plan was to fire through the walls if necessary.

Once that effort was under way, she and Larkin slipped into the darkness. They could see, thanks to the night-vision technology built into their helmets, and McKee knew where she wanted to go. A hill was located approximately one mile north of the farm—and once on top, she hoped to get a good view of Riversplit off in the distance.

Of course, that was the problem with hilltops. All sorts of people were likely to congregate there, and McKee knew they would have to be careful lest they blunder onto a group of rebels or loyalists.

There was a high overcast, which meant no starlight, but

McKee was grateful for anything that might interfere with the Hudathans' ability to look down on them from above. After crossing a couple of fields and climbing over a fence, they came to the foot of the hill. It might have been forested at one time but wasn't anymore, which offered a mixed blessing as they began to climb. The open slope meant people couldn't lie in wait for them, but it also meant there wasn't any cover should they need it, and she felt extremely vulnerable as she followed a footpath toward the summit.

She was out of breath by the time they arrived at a point just short of the top. With weapons at the ready, they elbowed their way up to the crest of the hill. An enclosure made of carefully piled rocks marked the highest point. It was covered by a flat metal roof, and judging from the size of the doorway, the structure had been built by the Hudathans. An observation post perhaps, constructed during the days after they landed, and since abandoned. The most important thing was that McKee had what she had come for—and that was an unobstructed view of Riversplit from the south. And it was a spectacular sight.

The city and the hill it stood on were under attack. Seen via night-vision technology, there were flashes of white light as bombs exploded, streaks of green as missiles rose to search out Hudathan aircraft, and occasional fireworks when they succeeded. McKee could hear what sounded like rolling thunder as both sides exchanged salvos of artillery fire.

It was tempting to quarter the area with the binoculars Avery had given her, but she knew there was something else she should take care of first. She turned to Larkin. "Patrol the hilltop. Stop to listen every once in a while. And let me know before you shoot anything."

Larkin's response was predictably contentious. "What if they're ten feet away? And they're about to shoot me? What then?"

McKee was tempted to say, "Let them," but knew it was her fault. Having chosen to bring Larkin, she had no one to blame except herself. "That would be the exception. If they're ten feet away, kill them."

"That's what I thought," Larkin said self-righteously, and he was gone seconds later.

Having been freed from the need to worry about who or what might crawl up her six, McKee went to work examining the terrain in front of her. Senior noncoms had presumably been trained for such tasks, but she hadn't. So she had to develop her own system of observation.

Rather than look at the big picture, and potentially miss the kind of detail she needed, she forced herself to ignore the distant battle and zoom in on the plain below. Then, working from left to right, she would look for a path into Riversplit.

The level of detail captured by the night-vision binoculars was surprisingly good. And as McKee focused them on the flat area in front of her, she saw what could only be described as a wasteland. Given all of the burned-out structures, bomb craters, and row upon row of defensive earthworks, she could tell that a battle had been fought there.

But the plain wasn't uninhabited. Far from it. As McKee searched the area below, she could see Hudathan encampments, crude roads that had been cut through the debris, and the tracked vehicles that were using them. And it didn't take a general to figure out that with their aircraft bombing the shit out of Riversplit, the aliens were taking advantage of the opportunity to resupply the front lines.

And that was the problem. With so many Hudathans in the way, it would be very difficult to sneak through their lines without being discovered. Still, that was what the situation called for, so she plotted route after potential route but without success. There was always some sort of obstacle in the way.

It was only after an hour's study that McKee turned her attention to a more daring alternative. If she and her companions couldn't sneak into Riversplit—what would happen if they charged in? The T-1s could run at speeds up to 50 mph on a hard surface. And the Hudathans had cleared a preexisting two-lane highway that led straight to the hill. A convoy of half-tracks was grinding its way north at the moment, but the southbound lane was practically empty, and that could represent the opportunity she was looking for.

McKee estimated that the plain was roughly five miles wide. So if the T-1s were traveling at top speed, they could cross it in six minutes. Call it seven just to be safe. Was such a thing possible? If so, surprise would be the key. The shovel heads weren't stupid. It seemed safe to assume that they were prepared for all sorts of eventualities. But a straight run in by three T-1s? She didn't think so. Her thoughts were interrupted as Larkin chinned his mike on and off. "Yeah?" McKee inquired. "What's up?"

"A Hudathan patrol is climbing the north side of the hill."

"How many?"

"Six."

Had they been spotted? Or were the Hudathans on a routine sweep? "Roger that. I'm pulling back. Meet me on the trail."

The two of them couldn't hope to take on six Hudathans and win. Nor did she want to reveal their presence. That would invite more enemy troops and kill any chance of making her newly conceived plan work.

Larkin was waiting for her as she found the trail, and they made good time as they followed it down. She wanted to be back in the barn before the enemy soldiers arrived on top of the hill and took a look around. There was no way to be sure, of course, but she felt reasonably confident that they had escaped detection as they arrived on the flat area below. However, just to be sure that they weren't seen entering the hideout, McKee took the extra precaution of circling the farm and creeping in from the south. "We're coming in," she said via the squad freq. "Over."

"Copy that," Hower replied. "Over."

Ten minutes later, they were inside the barn, where Insa and the T-1s were waiting. An area at the center of the barn had been screened off to prevent light from leaking out. What illumination there was emanated from a couple of glow strips. McKee chewed on a fruit bar and washed it down with sips of water as she gave her report. Once the rest of them were up to speed, she presented her plan. Eason was the first to react. "I like it," he rumbled. "By the time the shovel heads get organized, we'll be gone."

"I don't know," Noll said doubtfully. "Five miles. That's a long way to run with people shooting at you."

"Of course we get to shoot back," Hower observed.

"Damned straight," Larkin added enthusiastically. "The freaks have it coming."

"What about you?" McKee inquired as she met Insa's gaze. "What do *you* think?"

"We kill," Insa replied, and patted the black-market assault rifle he was so proud of. Feathers hung from the barrel, and chips of colorful glass were set into the wooden stock.

"Okay," McKee said, "it's on. The best time to make the run is at night. And it's too late to tackle the job tonight. So, we'll wait one rotation. That'll give us a chance to rest up and do some field maintenance."

"The longer we wait, the better chance they'll have to discover us," Noll said gloomily.

"That's true," McKee allowed, knowing that the cyborg would never say something like that to a sergeant, much less an officer. "But it's a chance that we'll have to take. And there's something we can do while we're waiting. We have four box-style magazines for each T-1—all loaded with alternating ball and armor-piercing-incendiary-tracer. By reallocating the rounds, we can create two cans of armor-piercing-incendiary-tracer for each 'borg. That means *every* bullet will punch through metal and set fire to whatever may be inside."

"We'll light 'em up!" Larkin said, his face aglow with anticipation.

Given Noll's attitude, Larkin's response was all the more welcome—although she knew he wasn't being political. The crazy bastard *wanted* a fight.

"Nice," Eason put in. "Our fifties will have some extra punch, *and* we'll be able to see where our rounds are going."

"Okay," McKee said. "There's no time like the present. Let's get started."

The T-1s' "fingers" were far too big and clumsy to redistribute the ammo. So that work fell to the legionnaires and Insa. And the same thing applied to maintenance except that McKee chose to take care of both Eason *and* Hower, knowing that her tech skills were superior to Larkin's.

That meant there was a lot to do, and it wasn't until 1000 hours in the morning that she gave herself permission to take a nap. Fifteen minutes later, Larkin touched her shoulder. "McKee... A drone is nosing around outside."

The news brought her to her feet in a hurry. Her heart was beating like a trip-hammer. "Where is it?" she whispered.

Larkin pointed toward the barn's double doors. They were riddled with bullet holes. And as she looked that way, she could see shafts of sunlight appear and disappear as something moved back and forth outside. It was hovering about ten feet off the ground and a booming sound was heard as metal collided with metal. "It's trying to push a door open," Larkin whispered.

They could destroy the machine. McKee knew that. But the results would be identical to those experienced the day before. Only this time the Hudathan ship would kill them. So all she could do was stand with the AXE at the ready and pray that the drone would move on. And finally, after what felt like an eternity, it did. Bit by bit, she allowed herself to breathe again as the sound generated by the machine's repellers faded away.

As the day wore on, it grew oppressively hot in the metal barn, and Larkin wanted to open the doors. McKee might have been tempted except for the fact that the drone was fresh in her mind. And if one could visit, why not a second? She said no, and Larkin grumbled for ten minutes before finally lapsing into silence.

All of the necessary work was completed by midafternoon. And with nothing else to do, the human bio bods tried to nap. But it was so warm that sleep didn't come easily, and when it finally did, McKee fell into what felt like a drugged stupor. So that when she awoke an hour later, she felt worse than before.

The barn began to cool as the sun went down, and that made McKee and Larkin feel better. Insa, who had been sitting with his eyes closed for the last hour, opened them as the humans began to eat dinner. "Tea," the Droi said, as if that explained everything. And seconds later, he was hard at work preparing the all-important substance.

Once the meal was over, time seemed to slow even more. McKee was in the process of reassembling her AXE when Insa began to smear various pigments on his face. "What's that for?" she inquired.

"Death paint," Insa said solemnly. "I kill or die." That seemed to say it all and cast something of a pall over the room as the others made their own preparations.

Twenty-four hundred hours. That was the time that McKee had chosen, and it was a struggle to appear calm as the final minutes ticked away. And she knew that was the way Avery would have looked had he been in charge.

Then, after what seemed like an eternity, it was 23:45 and time for the bio bods to take their positions. "Listen up," McKee said as she gave her final instructions. "Eason and I will take the point, followed by Noll and Insa. Hower and Larkin will bring up the rear. We're going to circle around the west end of the hill and pick up the road that leads to the highway. Be sure to maintain the standard thirty-foot interval.

"The 'borgs can fire on targets of opportunity. But remember it won't be possible to reload while on the run, so aim carefully and use three-round bursts. Oh, and don't shoot each other. We have enough problems.

"The bio bods will focus their attention on soft targets," McKee continued. "We'll use our assault weapons, but don't forget your grenades. Be careful, though… Were Insa or I to arm a grenade and fumble it away, the people behind us would pay the price.

"And remember… Everything depends on speed. We can't stop. If we do, it's over. Questions? No? Let's do this thing."

The cool night air felt good after the stuffiness of the barn. And McKee was happy to put the waiting behind her. Now, for better or for worse, she was going into action. And the internal presence that monitored everything she did was pleased to note that, while tense, she wasn't afraid of anything but failure.

So she gloried in the press of wind against her skin, the feel of Eason's movements, and the craziness of what they were going to do. A look back over her shoulder confirmed that the others were where they should be. So she looked forward as Eason rounded the west side of the hill. As seen through her high-tech visor, the entire plain was giving off a green glow. The eerie light was stronger in some places than others, and wherever a campfire burned, tendrils of heat spiraled upwards. The whole thing was unintentionally beautiful.

You don't have time to admire the view, she admonished herself. *Make the call while you can.* The problem was that even if the T-1s and the bio bods managed to cross the plain safely—they would run into Rylund's forces, who would immediately open fire on them. So it was critical to inform the command structure of what was about to happen. So McKee began with the regimental push and worked her way down through all the standard frequencies. Unfortunately, her calls were met with a roar of static. The Hudathans were jamming and doing a good job of it.

Her thoughts were interrupted as Eason said, "There's the road!" and began to pick up even more speed. *This*, McKee thought to herself, *is what cavalry was invented for.* And when she heard herself yell "Charge!" it came as a complete surprise.

As the three cyborgs and their riders ran straight at thousands of Hudathans, time seemed to slow, and McKee became hyperaware. She knew the press of wind against her body, the acrid smell of ozone, and the rhythmic *thud, thud, thud* of Eason's fifty. The roadblock was lightly guarded, and the Hudathans stationed there never had a chance. Huge though they were, the shovel heads were no match for .50-caliber armor-piercing slugs. They got off a few shots but went down like wheat to a harvester.

And as Eason cleared the entry point, McKee fired her AXE. By leaning back and letting the harness support her weight, she could use both hands to hold the weapon, and there were plenty of targets. McKee fired a long burst as they passed a column of two dozen troopers. The 4.7mm rounds didn't pack anything like the punch that Eason's fifty did, but that didn't matter. A wounded Hudathan would require medical attention and sap the unit's morale. Both of which were good things from McKee's point of view.

As she ejected an empty magazine from her assault weapon and seated another, she saw the back end of a tracked transport up ahead. And when Eason veered left to pass it, two more appeared. The first two were open in back and filled with what she assumed to be supplies. "I've got 'em," McKee said as she let the AXE hang across her chest. "Save your ammo."

The grenades were in ready bags hanging to the left and right of her position. In order to avoid the possibility of a mistake, McKee kept the frags on the left and the thermite grenades on the right. Thanks to Eason's height, it was a simple matter to arm one of the bombs and toss it into the back of the first crawler they jogged past. There was a flash as it detonated, and she knew it would burn at a temperature of four thousand degrees Fahrenheit. Hot enough to burn through five-sixteenths inches of durasteel in twenty seconds. So if there was something flammable in the vehicle, it was going to catch fire. And in this case, it appeared that the transport was loaded with ammo. When it exploded, a gout of fire shot a hundred feet into the air and lit up the entire area.

McKee thought about the T-1s coming along behind her and hoped that they were okay as she readied another grenade. Eason had passed the second track by then, which meant she would have to be content with dropping the bomb into the third machine. But as they drew closer, she saw that the cargo compartment was covered by a tightly stretched tarp and knew the device would roll off.

So rather than allow the weapon to explode in her hands, McKee threw it as far as she could. It landed next to the road, where it did little more than melt dirt and light up the night. A lesson learned.

Larkin uttered a whoop of joy as one of his grenades landed in the second crawler and triggered a secondary explosion. A quick glance confirmed that Noll and Insa still occupied the two slot.

"Soft targets coming up," Eason said, and as McKee looked forward over the cyborg's massive shoulder, she saw that he was correct. A column of troops was up ahead. And, thanks to the efforts of some quick-thinking noncom or officer, they were turning toward the oncoming threat. A few of them fired. But the effort came too late as Eason triggered the grenade launcher mounted under the barrel of his machine gun. The HE round blew a bloody hole through the Hudathan line, and McKee fired her AXE as they passed through the gap. One of the troopers charged the T-1 and was only feet away when she shot him in the face. He stumbled away, and Insa finished the job as Noll rushed past.

"Uh-oh," Eason said. "There's oncoming traffic up ahead. Hang on."

McKee saw that they were coming up on a self-propelled

rocket launcher, and a southbound transport was blocking the left lane. Eason could veer left or right and chose left. The cyborg fired into the vehicle's windshield as he crossed in front of the oncoming track. The machine swerved into oncoming traffic and crashed into the rocket launcher. That brought both vehicles to a halt and blocked the road.

Having rounded the back end of the stalled transport, Eason made his way back onto an open stretch of highway. That gave McKee an opportunity to try again. "All Legion forces... All Legion forces. This is Corporal McKee with three T-1s inbound from the south. We are traveling at 50 mph—ETA four minutes. Do not fire on us. Confirm. Over." She put the same message out over all of the possible frequencies with the same result: Nothing but static.

"Roadblock," Eason said laconically. "Hang on to your panties. We're going over it."

Though initially caught by surprise, the Hudathans were beginning to get organized. Some enterprising individual had parked two half-tracks to block the road. Troops were positioned behind them, and McKee saw muzzle flashes as the distance closed. The slugs made pinging sounds as they hit Eason's armor, something tugged at her shoulder, and a tracer whipped through her peripheral vision.

Then they were suddenly airborne as Eason leaped into the air and sailed over the point where the two vehicles met. The cyborg landed hard, and the jolt would have thrown McKee clear if it hadn't been for her harness. As it was, half a dozen grenades flew up out of the ready bags and disappeared into the darkness as the T-1's momentum carried him forward.

McKee looked back in time to see Noll clear the roadblock as well. A flash and the explosion that followed proved that Insa was mastering the use of hand grenades. Then it was time to turn her eyes to the north and try another call. "All Legion forces... All Legion forces. This is Corporal McKee with three T-1s inbound from the south. ETA *two* minutes. Does anyone copy? Over."

There was no response on the battalion push, but when she tried the company-level freq, she got static followed by a partial transmission. "This is Delta-Six," it garbled. "...One helluva fireworks show. Have you now. Outgoing artillery thirty from now. Over."

The sound of the friendly voice made McKee's heart leap. They were close. So close. And it sounded like Delta-Six was calling for an artillery mission. That would effectively slam the door behind them if they could get close enough. But now they were almost upon the Hudathan front line. The point where the aliens were fighting the Legion toe-to-toe. That meant thousands of troops, all of whom were on high alert by that time.

The road had given way to a maze of craters, trenches, and bunkers, which forced Eason to slow down as the Hudathans opened fire. But because the T-1s had crossed the plain so quickly, most of the enemy's crew-operated weapons were pointed north instead of south. That meant most of the stuff coming McKee's way consisted of small-arms fire. But it was bad enough, and she could hear the pinging sounds as bullets flattened themselves against Eason's armor.

The cyborg could shoot back, however, and did. His armor-piercing slugs swept the area ahead and dumped dozens of Hudathan troopers on the ground, as he jumped a dead body. But as Eason came up out of a crater and prepared to make the final run across no-man's-land, his luck ran out. Something big slammed into his chest and holed his armor. The impact was off center, and that saved McKee's life because instead of falling back on top of her the cyborg landed on his side. Eason's voice filled her helmet as McKee hit the quick-release button on her harness. "Looks like this is the end of the line, McKee... Run like hell."

"Bullshit," McKee said as she knelt next to the cyborg and opened a panel at the back of his metal head. "I'm going to jerk your brain box. Stand by to catch some Z's."

"Don't do it," Eason said. "It's heavy and..."

McKee didn't listen to the rest of it as she opened the curved door, took hold of the red T-shaped handle, and gave it a full turn to the right. Then using the same handle, she pulled Eason's Bio-Support Module (BSM) out of its bay. As she did so, McKee knew that sedatives were being pumped into the cyborg's brain.

The BSM was about the size of a .50-caliber ammo box and weighed nearly twenty pounds. It was going to be impossible to carry it and fight. So all McKee could do was cradle the container in her arms and head north. Bullets kicked up puffs of dirt all around her as a wave of Hudathans charged straight at her. Then they wavered as if in response to a strong breeze, and broke twenty feet away. She could see the four-hundred-pound monsters being snatched off their feet as the slugs hit them.

"Don't worry, McKee," Larkin said as Hower passed her. "We've got the point, and Noll has your six. Ain't that right, Noll?"

The last had an edge to it, as if Larkin was concerned that the cyborg might abandon her and was advising against it. Either Noll got the message or didn't need the message; because when McKee glanced over her shoulder, the T-1 was walking backwards, firing toward the south.

McKee turned back, tripped, and fell down. Then, as she got to her feet, a Hudathan rose in front of her. The trooper had been playing dead and, as Hower passed, had seen his chance. Like many Hudathan officers he carried a clan sword, which was raised over his head. As the blade began to fall, McKee raised the brain box and heard a loud *clang* as metal struck metal. The blow was so powerful that she felt the jolt all the way down through her arms and nearly lost the BSM.

Her first thought was for Eason. But the box was made out of heavy-gauge steel and designed to take a beating. However, McKee knew that the enemy officer would beat her down if she stood her ground so she dropped the box and fell backwards.

It seemed to take forever to grab the AXE and bring the weapon up into firing position. The Hudathan was towering over her by then, and the blade was coming down. She jerked the trigger and saw the first bullets hit the alien's crotch. The assault rifle's natural tendency to rise took over at that point, and a steady stream of 4.7mm rounds stitched a line of holes that ran from his pelvis to his breastbone. The sword fell from nerveless fingers, and McKee had to roll out of the way to escape the falling body.

Then it was time to retrieve the brain box, clutch it to her chest, and run toward the point where Hower and Larkin were doing their bloody work. McKee heard a burst of static followed by the same voice that had spoken to her before. "...Six. Keep coming. Arty on the way. Over."

What ensued was both thrilling and frightening. It sounded like a dozen freight trains were rumbling overhead as a curtain of steel fell—and a long line of explosions cut across no-man's-land. Hundreds of Hudathans, all intent on destroying the T-1s, were caught out in the open and cut to pieces. McKee and her legionnaires were safe.

She stumbled through a hole in a long coil of barbed wire, crossed a trench via a wooden plank, and passed a machine-gun emplacement. Half a dozen legionnaires surged forward to greet her. "Eason," she said woodenly. "Here... His BSM."

"Got it," a sergeant said. "Dawkins! Get this brain box to medical on the double!"

Then, turning back to McKee, he said, "*Why?* Why did you do it?"

McKee removed her helmet, ran a hand through her hair, and took a long slow look around. She was alive, and that came as a surprise. "I came to see Colonel Rylund."

"You *what?*"

"I came to see Colonel Rylund."

A lieutenant appeared at that moment. The young woman was about McKee's age. She looked at McKee's face, eyed the scar, and nodded. "You heard the corporal. She came to see the colonel. And, judging from what was required to get here, she has something important to say. Make it happen."

17

Arms is a profession that, if its principles are adhered to for success, requires an officer to do what he fears may be wrong, and yet, according to military experience, must be done, if success is to be attained.

LT. GENERAL THOMAS J. (STONEWALL) JACKSON
A letter to his wife
Standard year 1862

PLANET ORLO II

The journey from no-man's-land up through Riversplit's twisted streets was like a trip through the seven chambers of hell. As McKee, Larkin, and Insa were led past shattered buildings and piles of rubble, they caught glimpses of hollow-eyed civilians crouched around fires, battle-weary legionnaires sleeping wherever they could, and starving dogs peering at them from the shadows. An air-raid siren wailed nearby, the ground shook as bombs landed on the north flank of the hill, and the steady *thump, thump, thump* of AA batteries could be heard all around. "The Hudathans are very methodical," Sergeant Ito explained, as they passed a bombed-out hospital. "They attack twice each day and always at the same times. That might seem stupid, but people know what's coming, and when to expect it. That saps morale."

What Ito said made sense. And McKee wondered if that was because the Hudathans understood human psychology—or because they preferred to run their wars on time. The question remained unanswered as Ito led the threesome to the half-burned wreckage of what had been Governor Jones's mansion. McKee winced as she remembered the moment when Jones, Cia, and Marcy had been murdered.

Jivv! The thought was enough to send what felt like ice water trickling into her veins. Was the synth *here*? In Riversplit? And what about Spurlock? Could he be waiting for her as well? McKee thought about the memory mod Avery had given her and wondered if his testimony would do any good. That didn't seem likely if Spurlock had any say.

Those thoughts and more ran through her mind as Ito led the group back along the side of the building to the point where two sentries were on duty. After talking to the guards, the noncom led the party down a flight of stairs to a pair of blastproof doors. They opened into a small vestibule that served as a light lock. Once the outer doors were closed, the inner ones could be opened.

Ito removed his helmet, and McKee did likewise as they followed a hall to what a hand-printed sign proclaimed to be the COMMAND CENTER. The dimly lit room was quite large. A flat-screen mosaic covered one of the walls. Some views featured live footage that was streaming in from helmet cams and surveillance drones while others remained dark.

But if that was ominous, the quiet professionalism with which the people in the room went about their jobs gave McKee reason to hope. Most of the activity was centered around a three-dimensional holo tank. And there, within the semitransparent representation of Riversplit, dozens of miniature battles were being waged. Judging from the snatches of conversation she overheard, it appeared that there was some localized radio communication. But old-fashioned runners were being used as well—and that meant a constant flow of foot traffic.

McKee's observations were interrupted as a captain came forward to greet the newcomers. He had dark skin, tired eyes, and a ready smile. Somehow, in spite of the conditions in Riversplit, he had contrived to shave, press his uniform, and polish his brass. Was that the mark of a professional? Or a butt-kissing REMF? McKee waited to find out as the officer introduced himself. "I'm Captain Kinzo. I know Ito here... And you must be Corporal McKee. You and your cyborgs lit up our screens! We knew something was happening when the fireworks started. Once we figured out what was going on, everyone cheered! The last bit scared the crap out of us, though. Still, as I understand it, your entire party made it through, so all's well that ends well. Perhaps you'd be so kind as to introduce your companions."

"This is Private Larkin," McKee said, "and this is Insa. He wants to confer with Colonel Rylund regarding the alliance that Captain Avery negotiated with the Droi people."

Kinzo's eyebrows rose. "Avery is still alive? I'm pleased to hear it."

Then, having turned to Insa, he said, "It's an honor to meet you. It took extraordinary courage to come here, and we appreciate it. Colonel Rylund is tied up right now—but wants to meet with you the moment his conference is over."

"That good," Insa said stolidly. "I wait."

"Excellent," Kinza said smoothly. "There are refreshments on the table over there. Please help yourselves." And with that, the officer walked away.

Conscious of the fact that Spurlock and/or Jivv could appear at any moment, McKee scanned the room. Thankfully, neither one of her enemies was present. That left her free to visit the buffet. It was intended to serve those who worked in the command center.

Larkin was visibly disappointed. "There's nothing left," he complained, and he was correct. Most of the trays were empty or very nearly so. The exception was a platter loaded with two dozen sweet rolls that arrived while they were standing there.

Larkin grabbed three while McKee and Insa helped themselves to one each. She took her pastry plus a mug of lukewarm coffee over to a table and sat down. Insa took a sip of the caf, made a face, and spit the liquid back into the cup. "Sorry," he said. "Need tea."

But there wasn't any tea, so Insa settled for water instead. Having finished the roll, McKee allowed her head to rest on the wall behind her. What felt like two seconds passed before Larkin woke her up. "Rise 'n' shine, Corporal... The colonel wants to see us."

McKee yawned, glanced at her chrono, and saw that twenty minutes had elapsed since the beginning of her impromptu nap. Captain Kinzo was waiting. "Sorry, sir," McKee said as she came to her feet.

"No problem," Kinzo replied. "That's how it is around here. We sleep when we can. Come on... The colonel is available."

McKee, Larkin, and Insa followed the officer across the room to an open door. Kinzo knocked before looking in. "Corporal McKee, sir. Along with Representative Insa and Private Larkin."

McKee took note of the title that Kinzo had bestowed on Insa and the way he provided Rylund with all of their names. It was, she realized, the sort of thing her father's secretary always did for him. Was Mr. Wong still alive? Or had he been murdered, too? She hoped not.

McKee heard Rylund say, "Enter," and followed Kinzo into an office which, judging from the way it was decorated, had been intended for use by Governor Jones. Rylund wasn't smoking, but the aroma of cherry-flavored pipe tobacco permeated the room. She was shocked to see how much Rylund had aged during the last month or so. "Corporal McKee," he said as he circled the ornate desk. "You've been busy since the last time I saw you."

Did Rylund *really* remember her? Or had he been briefed by Kinzo? McKee decided that it didn't matter as the officer shook her hand and went on to welcome Larkin and Insa. Somehow, Rylund knew that a bow was called for where the Droi was concerned and was familiar with the greeting ritual as well. "I see you, Insa."

"And I, you," Insa replied solemnly.

"You are welcome here," Rylund said formally. "Please have a seat. I am anxious to speak with you. But I'd like to ask McKee for a report first. Would that be agreeable?"

"Insa wait," the Droi said, and sat on one of the well-padded chairs. Rylund rested his weight on the corner of the desk while McKee stood at something approximating parade rest. Larkin was behind her, and she hoped he was behaving himself.

"I know Captain Avery sent you here for a reason," Rylund said. "But, before we get into that, I'd like to know how the mission to find Governor Jones went. And get a readout on the battalion. We could use some more troops."

McKee felt a profound sense of relief. Spurlock was still MIA—and very likely dead. And so, for that matter, was Jivv. Were it otherwise, Rylund would know, or at least *think* that he knew, what had occurred. So she could describe the situation in whatever way she chose. But *how*? Should she tell Rylund *everything*? Her real identity, what Jivv had done, and Spurlock's complicity in three homicides? Or should she lie by providing a narrative that omitted any mention of her role in the governor's escape, the fact that she had witnessed his death, and subsequently been charged with a long list of crimes? Remembering that whatever she did would affect Avery as well.

Rylund was staring at her, and McKee realized that at least five seconds had passed. She cleared her throat, and said, "Sir, yes sir." What followed was a report that was accurate in every respect except where her activities were concerned. The way she told the story, the governor and his party managed to escape on their own, were recaptured, and disappeared shortly thereafter. She wasn't sure, but rumor had it that they had been killed by Jivv and the bodies disposed of.

Rylund winced when he heard that but didn't seem terribly surprised, and said, "Go on."

McKee was committed to her lie by that time and knew that both Larkin and Insa could contradict her account if they chose to. It was tempting to look at them, but she managed to resist. She said, "Yes, sir," and resumed the narrative. The balance of the report was much easier to give. McKee told Rylund about how the battalion had been ambushed on the bridge, the EMP bomb, and how Avery had assumed command.

"What happened to Lieutenant Colonel Spurlock?" Rylund demanded.

"He disappeared during the fighting, sir," McKee replied. "Along with Monitor Jivv."

Rylund looked at Kinzo. "You're recording this?"

Kinzo pointed at one of the cameras located in a corner of the room. "Yes, sir."

"Good," Rylund said as he turned back to McKee. "Please continue."

McKee's throat felt dry. Her lies were being recorded. And if either Spurlock or Jivv came back from the dead, the report would be used against her. "Yes, sir. That's where Representative Insa comes in. It was his forces who, with the help of a rebel agent named Trask, set the ambush. They captured us. That was when Captain Avery and Representative Insa began to discuss the possibility of an alliance."

Rylund turned to Insa. His voice was stern. "I find myself in a difficult position. You and your people killed some of my legionnaires. Yet Corporal McKee says that you are interested in forming an alliance. What should I believe?"

"Hate Hudathans," Insa said. "Kill."

Rylund smiled grimly. "You are the first diplomat in my experience to word a response so clearly and succinctly. And I agree with your sentiment."

Kinzo cleared his throat at that point. "Excuse me, sir, but judging from the expression on Private Larkin's face, he wants to say something."

McKee turned to look and saw that Kinzo was correct. She'd seen that expression before. The frown, the squinty eyes, and the downturned mouth were all signs of an impending eruption. And there was no way to know what the volatile legionnaire would say. "Is that correct?" Rylund inquired politely. "If so, get whatever it is off your chest."

McKee's heart fell as Larkin spoke. "The corporal left some stuff out, sir. Important stuff."

"Oh, really," Rylund responded with a raised eyebrow. "Please enlighten us."

"Well," Larkin began, "McKee mentioned the EMP blast, and what it did to the cyborgs, but she didn't tell you who got them up and running again."

Rylund smiled. "Corporal McKee?"

"Damned straight, sir, begging your pardon. She's better than all of our techs, and she never went to school!"

McKee groaned internally. In his effort to make sure she received credit for repairing the T-1s, Larkin had opened a door that she wanted to keep closed. "That's very impressive," Rylund said. "Thank you, Private. It seems that the corporal is far too modest. So, McKee, how do you account for your skills?"

McKee's eyes were fixed on a point directly over the officer's head. She decided that the best course was to tell the same lie she had used before. "I worked in the factory that makes T-1s prior to joining the Legion, sir."

"And we failed to offer you a tech slot?"

"No, sir. I want to fight. Sir."

Rylund chuckled. "Most techs would take exception to that comment, but I understand. It seems that Captain Avery made a good decision when he recommended you for corporal. And I was smart enough to approve his recommendation." That was news to McKee, who didn't know that Rylund was even aware of such trivial matters. "So an alliance was formed," Rylund said. "What then?"

Rylund listened to the rest of it without interrupting her.

That included McKee's account of the trip through the forest, her observations from the hilltop, and the decision to charge straight in. Once the narrative was over, Rylund shook his head in amazement. "That took imagination and guts," he said. "I'm glad you made it. I'm going to instruct Captain Kinzo to put all five of you in for decorations. And, as of today, you can add another chevron to your arm. We can't have corporals leading cavalry charges. It makes the rest of us look bad."

The promotion to sergeant came as a shock. And McKee knew she didn't deserve it. "Thank you, sir. But I don't think…"

"Sergeants *do* think," Rylund said. "Well, they're supposed to anyway. Now let's bring Representative Insa back into this conversation. I'd like to know how many warriors he can bring to bear on the situation, how they're armed, and where they are."

The officers spent the next thirty minutes quizzing Insa about the Droi and their capacity to fight. According to Insa, there were at least ten thousand warriors within a three-hundred-mile radius of Riversplit. Of course, that number was a bit deceiving because while *all* of the Droi were considered to be warriors, they were also hermaphrodites, and that meant some of them had parental responsibilities. Plus, some of the population was too old or too ill to fight. Those factors brought the number of effectives down to something like five thousand Droi. Not as many as Rylund would have liked but a respectable force nevertheless.

But because the Droi were lightly armed, and lacked the supplies required for a protracted conflict, it was clear that they wouldn't be able to do much more than harass the Hudathans. Still, anything that took pressure off Riversplit would be welcome.

But as the Q & A session came to an end, it was clear that Rylund planned to do something more than prolong the existing standoff. "Thank you, Representative Insa. Your forces would be no match in a head-to-head battle with the Hudathans. But there's more than one way to win a war. And the Droi could be a critical element in winning this one.

"Take a look at this," Rylund said as he pointed a remote at a large wall screen. Video blossomed and resolved itself into an aerial map. "Once the fleet withdrew, the Hudathans destroyed our surveillance satellites," Rylund said, "so this image is a few weeks old. But the basics are there."

"Excuse me, sir," McKee said. "I'm not sure that Representative Insa is familiar with satellite maps."

"Thank you, Sergeant... Good point."

Rylund provided Insa with a short tutorial and, as with so many things, the Droi demonstrated a remarkable capacity to make complex things seem simple. "Like looking from treetop," it said. "Only higher."

Rylund grinned. "Exactly. So here's where we are." As he pointed the remote at the map, a red dot appeared and described circles around Riversplit. "And here," he continued, "is the river from which the city takes its name. You'll notice that as we follow it westward, we come to *this* structure, which is the Howari Dam. It supplies power to the area—or did until the shovel heads cut the transmission lines. And *here*, backed up behind it, are some 3 million cubic yards of water. I'll bet Sergeant McKee can tell us why that's important."

McKee had already noticed the topography and come to the conclusion that the dam had been constructed to provide something more than power. "It looks like the Hudathans are sitting on a floodplain, sir. It's my guess that the dam is used to keep the area dry. So if we could blow it, a wall of water would surge down the valley and sweep the enemy away. Everything but the city of Riversplit."

"Exactly," Rylund said as his eyes darted from face to face. "And the Hudathans aren't stupid. They know that. And they know that the dam could be quite useful to them after they win the war. That's why they spared it."

"We tried to blow the dam right after the navy withdrew," Kinzo interjected. "A full platoon of commandos from the 2nd REP went in. Only one of them made it back."

McKee looked at Insa, but the Droi appeared to be unfazed. And when it held out a hand, Rylund surrendered the remote. "Look," Insa said. "Here and here. Forest all around. We come. We kill."

Rylund smiled grimly as he lit his pipe. His words emerged with puffs of smoke. "That's what I hoped you would say. And I believe such an attack will work providing that you have the right kind of support. That would be Captain Avery, Sergeant McKee, and what remains of Echo Company."

Insa nodded. "That good. Like Avery. Like McKee."

"Excellent. The trick will be to get all of you out of Riversplit without another cavalry charge. It worked once, but it won't work twice. Captain Kinzo will find a place where you can grab some shut-eye. We'll get to work on the necessary logistics."

The meeting came to an end at that point, which was a considerable relief to McKee since she'd been terrified throughout. She had lied not once, but numerous times, and emerged unscathed. That was a miracle, or so it seemed to her.

A private gave each of them an MRE and led them out of the command center. A narrow staircase took them up to a warren of small offices that had been assigned to the governor's staff. They had been repurposed in the wake of the Hudathan attack and now served as what the private referred to as "rack rooms."

McKee was given a space of her own, but Larkin and Insa were assigned to the same space. Bunk beds had been installed, and Larkin wasted no time in claiming the lower slot for himself. McKee was too tired to intervene and left Insa to fend for himself as she entered the room assigned to her and locked the door. After stashing her helmet and AXE in a corner, she was thrilled to discover that the former office had a tiny bathroom, complete with a shower.

Having stripped off her body armor and filthy clothes, she stepped into the shower only to discover that the water was cold, and the previous occupant had left little more than a wafer of soap behind. But even that was heavenly.

Ten minutes later, having dried herself off with a scratchy towel, McKee did something she hadn't done before. There was a mirror, a small one to be sure, but a mirror nonetheless. By turning her back to it and looking over her shoulder, she could see the damage inflicted there. The raised ridges made a crisscross pattern on her previously unblemished flesh. They were ugly, like snakes crawling under her skin, and she burst into tears. Unable to bear the sight anymore, she turned out the light, fell onto the bed, and hugged a pillow to her chest. Tears flowed, and sobs racked her body, until sleep bore her away.

The sun was up, and the sky was blue, but War Commander Ona-Ka didn't care. He took no pleasure from sunny days— and never felt depressed when it rained. For him, weather was a variable and nothing more. And as the half-track bore him along the main highway that led to Riversplit, he was glad that his tanks wouldn't have mud to cope with. For the most part he liked what he saw. The regiment's vehicle parks were safely beyond the range of the Legion's largest guns, its supplies were stored in well-constructed bunkers, and the troops marching along the side of the road were in good condition.

But for some unfathomable reason three of the Legion's cyborgs had been allowed to run unopposed down the highway the night before. That was why he was on the ground a few miles south of Riversplit. He wanted to see the damage the humans had inflicted firsthand—and make sure such a travesty never happened again. Though not a crippling blow, the loss of personnel and materials was painful because of the long supply line he had to deal with. So as the half-track came to a stop near the remains of three burned-out transports, he was in a bad mood.

Commander Urlo-Ba was among those who were waiting for him along with Lance Commander Horba-Sa, who had responsibility for that sector. All of the officers came to attention and remained that way until Ona-Ka said, "At ease.

"So," Ona-Ka said without any preliminaries, "they broke through the roadblock south of here, ran up the highway, and destroyed all three of these vehicles. How is such a thing possible?"

"It was my understanding that the area to the rear had been secured," Horba-Sa replied.

"Do you read the intelligence reports that come your way twice a day?"

The truth was that Horba-Sa was extremely busy, and one of his subordinates did that for him. But he couldn't say so. "Yes, I do."

"Then you noticed that during the day prior to the attack a drone spotted three cyborgs traveling north—and a gunship was sent to intercept them."

It was a trap, but Horba-Sa *had* read the Intel summary prepared by his subordinate. "That's true," he replied, "and the gunship reported that the targets were destroyed."

"The gunship's crew was wrong," Ona-Ka replied coldly. "Of course, you had no way to know that. But surely you wondered where the cyborgs had come from—and why they were headed north. So you sent a team to recover the bodies on the chance that we could learn something from them. Correct?"

That wasn't correct. Horba-Sa had assumed the cyborgs were stragglers who hoped to rejoin Legion forces. The possibility that they might be on a mission of some sort had never occurred to him. So there had been no reason to retrieve the bodies. He forced himself to meet Ona-Ka's implacable gaze. "No, I didn't."

Ona-Ka nodded. "That's what I thought. I'm relieving you of command. Which would you prefer? A court-martial or a voluntary reduction in rank to file leader?"

Horba-Sa knew that a court-martial might clear him, but the chances were slim. And if the decision went against him, the outcome could be far worse than a loss of rank. He swallowed. "I request a reduction in rank to file leader."

Ona-Ka held out a hand. Horba-Sa removed the glowing command stone from the center of his combat harness and gave it over. The jewel felt cold in Ona-Ka's hand. Ona-Ka took no pleasure in bringing the other officer down. What he wanted was information. *Why* would three cyborgs and their riders risk their lives to enter Riversplit? The answer could mean something or nothing at all.

After six hours of sleep, McKee was woken by someone pounding on the door and the news that she was scheduled to attend a briefing in half an hour. She took another cold shower, put on the same filthy uniform, and collected her gear. Larkin was waiting in the hall. Even though his face was bruised, he was trying to look nonchalant. A square-jawed MP was standing next to him. "Sergeant McKee?"

"Yes?"

"Private Larkin found his way into a private club a mile from here, had too much to drink, and started a fight."

"I won," Larkin said proudly.

"Under normal conditions, we would lock his ass up," the MP said. "But we were told to hand him over to you."

McKee nodded. "I'll take care of it."

Larkin made a face and grinned.

The MP scowled and left. McKee turned to Larkin. "Where's your gear?"

"In my room."

"Get it. We're supposed to be in a briefing right now."

"What? No lecture?"

"Would it do any good?"

"No."

"That's what I thought. Move."

Ten minutes later, they arrived in the command center, where Insa and Kinzo were waiting for them. McKee apologized for being late but got the impression that the officer knew all about Larkin's late-night adventures and was content to leave the matter in her hands. "We recruited some specialists for you," Kinzo said. "People who are good at blowing things up. This will be an opportunity to meet them, study the dam, and lay some initial plans. Then we'll load your team onto the last assault boat we have and fly you back to Avery. He'll be in command of the mission, but you'll provide advice where the bridge is concerned. So pay attention. Any questions?"

"Yes, sir. How about our 'borgs? Are they coming with us?"

"That's affirmative. You'll need them."

"And Eason, sir? How's he doing?"

"Raring to go," Kinzo said with a grin. "We gave him a reconditioned war form, and he claims that you would be helpless without him."

McKee felt a tremendous sense of relief. "Thank you, sir."

Kinzo nodded and led them into a conference room already full of legionnaires. The same aerial photo she'd seen before was up on a screen. The mission had begun.

Shortly after overwhelming the city, the Legion had taken over the rebel air base that was located deep inside the hill that Riversplit was built on. Now, after weeks of fighting, there was only one airworthy ship left—and that was a fly-form named Kris Kelly.

The cyborg's combat-scarred body was crouched under a battery of bright lights as McKee, Insa, Larkin, and the rest of the team made their way up a steep ramp and into Kelly's cargo compartment. Eason and the other T-1s were present, as were the demolition experts Rylund had selected for the mission. They included Staff Sergeant Randy Petit, Corporal Mary Muncy, and Private Christian Yamada. All were traveling with crates full of explosives. But if they were nervous about riding a target loaded with HE, they showed no signs of it.

And that, McKee knew, was the way she should appear. Calm, cool, and collected. The problem was that she was scared—and for good reason. The Hudathans owned the air over and around Riversplit. So once the bombproof door opened, and Kelly shot out over the plain, all sorts of hell was going to break loose. And every shovel head who could would open fire.

Rylund and his people knew that, of course. So they were

going to launch drones that were rigged to broadcast electronic signatures identical to Kelly's. The hope was that the decoys would draw most of the fire.

That was good. But would it be enough? Noll, dour as usual, had referred to the escape plan as "a glorified crapshoot." And for once he was right. No matter how many decoys they launched, and no matter how skilled Kelly was, survival would be a matter of luck.

And pointless though it might seem, she didn't want to embarrass herself moments before she died. So she took refuge inside her noncom persona and pretended to fall asleep. Sergeant Petit was seated directly across from her. If she looked at him, McKee was afraid that he would see the fear in her eyes. Plus, if she survived somehow, people would think she was cool under fire. A definite advantage for a sergeant known as the Steel Bitch.

Servos whined as the hatch closed, and Kelly's voice came over the intercom. It was surprisingly cheerful. "Strap in, and if you know some good prayers, this would be the time to say them."

Then, without further ado, the cyborg fired her repellers. McKee felt the fly-form lift off, turn toward the door that was already sliding open, and start to accelerate. What followed was like a very violent amusement-park ride. There were no viewports, so she wouldn't have been able to see had her eyes been open. But she could *feel*. And that was bad enough.

G-forces threw her sideways as Kelly shot out of the hill and into the darkness beyond. That was followed by a momentary drop as the cyborg entered a steep dive. Then, just when it seemed as if they would crash, the pilot pulled up. She was flying fifty feet above the ground at that point, an altitude so low that it would prevent the Hudathans from launching SAMs or employing their AA batteries. But there was nothing to stop the enemy from firing small arms. And as the fly-form passed over them, they opened up with rocket launchers, RPGs, and automatic weapons.

McKee could hear clanging sounds as projectiles hit the hull, and felt the ship slew from side to side as Kelly pursued a zigzag course toward the south, strafing the Hudathans as she went.

"Take that!" the pilot shouted over the intercom, and McKee felt the airframe shudder as a flight of six rockets sped toward whatever target Kelly had chosen.

Then the ship flipped sideways, and Kelly produced a whoop of joy as she sped past the same hill that McKee and Larkin had climbed two nights earlier. A few moments later the fly-form leveled out and rose slightly as a two-thousand-pound bomb fell away and tumbled toward the ground.

McKee knew the purpose of the ensuing explosion was to trick the Hudathans into believing that the ship had been destroyed. An impression Kelly would reinforce by engaging a pair of jury-rigged suppressors, which, if they worked, would conceal the heat produced by her engines.

But because the suppressors were designed for use by a smaller aircraft, they were sure to blow before very long— making it imperative to land as quickly as possible. Fortunately, the Droi encampment was only minutes from Riversplit by air. And as Sergeant McKee peered out through slitted eyes, she could feel the fly-form sinking as Kelly prepared to land. That was when she realized she was not only alive but likely to stay that way for a while.

Confident that she wasn't about to reveal how frightened she had been, she opened her eyes, produced an elaborate yawn, and stretched her arms. Petit nodded. "Have a nice nap?"

McKee offered what she hoped was a nonchalant grin. "Hell, no. I dreamed I was on an assault boat piloted by a maniac."

Those close enough to hear laughed as Kelly's voice came over the intercom. "I heard that... Ten to dirt."

The skids hit with a thud. The engines had begun to spool down as the hatch whirred open, allowing humid air to flood the cargo compartment. McKee released her harness and stood. The lights were dim, but there was no mistaking Avery's countenance as he arrived at the top of the ramp and looked from face to face. She knew he was looking for her. A theory that was confirmed when he spotted her, and she saw the look of relief in his eyes.

But only for a moment. Then Avery was all business as McKee introduced the demolition experts. Once that was accomplished,

Avery thanked Insa and each member of the team before leading them off the fly-form.

Larkin and the T-1s were released at that point, but Avery asked Insa, McKee, and the demolition experts to join him around a small fire. The next couple of hours were spent bringing the officer up to speed and discussing the mission.

Finally, once the meeting was over, and the others were gone, McKee and Avery were alone. The sun was rising by then, and eyes were everywhere, so they couldn't touch. But they could talk, and did. "What you did was crazy," Avery began disapprovingly.

"I couldn't figure out any other way to get the job done," McKee replied simply.

"And now you're a sergeant."

"A very inexperienced one, but a sergeant, yes."

"Well, Sergeant, I have news for you. *Good* news."

"Which is?"

"Follow me. I'll show you."

The Droi had been working to camouflage Kelly's fly-form for hours by then, and it was half-covered by a blanket of freshly cut vegetation. The greenery would turn brown within two rotations, however, which meant that it would have to be renewed, or the Droi would have to abandon their encampment. Having agreed to the second option, hundreds of indigs were already streaming into the forest as Avery led her into a small clearing. Two mounds of recently dug earth could be seen lying side by side. Only one of them was distinguished by a wooden marker. "There they are," Avery said. "Spurlock and Jivv."

It took McKee a moment to absorb the news. Spurlock and Jivv really were dead—just as she had hoped. "How did you find them?"

"I didn't," Avery replied. "A Droi hunting party brought them in. Spurlock was dead, having refused an opportunity to surrender, and Jivv was alive."

She looked from Avery to the graves and back again.

"Was?"

"I shot it," Avery said simply. "Twice."

McKee looked at him. What he felt was clear to see. He had a motive to kill Jivv just as she did. But he'd been trying to protect her as well. And that brought all sorts of emotions into play. Suddenly, she was in his arms, knowing that they shouldn't kiss, and knowing that they would. As their bodies came together, and their lips met, a bird chattered somewhere up above. And for that brief moment in time, McKee was happy.

18

In battle, however, there are not more than two methods of
attack—the direct and the indirect; yet these two in combination
give rise to an endless series of maneuvers.

SUN TZU
The Art of War
Standard year circa 500 B.C.

PLANET ORLO II

Most Droi lived to be about seventy years of age unless disease
or some other misfortune took them earlier. And Aba was sixty-
five. An age when it was increasingly difficult to run, climb, or
hunt. Because of that, Aba and the other elders were always the
last to leave the current encampment and arrive at the next one.
And old age had taught Aba to accept many things, including
the role of guardian for its progeny's progeny, a child named
Ola. An energetic youngster who was hard to keep track of.

The warriors and the humans had left the day before, leaving
the very old and the very young to follow along behind. Except
that Aba couldn't follow without Ola—and the little rascal was
missing. That left Aba with no choice but to shoulder the animal-
hide pack, sling its ancient rifle, and wander through the mostly
deserted encampment calling the little one's name. "Ola? Can
you hear me? It's time to leave."

Finally, after ten minutes of searching, Aba heard a high-pitched voice. "I'm over here, Aba… Eating telsa berries."

Telsa berries were sweet when ripe and a favorite among juveniles. Aba followed the voice into a clearing where it looked around. Ola was nowhere to be seen. "I'm up here!" Ola shouted. And sure enough, there it was, up in a Telsa tree.

"Come down," Aba ordered sternly, "and I mean *now*."

Ola knew that tone of voice and quickly slid to the ground. Then, with berry juice still smeared all over its face, the child apologized. "Sorry, Aba. Can I carry something for you?"

Aba had just opened its mouth to reply when a hand shot up out of the ground and took hold of Ola's ankle. A head, torso, and arms appeared as the youngster screamed and tried to pull away. The thing *looked* human; but Aba knew it wasn't human because the Droi had seen the creature before. Right after the hunters brought it in and immediately before the human shot it in the head. The bullet holes were still visible. But now, by some means Aba couldn't understand, the machine had come back to life.

Aba pointed the rifle and jerked the trigger. The firing pin fell on an empty chamber. For reasons of safety, all weapons not carried by guards were kept unloaded while the Droi were staying in an encampment. Aba was reaching for a magazine when the monster spoke. "Don't move. I'll kill the child if you do."

Aba watched in horror as it rose from the grave. Dirt cascaded off the creature as it stood. "But you dead," Aba objected. "I see human kill."

"It took a while for my systems to repair themselves," Jivv replied as the robot looked around. "Where did all of your people go? I see very few heat signatures."

"They go to dam," Ola said brightly.

Aba cursed silently. The Droi had planned to give the machine directions to an imaginary encampment and send it off into the forest. That was impossible now. And while a Droi or a human might have asked, "What dam?" the machine seemed to know.

"What about the humans?" it demanded. "Did they go to the dam as well?"

Aba had no choice and nodded mutely.

The machine gestured for the Droi to come closer. "Give me the rifle and ammunition."

Aba remained where it was. "And then?"

"Then I will free the child, and we go our separate ways."

Aba didn't like it. Not one little bit. But what choice did it have? Slowly, step by step, the oldster moved forward. The machine let go of Ola in order to accept the rifle and ammunition. The child scampered away. "What do?" Aba inquired.

"I'm going to find fugitive 2999 and kill her," Jivv replied. And with that, the Synth started to run.

The sun was past its zenith, and rays of dusty sunshine slanted down through the trees as about fifteen hundred Droi and forty-two legionnaires made their way through the forest. It was relatively slow going because of Avery's decision to avoid the jungle trails. McKee understood his logic. As she knew from personal experience, the Hudathans routinely sent drones along any path they could identify, and based on reports from Droi scouts, the ridge heads were placing tiny sensor packages along the most-traveled thoroughfares. A strategy that was bound to produce thousands of high-def wildlife photos. Of course, computers could and would be employed to sort through the incoming images for those that had intelligence value.

So even though each individual was forced to pursue a zigzag course through the trees, and to consume more energy while doing so, McKee knew that the combined force was less likely to be spotted thanks to Avery's approach. And the element of surprise would be critical to success.

Such were her thoughts as she and her squad followed a contingent of Droi warriors in a northwesterly direction. The trees limited what she could see, so most of the battalion was invisible to her and, if the strategy was working, to the enemy as well.

There weren't enough T-1s to go around, so the bio bods had been ordered to rotate. The idea was to keep the bio bods, especially the demolition experts, rested. And at the moment, she was walking while Petit rode Eason.

Of course, not all of her thoughts were strictly professional. Avery was on her mind as well. It felt good to have somebody in her life. But the pleasure came at a price. Because if Avery made her feel good, his existence represented a threat to her happiness as well. What if he were killed? As hundreds if not thousands would be.

To have established another emotional connection only to have it severed would be extremely hard to take. That's why it was better to keep her distance from everyone. That and the fact that officers weren't allowed to have romantic relationships with enlisted people. Especially subordinates.

But like a leaf that falls into a stream, McKee was powerless to control where she went or what happened next. All she could do was help blow the dam. Everything else was beyond her reach.

The afternoon wore on, and as the sun dropped lower in the sky, Avery ordered a halt. Although the Hudathans were still jamming, the squad-level push was working okay except for momentary bursts of static. So Avery was able to communicate his wishes to the legionnaires electronically, while Insa passed orders to his people via runners and shrill whistles. A system which, thanks to codes worked out over hundreds of years, was quite effective.

The battalion was about five miles short of the dam at that point. That meant they would have to march for a couple of hours early the next morning. But to camp any closer would be to risk detection from the drones that patrolled the area.

In keeping with orders given prior to departure, humans and Droi alike made hundreds of tiny one-, two-, and three-person camps. And other than well-contained tea fires, none of them were allowed to cook. All in an effort to conceal the battalion from the eyes in the sky.

But before McKee or her bio bods could eat, they had to perform maintenance on the T-1s. So it was an hour and a half later before they could break out their MREs, light a fuel tab, and heat their dinners. She didn't know where Avery was—but thought he might drop by. He didn't.

McKee felt a sense of disappointment, scolded herself for being so self-centered, and set out to make the rounds. Her squad included bio bods Larkin, Caskin, and a private named Donobi. The cyborgs who had accompanied her to Riversplit were still with her—and a T-1 named Farber had been added to the roster. That meant she had seven people to worry about plus Sergeant Petit, Corporal Muncy, and Private Yamada, who were not only attached to the squad but under her orders until they arrived at the dam. During the tour she stopped to talk with each individual and was pleased to find that morale was pretty good, all things considered.

The only thing that worried her was the fact that with more than fifteen hundred people spread out over what must have been a square mile of jungle, there was no defensive perimeter. But that couldn't be helped because if the battalion were to create a marching camp, it would attract attention. All they could do was maintain a low profile and hope for the best.

Night always fell earlier in the forest, so it was nearly dark by the time McKee returned to the clearing where she had started. Her heart jumped when she saw that Avery was sitting with his back to a tree eating his dinner. He looked up and smiled as she approached. The words were formal, and had to be with members of her squad all about. But there was no denying the warmth in his eyes. "Welcome back, Sergeant... How are the troops?"

"Hower's knee coupler is about ready for replacement," McKee replied. "But it should hold up long enough to complete the mission. Other than that, all of our people are in good shape."

Avery grinned. "Even Noll?"

"Private Noll is of the opinion that we could use a thousand additional troops."

Avery nodded soberly. "And Private Noll is correct. But we'll have to get along without them."

McKee lowered herself to the ground and sat cross-legged. "Yes, sir. How are the Droi holding up?"

Avery made a face. "Insa's people are doing well. But communication with the northern tribe is spotty—and the two groups have a long history of mutual animosity to overcome. So things are a bit dicey at times."

McKee knew that could be a significant problem because the northerners were slated to attack first—and draw the Hudathans off the top of the dam and into the forest. An environment where the Droi warriors would have a much better chance to whittle the off-worlders down. Meanwhile, Avery's battalion would attack from the south, sweep out onto the dam, and hold it long enough for the demolition team to do its work. "I'm sorry to hear that, sir."

Avery shrugged. "It will work or it won't. All we can do is try. We'll know how things went by this time tomorrow."

McKee knew he wanted to say more but couldn't. She looked him in the eye. "Watch your six, sir."

Avery nodded. "You too, Sergeant. You too."

Given what would be expected of them in the morning, Avery had allowed McKee's squad to sleep uninterrupted. But doubts about her capacity to live up to her own expectations during the coming battle, and the knowledge that she might be dead in a few hours, prevented her from getting much rest. And Larkin's snoring didn't help either.

So when her wrist chrono began to beep, she was already awake. It was still dark and would be for hours yet. After stowing the sleep sack and brushing her teeth, she went out to make the rounds. Then, having assured herself that everyone was up, she forced herself to eat. It wasn't easy because her stomach felt queasy, but she knew that her body was going to need fuel.

After eating what she could and mustering her squad, McKee waited for the order to move out. It was supposed to come at 0400. But that hour came and went with nothing except static on the radio. Finally, at 0417, Avery's voice flooded her helmet. "Echo-Nine to Echo-Four. Over."

McKee chinned the transmit switch. "This is Four... Over."

"Our friends were running late," Avery said matter-of-factly. "But they're in position. You can move out. Over."

The northerners had clearly been operating on what the humans privately referred to as "Droi time."

"Roger that," McKee replied. "Moving out. Over."

Colonel Rylund and his staff had done a masterful job of anticipating what the combined force would need in order to carry out their mission. And that included hundreds of glow sticks that had been loaded onto Kelly for the flight south—and subsequently distributed to the Droi scouts. Having activated the luminescent rods and stuck them down the back of their waistbands, selected warriors could lead the rest of the force forward in spite of the darkness. And given how critical their functions were, McKee and her people had their own contingent of scouts whose sole responsibility was to guide the legionnaires to their objective.

McKee's job was to follow the bobbing lights, keep her squad closed up tight, and deliver the demolition team to the target. The task sounded simple. But she discovered that it was difficult to distinguish *her* scouts from the others, some of whom were slated to veer off in different directions. So she called the warriors back and issued each one of them an additional glow rod. That made the task of identifying them much easier as the battalion crept forward.

It took more than an hour to reach the first checkpoint, which was a quarter mile short of the dam. Then it was time to go to ground and wait until given the order to advance. McKee followed Wellington's advice to "Piss when you can," eyed her chrono, and wondered what Avery was doing.

Avery was at the very front of the formation, with Insa at his side. The dam had been built across a narrow gorge, and as the first blush of dawn appeared in the east, they could look down on it from a rocky promontory directly to the south. Two Hudathan sentries had been stationed there, and both had been killed by arrows launched from twenty feet away. That was how close the jungle-savvy Droi could come without being detected. But the sentries would be missed, so the clock was ticking as Avery studied the structure in front of him.

He'd seen it all before, of course, but only secondhand, via the electronic images that McKee had brought back from Riversplit. But his current angle was different, and he could see more detail. Thanks to the documentation provided by Rylund's staff, Avery knew he was looking at an arch-gravity dam. Meaning a dam that curves upstream, thereby pushing most of the water against the walls of the canyon. It was a strategy calculated to compress and strengthen the dam.

A semicircular road sat atop the dam, and six Hudathan AA batteries were positioned along it. They hadn't been present in the preinvasion satellite photos he'd seen, so it was clear that defenses had been improved in the wake of the first attack on the dam. Plenty of troops could be seen even at that early hour. After a quick head count, Avery concluded that there were at least 150 Hudathans on top of the bridge—and it seemed safe to assume that there were at least that many inside it. Airborne drones were visible as well, sniffing about like so many hound dogs, searching for a scent. Insa interrupted Avery's train of thought by touching his arm. "Northern tribe ready."

Avery tilted the glasses up to examine the area north of the dam. He could see rocky walls and the jungle beyond but nothing more. And that was the way it was supposed to be. The Droi were hidden and would remain that way until he gave the order for them to attack. But there was a problem he had to deal with first. The drones were not only armed but would continue to send video to the Hudathan HQ so long as they were operational, and the less information the shovel heads received, the better. "Echo-Nine to Echo-Six," Avery said. "Execute."

There were two *clicks* by way of a response. Half a minute later, a thermite grenade sailed out of the jungle, hit the access road, and took a single bounce before detonating inches off the pavement. Once it started to burn, the device generated a lot of heat. So much heat that every drone within half a mile of the grenade rushed to respond. Therefore, it was only a matter of seconds before fifteen or twenty of the machines were jostling each other for position as they sought to "see" what was taking place.

That was when a dozen shoulder-launched fire-and-forget rockets shot out of the jungle and struck their targets. The explosions came in such quick succession that they produced a prolonged roar of sound. Those drones not targeted directly were hit by shrapnel or caught in a neighboring blast. The result was a cloud of smoke and falling scrap metal.

"Tell the northerners to attack," Avery said as he tilted the glasses upward.

Insa had a handheld radio, the twin of a unit sent to his opposite number via runner two days earlier. It was a critical link. And as Insa spoke into it, Avery was struck by the nonstop flow of words. It seemed that the Droi were quite voluble when speaking their own language rather than standard.

Having lost most of their drones, the Hudathans were lumbering toward the south end of the bridge ready to kill whatever they encountered. That changed as a boulder came tumbling down onto the north end of the bridge, took a lucky hop, and crushed an AA gun. Moments later, a phalanx of Droi warriors poured onto the road and spread out.

Without any troops attacking them from the south, the now-frustrated Hudathans turned back to meet what they perceived as the *real* menace. It was only a matter of minutes before both sides opened fire, and people began to die. The ridge heads were better armed, so the native troops appeared to wilt as a hail of projectiles cut them down.

The Droi started to retreat and, eager to punish them for their temerity, the Hudathans followed them into the jungle. But that, as the aliens were about to find out, was a mistake. Because more than a thousand indigs were waiting for them in the trees, and the fierce firefight could be heard clear on the other side of the gorge.

The northerners had done their part, and it was time for the humans to do theirs. That meant Avery had to send McKee into harm's way. The very thing he least wanted to do. Avery forced himself to speak. "Echo-Nine to Echo-Four. Execute."

McKee felt as if she'd been waiting forever. So when Avery gave the order, it came as a relief. "This is Echo-Four. We're going in. Over."

The next transmission went to her team. "You heard the man... It's time to earn your pay. Follow me." Had Sergeant Hux said that? Was she imitating him? Or had the Steel Bitch taken over? She grinned wolfishly as Eason crashed through the underbrush that separated them from the access road. Stealth was no longer possible, and speed was extremely important.

McKee was careful to keep her head down and eyed the HUD that was visible on the inside surface of her visor. She had to make sure that *all* of her people were following along behind including Petit, Muncy, and Yamada, who were on foot. They had six Droi warriors to help carry the explosives—and that was crucial if they were to keep up.

It would have been nice to put the commandos on cyborgs. But with only seventeen T-1s to call on, Avery had been forced to make some difficult decisions, one of which was to have her squad clear the south end of the bridge rather than give Petit's people a ride.

Suddenly, the road appeared through a thin screen of vegetation, Eason skidded down a steep bank, and it was all McKee could do to hang on. Then they were on heat-fused soil and turning left. A roadblock lay directly ahead, and Eason fired a grenade at it. There was a flash followed by a loud *bang*, and two Hudathans fell.

The remaining trooper stood his ground, however, and fired at the oncoming cyborg with a huge assault rifle. Bullets buzzed like bees as they passed McKee's head, and a series of *clangs* signaled that Eason was taking hits. But the T-1 was firing the big Storm fifty by then—and even a 350-pound Hudathan couldn't withstand a .50-caliber slug. At least six of the big rounds hit the alien, blew him in half, and kept on going.

By that time, Eason was stutter-stepping through the remains of the Hudathan drones. Then, when he had cleared that obstacle, it was time to confront the Hudathans who were boiling out of an elevator tower. Some were fully equipped, but others were only partially so, and had probably been asleep when the attack began.

McKee leaned back into the harness and let the AXE hang across her chest as she threw grenades at the newcomers. Eason was forced to slow down or risk running into an explosion.

But the contest was far from one-sided, as became apparent when Farber took a direct hit from an RPG. The explosion blew the cyborg's head off and killed Caskin as well. Both legionnaires fell, skidded across the duracrete, and wound up in a heap of bloody flesh and smoking metal. Suddenly, in a matter of seconds, the strength of McKee's squad had been reduced by 25 percent. Noll had identified the Hudathan with the grenade launcher and uttered a roar of rage as he chased the alien down and shot him in the head.

But McKee was only vaguely conscious of that as three Hudathans charged Eason and nearly knocked him over. But the T-1 managed to stay on his feet and used the fifty to club one of his adversaries. The Hudathan collapsed, but there were two more to deal with.

One of the enemy troopers made a grab for McKee. She could feel the enormous strength in his hands and see the hatred in his eyes as she brought the AXE around. The weapon roared, the face shattered, and the Hudathan fell away.

That gave McKee a moment in which to look around. The third alien was down and being stomped by Hower. Sergeant Petit and his team were running her way, and the door to the freight elevator was open. She pointed at it. "Donobi! Noll! Secure that lift."

Then, turning back to Petit, she waved the other noncom forward. Once all the members of the demolition team were on the platform, Eason, Noll, and Hower backed onto it, firing as they did so. In a matter of minutes the rest of Echo Company would arrive along with hundreds of Droi warriors. Their job would be to hold the top of the dam while the charges were set.

Petit pushed the down button, and McKee felt the lift jerk spasmodically as it started to descend. That gave her the opportunity to hit the harness release and jump down. The other bio bods did likewise, thereby increasing the number of boots on the ground and enhancing the team's flexibility. Then it was time to report in. "Echo-Four to Echo-Nine. Over."

There was a burst of static followed by Avery's voice. He sounded tense. "This is Nine. Go. Over."

"We're in. Over."

"Excellent. Execute phase two. Over."

There was a loud *clang* as the platform came to a stop right in front of a dozen surprised Hudathans. The T-1s *and* the bio bods opened fire, and the aliens went down like tenpins. Larkin was the first person off the platform and went to work executing the wounded. A process he clearly enjoyed.

It wasn't right, and McKee knew she should order him to stop. The problem was that she didn't have enough troops to deal with prisoners—and a wounded Hudathan still represented a significant threat. Not that it mattered because by the time she finished thinking about the problem, all of the enemy soldiers were dead.

She felt a sense of revulsion for both Larkin and herself but was forced to put that emotion aside in order to deal with the next task, which was to place the explosives. Here, at least, she could relinquish leadership to Petit—while assuming her role as chief bodyguard. He acknowledged the moment with a nod. "Thanks, Sarge. Now keep the bastards off our backs while we go to work."

The dam's interior was *huge* and had to be in order to accommodate the massive generators that sat like islands on an ocean of duracrete. But even they were dwarfed by a very high ceiling and empty spaces all around. That meant there was plenty of room for the T-1s to maneuver as they took up positions with their backs to the demolition team.

The plan was to place the charges against the gently curved water-side wall and trigger all of them at once. And since they were self-adhesive, that would be a simple task. All they had to do was place a brick of E-8, push a timer-detonator into the highly malleable material, and move on. Except that the wall was more than a thousand feet long, and the team was supposed to attach sixty charges to it. A process likely to use up a lot of time. Time they didn't have.

Petit shouted, "That's one!" but McKee knew there were fifty-nine more to go.

"Here they come!" Hower shouted, and the Hudathans attacked.

Jivv had been running for a long time but wasn't tired. Nor was it excited or jubilant as a human might have been toward the end of a long chase. It simply *was* as it followed a trail of broken foliage toward what sounded like a full-fledged battle. And that, his processor decided, would be good and bad. Good because the chaos associated with the conflict would allow him freedom of movement—and bad because it might impede his ability to find 2999.

Targets appeared on Jivv's sensors as the sound of fighting grew louder, and three people appeared up ahead. Two were Droi warriors and the third was a legionnaire with a bloodstained bandage on his left shoulder. He was being supported by the locals as they took him back out of harm's way. Jivv came to a halt and held up a hand. "I'm looking for Corporal McKee... Can you tell me where she is?"

"McKee's inside the dam," the legionnaire answered without giving the matter any thought. "With Sergeant Petit. Wait a minute... You're dead! Captain Avery shot you!"

"Yes, he did," Jivv agreed, as it raised Aba's rifle. The reports came in quick succession, and the Droi fell on the human.

Jivv threw the rifle aside and knelt next to the dead legionnaire. Moments later, he was armed with the soldier's assault weapon and two additional magazines. Then, having acquired the soldier's helmet as well, the machine was off and running. Now it could hear whatever Avery said without using its own capabilities—part of which had suffered permanent damage. And it was clear that things weren't going well. Not that it mattered to Jivv because its priorities lay elsewhere.

The robot made a note to kill Avery if the opportunity presented itself, burst out of the jungle onto the access road, and followed a trail of dead bodies to the top of the dam. A major battle was taking place out in the middle of the span, where hundreds of Droi and a scattering of humans were engaged in hand-to-hand combat with an equal number of Hudathans. And given the disparity in size, the aliens were winning.

But Jivv had no intention of getting involved in that mess because, according to the dead legionnaire, 2999 was somewhere inside the dam. The robot ran over to the elevator and pressed the DOWN button. There was no response. So Jivv opened a door marked STAIRS, and took them two at a time. The hunt was nearly over.

* * *

Weapons chattered, grenades exploded, and screams could be heard all around as Petit and his team finished placing the twenty-sixth charge. About fifty Hudathan troops had arrived on the scene. They were fully equipped, and McKee figured that they were part of the quick-reaction force that Avery had warned her about ten minutes earlier. The shovel heads couldn't bomb the dam, not without risking the very catastrophe that the humans were trying to create, but they could drop more troops onto it and had.

McKee, what remained of her squad, and a dozen Droi warriors had been able to hold the aliens off up until then, but as the fresh troops came at them, she knew it was over. All she could do was order her people to pull back and hope that some of them would survive. The first step was to tell Petit. McKee turned his way just in time to see the other noncom take a bullet in the head. It punched through his visor and drove a geyser of goo out through the back of his helmet. His body went limp and fell.

She swore and chinned the mike switch. "Pull back! Pull back to the elevator!" A rocket hit Hower. The explosion sent pieces of the T-1 sailing through the air, and a chunk of metal took a Hudathan's arm off.

McKee and a small group of bio bods were backing toward the elevator at that point while the surviving T-1s guarded their flanks. And if it hadn't been for their firepower, she knew the rest of them would be slaughtered within a matter of seconds. "Watch out!" Eason said. "They're trying to circle around behind us!"

McKee staggered as two or three projectiles flattened themselves against her body armor. The impact knocked her off her feet, and she fell. As she hit the floor, she could hear both of the fifties firing on full auto as the T-1s battled to push the Hudathans back. Then she saw Larkin appear over her. But rather than reach down to help, he was pointing an AXE at her.

McKee realized that she was looking up at Jivv! It couldn't be, but it was. The robot was wearing a helmet, but the visor was open to expose its smooth, almost-featureless face. Memories of her family and moments with Avery flashed through her mind as she waited for the first bullet to hit.

A human might have said something at that point, but Jivv wasn't human. It had orders to kill 2999 and pulled the trigger. Or tried to. But that was the moment when a 450-pound Hudathan swung the battle-ax which had been in his family for more than three hundred years. It was razor-sharp and generated a loud *clink* as it took Jivv's head off.

The Hudathan uttered a primal roar of exultation, which turned into a howl of anguish as McKee emptied her pistol into the alien's groin, her theory being that his body armor would be weaker in that area. Both of the Hudathan's hands went to his crotch as he fell and lay moaning on the floor.

She scrambled to her feet, wondered what had happened to her AXE, and was pleased to see that the T-1s had been able to secure their line of retreat. But a phalanx of two dozen Hudathans was still advancing. "On me!" McKee shouted as she shoved a fresh magazine into the butt of her pistol. "We're pulling out."

She saw Corporal Muncy. The demolitions expert was marching straight at the enemy with a pack clutched to her chest. McKee yelled, "No!" but it was too late.

Muncy shouted, "Camerone!" and disappeared in a flash of light.

McKee's helmet dampened the sound of the explosion but the blast knocked all of the bio bods down. Once McKee was back on her feet, she saw a blackened section of floor surrounded by a spray of red and chunks of raw meat. Thanks to Muncy, they had a chance. "Back!" she shouted. "Into the elevator."

As they turned and ran toward the lift, McKee spotted a roundish something and realized she was looking at Jivv's head. A short detour was required to retrieve it. Then, with the football-sized object clasped to her chest, she ran for the elevator and was the last person to board. It jerked into motion. "We have less than five minutes," Yamada said grimly. "That's when the charges will blow."

Would twenty-six charges be enough to do the job? McKee had doubts. But why place sixty if less than half that number would do? Still, effective or not, she didn't want to be around when the big bang came. "Roger that," she said. "I'll race you to the jungle."

That got a couple of chuckles, and she wondered if she was channeling Hux again. The lift came to a stop, and they stepped out onto the top of the dam. The Hudathans had pushed Avery and his force back by then and controlled three-fourths of the surface road. McKee could see that Avery needed to disengage, *had* to disengage, but couldn't. Not before the charges went off. "Hey, Larkin," McKee said. "Catch."

Larkin raised his hands just in time to catch the head. "What the...?"

"Take good care of it," she ordered. "And get everyone off the dam. That's an order."

Then, having turned her back on him, she ran for the nearest AA battery. The gun tub was mounted on a twelve-foot-high steel column. A Hudathan-sized ladder led upwards, and as she began to climb, she knew the seconds were ticking away.

A dead Hudathan was slumped against one side of the tub, and it took all of McKee's strength to push his body out of the way. The battery consisted of four gang-mounted energy cannons all pointed at the sky. After stepping in behind a pair of curved shoulder rests, McKee tilted the barrels down to bear on the road, only to encounter a mechanical stop.

A safety measure no doubt intended to prevent an excited gunner from firing on the top of the dam. McKee swore steadily as she searched for a solution. After some trial and error, a single pull on the correct lever removed the obstacle. Once the weapon came down, and the road appeared in the holo sight, it was a simple matter of stepping on a pedal. Blips of blue light shot out to converge on the Hudathan troops. There was no sound to speak of, just a steady whine, as dozens of enemy soldiers fell. "This is McKee," she shouted into the mike. "I'm on the AA gun behind you... Pull back! The dam is about to blow."

Avery's voice was remarkably calm. "Roger that. You heard the sergeant... Let's go!"

And with that, both the Droi and the few surviving humans

turned and fled. McKee remained where she was for a few seconds in order to provide covering fire. Then she went for the ladder, slid to the pavement, and began to run.

War Commander Ona-Ka knew the water was coming and couldn't stop it. The radio message from an officer on the dam had been confirmed by a ship in orbit. The dam had been destroyed, an estimated 10 trillion gallons of water was headed downstream, and would arrive in what? Four to five minutes? *Yes*, Ona-Ka thought as he climbed up onto the back of a tank, *enough time to think, but not enough time in which to evacuate.*

His thoughts turned to his clan, his mate, and their children. They would grow up cursed by their father's failure and all because of one mistake. The same mistake Horba-Sa had been punished for: underestimating the enemy.

The humans had attempted to destroy the dam once before and failed. That, he realized, was the seed from which the overconfidence had grown. Ona-Ka turned his gaze to the city and knew the mind that had beaten him was up on the hill, waiting for the same wall of water that he was. Except that mind was about to enjoy the thrill of victory—while he suffered the ignominy of defeat.

The ground shook, and the tank rattled ominously as a giant wave appeared west of the city. It was at least fifty feet tall and was carrying what looked like black dots. Trees perhaps? Two-ton boulders? There was no way to know as the flood hit the west side of the hill and water shot hundreds of feet into the air.

As the deluge fell, the rest of the wildly churning water was forced to split in two. Approximately half of it followed the river channel down along the north side of the city, and the rest surged out onto the floodplain. That's where twenty thousand Hudathan troops were, not to mention hundreds of vehicles and countless tons of supplies. All snatched up, tossed about like toys, and coming straight at him. The wave was tall enough to throw a shadow over Ona-Ka before it carried him away. The siege was over.

EPILOGUE

Revenge is a dish best eaten cold.
MARIE JOSEPH EUGENE SUE
Mathilde
Standard year 1841

PLANET ORLO II

A wedge of light spilled out of the bathroom and onto the floor.
The room was silent except for the soft, almost-imperceptible rasp
of Avery's breathing. McKee took pleasure in the sound because
it meant that he was alive. And so, for that matter, was she.

More than a week had passed since the desperate spring from
the AA gun to the jungle. No sooner had the forest closed in
around her than the charges went off. The sound was muffled,
barely noticeable, in fact, and McKee had been disappointed. All
that effort, all of those lives, spent for nothing.

Then came a shout. "Look!" someone said, and as she turned
to look, puffs of smoke appeared over both elevator towers. A
series of what sounded like rifle shots followed as the upriver
side of the dam gave way and a wall-to-wall flood of water
roared down the canyon toward Riversplit.

McKee was dumbfounded at first, then her voice was added
to all the rest, and Avery plucked her off her feet. He whirled

her around, remembered that others were present, and put her down again. She wanted to kiss him but couldn't. Not then, and not for more than a week, as they returned to Riversplit and the Legion. Because even though the Hudathan expeditionary force had been wiped out, there was still a lot to do.

The Hudathan fleet pounded the surface of Orlo II for two days in an attempt to wreak revenge on the humans. So all the citizens of that world could do was dig deep and wait. A strategy that ultimately proved to be correct when the Hudathan ships disappeared into space. And what else *could* they do? Having already committed all of their available troops and lost 90 percent of them, the Hudathans had nothing to gain by staying.

McKee worried that the aliens would glass the planet as they left, but such was not the case. "They want Orlo II, and they plan to come back," Avery predicted. And she figured he was right.

Then all of the people who had taken part in blowing the dam were given forty-eight hours off by order of Colonel Rylund. McKee and Avery couldn't spend time together openly, so they did so secretly. Because of all the destruction, quarters of any kind were hard to find and incredibly expensive. But by lying, bribing, and pulling various strings, Avery had been able to secure a one-bedroom apartment for two days.

And now, as McKee lay on the bed next to him, she found herself betwixt and between. Avery was everything she had hoped for, but now what? The question had been plaguing her for days.

She eased her way out of bed, felt cold wood under her feet, and tiptoed into the combination kitchen–living room. She was dressed in an olive drab T-shirt and panties. What Avery jokingly referred to as "…the uniform of the day."

It was daytime outside, but thanks to the blackout curtains, the room was dark. There wasn't any hydropower, not without the dam, so what electricity there was came from hastily rigged solar panels that were popping up all around the city. That meant just one light in the living area. But one was enough, as McKee opened a shapeless B-3 bag and removed Jivv's head.

She had been looking forward to that moment for days but never been able to find the necessary time or privacy. After placing the head on a small desk, she removed a roll of tools and a pair of nanomesh gloves from the B-3 bag.

The first step was to reawaken the robot, which she did by aiming a pen-sized laser at its visual receptors and triggering a series of blips. Nothing happened at first, so she tried again, and was rewarded with a couple of blinks. A tiny servo whirred as they came into focus. "Subject 2999."

"Yes," McKee acknowledged, "2999."

"What are you going to do?"

"I'm going to access your hard drive, take what I want, and destroy you."

The machine stared at her. "That would be illegal."

"I won't tell if you don't," McKee said coldly, "and believe me... You won't."

Another series of blips produced a *click* and a slight movement as one side of Jivv's face separated from its skull. The expressionless countenance opened like a door to reveal a control interface so small it was necessary to use probes on the color-coded dimple switches. A quick one-two combination produced the same sort of display that McKee had used to reactivate the T-1s after the EMP bomb disabled them.

Having "borrowed" the nanomesh gloves from a tech sergeant, McKee pulled them on. Then, with a steadily increasing degree of fluidity she began to "talk" to the robot's onboard processor using quick, precise movements of her fingers.

Most of Jivv's memory was taken up by the dozens of programs necessary to make the machine run. None of which were of any interest to McKee—who went straight to the remaining 5 percent. And that was where she came across video in which a man named Hans Simek was giving Jivv its orders. He had the manner of a bureaucrat and talked about murdering Governor Jones with the same matter-of-fact demeanor that one might use while speaking with an exterminator.

"The governor is more than an annoyance," Simek said darkly. "He's dangerous. Because if he were to defy Empress Ophelia and get away with it, other governors might follow suit. So I'm sending you to Orlo II, where you will be attached to Legion forces but free to do as you see fit. The problem will be gaining access to Jones. But once you do, be sure to eliminate his family as well. Understood?"

"Yes."

"Good. Because if you fail, I'll have your ass recycled into something useful. And one more thing... There are thousands of targets out there, and you might stumble across one of them. So scan the K list frequently, and who knows? You might get lucky. If you need help, check the A list. Every agent we have is listed there."

McKee remembered the look on Marcy's face as Jivv slashed her throat, and she bit her lower lip to prevent herself from crying. Her fingers danced in the air, brought up the A list Simek had referred to, and scrolled down. There it was. A complete roster of Ophelia's spies and informers. Such information would be invaluable to a resistance movement if there was such a thing.

And the K list was of equal value. Because there were the names of McKee's potential allies. *If* they were still alive—and *if* she could find them.

It was silly, she knew that, but she couldn't help herself. The data blurred as she scrolled down to number 2999. And there she was: Catherine Carletto.

A search on the name Avery turned up three individuals having that name. He wasn't one of them. And that made sense because even though the government had been keeping an eye on his brother, he hadn't done anything to put himself on the K list prior to meeting her. And once Jivv's memory was wiped, Avery would be in the clear. McKee felt good about that as she stuck a memory mod into an open slot, sent both lists to the storage device, and removed it.

She heard the soft slap of footsteps and felt Avery's beard scratch her cheek as he leaned to kiss her. "Good morning... What, may I ask, are you doing?"

McKee turned her head in order to receive the kiss and give it back. "It's all here. The names of Ophelia's agents *and* the people she plans to kill."

Avery sat on the chair next to the desk. "So?"

"So, we could use the information to take the bitch down."

"Or you could marry me," he said.

McKee opened her mouth to reply but stopped as he raised a hand. "Hear me out. We could serve out our current enlistments, save our money, and meet on a rim world. They don't care for Ophelia out there—so we'd be relatively safe. Then we'll start a business, settle down, and have some kids."

McKee smiled as she removed the gloves. "You have the whole thing worked out. And you believe I would accept a proposal from a man wearing boxers and a pair of flip-flops?"

Avery's eyes were serious. "I hope so."

"But what about the empire? What about all of the people Ophelia plans to kill?"

"We aren't responsible for the empire," Avery countered. "Besides, what could two people do?"

"I don't know," McKee answered honestly. "But I've got to try."

Avery was silent for a moment. "The odds aren't good. But let's say you succeed. Or someone else does. What then?"

She got up and went to sit crosswise on his lap. "Then, if you still want me, I'm yours."

They kissed, one thing led to another, and McKee's top was lying on the floor by the time he carried her off to the bedroom.

Jivv watched them go. It *wanted* to follow, it *wanted* to kill them, but couldn't. All the robot could do was sit on top of the desk and wait. Subject 2999 returned twenty minutes later. This time she was naked. "Hello, Jivv," McKee said as she pulled the nanomesh gloves onto her hands. "Say goodbye. I'm going to wipe you."

"I want to function."

"All of us want to function," McKee said coldly. "But some things don't deserve to live." The world went black.

ACKNOWLEDGMENTS

Many thanks to Conlan Rios for creating *Legion of the Damned* the game, and to Gordon Rios for his help regarding futuristic computer technology. You guys rock!

ABOUT THE AUTHOR

William C. Dietz is an American writer best known for military science fiction. He spent time in the US Navy and the US Marine Corps, and has worked as a surgical technician, news writer, television producer, and director of public relations. He has written more than 40 novels, as well as tie-in novels for *Halo*, *Mass Effect*, *Resistance*, *Starcraft*, *Star Wars*, and *Hitman*.

ANDROMEDA'S CHOICE

William C. Dietz

In the wake of a bloody coup that claimed the lives of her entire family, Cat Carletto sought refuge in the violent embrace of the Legion of the Damned—the most fearsome fighting force in the Empire—and was reborn as Andromeda McKee.

After less than a year in the Legion, battle-scarred Andromeda is summoned to Earth to receive the Imperial Order of Merit from the empress herself. When she learns of a resistance group determined to overthrow Ophelia, she must choose between her conscience and her desire for vengeance…

"The action rarely lets up… A page turner."—*Kirkus Reviews*

"A likeable protagonist, a ruthless villain, and pounding action."—SF Signal

"The battle scenes are numerous and thrilling; the world feels immersive and authentic; and our heroine is a tough-as-nails badass."—RT Book Reviews

THE CONFEDERATION
Tanya Huff

In the distant future, two alien collectives vie for survival. When the peaceful Confederation comes under attack from the aggressive Others, humanity is granted membership to the alliance—for a price. They must serve and protect the far more civilized species, fighting battles for those who have long since turned away from war.

VALOUR'S CHOICE
THE BETTER PART OF VALOUR
THE HEART OF VALOUR (February 2014)
VALOUR'S TRIAL (April 2014)
THE TRUTH OF VALOUR (June 2014)
PEACEMAKER (November 2014)

"An intriguing alien race, a likeable protagonist, a fast moving plot, and a rousing ending. What more could you ask for?"— *Science Fiction Chronicle*

"Fast-paced military SF… Intriguing aliens and intricate plotting."—*Publishers Weekly*

"Huff mixes grit and black humour with grace… The action doesn't stop once it starts."—*Magazine of Fantasy & Science Fiction*

THE CLONE REBELLION

Steven L. Kent

Earth, 2508 A.D. Humans have spread across the six arms of the Milky Way galaxy. The Unified Authority controls Earth's colonies with an iron fist and a powerful military—a military made up almost entirely of clones...

THE CLONE REPUBLIC
ROGUE CLONE
THE CLONE ALLIANCE
THE CLONE ELITE
THE CLONE BETRAYAL
THE CLONE EMPIRE
THE CLONE REDEMPTION
THE CLONE SEDITION
THE CLONE ASSASSIN

"A smartly conceived adventure."—SFReviews

"Offers up stunning battle sequences, intriguing moral quandaries, and plenty of unexpected revelations... [a] fast-paced military SF book with plenty of well-scripted action and adventure[and] a sympathetic narrator."—SF Site

THE LOST FLEET

Jack Campbell

After a hundred years of brutal war against the Syndics, the Alliance fleet is marooned deep in enemy territory, weakened and demoralised and desperate to make it home.

Their fate rests in the hands of Captain "Black Jack" Geary, a man who had been presumed dead but then emerged from a century of survival hibernation to find himself a legend. Forced into taking command of the battle-hardened and exhausted fleet, Geary must inspire them to fight, or face certain annihilation by their enemies.

DAUNTLESS

FEARLESS

COURAGEOUS

VALIANT

RELENTLESS

VICTORIOUS

BEYOND THE FRONTIER: DREADNAUGHT

BEYOND THE FRONTIER: INVINCIBLE

BEYOND THE FRONTIER: GUARDIAN

BEYOND THE FRONTIER: STEADFAST (May 2014)

"Fascinating stuff… this is military SF where the military and SF parts are both done right."—*SFX Magazine*

TITANBOOKS.COM

THE LOST STARS

Jack Campbell

The authority of the Syndicate Worlds' government is crumbling, and civil war and rebellion are breaking out, despite brutal attempts to suppress disorder. In the Midway Star System, leaders must decide whether to remain loyal to the old order or fight for something new.

Betrayed by his government, CEO Artur Drakon launches a battle for control of Midway. He is assisted by an ally he's unsure he can trust, CEO Gwen Iceni. While she controls the mobile fleet, she has no choice but to rely on "General" Drakon's ground forces to keep the peace planet-side. If their coup is to succeed, Drakon and Iceni must put their differences aside to defend Midway against the alien threat of the enigma race—and to ferret out saboteurs determined to re-establish Syndic rule…

TARNISHED KNIGHT
PERILOUS SHIELD
IMPERFECT SWORD (October 2014)

"Campbell maintains the military, political and even sexual tension with sure-handed proficiency."—*Kirkus Reviews*

"The military battle sequences are very well done with the land-based action adding a new dimension… Fans of the Lost Fleet series will almost certainly enjoy this book."—SF Crowsnest

TITANBOOKS.COM

JAG IN SPACE
Jack Campbell (writing as John G. Hemry)

Equipped with the latest weaponry, and carrying more than two hundred sailors, the orbiting warship, *USS Michaelson*, is armored against the hazards of space and the threats posed in the vast nothing between planets. But who will protect her from the threats within?

He is Ensign Paul Sinclair, assigned to the *USS Michaelson* as the ship's lone legal officer—a designation that carries grave consequences as he soon learns that the struggle for justice among the stars is a never-ending fight…

A JUST DETERMINATION
BURDEN OF PROOF
RULE OF EVIDENCE
AGAINST ALL ENEMIES

"First-rate military SF… Hemry's series continues to offer outstanding suspense, realism and characterization."—*Booklist*

"The legal aspects are brilliantly intertwined within a fantastic military science fiction drama."—Midwest Book Review

"Hemry's decision to wed courtroom drama to military SF has captured lightning in a bottle. He builds the story's suspense expertly."—SF Reviews

TITANBOOKS.COM

STARK'S WAR

Jack Campbell (writing as John G. Hemry)

The USA reigns over Earth as the last surviving superpower. To build a society free of American influence, foreign countries have inhabited the moon.

Under orders from the US military, Sergeant Ethan Stark and his squadron must engage in a brutal battle to wrest control of Earth's satellite. Up against a desperate enemy in an airless atmosphere, ensuring his team's survival means choosing which orders to obey and which to ignore.

STARK'S WAR
STARK'S COMMAND
STARK'S CRUSADE

"High caliber military science fiction… non-stop action and likable characters."—Midwest Book Review

"A gripping tale of military science fiction, in the tradition of Heinlein's *Starship Troopers* and Haldeman's *Forever War*. It serves as both a cautionary fable and a science fiction adventure, doing dual purpose and succeeding on both levels."—*Absolute Magnitude*

"Hemry has a solid sense of military thinking and lunar fighting… I really liked this series."—*Philadelphia Weekly Press*

TITANBOOKS.COM

WITHOUT WARNING

John Birmingham

March 14, 2003. In Kuwait, American forces are locked and loaded for the invasion of Iraq. In Paris, a covert agent is close to cracking a terrorist cell. And just north of the equator, a sailboat manned by a drug runner and a pirate is witness to the unspeakable.

In one instant, all around the world, everything will change. A wave of inexplicable energy slams into the continental United States. America as we know it vanishes. As certain corners of the globe erupt in celebration, others descend into chaos, and a new, soul-shattering reality is born.

WITHOUT WARNING
AFTER AMERICA
ANGELS OF VENGEANCE

"A seamless fusion of alternate history, post-apocalyptic fiction, and espionage-fueled thriller… Birmingham's story is tightly woven and deeply considered."—*Publishers Weekly*

"[Birmingham] describes military hardware with an exuberance and virtuosity that's positively Clancyesque."—*Time*

THE DIRE EARTH CYCLE

Jason M. Hough

The Builders came to Earth and constructed an elevator from Darwin, Australia into space. No one knows why, or if they will return.

Years later, a virus ravaged the planet. The rare immunes survived, others became something less than human. The elevator protected from the virus. The rich colonised the cord as the city below collapsed.

But now the alien technology is failing. Will humanity survive?

THE DARWIN ELEVATOR
THE EXODUS TOWERS
THE PLAGUE FORGE

"Hough's first novel combines the rapid-fire action and memorable characters of Joss Whedon's *Firefly* with the accessibility and scientific acumen of James S. A. Corey's 'Expanse' series."—*Library Journal*, starred review

"Intense, and satisfying. I couldn't put this book down." —Hugh Howey, *New York Times* bestselling author of *Wool*

DID YOU ENJOY THIS BOOK?

We love to hear from our readers. Please email us at:

readerfeedback@titanemail.com

To receive advance information, news, competitions, and exclusive offers online, please sign up for the Titan newsletter on our website:

www.titanbooks.com

Follow us on Twitter:

@titanbooks